LET'S KEEP IN TOUCH!

Don't miss a new release by signing up to my newsletter. You'll get sneak peeks, deleted scenes, and giveaways: https://landing.mailerlite.com/webforms/landing/p7l6g0

You can also join my Facebook readers' group here: https://www.facebook.com/groups/386830425069911/

DADDIES' CAPTIVE

LAYLAH ROBERTS

Laylah Roberts.

© 2023, Laylah Roberts.

Laylah.roberts@gmail.com

https://laylahroberts.com

ALL RIGHTS RESERVED. This book contains material protected under International and Federal Copyright Laws and Treaties. Any unauthorized reprint or use of this material is prohibited. No part of this book may be reproduced or transmitted in any form or by any means, electronic or mechanical, including photocopying, recording, or by any information storage and retrieval system without express written permission from the author/publisher.

Editors: Woncas Creative; Celeste Jones

Photographer: Wander Aguiar

Cover Models: Andrew, Megan, and Pat

Cover Design by: Allycat's Creations

❋ Created with Vellum

BOOKS BY LAYLAH ROBERTS

Doms of Decadence

Just for You, Sir

Forever Yours, Sir

For the Love of Sir

Sinfully Yours, Sir

Make me, Sir

A Taste of Sir

To Save Sir

Sir's Redemption

Reveal Me, Sir

Montana Daddies

Daddy Bear

Daddy's Little Darling

Daddy's Naughty Darling Novella

Daddy's Sweet Girl

Daddy's Lost Love

A Montana Daddies Christmas

Daring Daddy

Warrior Daddy

Daddy's Angel

Heal Me, Daddy

Daddy in Cowboy Boots

A Little Christmas Cheer (crossover with MC Daddies)

Sheriff Daddy

Her Daddies' Saving Grace

Rogue Daddy

A Little Winter Wonderland

Daddy's Sassy Sweetheart

Daddy Dominic

MC Daddies

Motorcycle Daddy

Hero Daddy

Protector Daddy

Untamed Daddy

Her Daddy's Jewel

Fierce Daddy

A Little Christmas Cheer (crossover with Montana Daddies)

Savage Daddy

Boss Daddy

Daddy Fox

A Snowy Little Christmas

Saving Daddy

Daddies' Captive

Harem of Daddies

Ruled by her Daddies

Claimed by her Daddies

Stolen by her Daddies

Captured by her Daddies

Haven, Texas Series

Lila's Loves

Laken's Surrender

Saving Savannah

Molly's Man

Saxon's Soul

Mastered by Malone

How West was Won

Cole's Mistake

Jardin's Gamble

Romanced by the Malones

Twice the Malone

Mending a Malone

Malone's Heart

New Orleans Malones

Damaged Princess

Vengeful Commander

Wicked Prince

Men of Orion

Worlds Apart

Cavan Gang

Rectify

Redemption

Redemption Valley

Audra's Awakening

Old-Fashioned Series

An Old-Fashioned Man

Two Old-Fashioned Men

Her Old-Fashioned Husband

Her Old-Fashioned Boss

His Old-Fashioned Love

An Old-Fashioned Christmas

Bad Boys of Wildeside

Wilde

Sinclair

Luke

Rawhide Ranch Holiday

A Cozy Little Christmas

A Little Easter Escapade

Standalones

Their Christmas Baby

Haley Chronicles

Ally and Jake

TRIGGER WARNING

This book involves the loss of loves ones (in the past). Spankings, DDlg, mmf, mild voyeurism (between our heroes and heroine) and touches on somnophilia.

1

She was going to puke.

Effie stood in the parking lot and stared at the attractive brick building with a simple neon pink sign above the double doors.

Pinkies.

I can't do this.

There's no way.

Putting one hand on her tummy and the other over her mouth, she tried to calm her breathing.

This was ridiculous! If she couldn't even go inside, then she was utterly screwed.

Her phone rang as she stood there, shivering. Montana in February wasn't exactly warm. Plus, it was eight at night and she was wearing a threadbare coat that had definitely seen better days.

And underneath that coat . . . yeah, she was wearing pretty much nothing at all.

What was she thinking?

Drawing her phone out of her handbag, she groaned as she

saw who it was. Not because she didn't love the person calling, but because she knew she'd have to answer or April would just keep pestering her until she did.

"Hey, Hairy Tits," she said.

"Are you there yet?"

"Uh, yeah." Effie eyed the building. "I'm here."

April sighed. "You're standing outside, aren't you?"

"That would be affirmative."

"Droopy Bum, you need to go in if you're going to get the job."

She bit her lip. She knew that. But she still couldn't get her feet to move.

"I'm scared."

"Effie," April said softly. "You don't have to do this."

Except she kind of did. She had seven hundred and eighty-three dollars in her bank account. Which didn't sound too bad. Except her rent was due next week. And that was six-fifty for the month. Then there were the gas, electric, and co-pay bills. Plus, she had to feed Brooks. She could go without food, but her nephew needed to eat. Thank God the scholarship he'd won covered his meal plan at school. It was one less meal she had to worry about.

But he was a sixteen-year-old boy. He needed healthy food and plenty of it.

She was failing him.

"I wish I didn't have to, but I do," she replied.

"You know that you and Brooks can come and live with me and Daddy."

It was sweet of April to offer. She lived in Wyoming with her mountain man husband, who was also her Daddy. And while she knew that Trent would agree with April, she also knew it would be an imposition to have her and Brooks come stay with them.

"Brooks is in an excellent school here. One of the best. He has an amazing scholarship. We'd have to start over in Wyoming. I don't know if I could give him the same there."

"Honey, Brooks will do well wherever he is. You know that. I don't think Brooks is the real issue."

No. He wasn't. April was right. Brooks would adapt. She was the one who didn't want to move, who couldn't leave the place where all her memories of Joe were.

"I n-need to try to make it work here. Last s-shot." For her. For Brooks. And for her memories of Joe.

"You need to get inside before you catch pneumonia and Daddy and I have to come get you and force you back home with us."

"Right." Good plan. Since parts of her were starting to grow numb and she could feel her nose running.

Not a good look.

"You got this, Effie. Chardonnay said Pinkies is a great place to work. The owner treats the girls well. They make awesome tips."

Chardonnay was April's cousin and the only reason that Effie was here right now.

"You can do this. You're an amazing dancer. And you will knock their socks off. All you've gotta do is show a bit of skin."

She *had* been an amazing dancer. Before everything in her life had imploded. Now, the only dancing she did was in the living room of her one-bedroom apartment.

"I've never danced while taking off my clothes. What if they don't like what they see? I'm not as young as I used to be. I have cellulite and my tummy is round rather than flat. What if I'm taking something off, trip and fall, and show everyone my hoo-ha?"

"Then I'm sure you'll get excellent tips."

"April, I'm not joking. This is . . . I can't."

"Then come here."

"I . . . I . . ."

"Effie, have you got any other choices?"

April knew she didn't.

"It's not nice to be right all the time."

"Sorry," April replied, but Effie could tell she was grinning.

"Next time we talk, it's my turn to be right," Effie informed her.

"Problem with that is that I'm always right. Have you got your outfit?"

"I've got it on under my coat." There wasn't much to the outfit, which was part of the reason she was freezing. She hadn't been able to afford anything new, and so she'd bought material from thrift stores and managed to create it with what she got. It was neon pink, and she thought it looked pretty good.

At least it covered the major things and still showed skin. She just hoped it was enough.

"Done your stretches?"

"Yes."

"Got Slowly with you?"

"Yep, he's in my bag." Hopefully, Slowly the Sloth brought her some good luck. Joe had given him to her years ago, and the stuffed toy was her most prized possession.

"Celebratory jelly beans?"

"Yep."

"Just pretend you're acting a part. You used to love acting and dancing."

She had.

She wished she could find that joy again. She used to always be happy, smiling, seeing the good in life.

That had become harder the more life beat her down.

"If it makes you feel better, I'm off to do something I don't want to do either," April told her suddenly.

"What's that?"

"Corner time. It's the pits. Way worse than having to take your clothes off for money."

Effie had to grin. "I'm sure it is. What did you do this time?"

"I might have gone out on the ATV. On my own."

"April." Effie shook her head, dancing around to warm herself up. Even though her feet protested. The only shoes she'd been able to find at the thrift store were a size too small, and they were killing her. "You know you're not allowed to do that."

"I know. Now I'm in trouble. It's corner time and a spanking for me."

"I'm surprised you were allowed to call me."

"Hmm, I might have lied and told Trent that I needed to make an urgent work call."

"Did you just?" a deep voice said.

April squealed. "Daddy! I didn't see you there."

"I bet you didn't. Work call, huh? Little one, you just added on ten with my belt for lying."

Ouch.

Effie couldn't imagine anyone taking their belt to her backside. That seemed like it would really hurt. She'd never even been spanked before. Joe had threatened to several times when she did something he thought was dangerous. But that was all it was.

Joe had been a Daddy Dom. And while he'd sometimes taken care of her while she was in Little headspace, it had all been very platonic. One friend looking out for another.

Even though one of those friends had wanted more.

Had he ever known that she'd wanted more than friendship?

Maybe you should have told him.

Maybe. And perhaps she would have lost him. She'd never know now. What she did know was that he had trusted her to take care of his son. Which meant that she needed money so she could give Brooks the best life possible.

"I better let you go," Effie said quickly.

"Get in there and kill it, babe," April said quickly. "Don't worry about anything else but dancing, yeah?"

"Effie's going dancing?" Trent asked. "On her own? Where is she going?"

She could feel tears fill her eyes at the concern in his voice. Lord, she missed that. Having someone who cared.

"I'll explain later, Daddy," April said. "Get inside before you freeze, Droopy Bum. I'll call to see how it goes. If I'm not grounded. Daddy's got his grumpy mountain Daddy face on, so I might not be able to call for the rest of the year."

Effie ended the call with a grin, before she looked back at the building and grew serious.

I have this.

I can do this.

After wiping her nose with a tissue, she walked up to the door, pressing the buzzer. The club wouldn't open for another hour, but the door opened quickly and a gorgeous, tall woman with long dark hair stood there. She wore tight, black faux leather pants and a red shirt that was partially unbuttoned so you could see the black bra underneath.

She might have been beautiful if the look on her face wasn't so mean.

"Yes?" she asked snootily.

"Um, hi, I'm Effie."

The other woman continued to stare at her.

"Effie Stephenson. I have an audition at eight-fifteen."

"You're late."

Effie spotted a piece of spinach between the other woman's two front teeth. She should really tell her about that.

Except . . . she wasn't late.

Effie glanced at her watch. She had two minutes to spare. She usually liked to be early. But she didn't think this woman would want to hear how she had spent the last fifteen minutes freaking out in the parking lot.

The urge to turn tail and run was strong. She'd been looking for an excuse and now she had one.

But . . . what other choices did she have?

So she forced herself to push her fears aside and smile brightly. "Who are you?"

The other woman just sniffed and looked down her nose at her.

Right.

"It's not eight-fifteen yet," Effie pointed out.

"Everyone else was here early."

Effie smiled cheerfully. Kill them with kindness. "That's awesome! I'm here now, though. And I'm not actually late."

The woman's face tightened, then she looked her up and down. "Interviewing you would be a waste of time. You're too old and fat."

Ouch.

Just fucking ouch.

Yeah, okay, she was carrying more weight than she probably should be. Stress made her eat. And what she chose to eat was crap. But if she got this, then she'd be moving more, right? And she could finally afford to buy better food.

She was pretty sure that her teeth would rot if she kept eating candy, and just this morning, a huge clump of hair had come out.

Of course, she had been tugging on her hair at the time as she'd tried to work out her finances.

Adulting was so hard sometimes.

She envied April. Sure, would probably have trouble sitting tomorrow, but she had a man who loved her. A Daddy who took care of her. Who gave her a safe space to be who she wanted to be.

She threw her shoulders back. She wasn't going to let this woman make her feel bad. What was wrong with boobs and ass and a bit of a belly? Well, maybe more than a bit.

Now, she was glad she hadn't told this woman about the piece of spinach between her teeth.

That's not very nice, Effie. People won't like you if you're not nice.

The last thing she needed right now was Nan's advice.

And she still wasn't telling this woman about the food between her teeth. She'd called Effie fat.

There was a line.

And being told that she was fat and old crossed that line.

"Effie?"

She turned and saw a tall woman strutting toward her. This woman could only be Chardonnay. Effie wasn't sure if that was her real name or her stage name, but she rocked it.

Long, bright red hair fell down her back in waves; her make-up was on-point. She had a generous cleavage and wore a tracksuit in a green velvet that was totally awesome.

"Chardonnay?" she asked.

"Yep." Chardonnay gave her air kisses. That had been something Effie had never managed to pull off. The last time she'd tried to do that with a friend, she'd ended up whacking her nose so hard that it had bled.

So she stayed still while Chardonnay did her thing.

It was safer that way.

"You two know each other? Figures," the rude woman muttered.

"I see you've met Satan's mistress," Chardonnay said.

"Oh, that's her name? She wouldn't tell me. She called me fat and old." Shit. Why had she blurted that out?

Chardonnay glared at the other woman. "You're such a bitch, Lucy. Why don't you go sacrifice a goat to the dark gods?"

"You can't talk to me like that! I'm your boss!"

Was this woman really in charge? That wasn't good. Dread filled her.

Chardonnay wrapped her arm around Effie's. "No, you're not. You're just on a power trip because you think you're going to get into Steele's pants. News flash, he ain't interested in your pants or any other part of you. Oh, and you've got spinach in your teeth!"

There was a screech as Chardonnay led her away.

"Wow, she's . . . intense," Effie said, coming up with the kindest word she could think of.

"She's a bitch is what she is. Hates us dancers because we make more money than she does. And she knows that even if she got up on stage and started stripping, ain't no one who wants to see what she's got under her clothes. There's probably a portal to hell between her legs."

Effie let out a surprised giggle as Chardonnay winked at her. "Come on, let's head into the main room. They've already started."

"I'm sorry I'm late."

"Pfft, you're not late. Don't let Lucy get to you. She's like that with everyone who isn't Steele or Grady."

Steele was the owner, but who was Grady? A manager?

They stepped into what was obviously the main area of the bar. A stage with a long catwalk went out into the middle of the room.

Seating went around the edge of the catwalk, and more chairs with tables were scattered throughout the room. Booths lined two walls.

A long bar took up most of the wall to the left. It was all done in shades of black and red.

Honestly, it was pretty much what she'd expected for a strip bar.

"For some reason, I thought there would be some pink," she muttered as Chardonnay led her toward the back of the room where a few other women were sitting.

"Wouldn't that be awesome? But no . . . it was named after the original owner. I don't think the clients would appreciate a pink overload, anyway."

Effie nodded as they sat to watch the woman on the stage. She was an okay dancer. Good body. But her face was stony, as if she didn't want to be here.

"I was kind of freaking out in the parking lot."

"April said you're an amazing dancer, but it's your first time stripping?"

"Uh, yeah. Do you . . . do you think I'm too old and fat to strip?"

Chardonnay turned her, putting her hands on her cheeks. "Do not listen to that bitch. You're freaking gorgeous. Seriously. Men dig curves. And all that hair and those cheekbones. By the way, I love what you've done with your eyeshadow. You think you could do something like that on me?"

Effie nodded enthusiastically. Even if she didn't love helping people, Chardonnay had just saved her from Satan's mistress. So she'd do anything she asked.

"You'll be on after the next dancer. I think Grady is going to enjoy watching you."

"Who is Grady?"

"He's Damon Steele's right-hand man. Steele owns this place, but Grady mostly runs it after our old manager, Mitchell, left. Don't worry; no loss. He was a rat bastard."

Right. Okay.

"And Lucy?"

"She's the bar manager and the reigning queen of hell."

The next woman moved onto the stage. And she was good. Sultry and sexy. There were a few moves she could tweak to make it even better.

But she was rocking it.

Effie watched her in awe. She hoped she looked that good. She also hoped like hell that her body didn't give up on her. But she hadn't had a back spasm in a long time.

When the dancer finished, Effie clapped until everyone turned to stare at her.

Oops. Was she not supposed to clap? Okay, so technically, the other woman was her competition. But she deserved to know she'd done a great job, right?

Chardonnay grinned over at her. "Just like April said."

"Uh-oh, what did April say?"

"That you're a bit nutty with a heart of gold."

Great. Nutty.

"Come on, you're up next. Let's head backstage."

As Effie got up to follow her out, she felt someone watching her. Turning, she looked to a back booth where a man sat. He was partially in shadow, but what she could see she approved of. Muscular, dark hair, trimmed short beard, well-dressed.

His gaze was intense as he stared at her. Then he looked away, dismissing her.

It was silly, but she felt a stab of disappointment. Chardonnay tugged her along and she nearly lost her footing.

"That's Grady," Chardonnay whispered to her. "Sexy, right?"

"Uh, yeah." She probably shouldn't be saying that about her hopefully soon-to-be boss.

"He's a little odd. Standoffish. He isn't the sort of boss you could sit and chew the fat with. There's a definite barrier between him and us."

Huh. That didn't sound like he was that great of a boss.

"But since he took over for Mitchell, things have been much

safer here. He insists that all the girls, dancers, and bar staff, are escorted to their cars. If they don't have cars, then Pinkies covers their transportation home.

"Really?" That seemed amazing. She hadn't been sure how she'd get home at night, seeing as the closest bus stop to her place still meant a four-block walk.

"Yep. Grady is really big on making sure we're safe."

All right. She was starting to like him more.

"And he hired additional bouncers. One that stands by the door to our dressing room and one out by the stage to make sure no one touches us. Some people think that being a stripper means you're all for being groped or that you're selling yourself in other ways. Not the case. I got a man back in my bed waiting for me, and he doesn't want anyone else touching what belongs to him."

"He's all right with you doing this?"

Chardonnay raised her eyebrows. "I just paid off our condo, and I'm saving to take us on a cruise around the Caribbean. Yep, he's fine with this. Show me what you got under the jacket."

Nerves filled her.

Stupid. She was about to dance in this outfit in front of a bunch of people she did not know. And she was going to have to show more than a little bit of skin.

Which was terrifying.

Because while she thought her boobs were nice. They were also big. And they had stretch marks.

"This was a bad idea. I can't do this."

"Show me," Chardonnay said in a surprisingly kind voice.

Taking a deep breath, she opened her jacket and let it fall off.

It was far warmer there than outside, but she still felt a bit chilled.

"This outfit is . . . interesting. Where did you find it?"

"Ahh, I made it."

"It's bright."

"I like bright colors. Is it too much? Should I have toned it down?"

"Hey, it's different. And different isn't always bad."

Not in her experience.

Nerves filled her. "This was a terrible idea."

"What? No!" Chardonnay cupped her face. "Seriously? Babe, you have got it going on. And these curves? The patrons here are going to love you. If Steele was here, he would cream his pants."

Jesus. What a thought.

"You are just his type."

Effie wasn't sure she wanted to be Steele's type.

"I've got stretch marks," she blurted out.

"So? Me too. Don't worry. Ain't no one going to be focused on a few stretch marks when you have these girls out."

Right.

There was a change in the music.

"That's your cue, babe. Good luck."

Fuck. Luck was something that had never been on her side. In fact, she'd always been seriously unlucky.

But maybe things were changing. Effie set her bag down by her jacket and took a deep breath.

Then she forced a smile onto her face. She could do this. She could rock this.

She had to.

2

Thomas Grady watched from the shadows as she walked out onto the stage.

Interest filled him. This was . . . strange. He couldn't remember ever feeling attracted to anyone else like this.

Well, other than Steele.

And nothing could ever come of that.

She'd clapped for her competition.

That said something about this girl . . . no, woman. Because she was all woman. Curves he would love to run his hands over. Piles of blonde hair that lay in soft waves down her back.

Lips that would look perfect wrapped around his cock.

Fuck. He was being a complete dick.

This was part of the job, although not a responsibility he particularly relished.

He was not supposed to get turned on.

None of the other women interested him. That didn't mean they weren't attractive. That they weren't good dancers. That they wouldn't be popular with Pinkies' regulars.

It worried Grady because it was very rare for him to be

aroused by any woman . . . unless he was sharing her with Steele. He'd long since given up trying to have sex without Steele. Not that he'd ever told his best friend that.

It was bad enough Grady knew it. He didn't need Steele knowing how fucked in the head he was.

Except . . . now there was her. She stepped out slowly onto the catwalk, looking like she couldn't decide whether she was about to vomit or not. Her heels were too low and her outfit covered her almost entirely from chest to ass. Sure, it was made with see-through lace, but all the other women interviewing for this job had started out in G-strings and tiny bras that barely covered their nipples.

The outfit was so pink that it made him wince. And it looked like it was made of several different pieces of material sown together.

"She's so far out of her fucking depth. What a joke," Lucy said snidely as she sat across from him in the booth.

Fuck. Why had he kept Lucy on?

Because other than being a total cow, she hadn't given him a reason to fire her. And if he got rid of her, he'd need to find someone to replace her. Which meant taking on more responsibilities until he did.

Which was something he didn't need.

So for the moment, he put up with her cattiness and the way she continually tried to stick her nose up Steele's ass.

But as soon as she messed up, she was gone.

He didn't reply. He knew she wasn't expecting him to because he gave Lucy even less than he gave most people.

Which wasn't much to begin with.

"And what is she wearing? It's probably a good thing she's covering herself up. Why would she think anyone would want to see her strip?"

"Go away, Lucy."

"What?" She jolted and then gaped over at him. He tried not to swear at women. His father had always cussed at his mother. And Grady worked hard to never be like his father.

However, with Lucy, he was really close to breaking that rule. It was hard to get through her thick skull.

"Go. Away."

The woman started dancing. What was her name? He glanced down at his list. *Effie*. Unusual, but it suited her.

To his shock, once she started moving, she lost her nerves. That sick look disappeared. And as she relaxed . . . she could move.

Fuck. His dick was so hard that it hurt.

"But Grady," Lucy whined. "I'm supposed to help you. Damon said."

Steele said nothing of the sort. Grady also knew that the other man would never have told Lucy she could use his first name.

"Lucy, go away. And don't let Steele hear you calling him Damon."

She swallowed and stood, stomping over to another chair. It wasn't far enough away, but it would have to do.

It gave him a chance to watch Effie. His balls fucking ached. He couldn't remember the last time he'd gotten off. Lately, he hadn't felt like joining in with Steele. It wasn't that the other man had a parade of women through his bed. But he also wasn't celibate. Yet, for the last few months, Grady had been.

But this woman . . . she was making him feel.

And he wasn't sure that he liked that.

Because that made him vulnerable to being hurt.

Fuck.

She's just a chick trying out for a stripper job. She's not going to change your life.

But damn . . . watching her was . . . it was almost a gift. Which sounded ridiculous. But the way she moved, the look on her face, she loved to dance.

And then she moved to the pole. He tensed. Soon, she'd have to strip off that outfit she was wearing. And he didn't want anyone else seeing her.

Stupid.

It was part of the job.

She grabbed the pole and spun. It was an okay move. Nothing amazing. She reached high and attempted a basic invert.

He swore he sensed it before he saw it. Her face twisted in pain and she suddenly crashed to the floor. There were a few gasps and a laugh that he knew was coming from Lucy.

Bitch.

Without thinking, Grady jumped to his feet and rushed toward her.

∼

Fuck.

Fuck. Fuck. Fuck.

Effie closed her eyes as she lay on the stage. Her back was spasming and it hurt. Why the hell had she attempted that move? Why had she thought this was a good idea?

Dumb. So dumb.

At one stage she would have kicked ass at this.

That was before.

It felt like her life had two acts. Before the accident. And after. And the after was complete and utter shit.

She had to move. She'd already humiliated herself. Now, she had to pick herself up, get off this stage and take the bus home. Walk several blocks. Then, cry herself to sleep without Brooks hearing her.

And considering he was the most observant sixteen-year-old she'd ever met, and they lived in a tiny one-bedroom apartment that was going to be pretty impossible.

"Oh, babe. Are you all right?"

She opened her eyes to see Chardonnay standing over her, concern on her face. That was nice. At least she wasn't laughing at her. Yep, she'd heard someone laugh after she'd fallen.

Who did that?

"I could use a hand to get up," she said in a husky voice. This wasn't good.

Not good at all.

Why did you think it would be? Why did you think your back would be able to take this?

It could have handled the dancing if she didn't get too carried away . . . but pulling herself up and down and twisting around a pole?

No. Just no.

Chardonnay didn't move to help her, though. Instead, she tensed, looking away.

Awesome. She guessed she'd crawl her way out of here. At least she never had to see these people again, right?

"Are you hurt?"

Fuck.

Don't be him. Don't be him.

She turned her face toward that cold voice.

Fuck it.

She really had the worst luck, didn't she? It was definitely him. He was now staring down at her with concern.

He's probably wondering how the hell he's going to get you off the stage so he can continue with his night.

"Effie, right?" he asked.

"You know my name." Wow.

His face softened. "It was on your interview form, sweetheart."

Well. Hell.

Too much to ask that he'd seen her across the room, fallen instantly in love, and questioned everyone for every detail he could find out about her so he could whisk her away on his yacht.

Urgh, no, not his yacht.

"I get sea-sick."

"What?" he asked. "Did you hit your head?"

"It would seem that way, but no."

"Are you sure? What hurts, then?"

"Nothing. I'm fine. Sorry. I'll just get out of the way."

His eyebrows rose as he crouched next to her. Wow, he was even sexier close-up. "Who said you're in the way?"

"So. Darn. Pretty."

"Did you just call me pretty?"

Uh-oh. Damn you, mouth.

"Nope. I was talking to Chardonnay."

Chardonnay started laughing. "Nice as that is to hear, I don't think you were talking about me."

Yeah. She really wasn't.

"What do you need? Grady asked.

"I think I'm okay, other than my pride. And my butt. It's okay, it can take it. It's well-padded."

He frowned. "Don't speak about yourself like that. Are you sure you're not in pain? What caused you to fall?"

"Uh, just slipped, I guess." She decided to ignore his small scolding about how she'd talked about her bottom.

"Hmm." He didn't look convinced. Which didn't make sense. "It looked like you were in pain before you slipped, Twinkletoes."

Twinkletoes? That was cute. Even if wrong.

Focus, Effie.

Sometimes, it was hard to get her brain to think about one thing. Scatterbrained is what Nan used to call her.

"Ah, I'm fine."

"Is that so?" he murmured. "Then can I ask why you haven't moved?"

"Um, well . . . I . . ."

"Babe, just tell us what hurts," Chardonnay told her. She didn't sound impatient, just concerned.

"It's my back. I'm so sorry. If you just give me a moment, it will stop spasming and I'll be able to move."

"Will I make it worse if I pick you up?" he asked.

"Ahh, no. But you don't want to pick me up."

"Have you got a flesh-eating disease that I might catch?"

"Oh no, I got that cured last week."

His face softened. There wasn't a lot soft about this man, so she took that as a win.

"So there's no reason for me not to pick you up?"

"I know I'm holding everything up. And everyone is probably staring at me, wondering why I'm lying here like a beached whale, but really, a few minutes is all I need."

She hoped.

Because the stab of pain that just went through her back told her that things were worse than she'd thought.

"Is she all right?" a fake-sweet voice asked.

"Fucking Lucy," Chardonnay muttered.

"It's just . . . we're opening in half an hour. So if we need to get an ambulance and someone to help move her, then I need to get onto that."

Wow. She was so kind.

"Lucy," Grady snapped.

"Yes, sir?" Lucy simpered.

"That was uncalled for."

"I don't know what you mean. I was only trying to help."

Chardonnay snorted. "And my man has a small dick and doesn't know how to use it."

"Take it he's well-endowed and knows how to use it?" Effie asked with a grin.

"Oh yeah, he sure does. And even if he wasn't big, it wouldn't matter. Because he's all about making me come first."

"Total keeper," Effie replied. She managed to half-lift her arm to fist-bump Chardonnay.

Ouch. That hurt.

"Careful," Grady snapped. "That's hurting her."

"Sorry, babe," Chardonnay said with a wince. "How about I help you?"

She reached down to grab Effie's arm.

"No, wait!" Effie said.

But before she could grab at her, Grady moved. He did it quickly and without hesitation. Suddenly, she was in his arms, and then he was walking toward the back of the stage.

"That's seriously hot," she whispered.

"A man carrying you?"

"Well, yeah. You must work out because I'm not exactly a lightweight."

He shook his head. "You better not let Steele hear you talk like that."

"Like what?"

"Putting yourself down. It's something he's not a fan of in women. Something I'm finding I'm not a fan of either."

Meaning neither of them were fans of her. Right. She got it.

She bit her lip as Chardonnay rushed ahead of them.

"Sorry," she told him. Even though she wasn't quite sure why she was saying it.

"Stop chewing your lip."

"Sorry," she whispered.

"And stop saying sorry."

"Is there anything you do like about me?" she asked with exasperation.

"Don't really know you, sweetheart."

"And yet you think you get to boss me around."

"I'm not the bossy one. I leave that up to Steele."

"You could have fooled me," she muttered. If Damon Steele was bossier than this guy, then it was probably good he wasn't here.

"I'll open the dressing room door," Chardonnay said.

"We're going to my office," Grady stated.

Chardonnay stopped and turned to stare at them. "What?"

"We are going to my office," he repeated in a low, calm voice. But one that didn't invite the other woman to argue with him.

"Why're we going to your office?" she asked.

"Because that's where I want to go."

"Do you always get your own way?" She was guessing yes.

"Most of the time."

She sighed. "That must be nice. I rarely get my own way."

"It is nice."

"I can only imagine."

3

Grady carried her into an office. It was pretty bare. It didn't really match the well-dressed, gorgeous, confident man holding her.

"Can I get you something? Ice? Heating pad?" Chardonnay asked as Grady lowered her onto an old leather chesterfield sofa with some cracks in the material.

Yeah. It had definitely seen better days. As had the beaten-up wooden desk in the middle of the room and the old shelves along the back wall.

"I'm good," she replied. "But could you please get my stuff for me?"

She was really feeling the urge to run. Well, not that she could actually run. But getting out of here was high on her priority list.

And she wanted to get out of here about twenty minutes ago. Before she'd gotten up on that stage and made a fool of herself.

Her feet were aching from her stupid shoes. But the worst pain was in her back which hadn't stopped spasming.

"Sure thing!" Chardonnay ran off, which was quite a feat in her high shoes.

Effie remembered what it was like to wear high heels. She could move in them even better than Chardonnay.

Before.

"Right. Now, tell me what you really need. Shall I get a doctor in here?" Grady asked.

"Um, pretty sure doctors don't make house calls unless you're like the queen or something."

"They do if you pay them enough."

Wow. "You shouldn't be paying them to come in for a simple back spasm. I'm fine."

"You keep saying that, sweetheart. But I don't believe it. And I don't like people lying to me."

"Let me guess, Mr. Steele likes it even less."

His lips twitched. "You catch on quick."

"Not always," she muttered.

He gave her a curious look. This man was sharp. Way too smart for her.

A knock on the door had her stiffening and she had to swallow a gasp of pain. Grady didn't look happy at the noise she made. He looked even less pleased as he glared over at the door.

"Who is it?"

"Oh, Thomas, it's just me." The door opened and there she stood. Lucy.

Awesome.

"Don't call me Thomas," Grady replied sharply.

Ouch. She'd probably slink away and cry if he ever used that voice on her.

"Sorry, Grady."

"Mr. Grady," he said.

"Mr. Grady." This time, Lucy's voice was harsh. It seemed like it wasn't as easy for her to hold on to the sweet act when he wasn't buying it.

"Right. What do you want, Lucy?"

"Everyone is waiting for you. What do you want me to do?"

"Send them home and tell them we'll be in contact," Mr. Grady replied.

"I think they'll want to hear from you. Plus, the alcohol rep just turned up and wants a word. I mean, she's not too badly injured, right?" Lucy stared down at her with mock sympathy.

Right. Like she was seriously concerned about Effie.

"I'm fine. Really. You should go talk to them," she said to Grady.

He sighed and glared at Lucy. His face softened as he turned to Effie.

That was nice.

Really nice. What was even nicer was that Lucy saw it and her face tightened in anger. While Effie didn't usually enjoy other people getting upset, it was hard to feel sympathy toward Lucy.

"Sure you'll be all right, sweetheart?"

Lucy's mouth dropped open.

Oh yeah. That stab of satisfaction Effie got at seeing Lucy's face definitely made her a bad person.

But she didn't care. Not one bit.

"I'm fine."

Grady stood and nodded to her. "Stay there. Do not move."

And he didn't consider himself bossy?

Sheesh.

As soon as he was gone, she attempted to stand. Ouch. This was bad. Taking the bus was going to be painful. But she couldn't sit here and wait for him to get back. She needed to go home and hide under the covers for about a week.

That would fix everything.

"What are you doing? Are you all right?" Chardonnay rushed into the room and grabbed her arm, helping her up.

"Not really. But I will be. Thanks for getting my stuff. I'm really sorry I messed everything up."

"Girl, you were dancing like a dream. I couldn't keep my eyes off you until..."

"Until I messed it all up. Story of my life."

Chardonnay bit her lip. "Where did Grady go?"

"Lucy came and got him."

Chardonnay's lip curled. "Say no more."

"I'm supposed to wait here."

"Yeah?"

"But I don't think I want to wait here." Because with each moment that passed, with each flashback of her falling off the pole, she became more agitated.

"So what do you want to do?"

She chewed at her lip. What did she want to do? Lord, making decisions sucked sometimes. But she had to suck it up and make them. She was an adult. She was in charge of a child. Well, not so much a child since he was taller than she was and was fond of bossing her around.

Still, at thirty-five years old, it shouldn't be this hard to make decisions.

"You want to leave?" Chardonnay asked kindly.

It was for the best, right? Grady was probably hoping that he'd return and find her gone. So, really, she was doing what he wanted.

That made her feel marginally better.

She nodded. "Yeah. I want to go."

"I want to tell you that it doesn't matter that you fell but I can see that it does," Chardonnay murmured quietly.

"You're very observant. And kind."

Chardonnay shrugged. "At the end of the day, I've got to look myself in the mirror. I'm not always nice. I don't always make the right choices, but I'm trying to be a better person."

"Well, I think you're awesome. But you'd be even better if you could show me where the back entrance to this place is."

Chardonnay grinned. "You got it."

Ten minutes later, Effie set out toward the bus station. It was only two blocks from Pinkies, so at least she didn't have too far to walk. Just as well with the pain slicing through her.

She'd had to lie to Chardonnay and tell her that she'd parked down the street to get her to leave. The only reason Chardonnay hadn't walked her to her fake car was because she had to get ready for tonight.

But she'd given Effie her phone number. So while everything else might have turned to shit tonight, at least she'd made a new friend.

That was never a bad thing, right?

What was a bad thing was the pain in her back, making her shuffle along, and the fact that she didn't know what time the next bus came. And it was cold.

Really fuckin' cold.

Tears threatened, but she wouldn't give in to them.

No. Nope.

She could make it to the bus stop and wait for the bus. Then, she could sit for a while on the bus. Then walk on sore feet to her crummy apartment, where the best thing in the world waited for her.

Her nephew, Brooks.

He wasn't her blood nephew, but that didn't matter. He was Joe's. And Joe had always been hers as much as she'd been his.

So Brooks was hers too.

Sometimes looking at Brooks hurt, because he was the exact image of Joe. But it hurt in a good kind of way, because having Brooks meant she also always had a piece of Joe.

And if she got under enough blankets on her crummy bed, well, she might just be able to warm up.

Shivering, she moved slowly through the parking lot to the street.

"You're not very obedient, are you?" a deep voice asked.

She gasped, then turned, letting out a pained cry as her back protested. Her legs gave way and she knew she was about to eat gravel.

Muscular arms surrounded her, lifting her against a firm chest.

This time, the tears leaked out of her eyes and down her cheeks.

"Damn it."

"What is it? Is it your back?"

"My eyes."

"Your eyes?" he asked. "What happened to your eyes? Jesus, I was only gone twenty minutes."

"They're leaking."

"Leaking?" He stilled and stared down at her. The parking lot was well lit; however, she still couldn't figure out what he was thinking. "Do you mean that you're crying?"

"Yes. If that's what you want to call it."

"Pretty sure that's what it's called, sweetheart."

She sniffled. "I don't like it. I want it to stop."

"It's all right to cry."

"Do you cry?" she asked incredulously.

"No. I can't remember the last time I cried."

"Well, then, when you cry, come back to me and tell me it's all right. Because it's really not. If it gets bad, then I'll start to sob. And if I start sobbing, then I'll get all snotty. And my cheeks will go blotchy. My make-up will run. It's a whole thing, and none of it is . . . is pretty!" she wailed.

"Do you get louder as well?" he asked as he entered Pinkies.

"Yes!" she cried. "Oh God, people are going to see me."

"Yes, they're probably wondering how a fox got in here."

"A fox?" she asked as he carried her down a passage and into his office. At least they'd come in the back way.

"Hmm. A female fox can sound like a person in distress."

"Really?" She wiped at her tears, trying to hide her face. She didn't need to scare the poor guy half to death.

"Yes, they let out a similar sort of cry when they want to mate."

She gaped up at him. "You're kidding me!"

"I assure you, I am not." He set her down on the sofa before sitting on the old coffee table in front of her. He grabbed the box of tissues from next to him.

"Thanks," she muttered, taking a few tissues.

He watched her as she cleaned herself up, which was kind of embarrassing. When she was finished, she glanced around for a garbage bin.

"What are you looking for?"

"Um, somewhere to throw my tissues."

He held out his hand. She looked down at it, wondering what he wanted. A high-five. Weird, but okay.

She slapped her hand down on his.

"What was that?"

"A high-five. That's what you wanted, right?"

"I want the tissues."

"Why would you want the tissues? They're used."

"To throw them in the bin."

Dear Lord. There was no hope for her. None at all.

"I can throw them in the garbage."

"Effie."

It was all he said.

It was enough. After all, she'd just given him an unwanted high-five. If it hadn't been for falling over on stage while wearing next to nothing, this would be the most embarrassing thing to happen to her.

"It's all right, I'll just hold on to them."

"Effie. Give me the tissues."

She handed them over. There was no denying him when he used that tone.

And that tone was bossy and hot.

She was a total goner.

4

"Where are your gloves?" Grady asked with a frown as he took the tissues, throwing them into a bin that she hadn't seen from her angle.

"I don't know. I couldn't find them before I left the house."

He eyed her. "You went outside in February in Montana without gloves?"

He made it sound like she'd gone outside while naked. That had nearly happened once. She'd missed putting out the garbage bin the night before. Oh, she'd had panties on, but still . . . she was grateful she'd realized her error when she'd opened the doors and the cool air hit her nipples.

"I've lost you again."

"What? I'm here. I'm good."

"Are you?" he asked.

"Uh-huh. Are you good?" It was nice to ask people how they were doing, right?

"What I am is angry."

"You are?"

He didn't look or sound angry.

"I am."

"You don't look it," she told him.

"Then you'll have to take my word for it. I am upset. With you."

Ouch. That felt like a punch to the gut.

"Mr. Grady—" she started to say.

"It's just Grady."

"Oh. Uh, that's not what you told Lucy."

He just looked at her. "That's for Lucy. For you, it's just Grady."

That turned the pain in her stomach into something warmer that filled her whole body.

"All right, Grady. Why are you upset with me?"

"Are you kidding me?" he asked, turning her words from earlier back on her.

"Um, no," she said. "Why are you mad?"

"You left."

"Oh. But you left first."

Lame, Effie. Really lame.

Lord, she really could use some jelly beans right now. And a hug from Slowly. And some painkillers.

"I left, but I was coming back. Were you coming back?" he asked.

"I might have been?"

"I believe we have discussed lying. What did I say to you before I left?"

"It was more like what did you order me before you left."

"Yes, it was," he replied calmly. "And what did I order you?"

"To stay here and not move."

"Did you stay?"

"Um, no."

"You disobeyed me."

Damn, he had this whole stern professor thing going on

right now.

And she could be the naughty college student . . . uh-uh, no. Stop, Effie. This was not the time for her imagination to run wild on her.

"Effie? Why did you leave?" he asked.

"Well, I didn't see much point in staying. I didn't get the job and I need to get home." So she could scour the internet for another job. Or bus tickets for her and Brooks to get to Wanton, Wyoming.

Yep, that was really the name of the town where April lived.

Pretty awesome.

"You didn't see much point in staying?" he repeated.

"Um, yeah."

"What about the fact that I still needed to check whether you were well enough to move around by yourself?"

Uh. Right.

Now she felt terrible.

It wouldn't have hurt her to wait around a few minutes for him to return.

Except . . . he'd been gone a while and she'd grown more embarrassed with each passing second.

"And that I came back expecting to see you where I put you."

Okay, she wasn't feeling so terrible now. In fact, she was feeling kind of mad.

"Where you put me?" she asked in a quiet voice.

"Yes, Twinkletoes, where I put you." He leaned in and she felt her heartbeat quicken at his closeness.

Not in fear. Or anger.

Nope. It was another emotion rushing through her. One that had her pressing her thighs together as her clit throbbed.

"I don't think I have to stay where you put me when I don't belong to you."

He leaned back and she missed having his face near hers.

Seeing those tiny flecks of brown in his amazingly green eyes.

Shoot. Why did she go and say that?

"What about if you worked for me? Would you need to stay where I put you then?"

A shiver ran through her.

"You're still cold," he said, misinterpreting her shiver. "You shouldn't be walking around in this weather without gloves. Or a scarf. Or a hat. Or without shoes that fit, for that matter."

He got up, opened a cupboard at the wall behind his desk and pulled out a soft-looking deep blue blanket.

Which he placed around her shoulders, then pulled it around her so she was covered in it.

"Now, back to what I was saying about you working for me—"

He was interrupted by voices on the other side of the door, which he'd left open a few inches.

"Oh, Steele, you should have seen her. She was far too old, and well, if I can be blunt, fat to be stripping. She tried to hold herself up on the pole, then she just fell to the stage. I was so embarrassed for her."

Effie felt her face growing bright red. She kept her gaze on her lap since the last thing she wanted was to look up at Grady and see his pity. Or worse, his agreement.

"She fell? Is she okay?" a deep voice rumbled.

Whoa. That was one sexy voice.

"Fucking bitch," Grady said, standing.

"Yeah, she's fine. She won't be suing or anything. She didn't look like she had the money for the bus home, let alone an attorney. And besides, she was faking being hurt to feel less humiliated. But it was completely humiliating."

Lucy started laughing and shame rolled through Effie. She hadn't been faking an injury.

And this bitch didn't get to make her feel bad.

By the time she'd given herself a pep talk, Grady was at the door, swinging it wide.

"Shut up, Lucy."

Lucy gasped at his harsh words. Even Effie looked up at him in shock. No one had stood up for her since Joe died. Well, other than April, but she lived thousands of miles away. Although she wouldn't have hesitated to get in this bitch's face.

April had fire. Because not only did she known her own worth, but she also had a man at home who wouldn't hesitate to take her back.

Effie didn't feel like she'd ever known her own worth. Maybe when Joe was alive. But even then, she spent most of her time trying to be nice and not rock the boat.

Things her Nan had ingrained into her.

"Grady? Everything good?" the deep voice asked.

"It will be as soon as Lucy leaves my eyesight," Grady countered.

Whoa.

Grady was mad.

Really, really mad.

He'd said he was angry before because she'd taken off. But she thought he might have been exaggerating.

Because this . . . this was angry.

And he was mad because of what Lucy was saying about her. She could feel a crack in the shield she'd put up to protect herself. An armor that few people could get through, that they even noticed was there.

But it was there. And it was cracking.

"How rude! Why are you talking to me that way, Mr. Grady when all I've ever done is try to do a good job for you."

Dear Lord. That was a terrible acting job. Did Lucy really think that people would buy that?

"Grady," the other voice warned.

Whoa. Was the other guy buying her act?

"Steele, she needs to get far away from me right now. I am not going to stand by while she talks badly about Effie."

"Effie?"

She liked hearing her name being spoken by Steele. She couldn't see him, nor did she know him, so there was no reason why she should react that way.

But she liked it a heck of a lot.

"Let's go talk in your office," Steele added.

"No, we won't be talking in there," Grady replied. "We need to talk; we'll do it somewhere else."

There was a beat of silence.

"It's fine, really," Lucy said. "I'm all right, Steele."

She rolled her eyes. Lucy was laying it on thick.

"Hey, Grady, Steele, there's a problem with the alcohol order," an unfamiliar voice said.

Grady sighed. "I'll be there in a minute." He stepped back into the office and shut the door before turning to look at her. "You. Stay here."

Then he grabbed a set of keys out of his desk drawer and left.

But not before she heard a key turning in the lock.

Did he . . . did he just lock her in here?

Getting up slowly, she moved to the door and tried it.

Shit. Fuck.

That asshole. Obviously, he thought she was going to run.

Which you were.

Yeah, but that didn't mean he got to lock her in.

She tried to find a comfortable position with her back spasming. But nothing helped. Also, her feet were aching from her stupid shoes, but she didn't want to take them off. She looked at the clock.

God damn it. He'd been gone a long time now.

Where the hell was he?

5

Damon Steele eyed his best friend curiously.

Grady was usually a closed book to everyone but him. He kept his true feelings and emotions locked down tight. Only letting things slip through his guard when they were alone.

Except for right now. He was glaring down at Lucy. Steele wasn't sure why, exactly. Sure, Lucy was annoying. But Grady didn't usually look at her with such fury in his eyes.

Steele couldn't quite work out what she'd done. Was it because she'd been unkind to the woman who'd fallen while doing her interview? Steele had never known Grady to be protective over someone he'd just met.

Grady wasn't really that protective of anyone. Sure, he took care of the staff that worked here. But he didn't favor one over the other. He just considered that part of his job. He didn't feel anything for them.

Curious.

And why did he lock his office door? He never locked his office door unless . . . unless he had a woman in there.

Grady wasn't known for mixing business and pleasure. So the rare time a woman had been in there for anything other than business was when Steele put her there.

In fact, he couldn't remember the last time Grady had slept with a woman without Steele instigating things.

Hmm. That didn't seem healthy now that he thought about it. Maybe he needed a word with the other man.

Maybe you haven't been looking after Grady as well as he takes care of you.

And perhaps he should head back to the office to see why Grady had locked it.

If he has a girl in there, it's none of your business.

Yet, he was curious.

And he hadn't been curious about anything in a long time.

Life had become monotonous, with only brief bursts of color to intersperse the gray. Sometimes, he thought the only reason he got up in the morning was because Grady wouldn't let him wither away.

And because Grady wouldn't do well without him.

He was all Grady had.

So, yeah, feeling curious wasn't normal for him. The last time he'd been this interested in a woman was when Millie came into Pinkies that first time.

Now . . . there was a woman who made life interesting.

He envied Quillon. His life would never be boring. Although, he also had a lot on his hands. Millie ate life and didn't always stop to think before doing something.

That was something that Steele would have squashed straight away. Because any woman of his wouldn't be putting herself in danger.

No fucking way.

But since he never intended to have a woman of his own, that shit didn't matter.

He watched Grady breathing ice at Lucy, who actually looked slightly concerned. He should interfere. Even though he didn't really care about Lucy, he knew that if she quit, Grady would have more on his plate that he didn't need.

"Grady, didn't you need to go deal with the alcohol issue?" he asked.

Grady turned to eye him. Then, he seemed to gather himself. "Yes, I'll get onto that. But you need to remember this, Lucy. Do not speak about anyone who works here like that."

"She doesn't work here," Lucy replied.

"She was interviewing for a job. And you need to watch the way you speak to people, or you are gone."

Something flashed in Lucy's face. Something ugly. And Steele made a mental note to watch her.

"Steele?" Lucy turned to him, her eyes wide and pleading.

Was she serious with this shit right now? Was she expecting him to side with her? Over his best friend? The person he cared about most in the world?

"Go back to work," he ordered.

Her face filled with shock.

"And you might want to take Grady's words to heart."

Yep. She wasn't expecting that. She turned and stomped away.

Steele turned to the other man, who was scowling. "You want to tell me what that was about?"

"It was about Lucy being a bitch and talking to people in ways she shouldn't."

"Never seemed to bother you before."

"It's always bothered me."

Yeah, that he didn't like. "You should have told me. You want her gone?"

"Not right now. I don't have time to do her job as well."

"We'll hire someone else."

"Actually, I've got another plan for that—"

"Grady? Sorry to interrupt, but we need you," Nate, the head bartender, interrupted them.

"Go take care of that," Steele ordered. That would give him time to do what he really wanted.

Check out whoever Grady had in his office. Who had him twisted up in knots.

∼

EFFIE WAS ready for the door to open, and as soon as it did, she stepped forward, her finger up in the air. "Listen up, mister. You might be stronger than me, smarter than me, and richer than me, definitely prettier than me, but that does not mean you have the right to lock me up!"

She stilled as she got close to the broad chest before her. A wide chest that was even bigger than she'd been expecting. In fact, all of him was larger than she'd been expecting.

Because the man standing in front of her was not the one she'd been expecting.

Oops.

"Never been called pretty before."

She gazed up into a hard face. One that was striking. Intriguing. Certainly sexy.

Not as classically handsome as Grady's face. And most certainly not pretty. But that didn't make it any less mesmerizing.

Also, slightly terrifying. Because this man was enormous. He looked like he could squash her with one of his pinky fingers and not even break into a sweat.

She stumbled back a step, then let out a wince as pain shot through her back.

"You all right?" he asked.

"Hunky-dory."

Hunky-dory? Really? Could she be any more of a dork?

She studied him. This had to be Steele. And he really suited his name. Because there didn't look to be an inch of him that wasn't hard.

Hmm. There might be a few inches. Her gaze dropped to his crotch.

"No, you're not okay, Spitfire. I don't know you, but you've already gotten up in my face with your finger, which you won't be doing again. You've called me pretty and a whole bunch of other things. Plus, you've just lied to me. And all of those things are spelling trouble for you."

"I well . . . I don't even know you!"

"No, you do not. But what you need to learn very quickly is that I don't appreciate having a finger in my face. Or being lied to. Especially when you are not okay."

"I was expecting someone else to walk through the door and . . . well, it was a little white lie."

"A little white lie."

"Yeah, because it's the polite thing to say. If someone asks you if you're okay and you don't know that person well, then you say you're fine. Because they don't really want to know if you're in pain, they're just being polite."

"I'm very rarely polite."

Right. Good to know.

Also, she wasn't sure how to reply to that.

And she wasn't sure she liked being called a Spitfire, either.

"I take it you're Mr. Steele."

"You'd be right. Damon Steele." He held out his hand, which surprised her.

But she reached out to take it, only to have him grab hold and not let go.

"Uh, can I have my hand back?"

"No."

She gaped up at him, noticing his eyes were a striking blue color. He had short dark hair, a short beard, and shoulders that went on forever.

Seriously, he had to be twice as wide as she was.

"You look like you could bench press a small car."

Something changed in his face. "Not quite. But I can easily pick you up and put you where I want you."

"Now you sound like Grady."

"Do I?" he asked curiously.

"Yes, he told me I should stay where he put me. And then he locked me in his office."

"Obviously, he thinks you're a runner. Are you a runner?"

"I can't run. I try to run and I look like Donald Duck. Big butt waddling along. Boobs flying all over the place because no sports bra can tame these girls. It's not a pretty sight. Then I usually trip over something or twist my foot, and my body will warn me that it wasn't made for running. And then I'll stop running for another few years. Until I get the hare-brained idea that I need to run in order to lose a few pounds. And the cycle starts again. What was my point again?"

He was standing, leaning against the door with her hand still in his. She gave it a tug, realizing just how warm her skin was where she was touching him.

He didn't let her hand go.

She wanted to frown at him. Instead, she smiled brightly. If she asked nicely enough, then he'd have to do what she asked. It was just good manners.

And she was going to ignore the fact that it seemed like he didn't have any.

"Could I please have my hand back?"

"No."

"No?"

"No."

"But I said please."

He leaned in closer. "No. When I asked if you were a runner. I wasn't talking about actual running. I meant, are you going to try and leave?"

"I can't leave with you standing in front of the door," she pointed out.

"True. Which is why I'm standing here. But if I wasn't, would you try to leave?"

"You also have my hand. Which is kind of unnecessary with you standing in front of the door."

"Figure it's added security against you trying to leave."

"You know you can't just hold on to me. And Grady can't just lock me up! That's not legal."

"Never been much to worry over what's legal, Spitfire."

"I'm not sure I like that nickname."

"You like it."

Shoot. She did. And Effie didn't think trying to deny it was going to help matters.

Suddenly, he moved toward the couch. And she had no choice but to go with him since he still had a hold of her hand. He sat and she stared down at him. It should have put her in a position of power, considering that she was standing and he was sitting. But he was so big that even sitting she wasn't that much taller than him.

"I didn't know it was possible to get muscles that big," she muttered.

"Do you always say what you're thinking?"

"I'm trying to do that less."

"Why?"

"It tends to get me in trouble."

He eyed her. "And when you get into trouble, who gets you out?"

"I do." She straightened her shoulders and her back gave another twinge. Nausea rolled in her stomach.

Great. She needed to get home and grab a heat pack as well as take some stronger painkillers.

"Got no man, then?"

"What makes you think that?" she asked.

"Well, if you do, he's a shit man."

"What? Why would you think he was a shit man!"

You don't even have a man. So why are you trying to defend him?

"So there is a man? Doesn't matter. He won't be around for long."

"Are you threatening my man?" she asked, alarmed.

"He's not much of a man if he lets you get into trouble. He's even less of a man if he doesn't help you get out of that trouble."

"I can take care of myself." Wow, he was sexist, wasn't he?

"Yeah, I don't think you can, considering you just got yourself locked into an office at a strip club."

She swallowed heavily. "Are you saying I'm in trouble?"

"Not the sort of trouble you're thinking about," he soothed. "The sort of trouble where I don't like being lied to or listening to you put yourself down or knowing that you're with a shit man. That's the sort of trouble you're in."

"I don't know you."

"Yes, I think we've already discussed that part, Spitfire. I'm just letting you know the things that I don't like."

"But why?" she whispered. "I'm going to leave soon and you're won't see me again."

"Somehow, I don't think that's true."

The door rattled and then opened before Grady stepped in. His frowning face went from Steele to her. Then it dropped to where Steele was still holding her hand.

"What the fuck is going on in here?"

6

Grady was in a bad fucking mood.

Everything that could go wrong was going wrong tonight and on the one night he had something else to do.

And that something else was dealing with the girl in his office. He took a deep breath and reached for his keys. Only to hear the murmur of voices from behind the door.

Who the fuck was she talking to? He tested the door. Unlocked.

There could only be one person in there.

What the fuck was Steele up to?

He stormed into the room and took in their coziness. Steele was sitting on the sofa, which was where she was supposed to be. Because that's where Grady had put her. And she was standing close to him. With her hand in his.

"What the fuck is going on in here?"

Effie's eyes were wide as she stared at him.

"Ahh, good, you're here," Steele drawled. "I was just having a conversation with Spitfire."

"Spitfire?" Grady asked, trying to pull himself together. "And what sort of conversation?"

"The sort of conversation that we don't need to be having," Effie replied. "Because right now, I should be at home, in bed, with a heat pack on my back."

"You're still in pain?" Steele asked sharply. "It wasn't just because you moved too fast before?"

What was up with him? Steele didn't usually pay a lot of attention to his employees.

But Effie wasn't an employee.

Not yet.

Grady had plans to change that. But now he was wondering how Steele would feel about those plans. They had a rule about getting involved with employees.

Lucy seemed to think she was beyond that rule. She wasn't.

And Effie wouldn't be either.

So considering that his hand was still holding hers, Grady's next play might piss Steele off.

But that didn't matter if it was best for Effie. And he had a feeling that what Effie needed most was a job.

Not to end up in bed with the two of them for a weekend. They'd take care of her. They'd show her a good time. But it wouldn't be permanent.

Because Steele didn't ever want permanent.

And Grady couldn't be in any sort of relationship without Steele.

"Did you injure yourself when you fell? And do not tell me that you're fine, Spitfire."

"I didn't injure myself when I fell," she muttered, looking stubborn.

Steele thought he wanted someone who would jump when he barked. That he wanted instant obedience and no arguments.

But that shit bored him after a day.

He needed someone sweet. But also with a bit of sass. And when Effie forgot to be scared or worried, she had sass.

"She was in pain before she fell," Grady explained. "Back injury?"

She stared between them both.

"Effie?" Steele pressed. No one denied him when he used that tone, so Grady just waited for her acquiescence. "Tell us. Right now."

Instead, she looked to the ceiling. "Why? Why me? What did I do? I'm certain I've never done something so bad that I'd end up stuck in an office with two cavemen."

Grady moved his gaze to Steele.

To Grady's shock, the other man's lips twitched. "I can see why you're calling me a caveman, but Grady? Nope. Not a caveman."

Effie glared at Steele. "When I tried to leave before, he chased after me, picked me up, and carried me back to his office. Before locking me in it."

Steele's gaze hit his, assessing. "Did he, just?"

"She was hurt," Grady told him. "And she was walking along the road in the cold with no gloves, scarf, or hat."

"Spitfire, it's fucking thirty-five degrees out there," Steele rumbled, looking seriously unimpressed.

"I forgot them." Sort of.

That blue gaze turned icy. "You forgot them?"

"Ah, yep."

"It's not even forty degrees out there. What are you doing going out without your hat, scarf or gloves?"

Her mouth dropped open. "Is this . . . is this some sort of prank? Like, are you filming for some shitty reality show? Because I can tell you right now, I'm not signing any waivers."

There was a note of panic and hurt in her voice, which made

something in Grady melt. Something that he'd long since thought had turned to solid ice.

"No one is pranking you. I promise. Look at me." He waited for her dark-brown gaze to move to his. "I promise."

Her rapid breathing slowed. Grady didn't like how pale she was. She was still in pain, he could see it in the lines bracketing her mouth.

"Then why do you . . . why do you care whether I'm hurt or whether I'm warm or anything else about me?"

That wasn't something he had a ready answer for. Not a proper one. So he said the only one he could think of.

"Because you're going to work for me."

Effie gaped up at Grady.

"She's what?" Steele asked in a low rumble.

She was trying really hard not to show how much his voice affected her. But sheesh, if it was possible to come from just listening to someone's voice . . . it would be Steele's.

"She's going to work for me," Grady repeated firmly.

"As . . . as what?" She didn't let hope fill her. Because she had no idea what this job was. It could be shining his shoes and cleaning his toilet with a toothbrush. Not that she wouldn't do that. She just needed to know what it was first so she could prepare herself.

Also, because these guys were clearly a few cans short of a six-pack. They seemed to think being bossy and touching her and locking her up was normal behavior.

Speaking of touching her . . . she tugged at the hand that Steele was still holding.

And he let her go.

That shouldn't have upset her. She should be rejoicing that finally he'd stopped touching her.

But she really missed his touch.

She should probably turn this job down. Except she was desperate. Which is why she was here in the first place.

Desperation made people do things they otherwise wouldn't.

"My assistant," Grady replied coolly. "I'm overworked and I need help. As well as Pinkies, I also run several more of Steele's businesses. And I need an assistant."

"An assistant?" she asked.

"Yes."

"How do you know she's qualified to be an assistant?" Steele asked.

Shit. She guessed that Grady needed Steele's agreement to hire her, since he was the big boss. Although they didn't really act like employer and employee. Nope, there seemed to be a whole other vibe to their relationship that she didn't quite have her finger on yet.

It's also none of your business.

"Effie, do you think you're capable of being my assistant?" Grady asked. "Can you answer the phone, keep track of my calendar, organize stuff, and just generally do whatever I ask you to?"

Fuck yes.

Well, she'd need to be careful because sometimes she went into her own head and got lost in there. But not this time. She needed to stay in the here and now.

"I can do that! I can do the shit out of that!" She smiled wide.

Steele still seemed bemused. Oh no, was he going to say no? She stared at him, willing him to agree.

"When can you start, Effie?" Grady asked.

"Now."

His face softened. "I like that you're eager, sweetheart. But after the night you just had, you need to go home, put a heat pack on your back, take some painkillers, and get some rest."

"How come she hasn't already taken some painkillers?" Steele asked, surprising her.

Grady's face hardened.

"It's all right," she said hastily before Grady could snap. Which is what he looked like he was about to do. "I'm fine."

Now, both of them turned to look at her. And whoa, their attention made her legs go weak. She started moving back and forth to relieve the pain in her back.

"I think I've told you how I feel about you lying, Spitfire."

"My back really isn't that bad anymore. I actually have some painkillers in my bag. I was going to take them on the way home."

"You'll take them now," Steele ordered, getting up from the sofa. "And you'll sit."

She thought it was wise not to argue.

No one will like you if you argue all the time.

Thanks, Nan. Although, this time, she thought that not arguing might be the best idea.

Winning a fight against Damon Steele seemed pretty impossible. He definitely looked like he'd fight dirty.

She moved to the sofa and sat as Steele disappeared into an attached bathroom.

"If she had stayed where I put her, then she'd already be sitting down," Grady commented.

She wanted to glare at him and tell him she wasn't a darn dog to be told to stay. But he was her new boss.

Be nice. You need this job.

Steele returned with a glass of water. She gave him a surprised look. Even Grady stared at him funny, so she knew this wasn't normal.

"Where's your bag?" Steele asked as he handed her the drink.

"Um, over here." She turned to where it sat on the floor. But he got there first, opening her bag so he could search through it.

"Hey! What do you think you're doing?" she demanded.

"Looking for your painkillers."

"You can't just go through my handbag." She gaped at him, aghast, as Grady groaned and ran his hand over his face.

"Why? What do you have to hide?" Steele asked.

"I don't have anything to hide," she fired back. "But that still doesn't mean it's okay to go through a woman's handbag. My handbag is my life. It's private. It's sacred. And it can only be held by a man when necessary. Like when you're doing some shopping and you have your arms full of clothes and no room to hold your handbag. But still… it should never be breached by a man's giant paws."

Steele just stared at her for a long moment. Was that too much honesty? Then he shook his head and handed her the bag. "Get your pills out."

She frowned as she searched through her bag and found the bottle. He took them from her, looking at the label.

"Steele," Grady said warningly.

"These are strong. And they say that you shouldn't take them on an empty stomach. Or while drinking alcohol. Have you done either of those recently?

"I don't really like alcohol."

And did a cup of noodles at lunchtime count as eating recently?

Please do not rumble, stomach.

"I'll be fine."

"You lying about being fine?" Steele asked.

"I think we should stop staying fine," she suggested. "It's starting to sound weird to me. Fine. Fine. Fine."

"Okay, I think that's enough," Grady suggested.

Probably wise.

"You're not swallowing these until you eat," Steele dictated. "I'll go get you something. Grady, make sure she stays."

She gaped at him as he stomped out of the room.

"You were right, I was wrong."

"That could pertain to many things, sweetheart," Grady drawled. "Exactly what are you talking about?"

"The fact that he's bossier."

"Hmm. He is. But I have to say that he's being even bossier than usual."

"Really?" she whispered.

"Yes."

"That doesn't seem to be a good sign."

His eyes zeroed in on her. "I can't be certain, since I don't know you well, but I think you might need some bossing."

"I do not."

"And since I'm about to be your boss, you won't be able to argue with me when I boss you."

"I don't think that's how it works." But she knew she'd take it. She'd take whatever was thrown her way as long as it didn't involve rollercoasters, going out on a boat, any food starting with s–especially vegetables–or selling her body or soul. And to be honest, she'd consider the last two at this point in time.

"It does."

"Mr. Grady?" she asked.

"We've already had this discussion, Effie," he said firmly. "What do you call me?"

"Grady," she whispered.

"Right. And yes?"

"Is there really a job? Or do you just feel sorry for me?"

"Why would I feel sorry for you?" he asked as Steele walked back into the room holding a bag of chips.

"Chips?" Grady asked incredulously.

"Don't start. It was all I could find. The kitchens have just opened and I didn't want her to wait ten minutes while they made her a salad."

"It would probably be half an hour since they'd have to run out and get the ingredients for a salad," Grady replied.

"Chips are fine," she said hastily. "Chips are good. Salad is not."

Both sets of eyes shot to her again. Shoot. She really felt that like a lightning bolt straight to her clit.

These guys were potent.

"Chips will do for right now," Steele said. "They aren't a substitute for dinner, though."

They were for her. Since dinner was going to consist of a bag of celebratory jelly beans.

She ate a few chips, trying desperately not to go at them like a dog who'd raided the garbage bin and found some leftover Hamburger Helper. She was hungrier than she'd thought.

Steele gave her two pills. "Swallow."

Effie barely managed not to roll her eyes at him. She swallowed and then poked out her tongue.

"Happy?" she asked.

Something strange filled his face. "Not exactly."

She didn't know what that look meant and she wasn't sure it was a good idea to find out. But it sent another bolt of arousal through her.

She was in so much trouble.

"Effie," Grady said after a few moments.

Crap. She just realized that she hadn't offered them any chips. And that they'd stopped talking, so they'd all been listening to her chew.

Embarrassing.

"Um, would you like some?" She held out the packet.

They both shook their heads. Steele even wrinkled his nose.

That was really cute when she didn't think a man who looked like him could pull cute off.

"No, thank you," Grady replied. "Now, we were discussing whether there really is a job or I just feel sorry for you."

Great. They were just laying things out, were they?

She glanced over at Steele, who leaned back against the desk, not looking like he was going anywhere.

Well, she guessed he owned the joint.

"Um. Yeah."

Lord. Why did she ask him that? Was she a glutton for punishment? Now, she'd given them an out, would they take it?

You're an idiot.

"There's really a job," Grady told her immediately. And in a voice that didn't invite any argument.

She glanced over at Steele, wondering if he might have anything different to say. But he just stared down at her steadily.

That tight knot in her stomach dissipated.

"That's good then," she whispered.

"It is. And we'll discuss all the details tomorrow. Over dinner."

"Dinner?" she asked in a high-pitched voice.

"Dinner," Grady said in that same tone of voice that allowed no arguments.

"Um, I could just come in at any time. We don't have to meet for dinner."

Mainly because she had no idea how she was going to afford dinner. The rent was due, but she could probably push back the electric and gas for a while. Spare a few dollars for a burger or something.

"We're meeting over dinner," Grady repeated. "I'll pick you up."

"No, that won't be necessary," she replied.

"It is."

"I'd rather make my own way to dinner. Thanks."

Steele grunted. "You want the job, then you'll let our driver pick you up. If you're worried about letting us know your address, then you probably shouldn't agree to work for us."

Fuck. He had a point.

And it wasn't that she was worried about them knowing where she lived. It was more that she didn't live in a great area of town. It was okay. It wasn't the worst part of Billings. But still . . .

"All right."

Grady's phone beeped. "I have some things I have to do. Raul's free?"

"Yep," Steele replied, that gaze still on her.

Grady nodded. "Raul will take you home. I'll be at your place tomorrow at seven."

"I'll walk you out," Steele said suddenly. "Since Grady is busy."

They shared a look that she couldn't read. Then Grady nodded. "Goodbye, Effie."

"Goodbye. Thank you so much for hiring me. I promise I won't let you down." She gave him her biggest smile, which wasn't hard since she was truly happy.

He just gave her a strange look back, nodded, then left.

7

She gave Steele a worried look.

"Feel like he left you with the big bad wolf?" he asked, quirking an eyebrow.

"More like a lion or a tiger. Maybe an ogre."

His eyes widened. "An ogre?"

"A good ogre," she said hastily.

That probably wasn't the best thing to call one of your new bosses, Effie!

"An. Ogre."

"Like Shrek."

He sucked in a breath and she closed her eyes.

"Shrek? Like an ugly, green, grouchy ogre?" he asked.

"I didn't think he was that ugly. I kind of thought he was cute," she said.

Dear. Lord.

She was digging herself a bigger and bigger hole.

"Cute?"

"Yes, cute," she said. "And ogre was just one of the options I threw out there. There was also a lion or a tiger or a whale—"

"A whale? There was no mention of a whale."

"I'd just like to point out that I'm on drugs. Strong drugs."

"They've barely hit your system."

"They work quickly on me. And there's nothing wrong with whales. They're really very intelligent and cute—"

"Stop."

Oh, thank you, God.

"Take a breath."

She took a breath and let it out, staring up at him.

"We're gonna forget this conversation ever happened."

Her eyebrows rose. "We are?"

"Yep."

"You think that's possible?"

"I'm really, really hoping it is," he said.

To her shock, his lips quirked.

"You're not angry?" she whispered.

"More amused by you."

"That's good. Hold on to those feelings." He was going to need them. She knew she could be a lot.

Which is why Nan often advised her to be . . . less.

He raised his eyebrows. "Let's get you out to Raul, he'll take you home."

"Who is Raul?"

"My driver."

"You have a driver?" she asked.

"Yep. His name is Raul."

She narrowed her gaze. "Are you teasing me?"

"Good. I wasn't sure it was obvious."

Her mouth dropped open. Oh, he was a smart-ass.

And she really, really shouldn't call him that.

"You all right to move?" he asked.

"Yes, of course."

"You going to tell me what's wrong with your back?"

"It just twinges sometimes," she said vaguely.

"If I'm going to be your new boss, I need to know whether there's something that will affect your health."

"I won't let anything affect my ability to do this job," she told him fiercely. She wasn't going to give him an excuse to back out of this. "I'll work really hard and you won't have any reason to find fault with my work."

"Easy, Spitfire," he said in a voice that held a hint of softness. Which was shocking in a man who looked and spoke like he did. "Wasn't asking to find an excuse to get rid of you before you even started."

Do you believe him?

To her surprise, she did. "It's an old back injury. Really, my back is good most of the time."

"All right. Come on," he said gruffly. "I've got work to do and you need to go home to bed and sleep off your twinge."

She stood, trying to hide her wince. She really did need to get home. Those pills would make her sleepy and she wanted to get home to bed.

She held onto the bag of chips. She'd take the rest home for Brooks. He loved chips.

Then she heaved her handbag up over her shoulder.

Steele held out his hand. What did he want? A high-five?

She slapped her hand down on his.

He stared at his palm, then up at her. "What was that?"

"A high-five?"

"Yeah, Spitfire. Wasn't after a high-five. Give me your handbag."

"Uh, why?"

"I've had a sore back before. I know what makes a sore back worse. And one of those things is carrying unnecessary weight. So give me your handbag."

"You can't carry my handbag. That's . . . that's preposterous."

His lips twitched. "Big word there."

"I know some big words," she muttered. She wasn't completely ignorant.

He eyed her curiously. "Was just teasing you, Spitfire. Didn't mean to hit a sore spot."

Crap. She was being too sensitive. "Sorry." She smiled up at him.

"Now, I've got shit to do. Handbag. Let's go."

"It's not heavy."

He sighed. "Handbag. Go."

Okay, when he got grouchy, his sentences grew shorter. That was good to know.

She handed it over.

"Jesus, Spitfire. Doesn't weigh much? This thing weighs a ton. What have you got in here?"

"My life," she replied. And it was true.

"If that was the case, wouldn't you also have your hat, scarf, and gloves in there?" Steele grumbled. "Forgetting them in this weather isn't smart."

Hmm. He seemed rather upset about this, so she decided to keep quiet.

"Come on. Let's get you quickly out to the car."

It was a sight she'd never forget for the rest of her life. Her handbag in Damon Steele's hand. Utterly ridiculous. He made her handbag look small when it was anything but.

And had she mentioned that it was bright pink? Almost neon, it was so intense. And he carried it like he was carrying a briefcase. Without a care about the way he looked.

That sort of confidence was . . . so sexy.

He walked her out the back to a smaller parking lot that was obviously for employees and over to a large town car.

Then he surprised her by opening the back door.

She stared at him, then at the door.

"Get in, babe. It's freezing out here and you're half-dressed." His tone was gruff, a bit impatient. But she understood it. He had other things he needed to do, and she was standing there, staring at him like an idiot.

But there was something she needed to ask. "He's a good driver?"

Steele stared down at her for a moment. She waited for him to get impatient with her. But he simply nodded. "Yeah, babe. Wouldn't have him as my driver if he wasn't the best there was."

She tried to ignore the babe. He probably called everyone that. But it went to her head, making it spin.

To try and hide her reaction, she quickly climbed into the car.

A broad-shouldered, dark-haired man sat in the driver's seat. He looked back at her through the rearview mirror.

Steele leaned in. "Seatbelt."

She always wore her seatbelt and she'd barely just sat down, so he hadn't exactly given her a chance to grab it.

"Raul, take Spitfire home. Drive careful. Precious cargo."

Holy. Heck.

Warmth filled her belly.

Precious cargo.

He couldn't know what those words meant to her. Maybe this was like his 'babe', something he said to every woman Raul drove home, but it still felt nice. And she didn't want to think about how many women there had been in this car.

Nope.

"You got it," Raul replied.

Steele shut the door before she could say goodnight.

Okay. That was a bit rude.

She gave her address to Raul and he drove her silently through the streets. While Raul was very careful, she still found herself clenching her hands together and chewing on her lip.

By the time they got to her neighborhood, she felt exhausted from all the stress. The pills had kicked in, so her pain level was low, but she was sleepy as hell.

"Thank you," she told him, undoing her belt and reaching for the door as he came to a stop.

"I'll walk you to your door."

"That's not necessary."

"In this neighborhood, Miss, it certainly is."

Okay, seemed even the mysterious Raul was bossy and protective. Good to know.

He walked her to the door, which Brooks opened as she got there. She gave him a surprised look, but he was glaring at Raul.

"Who is he? What's going on?"

"Nothing, honey," she said. "Raul just drove me home. Thanks. Oh, let me get you some money."

Raul just shot her a look. He was a good-looking guy in his late forties with a fit build. And that look he sent her was pure alpha male.

"No money."

"But you'll need a tip."

"No money. Go in, lock your door, don't answer it to anyone you don't know."

"Um. Okay."

He was still standing there, so she guessed he was waiting for her to do just that. She gently pushed Brooks inside, then turned to lock the door. She watched out the side window as Raul walked back to the car.

Then she turned to where Brooks was waiting. His foot was tapping, his arms crossed over his chest.

An alpha male in the making.

"Hey, honey. How was your day?"

"My day was good. Uneventful. I'm guessing yours wasn't. Who was that?"

"My new boss' driver," she said.

Urgh. Maybe she should have made something up. But she really hoped this job would work out, so Brooks would soon find out if she lied. And she tried not to lie to him. And not just because he seemed to have some sort of lie-radar.

"New boss? You got a new job?"

"Yep. Maybe we should crack out the hot chocolate to celebrate."

"New job doing what?" Brooks asked as she moved through the living room, which also doubled as her bedroom since she slept on the sleeper sofa. Teenage boys needed their privacy and she'd rather Brooks have the bedroom.

Once she was in the tiny, avocado-green kitchen, she turned to him. There was a look of disapproval on his face.

"What type of job do you think I got?"

"I don't know, but interviews for most jobs don't usually happen at this time of night."

Shit. He had her there.

And while she tried not to lie to Brooks, she didn't want him to know what she'd been interviewing for tonight.

Yeah . . . and what were you planning on telling him if you had to work at night?

Plus, he was probably wondering why she still had her coat on.

Suffice it to say, she hadn't thought things through all that well.

She heaved out a breath. "I got a job as a personal assistant. But the guy I'm going to be working for, well, I think he mostly works late at night."

"What sort of job does he have where he works late at night?"

"He runs a bar."

"Which one?"

"Brooks," she said, turning the kettle on.

"You don't want to tell me. Which bar? Where is it? What time are you going to be working? And will his driver be bringing you back every night? Because it's not safe to take the bus this late."

"You know that I'm the adult, right?" she shot back.

"I'm sixteen years old, Aunt Effie. I'm not a child."

She closed her eyes at the hurt note in his voice. Then she opened them again as the water boiled.

"You're right, you're not." She attempted to reach up for the hot chocolate that was stashed up high so that she wouldn't drink it all the time, but she let out a pained grunt.

Then she felt him behind her, reaching up to grab the tin.

"Thanks, honey," she murmured.

"Your back hurting?" he asked.

"I had a bit of a fall caused by a spasm in my back. But I took some pain pills."

"Did you eat with them?" he asked worriedly.

Turning, she wrapped her arms around him. He stiffened, then he awkwardly patted her back. He wasn't big on hugs anymore. She missed six-year-old Brooks, who'd hugged her all the time.

"I had some chips. You want some?"

"Nah, I'm good. Thanks."

Letting go, she leaned back to look up at him. "How'd you get so tall?"

"It's all that spinach you made me eat."

"Gag. We don't even say that word in this household, you know that."

He grinned down at her. Then, that grin slowly faded. "I know things are bad money-wise since you lost your job."

"Brooks, that's not for you to worry about."

"Hard for me not to worry about when I know you're going without just to make sure that I have enough."

Fuck. She should have known he'd catch that. Her boy was smart and observant.

"I'm going to quit school and get a job."

Her eyes nearly bugged out of her head. "You are not."

"We need the money. It's not right that you're not sleeping and stressed because we're running out of money. And I don't like that strange men are bringing you home at night."

"Okay, let's just take a moment to talk about this. I'm going to get into my pajamas and take off my make-up. You make the hot chocolates."

"There's no whipped cream."

"Which is a huge tragedy, but I'll be able to buy more. Because I have a job now."

He didn't look much happier, but he nodded.

After she got ready for bed, she came out to find he'd already folded the sleeper sofa out into a bed for her.

Damn, he was a good kid.

He handed her a hot chocolate as she walked up to where he stood at the end of the bed.

"I just want to help." He gave her a stubborn look.

"I know you do." Reaching up, she put her hand on his cheek. "Listen to me. You are the smartest, kindest, best kid I know. And you're pretty damn mature for sixteen. But you're still the kid and I'm the adult. It's up to me to provide for you. Got me?"

"Not if you are putting yourself at risk or doing something you shouldn't do."

"I'm not doing anything I shouldn't be doing."

He eyed her.

"I'm not. I really am going to be working as a personal assistant to a guy called Thomas Grady. And . . . all right, one of the bars he runs is a strip club called Pinkies." She wasn't sure if that was the smartest parenting move. But when you were a thirty-five-year-old with a tendency to eat too much junk and you slept with a sloth soft toy and were raising a super smart kid who was sixteen going on forty, you had to do the best you could.

And she'd learned that honesty often worked best.

"Strip club?"

"Yes. Among other businesses."

"That's why you'll have to work at night?"

"I'm not actually sure of my hours," she admitted. "I'm having dinner with him tomorrow night to discuss that."

"Dinner?"

"Just dinner."

"He doesn't expect anything else?" he asked.

"No, honey."

He nodded solemnly. "I'm not going to be here tomorrow night. I'm going out."

"Oh, yeah?" she asked with a teasing grin. "Got a date?"

"Maybe."

"Well, you have fun. Treat her right. I hope she knows that she's going out with the sweetest, smartest, most handsome guy at school."

He rolled his eyes. "Jesus, Aunt Effie. You have to say that shit."

"I say it because it's true. But enough mushy stuff, let's move on." She said that last part because she knew that despite being mature for his age, he was still a teenage boy.

And teenage boys didn't like mushy stuff.

"You're going to need money for this date. I'll put some in your bank account." That would hurt, but she wanted her boy to have everything she needed.

"I've got money, Aunt Effie."

"You do? How?"

"Logo work."

She nodded. Her boy was smart and artistic. A while back, he'd set up a webpage to sell his graphic skills. "That's good."

"I'll give it all to you, if you need it."

Her gaze hit his. "You need it for your date."

"I can bring my girl back here instead."

"Thanks, darling. But you don't want to bring your girl back here. You'll scare her off." If she went to Brooks' school, that likely meant her family was well off. Well, unless she was a scholarship student like he was. But there weren't many of those.

She sipped her hot chocolate.

"If I stayed here, I'd be able to meet your new boss. Make sure working for him is a good idea."

Darn it. Definitely an alpha male in the making. So protective.

"I'll be fine, darling. I promise. Besides, I'm a good judge of character."

"Surprised you can say that with a straight face."

"Hey, brat. I can still ground your ass."

He shot her a look that clearly told her to try. What was she going to do in a few years when he went off to college?

She didn't want to think about that.

She yawned. Tonight had been exhausting.

Brooks took the mug from her hand. "You need to go to sleep. I'll get your heating pad."

"Thanks, kid," she murmured as she reached into her handbag and pulled out Slowly. "You're my favorite kid, you know that?"

"I'm your only kid."

And he was her kid. Blood or not. And she'd do whatever it took to take care of him.

8

"You gonna tell me what that was all about?" Steele asked.

Grady didn't bother looking up from his phone. They needed a new alcohol rep, their current one was shit.

He was someone that Lucy had put them on to. So Grady didn't trust him as far as he could throw him.

"What?"

A large hand landed on his phone, tugging it away.

"Hey!" He scowled up at Steele. His best friend. The most important person in his life.

And he wished he could touch the other man like he wanted to.

He didn't let that thought show. He'd learned long ago to put on a mask, wearing it so much that sometimes he wasn't sure what he looked like underneath that mask.

"Look at me when I'm talking to you."

He straightened his suit jacket and stared up at Steele. "You might want to reword what you just said and the way you said it.

Because you might be the big man in charge, but you are not in charge of me, and I am most definitely not your sub."

Steele glared back before closing his eyes and letting out a deep breath. "Fuck. Sorry."

"My phone?"

Steele handed it over, then sat in the chair across the desk from him. Pinkies had just opened and they were in Grady's office. Typically, Steele would head upstairs to keep an eye on things. Or he'd be out, keeping track of other parts of his operation.

So Grady knew he had something pressing that he needed to discuss.

And he knew what it was about.

Her.

"Why'd you offer her a job when we never discussed getting you an assistant?"

"Are you saying you don't think I need one?"

Steele frowned. "You never mentioned it. But if you need help, why don't you give Lucy more responsibility or hire her as your assistant? Better than taking on a stranger who we know nothing about."

"I'm doing a background check on her," he said, pointing to his computer. "But if you're worried that Effie won't be good with everything that goes on here, I intend to keep her working on the legitimate side of things. Oh, and I wouldn't hire Lucy if you held a hot poker to my balls."

"You want to expand on that?" Steele asked.

"Not sure there's much to say. She's a bitch. A bitch who thinks she can be sweet as pie to your face and you'll open up your pants and your wallet to her while behind your back, she's horrible to everyone else. And I'm pretty sure she's after your fat bank balance more than your fat cock."

"She thinks she's getting in with me?" Steele frowned.

"Uh, yeah. Have you not noticed how fake she is around you?"

"I noticed. Figured it was because I was her boss."

"Lucy is a bitch who is trying to hide that she's a bitch in front of you to get hold of your dick and wallet."

"Guess I wasn't really paying her much attention."

Something that would shock and anger Lucy, but Grady knew that was precisely what was happening. Lucy didn't matter to Steele. She didn't even register on his radar when she wasn't in his direct sight. She wasn't ever getting in there.

"I'll get rid of her. If she annoys you, that's good enough for me."

That was part of the reason he loved the big bastard.

Because he always had his back. No matter what.

"I can deal with Lucy." Because Steele might be the big man, but Grady was still a man.

"Right, so you need some help and you don't want Lucy. Still doesn't explain why want to hire her."

Didn't he see it? Grady thought he would.

"You really don't know why?"

Steele's gaze narrowed. "I know what I wanted from her and now that you've hired her, I won't be able to get that."

Because Steele had a policy against fucking employees.

"She's not a one-night stand kind of girl," Grady warned.

"I wasn't thinking of just one night."

"Fine. She's not a weekend type of girl either."

"You barely know her."

"I know that she had scuffed shoes that were a size too small for her."

Steele frowned.

"And that her coat was threadbare."

"Fuck."

"She didn't drive here. And she wasn't waiting around for an

Uber. She was walking down the street. With no hat, scarf, or gloves, and in a threadbare coat."

"Grady," Steele said in a low voice.

"That could be me. If it wasn't for you."

Steele shook his head. "I didn't do anything."

Grady leaned forward. "You saved me. Before I could get to the stage of desperation. Which is what I saw in her face."

"You can't save everyone."

"I know that. I'm not a selfless person. But I can save her. And I want to. So she's coming to work for me and I'll be paying her wages myself."

Steele's eyes widened. "You what?"

"I'll be paying her out of my own money. I'll get her to sign an NDA, don't worry."

Steele stood and then placed his hands on the desk, leaning toward him. "You won't be paying her fucking wages. That will be paid for through the business. Like it would for any employee. Got me?"

Grady bit back the need to snap at him. Cool and calm.

"And I'll be coming tomorrow night."

"There's no need," Grady said coolly.

"I think there's every need." Steele stared down at him for a long time. "She had a soft toy in her bag."

"What?" Grady asked his gaze up to Steele. "What are you talking about?"

"When I was looking through her bag, I saw it."

"And what do you think that means? She could have a kid." Shit. Did she? Had she turned up for the job interview because she had a kid at home to feed?

"Possibly. Or it could be something else."

"It doesn't mean she's a Little," Grady warned, knowing where Steele's mind had gone.

Steele's brother-in-law, Spike, was a Daddy and his girl,

Millie was a Little. Spike's wife, Jacqui, had also been Steele's adored baby sister. When she'd died, well, Steele had changed.

He'd given up the idea of ever falling in love, ever having a family, of ever having a Little.

Grady had gone to BDSM clubs with Steele. And there were parts of it he had definitely enjoyed. He liked having control. It had just felt right to him. He didn't even need to get off, but tying up a partner and getting her off or punishing her was enough to satisfy him.

He wasn't so certain about being a Daddy Dom. That required more nurturing and care than he thought he was capable of.

It was hard to care for someone when you were frozen inside.

"No signs that she's not either."

"You have a rule about getting involved with employees," Grady reminded him.

"Yep. Which is why I wasn't planning on letting her become an employee."

"And you don't want to be a Daddy Dom anymore."

"No. I don't." There was something strange about the way he said that. Something that had Grady studying him closely to see if he could understand what was going on. But then Steele turned away. He left, slamming the door behind him.

Well. That could have gone better. Could have gone worse too. Leaning back in his chair, Grady closed his eyes and rubbed at his temples. He knew Effie had gotten home safe because he'd already checked in with Raul.

The other man hadn't been all that impressed by her neighborhood. Which meant Grady was going to need to make sure she got paid enough to be able to move.

He turned to his computer to see what he could find on her.

Shit. Not a great credit score. Not awful, but still not great. They'd need to work on that.

Nothing came up about her back injury. Likely, he'd have to search deeper to find any information about that. Which he wasn't prepared to do yet. Her former job had been running a small team at a grocery store. She'd lost it when they'd sold out to a big chain and that chain had closed them down.

Fuck. He hated that sort of shit.

And yeah, she did live in a crappy neighborhood. But it wasn't the worst neighborhood.

Something else came up and he frowned, staring at an older image of her with her arm wrapped around a dark-haired kid. This had to be the boy Raul had mentioned when he took her home. He looked to be about thirteen but was already bigger than her. The article was from three years ago. And it was about a scholarship he'd won to some fancy school.

Was that her son? He didn't really look like her, and they had different last names, but that didn't mean anything. Okay, unexpected, but not a problem.

Grady shut down the search and got back to work. Tomorrow night would be soon enough to find out more about Ms. Effie Stephenson. Not that he needed to know everything for her to work for him.

But that didn't mean he didn't want to know more.

Which could be an issue.

9

Effie stood outside in the cold.

She'd managed to find her scarf. But her gloves had given up the will to live about two weeks ago and she didn't want to put a hat on and ruin her hair. She'd spent time curling it into soft waves that fell down her back. Her hair was her best feature, if she did say so herself.

Which she never would. Because that seemed rude.

This morning when she woke up, she'd been a bit stiff but not really in any pain. And let's face it, she was a thirty-five-year old, sleeping on a pull-out sofa. Being stiff in the mornings was to be expected.

It was five minutes to seven, and the sensible thing would have been to wait inside until she saw the car pull up. However, she didn't want to give Grady any excuse to try to get inside her apartment. It actually looked better on the outside than it did on the inside. It was a big house that had been cut up into four one-bedroom apartments. She and Brooks lived on the bottom floor, which was good for her back. Going up and down stairs all the time wasn't ideal. But the downside was that she could hear every time her neighbors moved around upstairs.

Including when they got overly enthusiastic in bed.

And considering the upstairs neighbor was a guy in his twenties, that happened a lot.

The car pulled up and this time, it was a longer car. The door opened as she moved toward it, and to her surprise, Steele got out.

He was dressed in a huge peacoat that must have been made for him. It fit him perfectly, and those broad shoulders didn't dress in off-the-rack clothing.

He looked around, scowling at her.

Uh-oh.

Was he here to tell her that she was fired before she'd even started? She'd expected Grady, not him.

But she managed a big smile. "Good evening."

"Not a fan of your neighborhood, Spitfire."

Okay. So they weren't doing pleasantries?

"It's fine. Really. It looks worse than it is."

He shot her a look that told her he thought that was pure bullshit. "Not a fan of you waiting out in the cold either."

Right.

That made her feel surprisingly warm. Well, inside at least. She was still freaking cold.

"I'm good."

His gaze moved over her. "Especially when you've got no hat on again." He stared at her hands. "You got gloves on?"

"Um, no. They kind of fell to bits a few weeks ago, and since it's nearly the end of winter, I didn't bother buying any."

"You didn't bother buying more?" he asked in a low voice.

"Nope. But you know what would warm me up?"

"What's that?" There was a decidedly sexy note to his voice that made a shiver go through her.

Bad Effie.

He's your boss.

"Getting into the car and out of this cold."

His eyebrows rose. "By all means, Spitfire."

She still wasn't sure about that nickname, but she didn't protest as she grew closer.

He held out his hand to her.

"You want my handbag?" she asked.

"Nah, I was thinking of a high-five. You going to leave me hanging?"

Was he teasing her?

His lips twitched. "I was holding out my hand for you to hold on to while you climbed in."

"Why?" she asked.

"Seemed the gentlemanly thing to do."

"Are you often a gentleman?" she asked.

"No. And I'm beginning to see why I've never bothered."

"What?"

"Being a gentleman takes patience and doesn't always get you what you want straight away. Next time I need to get you somewhere, I'll just pick you up and put you there."

"Uh, well, that's nice. But I'm not sure that's something a boss is allowed to do."

"I'm not a normal boss. And I'm not nice."

No, he wasn't. And she quickly climbed into the car, nearly tripping over the doorway in her haste.

Large hands grabbed her waist, steadying her and he lifted her in.

Shoot.

"Definitely going to just do what needs to be done next time," he muttered.

And she was definitely in trouble here.

She nearly sighed in relief as she climbed into the back to

find Grady sitting there in the corner. He was on his phone, seemingly uninterested in her and Steele's conversation. She sat across from him, knowing it was likely a bad idea for her to face backward. She could get motion sickness just by watching a fishing show on TV. And she could never sit on the sideways seats on the bus.

"Took the two of you long enough. You've let out all the warm air."

"Sorry," she whispered as Steele folded his massive frame into the car, sitting beside Grady. "Hello, Mr. Grady."

He glanced up at her. "Haven't we had a conversation about what you call me?"

"Uh, yes, but that was before I was about to become your assistant. Shouldn't I call you Mr. Grady?"

"No."

Oh.

All right then. Effie guessed it was cool if he didn't expect her to be formal with him.

Suddenly, he reached over toward her and hit a button that lowered the privacy screen.

"Raul, pull over," he ordered, his gaze on her feet.

Was something wrong with her shoes? They were the same ones she'd worn last night. She didn't really have anything else suitable.

"This isn't happening." Grady waved a hand down at her feet. "Don't you have better shoes?"

Ouch. That hurt.

"No," she replied quietly. "The only other shoes I own are a pair of sneakers. That's all I ever wore at my other job. Oh, and some flip-flops. I realize I'll need to get other shoes for this job, I just didn't have a chance today."

Actually, she'd hit the thrift stores today, but hadn't found anything in her size. The only shoes she'd seen were for women who had dainty feet.

Not elephant feet like hers.

Grady started tapping on his phone. "Raul, we're going shopping first. Do you know anywhere that is likely to be open?"

"Yep," Raul said. "I know someone who will stay open late for us."

"Won't we be late for dinner?" she asked.

"No," Steele replied.

No?

"Um, what are we going shopping for?" she asked.

"Shoes."

Her eyes widened. "Shoes?"

Grady put up a finger as he spoke quietly into the phone. She glanced over at Steele, who was staring at Grady curiously.

"We can't go shopping for shoes," she said desperately. Surely, Steele would be the voice of reason.

"Sure we can," Steele said. "Raul knows someone. Raul knows everyone."

She turned back to Grady as he ended his call. "I can't afford new shoes."

Grady eyed her calmly.

"I'm paying," Steele told her.

"No." She shook her head. "You cannot buy me new shoes."

"I can."

"Signing bonus," Grady said.

"A signing bonus for a personal assistant job? That doesn't happen."

"This won't be the easiest job," Grady told her. "It will require you to work odd hours. To do a number of different tasks. You're going to need to be dressed appropriately at all times."

She felt herself growing red. Grady was dressed as impeccably as he had been yesterday. In clothes that looked expensive. So was Steele. While she was in a ten-year-old coat that had definitely seen better days.

"I don't need a signing bonus. I've already agreed to work for Grady. I think you've already figured out that I'm desperate."

"We need to teach you how to negotiate better," Steele told her. "Aim high and allow some wriggle room to be negotiated down. But never tell someone you're desperate."

She pulled at one of her earrings. They were cute teddy bears. Steele reached over to pull her hand away. Oh Lord, what was happening here? This wasn't normal boss-employee behavior. And she didn't know what to say to stop it.

Or if she even wanted to stop it.

"Feet," Grady commanded, setting his phone down.

"Sorry?"

"Give me your feet."

She continued to stare at him.

"Now."

She raised her feet into the air and he grabbed them with his firm, warm fingers.

"Your feet are freezing. You won't be wearing these again."

Dear Lord, he was bossy. She turned to look at Steele. "And he said you were the bossy one."

Steele just nodded. "I am."

That did not bode well for her. She swallowed heavily. Then Grady drew her heels off.

"Wait, I still need them," she said as he threw them onto the floor.

"No, you don't."

Then how the heck was she going to get from the car to the shoe store?

The car turned and she put her hand on her stomach with a muffled groan.

"Everything okay?" Steele asked.

"Can we crack a window?"

Grady's gaze shot to hers right as Raul took another turn. He wasn't driving erratically or anything. But riding backward, combined with the fact that she'd eaten nothing but candy today, was making her stomach turn.

"Raul, pull over," Steele commanded.

Grady leaned over and undid her seatbelt. She didn't have it in her to protest as he opened the door and jumped out. Reaching in, he grabbed her. Suddenly, Steele was there, taking hold of her and carrying her over to the side of the road. He put her on her feet and she leaned over, dry-retching.

At least there wasn't anything in her stomach to come up.

"Here. Sip this," Grady commanded, coming up next to her.

She turned to see him holding out a bottle of water to her. She reached for it, but he drew it back.

"No. I'll do it. You just drink."

This was definitely not boss-employee behavior. But she wasn't feeling well enough to protest. Steele had his thick arm around her waist, holding her against him. And she knew that if he let go, she'd probably fall to the ground.

Grady tipped the bottle of water up so she could sip at it.

"Slowly," Grady warned. "You don't want to throw it back up."

She took some cautious sips, then attempted to stand, only to realize that Steele held her up in the air so her feet were dangling inches off the ground.

"I can stand now," she said.

"No, you can't," Steele countered.

"Yes, I can. I won't collapse."

"You aren't standing, Spitfire, because you've got no shoes on."

Oh. Right.

She didn't. Crap.

"Are you still feeling ill?" Grady asked, moving in front of them.

"No, I'm all good."

Grady's eyes narrowed. "Another way of saying fine. Which we weren't going to say anymore."

Drat. He was right.

"Should have told us you weren't feeling well, Spitfire," Steele scolded.

Oh no. Did they think she was actually ill? Great, they probably thought that she was giving them her germs.

"I'm not ill," she said quickly. "It was just all the swaying and stuff."

Grady raised his eyebrows. "You got car sick?"

"Ah, yeah. That happens sometimes. All right, a lot. But especially when I'm riding backward."

Steele's arm tightened around her waist, squeezing her to the point where she might throw up again.

"Um, if you don't want me to puke again, you might want to ease up," she said, tapping his arm.

Steele eased up. Then, to her shock, he picked her up and carried her back to the car.

But he didn't hold her bridal style. Nope, he moved her to his side so she was sitting on his hip. Like a child.

A flush of pleasure filled her. Even though she knew she couldn't read anything into it, she couldn't help but wonder what it would be like if he were her Daddy Dom.

Sure, he was kind of gruff and to the point. Bossy as hell.

But if she was his, she knew that no one would ever dare harm her. Because Steele wouldn't allow it. She gave herself a few seconds to live in her fantasyland.

But reality always found a way to intrude.

Which really, really sucked.

When Steele settled her in the car, she was in his seat.

Damon Steele was going to give up his seat for her?

Then she realized that, nope, he was not. Because he slid her along into the middle seat before climbing in. And then Grady got in on her other side.

I'm in the middle of a Steele-Grady sandwich.

And there went her mind again, off to fantasyland where she got to be in a Steele-Grady sandwich but this time it was a naked sandwich.

Yikes.

This wasn't good. The heat coming off them was incredible and there was no way for her to not touch them. Steele was far too wide to avoid. In fact, they were both kind of pinning her back with their shoulders.

"Seatbelt," Steele said gruffly.

She tried to reach it, but his shoulder was in the way. In the end, he half-spun, facing her, and then she was able to grab the belt. However, the intense look on his face made her fumble.

Grady grabbed it and drew it over her, clicking it into place.

"I . . . um . . . you guys . . . this is weird," she blurted out.

"What is?" Grady asked.

"Um, I don't know. Maybe sitting like this between two men I barely know who are taking me shoe shopping."

And had just held her while she heaved.

Shoot. She needed a mint. Where was her handbag?

"Don't forget about gloves," Steele muttered. "You need new gloves."

"No one said anything about gloves," she squealed, feeling herself getting slightly hysterical. "I draw the line at gloves."

"Hear that, Grady?" Steele asked, sounding far too amused for her liking.

"Yep, she draws the line at gloves."

"Nice to know where the line is, Spitfire. But gotta be honest, I like pushing boundaries."

She closed her eyes.

"Probably not a good idea to close your eyes while in the car if you have motion sickness," Grady pointed out as he tapped on his phone. "It's more likely to make you sicker."

"Should she be sitting in the back?" Steele asked.

"Hmm, she's less likely to get sick while sitting in the front passenger seat," Grady replied.

She wasn't normally the sort of person who looked at what others were doing on their phones. But she happened to glance down and see that Grady was on a site about limiting the effects of motion sickness.

Well, that was sweet, even if it was strange behavior for a boss.

"But it's safer for her to be in the back in the event of a crash," Grady added. "Although we probably should have put her on the side."

"I like her better between us. Feels safer," Steele said.

"She's certainly not moving." Grady stared down at her. "Are you all right there, sweetheart?"

"I can barely breathe."

It was Steele's turn to stare down at her. "You look like a little kid. Maybe what she needs is a booster seat, since she's so tiny."

"Tiny? Me? Have you seen my ass?"

Suddenly, they both grew still and it seemed like the air had been sucked out of the car.

"Not liking the way you keep putting yourself down," Steele said in a dark voice. "And you might want to stop."

Don't ask. Don't ask.

"Or what?"

Shit. She had to ask.

"Or I'll turn your ass red."

"Steele," Grady warned.

Steele sighed. "Fuck. Employee."

"Employee," Grady repeated.

Huh?

She wasn't keeping up. Sometimes it seemed like they were having a conversation between the two of them and she was missing the secret code.

"That sucks. She needs a good spanking."

"You want to spank me?" she asked in a high-pitched voice.

"Yeah, my hand is really twitchy." Steele held his hand up.

"Oh no. Do you need to see a doctor about that?" she asked.

"Doctor? No, Spitfire. Only cure for this twitch is to spank a naughty bottom."

"That sort of twitchy," she whispered.

"That sort of twitchy," he confirmed.

"Which he will not do as you are going to work for us," Grady said firmly.

"She doesn't work for us yet," Steele said.

"And she won't if you spank her," Grady countered.

"Wait, you seriously want to spank me? You . . . you can't do that without consent, right?"

Steele turned again so his back was against the door and he could stare down at her. "I might be reading you wrong, but I don't think you're opposed to that idea."

Effie swallowed heavily, trying to search for calm. Inwardly, she was kind of freaking out.

But it was the good kind of freak out.

It doesn't mean anything.

Well, it meant something. It suggested that Steele was a man who liked to spank. It shouldn't come as much of a shock, they were both super-dominant men. But in different ways. With Steele, it was more in your face. With Grady, it was a cooler, calmer need for control.

But no less potent.

Or worrying. Because keeping up with these two guys meant she'd always have to stay focused and be on alert.

Not her strong points.

"Yes, there has to be consent," Grady said.

"I mean, you could give your consent for there to be no consent," Steele said.

Huh?

"Steele," Grady warned.

"Yeah, yeah. I get it. She doesn't get it." Steele moved back so his shoulder was basically covering half her chest.

Effie tried to hunch down, which was pretty hard considering how squished she was.

"Still think the booster seat is a good idea, though," Steele muttered.

He wasn't truly serious, right? She glanced up at Grady, who was giving the other man a look filled with exasperation . . . and affection? Yes, a lot of affection.

That look almost made it seem as though he felt more for the other man than just friendship.

None of your business, Effie. You have enough of your own problems going on without borrowing more.

10

The car came to a stop, and looking out the window, she saw they had stopped in front of a shoe shop.

"Here you are," Raul said. "My friend owns it. Her name is Alice. She's going to stay open so you can shop in private."

"We won't be long," Steele told Raul before he undid his belt and slid out.

She grabbed her handbag and then reached for her own belt, but before she could slide out, Grady spoke.

"Effie, wait for a moment."

She paused and looked back at him.

"Steele has a big personality, but he won't ever harm you. Normally, he leaves employee stuff up to me. But you've caught his attention."

"Is that a good thing or a bad thing?" she joked, nerves filling her.

"That, sweetheart, remains to be seen."

Well, that wasn't fear-inducing or anything.

After slipping a mint into her mouth, she slid further along the seat, toward the door. She was not looking forward to walking on the cold ground barefoot.

She should have known better.

But she was still shocked when Steele swooped in and lifted her up into his arms.

"What are you doing?"

He looked at her, then over at Grady. "Is it not obvious?"

This question wasn't aimed at her but at Grady.

"I think it is," Grady replied.

"Thought so too. I'm carrying you, Spitfire."

"Yes, but why?"

"If you wanted to know why, then why didn't you ask why in the first place?"

"Has anyone ever told you that you're annoying?" she grumbled before she thought better of it.

"Nope," he replied as Grady opened the door to the shop for them.

"Surprising," she muttered.

"The only person who'd dare call me annoying is Grady. And he doesn't find me annoying."

"Not necessarily true," Grady muttered.

She shot him a grin before it fully registered what Steele had said.

No one would dare?

Except for Grady and her . . . the woman who hadn't even secured a job with this guy yet.

She really needed to watch her mouth.

People won't like you if you're you, Effie. Be more agreeable. More pleasant.

Thanks, Nan.

"Why have you gone all stiff? Don't you like this shop?" Steele asked.

Effie took a moment to look around. There was nothing

wrong with this shop, except that the shoes looked far more expensive than she was used to.

Then she realized she was still in his arms.

"I'm good. You can put me down now." She blushed as she saw an older woman eyeing them curiously as she spoke quietly to Grady.

"Not until you tell me what's wrong."

"Nothing is wrong."

He just stood there, not moving. Not setting her down. And not saying anything.

Grr.

"Anyone tell you that you're stubborn?"

"Hmm, I have heard that once or twice."

"Grady?" she asked.

"Yeah, and my sister." A strange shutter came over his face as he said that.

To her surprise, he set her down on her feet, holding her steady as she wobbled slightly.

She opened her mouth to say something . . . she wasn't sure exactly what, but then Grady spoke up.

"Sweetheart, come here." His tone was velvet but with a core of steel. And she instinctively went to him even as she wondered whether she ought to be doing something about the way Steele had shut down.

Not your business.

You barely know these guys and you're about to work for them.

Be professional.

"Yes, Mr. Grady?"

Oh, the look he shot her had her clenching her butt cheeks together.

"I mean, Grady?" she said in a high-pitched voice.

He leaned into her, speaking quietly so the older woman

couldn't hear them. "I'm not going to give you any more warnings about that, sweetheart."

Yikes.

"Now, please sit. Alice is going to get you some shoes to try on." He nodded at the older woman.

"What size are you, dear?" she asked.

"Uh, I'm a nine and a half," she said softly. She waited uncomfortably for the woman to tell her that they didn't stock much in that size.

But Alice just nodded. "Style?"

"Something that covers her feet to keep them warm. No heels," Steele said, coming forward.

Obviously, he had gotten over whatever had been going on with him since he was back to being the bossiest of the boss men.

"A small heel will work better with this outfit," she said.

"No heel," Steele said.

"Right." Alice smiled and disappeared.

"Mr. Steele—"

"Nope."

"Nope?" What did that mean?

"Not listening to any arguments."

Dear Lord.

All right, she needed to see the bright side. She was getting a new pair of shoes–as a signing bonus. Sure, maybe they were giving her a signing bonus because they pitied her, but she was going to take it.

Because that money could be used to help her kid.

And when it came to Brooks, she had no pride.

So she smiled brightly at Alice as she returned with several pairs of shoes. "Thank you."

To her surprise, both Grady and Steele stuck around as she

tried on the first pair. In her experience, men weren't usually interested in shopping. Joe had never gone shopping with her.

However, they both watched as she got up and walked around in a sensible pair of black shoes with very low heels, which didn't exactly go with her outfit, but were comfortable.

But then her gaze caught the shoes of her dreams. They had a solid, thick heel and were a pure white, which was incredibly impractical. Then, there were colorful dots all over them. Like they'd been dipped in confetti.

And the laces were just as awesome. They were a pair of thick rainbow-colored ribbons.

She bit at her lip as she stared at them.

Grady came up beside her. "You like them?"

"The shoes I have on? Yes, they're great. Sensible and practical."

"So boring?" he asked, sounding amused.

"Not at all," she said hastily, not wanting him to take offense. "Is it all right if I get these ones?"

Grady glanced at her, then down to her sensible shoes before nodding.

She turned away from the confetti shoes, wincing slightly as her new sensible shoes rubbed against her blisters. They were stiff, but she knew they'd loosen up with wear. Although right now they were aggravating all the sore spots on her feet.

Suddenly, she was swept up again against a broad chest.

She gaped up at Steele.

"Take them off," he said gruffly to Grady.

"Something wrong?" Alice asked.

"They're hurting her." This was said in a voice filled with accusation.

"It's not the shoes' fault," she said quickly as Alice's face dropped. "They fit fine. It's just that I've got a couple of blisters."

Grady slid the shoes off and inspected her feet before looking at her with a frown. "You should have said something."

"You got something she can wear now that won't hurt her feet any further?" Steele demanded as he set her down.

"Um, well. Not really. Unless she wants to wear sandals."

"In this weather?" Steele said, sounding like she'd asked him if he wanted to go to war.

"Or slippers."

"Slippers," Steele said thoughtfully.

"I cannot wear slippers to a restaurant," she said.

"Why not? We'll take a pair of your warmest slippers as well as these," he said.

"Steele! You can't!" she said insistently, but he wandered off to the front of the store as his phone rang. She turned to the only person in the store who might be able to stop this lunacy. "Grady."

"Yes?"

"I'm not wearing slippers."

"You're wearing the slippers or we go back to your place to discuss all this."

Shit.

"I'll find a pair that looks nice," Alice assured her. "I've got a pair that kind of look like boots with fluff inside. No one will know they're slippers."

"They'll know they're slippers."

"We have a private room," Grady told her. "Not many people will see you."

Okay, that was something at least.

Alice found her some very boot-like slippers. They wouldn't go with her outfit, but it seemed she didn't have much of a choice.

"They're very concerned about your comfort. It's so sweet,"

Alice whispered as the two men stood across the room, talking. "Which one are you dating?"

"Neither. They're my soon-to-be-bosses."

Alice gave her a shocked look. "Really?"

"I only met them yesterday. I'm in way over my head."

"Girl, drowning in that much gorgeousness and testosterone . . . what a way to go."

Yeah, she wasn't wrong there.

"You won't ever be bored."

She wasn't sure that was a good thing.

You got this, Effie. You can do this.

"Let's get back into the car. Steele will take care of this." Grady ushered her outside. At least she got to walk this time. Even if she was in what amounted to slipper boots.

After a few minutes, Steele climbed in beside her.

"Thanks for my shoes," she said.

Steele nodded while Grady was on his phone. Shoot. Was he upset with her?

Say you're sorry. You were rude.

"I'm really sorry I called you stubborn."

Steele grunted.

"And I'm really, really sorry I called you annoying."

Grady made a strange noise and she tried to turn to see if he was all right. But she was kind of pinned back against the car seat again.

"Are you all right, Grady?"

"Yep," he said in a strangled voice.

"Okay. Um, and I'm sorry that I called you bossy too."

"You didn't mean any of what you said?" Steele asked after a moment.

"Oh, ah, um . . ." Crap.

"Truth," he demanded.

She heaved out a breath. "No, I meant it. I mean, maybe not the annoying part."

"You meant the annoying part."

Damn it. She probably shouldn't say anything more. "Maybe we should talk about something else."

"And you think I'm stubborn."

Well, yeah, and that was evidenced by the fact that he wasn't letting this go.

"And bossy."

"But I'm sure you're a nice guy too," she said.

There was a beat of silence, and then Grady made another strange noise.

"Nice?" Steele asked in a strangled voice.

"Uh-huh. I mean, you can be nice sometimes. You bought me these awesome slippers."

"You didn't want the slippers," Grady pointed out.

"Well, it's not that I didn't want them," she prevaricated. "I just don't think I should wear slippers into a restaurant."

"When else has he been nice?" Grady asked.

"Uh, well, um . . ." Shoot. "He held me while I was vomiting. That was nice."

"Was it?" Grady said.

"Sure. And he made sure that my feet didn't touch the ground."

"Yes, he is most definitely a nice guy," Grady said.

"Shut up, Grady. And I'm not a nice guy. Call me that again, and you're fired, got me?" Steele said grumpily.

"Seriously?" she whispered.

"Not seriously." Grady frowned at Steele. "He's joking."

"I never joke."

No more calling him nice. Got it.

11

"You okay?" Steele glanced over at Grady. "She called me nice."

Grady's lips twitched and Steele sat back with a sigh. Effie had just headed off to the restroom. Thankfully, they had a private bathroom attached to this room.

That was because he owned this restaurant and no one used this room but him. Which was also why they could come in through the back entrance. Steele could count on one hand the amount of people he liked and wanted to spend time with.

Yet here he was at dinner with Effie. Voluntarily.

She intrigued him. Stirred him. Very little interested him anymore. The only people he truly cared about were Grady, Quillon, and Millie.

"Hmm, she did."

"Nice. Me? Is she blind?"

Grady stared thoughtfully over at him. "Not blind. But I think she likes to see the good in people."

"Naive."

"Perhaps."

That wasn't good. Especially if she was going to work for them. It meant he'd have to make sure she was protected.

"She could get walked all over."

Grady nodded. "That's the feeling I get too."

"Don't like where she's living." And that worried him as well. Because he had no idea where any of his other employees lived.

Didn't give a shit about their neighborhoods.

Maybe that made him a terrible person . . . but he already knew that. He wasn't destined to end up in the clouds with the angels, and he was okay with that.

That was the life he'd chosen to live.

So why did he care about where she lived? Why did he care that she didn't own any gloves? That her shoes were too small and hurting her feet? That she got motion sickness when she sat backward in a car?

This was confusing as hell.

It's because you want to fuck her.

Probably . . . except he'd never cared this much about anyone he'd wanted to fuck either.

So yeah, he was confused.

"Neither do I," Grady said. "But it's not our business where she lives."

To anyone else, Grady might sound callous. But Steele understood where he was coming from.

He was trying to remind Steele that she wasn't theirs. And that she would never be theirs.

Because they didn't do relationships. Steele, because he didn't want to ever risk losing someone the way he'd lost Jacqui. And Grady because . . . well, Steele wasn't completely sure why Grady had never found anyone.

"She's not our problem," he muttered. "Beyond being an employee." That gave him some rights to dictate to her. But not much. Then again, Steele wasn't a typical employer.

"Is that going to be a problem?" Grady asked.

He leaned back in his chair. "I'm not going to curb who I am. Not for anyone."

"So what you're saying is that you won't stop being stubborn, annoying, and bossy?"

"Exactly."

"Christ," Grady muttered. "You can't fuck her."

He knew that. It was against the rules.

That didn't mean that he didn't want to.

He watched as she walked out of the bathroom. She was wearing some sort of pant suit that didn't fit her properly and was the wrong color for her skin tone. Along with those ridiculous slipper boots.

And he still thought she was hot as fuck.

This was definitely a problem.

A server walked in and Effie smiled at him.

The server smiled back and moved to pull out her chair. Grady stood and got to the chair before the server could get there, pulling it back for her.

Her face grew startled as she stared at Grady.

"Please sit." It was worded politely, but Steele could hear the command and so could she.

She sat.

Unfortunately, she sat too early and the chair was still quite a bit away from the table.

Steele could see her face growing red in embarrassment. Just as he was about to get up and help her, Grady pushed on the back of the chair.

"Let's just scoot you a bit closer."

Steele was surprised by the way Grady watched over her. Generally, he was happy to step back and let Steele take the lead with any woman who took his eye.

Then again, Effie wasn't just any woman.

The server, whose name he still couldn't remember, handed out the menus.

"Thank you, Lee," she murmured quietly.

The server gave her a pleased smile and stepped away.

"How do you know his name?" Steele demanded.

Her eyes widened as she stared at him, then over at Grady. "Is he serious?"

"Yep."

"I want to know. How do you know his name?" He crossed his arms over his chest in irritation.

"It's on his name badge."

Name badge?

He didn't have a name badge . . . right?

"It is?"

"Um, yep. Maybe you need glasses."

"I do not need glasses," he muttered. "Every part of this body is in excellent working condition."

"Well, I already know that your eyes aren't in excellent condition, so I'm a bit worried about your threshold for what you consider excellent."

"She's got you there," Grady said.

Steele shot him a look. "It is *all* in excellent condition. And if you doubt my word, Spitfire, I would be happy to show you."

He had to hide his grin as a blush filled her face. Her face was crimson and the blush traveled down her neck. Hmm, he wondered how far her blush went.

That thought made his dick grow hard and he had to reach down to adjust himself discreetly.

Well, he thought he'd been discreet, but Grady sent him a knowing look.

"I don't think that will be necessary," she said primly.

Grady gave him another look. Employee. Right. Fuck. Why had he made that rule? Oh yeah, to ensure there weren't any awkwardness or misunderstandings.

For some reason, that rule had never been hard for him to follow.

Until her.

Because all he could think about was getting her in his bed... stripping off the ugly mustard-colored pant suit she was wearing and chasing that blush with his tongue.

Grady raised an eyebrow at him. What was his problem? Steele was behaving himself.

And it wasn't easy.

"The two of you do that a lot," she said as she picked up her menu, reading it with a frown.

"Do what?" Steele asked.

"Have conversations silently. I guess you've known each other a long time."

"Yeah, a long time," Grady said.

Steele frowned slightly, unable to read his tone.

"My best friend and I were like that," she said.

Grady narrowed his gaze on her. "Were?"

"Yeah. He died in a car accident a long time ago."

"He?" Steele asked.

She raised her gaze, looking slightly confused. "Uh-huh. His name was Joe. He was my best friend for years. We were driving home one night after we'd been to a wedding. Joe asked me to go as his date. A car tried to overtake another car going the other way, and we couldn't get out of the way in time. That's also how I injured my back."

"Sweetheart, I'm so sorry," Grady told her.

"Me too. Brooks got the worst of it."

"Brooks?" Steele asked. Even though he knew that she was the guardian of a sixteen-year-old boy, Steele figured she wouldn't be impressed to learn that Grady had done a background check on her.

"Yeah, Joe's son. He came to live with me after Joe's death."

"What about his mom?" Grady asked.

Her face grew closed-off, anger flooding her features, which was surprising when she was usually so happy. "In jail."

Christ. That poor kid.

"How long has Brooks lived with you?" Grady asked.

"Six years now."

"What did his mom get put away for?" Steele asked.

"I don't want to talk about that anymore. What's celeriac?"

"It's a variety of celery," Grady told her.

Her nose wrinkled adorably. "Eww."

"You don't like celery?" Steele asked.

"It's a vegetable, so no."

"You don't eat vegetables?" He gave her an alarmed look. That wasn't healthy. He liked sweet things, but he still ate well.

"Hmm. I like raw carrots with dip. But not cooked carrots. They should be illegal."

"Illegal?" Grady repeated.

"Uh-huh. Oh, and I like potatoes. All sorts of potatoes, really. I like fries, curly fries, mashed potatoes, potato skins, potato wedges, roasted potatoes. I mean, they're basically their own food group. Oh, and sweet potatoes are good too."

"Right. So potatoes and raw carrots?" Steele asked.

"Uh-huh. What is creamy Tuscan chicken?"

"It's delicious," Grady replied.

"It basically has cream, spinach, garlic, chicken, tomatoes, and parmesan in it," Steele added.

"Oh no, I can't eat that."

"You don't eat tomatoes?" Grady asked.

"What? Of course I eat tomatoes! What sort of crazy person wouldn't eat tomatoes?"

There she went again. When was the last time he'd felt this amused? The last time someone had held his attention this long?

Steele couldn't even remember, it was that long ago.

"It's the spinach," she muttered.

"You don't like spinach?" Grady asked.

He guessed a lot of people didn't like spinach.

"I don't eat anything that starts with an S," she replied. "What's carpaccio?"

"Thinly sliced raw meat or fish. In this case, it's tuna," he replied. "Were you joking about not eating anything starting with S?"

"That's disgusting," she muttered. "And of course I wasn't joking. Why would I joke about something like that? It's very serious."

"You can't not eat things that start with S," Grady said.

"Why not?" she asked, looking like it was a reasonable thing to do.

"Because that's crazy," Steele told her. "What about salmon?"

"Nope."

"What about Swiss cheese?" Grady asked.

"Well, it doesn't really start with S because it's cheese. So really it's a C."

"Is that your same reasoning with sweet potato?" Grady asked.

"Yep."

"Then what about a Snickers? You have to eat those." Steele smirked, knowing that he had her now.

Everyone liked Snickers.

"It's not really a food name, though, is it?" she said. "Not like sardine or sauerkraut. Also, things I don't eat."

She was bonkers.

And for some reason, he found that fucking adorable.

12

"I have decided what I'm going to order," she said.

"What's that?" Steele asked.

"Baked Alaska."

"Baked Alaska?"

"Uh-huh, food starting with B is always good." Her eyes were twinkling with laughter.

"So what other B foods do you like?" Grady asked.

Steele eyed him. He'd never seen the other man this interested in a woman. Hell, in anyone else. Grady didn't really like people.

Damon wasn't a fan either. People could be dicks.

"Burgers. Bread. Buns. Bratwurst. Do I need to go on? Ooh, bon-bons, berries, butter, baklava, banana bread. That's a double B. Yum. Oh, and we can't forget bagels."

Steele shook his head. "You can't eat Baked Alaska for dinner."

"Why not? It's the best thing on this menu. Whoever owns this place might want to revisit their options."

He gaped at her.

"What is it?" she asked. "Did I say something wrong?"

"Steele owns this restaurant," Grady told her gently.

Her mouth opened. Then closed. Then she winced. "Sorry, sometimes I need to think more before I speak. I'll do better. Really. I'm really sorry."

Fuck. Steele didn't like that. The way she kept apologizing, as though she was scared.

Of him.

She was tugging on her earrings. They were little zebras today.

Fuck, he needed to say something to put her at ease. "You like kale?"

"Umm." She eyed him as though she was worried about insulting him. "I, uh . . ."

"Steele makes these kale chips that are out of this world delicious," Grady explained. "Better than potato chips. I can't get enough of them. Although he hasn't made them in a long time."

She wrinkled her nose, her shoulders relaxing. Back to being adorable. "I really don't think kale chips can possibly be more delicious than potato chips. That's impossible."

"You'll change your mind when you try my kale chips," he told her.

She gave him a startled look, probably wondering when she'd ever have the opportunity to try his kale chips. But she would try them. And like them.

"Do you think Lee is coming back?" she asked, peering over at the door.

"Who?" he asked, confused.

"Um, Lee. The waiter."

"Maybe you should get your memory checked, as well as your eyes," Grady joked.

Something Grady rarely did. Effie gave Grady a startled look before her eyes twinkled.

"Here comes Lee," Grady murmured.

"What are you really going to have for dinner, Miss Effie?" Steele asked, aware of Grady's warning look but not caring.

She hadn't signed on to work for them just yet.

And she really couldn't have Baked Alaska for dinner.

"Baked Alaska."

"How about the steak?" he countered.

She looked pale and he knew money was tight.

"Steak? It seems expensive."

"Then that's what you should get," Grady said smoothly. "Since Steele is paying."

"Oh. That doesn't seem fair. I can pay."

"You being serious right now?" he asked grumpily. Was she trying to insult him?

"Uh. Um. Yes?"

She was back to stumbling over her words and looking unsure, but he was too upset to care right then.

"You're not paying."

"I, uh, I'm not?"

"If I didn't let you pay for those slippers on your feet or the shoes, you're definitely not paying for your steak and overload of sugar."

Grady sighed. "I'd actually like her to agree to work for me, you know."

Like Steele would allow her to say no. Now, he expected her to apologize for having the audacity to think that she would pay for her own meal. And then give in graciously.

"About the slippers—"

"No." Dear Lord. Was she trying to give him a stroke?

She frowned. "No? What do you mean, no?"

"I mean that we are not speaking of the slippers. They are yours. As are the other shoes."

"What other shoes?"

"The ones he was supposed to wait to give you until you got home," Grady said stiffly.

Grady was getting pissed at him. It wasn't noticeable to anyone else. But he could see it in the slight twitch in the other man's fingers.

"You bought me other shoes?" she asked.

"Those ones that look like a clown threw up on them," Steele told her

"W-what?"

"Or like a unicorn farted on them. That seems more accurate."

A small groan escaped Grady.

"A unicorn farted on my shoes?" she said as the server cleared his throat, reminding them that he was still standing there.

"Shall I come back?" he asked.

"Nope. I'll have the steak, baked potato, vegetables. Grady will have the seafood risotto. And Effie will also have the steak with a baked potato and salad."

"No salad!" she said quickly. "It's an S word. And I want mashed potatoes. Thanks."

Lee nodded and took away the menus.

"Well, that wasn't that hard to decide, was it?" She smiled widely at them both.

Yep. She really was nuts.

∼

Effie grew slightly nervous as they drew closer to her apartment. She knew the polite thing to do would be to offer them a drink.

But the only drinks she had were pop, hot chocolate, and coffee. Men like this probably drank fancy things. Like Scotch.

She might have some peach schnapps somewhere. But that would be the best she could do.

And anyway, it didn't matter what she had to drink because the main reason she didn't want to invite them in was because of her apartment.

And Brooks. She wasn't ready to introduce him to her new bosses.

Because, yep, she'd signed the contract. As soon as she'd seen what they were paying, she knew there was no way she could ever turn them down.

It didn't matter much to her what she had to do. She would be making nearly three times as much as she had been at her old job. Which might mean she could get into a nicer rental in a better part of town.

Maybe a two-bedroom place. That would be amazing.

She could see how their life was going to improve.

"Effie? Effie?"

She snapped back to attention as Grady spoke to her. Of course, she had to focus and pay attention in order to keep her job. But she was going to do this. She was going to be the best assistant that she could be.

Maybe she should bring cookies. That seemed like something the most amazing assistant in the world would do.

Right?

"Effie?" Grady repeated.

"Sorry?"

"Are you all right?" he asked.

"Yes, sorry. I'm just a bit tired. What is it?"

"We're here."

"Oh." Now, she felt like a complete idiot. "Wait, where's Steele?"

"I got sick of him so I left him behind at the restaurant."

"What? No, you didn't. He was in here with us."

Wasn't he?

"That was a joke, sweetheart," he said gently.

She covered her face with a groan. "I'm such a doofus."

"Not a doofus. Don't call yourself that." The scolding was light but with a hint of steel. Seemed these guys weren't real big on her saying bad things about herself.

"I was just joking around," she said.

"It can still hurt. Whether you were joking around or not."

"I'd never say it about someone else."

The door suddenly opened and Steele stood there. "Come on, babe. Walk you to the door." He sounded gruff, impatient.

Shoot. Had she done something?

You've got to focus and stop daydreaming.

"I'm sorry," she blurted out.

"Huh?" Steele frowned down at her, a blast of cold air filling the car.

Get it out quick, Effie.

"I'm sorry I said you need glasses and implied that some parts of you weren't in excellent working condition. I won't do that again."

"What the hell? Grady? What's she going on about?"

Grady was studying her closely. "Effie, that wasn't what I meant."

"I should let you both go. It's late and cold." She slid out of the car. "Thanks for the slippers and the dinner. I'll see you Monday." It was only Thursday night, but they said there was no point in starting work tomorrow. She understood that even if she was keen to get started straight away.

"Whoa, babe." Steele caught hold of her arm as she went to move past him. "What the hell?"

Grady sighed and got out too, crowding in behind her. Steele eased her forward gently so they were all standing outside. She had to work hard not to let her teeth chatter. It was freezing out here, though, and her coat was thin.

With her first paycheck, she'd buy herself a coat. Although it was near the end of winter, so maybe she should wait. Then again, that meant end-of-winter sales.

"Babe?" Steele clicked his fingers in front of her face.

"You know, it's quite rude to click your fingers in front of someone's face."

"Is it?" he asked. For some reason, amusement filled his face. "Where does ignoring someone while they're talking to you fall in the manners spectrum?"

"Oh, that's bad. You shouldn't do that."

Now he looked like he was fighting a grin. She really didn't understand him.

"Effie, look at me," Grady said firmly.

She glanced up at him in surprise.

"Good girl."

Whoa. A rush of heat went straight through her. Effie had always been a good girl. She'd always done the right thing. But no one had ever told her that she was a good girl in that tone of voice.

And it was her boss. Who was off-limits.

Typical.

"Now, focus on me," Grady said. "It's cold and you need to get inside."

"Oh, I'm so sorry. You should get back into your car."

"Effie, when I told you that I didn't like you calling yourself a doofus, I didn't mean to make you feel bad for teasing Steele about going blind."

"So that's what happened." Steele crossed his arms over his chest. "You called yourself a doofus?"

"I was just joking around."

"And when I said you shouldn't joke around, I meant with

what you say about yourself. Not about what you say about Steele."

She bit her lower lip.

Steele reached out to pull it free. "Stop."

Sheesh. Bossy.

"I didn't hurt your feelings?" she asked.

"I got a dick, Spitfire?"

"Um, I assume so." Lord, she hoped this wasn't some big reveal where he told her he was a eunuch. That wouldn't be pleasant. It would be disappointing.

You should not be thinking about your boss's dick, Effie.

She bet it was nice, though. And big. Like him.

"I've got a dick," he confirmed. "You make a joke about my eyesight, I'm not going to cry into my cornflakes."

"You eat cornflakes?"

"Course not. Think we've established I've got a dick."

"Well, I've only got your word for it." Shoot. What was wrong with her? It was like her mouth ran away from her around them.

Steele opened his mouth, but Grady got there first. "Let's get Effie inside before she catches pneumonia."

Steele cut her a sharp glance, then nodded. His hand was still around her arm, which he used to lead her toward her apartment.

How was he not shivering in the cold? She guessed when you were that big, you generated your own heat. And what had he been doing out here on his own?

She tripped over a crack that she shouldn't have tripped over since she knew it was there. She would have gone down if Steele hadn't had a hold of her.

"Whoa, Spitfire. You all right?"

"Just not used to wearing slippers. Where's Grady?"

"He's grabbing your stuff."

Shoot. She should have done that.

"How many apartments in this building?" Steele asked.

"Four."

"Four? Shit. They must be small. How long has the security light been broken?"

"What security light?"

"Not liking that, Spitfire. Not liking it at all."

Well, she didn't either. But since the landlord was an older guy with bad arthritis and she really didn't want him getting up on a ladder, there wasn't much she could do.

Except get up there and do it yourself.

Well, that was true. She could do that. If she had a ladder and knew how to put up a security light.

Maybe she could find a video to tell her what to do.

"I'll arrange a security light," Steele said.

"What? No! I mean, the landlord said he's onto it."

Yeah. That was a total lie.

He cut her a side look, but Grady appeared, carrying a shoe box.

Oh God. The confetti shoes. They'd really bought her the confetti shoes. She couldn't believe it.

Steele's phone started ringing as she reached in for her keys.

"I got to take this. Raul will pick you up Monday at eleven-thirty," he told her.

"Uh, I can get myself to work."

"You got a car?" Steele countered.

"No."

"Then Raul will pick you up." He stepped away, talking into his phone.

"Don't fight him on that, sweetheart," Grady told her as she stared after him in shock. "Unlock your door."

"Uh, I'd invite you in, but the place is in a state."

"It's all right."

She got the feeling he understood exactly why she didn't want them coming inside. Shame had her shoulders slumping.

"Effie. Look at me."

She glanced up at him.

"Go inside. Lock the door behind you. Get warm. Rest. Okay?"

"Okay."

"Be a good girl over the weekend. I'll see you Monday."

She unlocked the door and took the box in a bit of a daze. After walking in, she just stood there until there was a knock on the door.

"Yes?" she asked.

"Have you locked the door?"

"Oh, yes! Done! Thank you for dinner! And my slippers!"

"You already said that, sweetheart," he reminded her. "Sleep well."

She leaned her forehead against the door. How long since someone told her to sleep well?

And he'd told her to be a good girl. Sure, it was a bit strange for a boss to say that to his employee. But she got the feeling these guys weren't going to be ordinary bosses.

It wasn't until later, when she lifted the lid on the shoe box to look at her new confetti shoes, that she found them.

A pair of super warm gloves with red leather on the outside and sheepskin inside.

She had no idea how or when they'd managed to buy them. But they fit perfectly and they were so warm.

Definitely not your typical bosses.

∽

"WHAT'S GOING ON?" Grady asked as he joined Steele in the car.

The other man scowled. "Fucking Wolfe wants a meet."

"Wolfe? Rykers' Wolfe?" he repeated in surprise as the car pulled away from Effie's apartment.

For some reason, Grady felt a strange wrenching. As though he shouldn't be leaving her.

As if he should be holding her tight and never letting go.

Which was ridiculous. And stupid.

He needed to take a step back from this girl and get some perspective.

And so did Steele.

"Why would Wolfe think you'd want to meet with him?" Grady asked.

Wolfe was the leader of a gang called the Rykers. They were small-time assholes with inflated egos. Petty, dumb, and dicks.

They'd been causing problems at Pinkies a while back, coming in and hassling the girls. The bouncers had thrown them out, of course. The following night, more of them tried to get in.

They'd been thrown out. And they hadn't appreciated that even though they'd been in the fucking wrong.

They'd vandalized the building after hours, driven by on their bikes to intimidate their customers and girls. They'd started selling heavy drugs, having attached themselves to this dickhead called Edmund James. But now Eddy was dead, and Steele had his guys coming down on their gang.

Hard.

"He's bleeding men and money," Steele said gruffly. "We've all but destroyed the Rykers and he knows that the bullshit he let his men pull was over the line."

"So you think he wants to suck up to you? Apologize?"

Steele snorted. "He can get down on his knees and offer to suck me off . . . still not happening."

Grady drew in a breath. Because the idea of another man sucking Steele off filled him with rage. He didn't think Steele had ever been with another man. Grady had experimented a few times. He'd wondered if his disinterest in being with a woman without Steele was because he wanted to be with men.

But nope, he hadn't been any more interested in those men.

Seemed he just wanted a person. And that person was Steele.

You're interested in Effie.

"The Rykers are dying and he knows it. Fucker can't come begging to me now to help him."

"Let me know if you need anything."

Steele nodded.

"You need to ease back with Effie," Grady warned.

Steele gazed over at him. "I could say the same thing to you."

"Just as long as we're on the same page. Effie is off-limits. To both of us."

And he'd just have to keep reminding himself of that.

13

Effie peered down at the spreadsheet on her laptop. She was sitting on the ergonomic chair that Grady had told her that he'd bought for himself. But which she knew he'd bought for her. Because he was surprisingly thoughtful.

She'd been working for him for three weeks and she was enjoying it. He was demanding and exacting, but he wasn't a jerk.

She still couldn't believe that they'd bought her slippers and confetti shoes and gloves. Every morning, she woke up and pinched herself, certain she was living a fairy-tale.

Actually, she should probably stop doing that since that skin was starting to bruise.

"Yo, Effie."

She glanced up with a smile as Chardonnay walked in, followed by Tessie and Cilla. Her posse.

That's what she called them.

Cilla was another dancer. She was gorgeous with long blonde hair that she probably bleached a bit too much for it to be healthy. And big blue eyes. She spoke in a soft, breathy voice, but she was no pushover.

Tessie was a server. She was tiny. Super tiny. And she had short, black hair that was longer on one side than the other. She was pure biker babe. She usually dressed in jeans and some awesome biker T-shirt as well as a leather jacket when she wasn't in her Pinkies uniform, which consisted of a tight top and short shorts.

Tessie might be tiny, but she was strong. The other night some asshole had tried to grab her and she'd had him in a headlock before the bouncers could even get there.

"What'd you make today?" Tessie asked, coming over to open the container on her desk.

"Brownies. With white chocolate and pecans. They're delicious."

A bit too delicious. Effie's clothes were starting to get rather tight. It might be time to try some of those sugar-free recipes she'd been researching.

Or gain some willpower. However, she didn't have much of that. As soon as her first pay check had cleared, Effie had started bringing in her baking for everyone. And to her surprise, everyone seemed to love it. Not just Brooks, who she thought would tell her it was good no matter what. But each of the servers and strippers who made their way back here.

And they were back here a lot. That surprised her too. How friendly everyone was.

"Tessie, I scheduled that time off you wanted. I've had to use Vanessa for some of the shifts, though."

Tessie groaned. "She's going to make a mess of it."

Effie sighed. This was likely true. Vanessa wasn't good at her job. She had big hair, a rocking body, and she knew it. She was more interested in having a good time rather than working.

Which is why she only worked shifts at Pinkies when they needed someone to cover other servers.

"If I had someone else, I'd use them."

Tessie nodded.

"And you need to go on vacation and not worry about any of this."

Tessie was off to Greece. Alone. That was so brave. Braver than Effie could ever imagine being. Effie hadn't left the state of Montana in years. And not because of finances.

But because the idea of traveling alone kind of scared her.

"You better bring us back some good gifts," Chardonnay told her.

"I want a hot Greek man," Cilla added. "Apparently they have stamina. And they're hung."

Effie giggled.

"I don't think every Greek man can be well hung," Tessie told her skeptically.

"Find that out for us, will you?" Chardonnay said with a grin.

"I just might," Tessie said.

"I bet none of them would be as well hung as Steele," Cilla said.

"Cilla!" Tessie scolded.

"What? He's got to be huge all over. And I reckon Grady is too. Imagine being in that man-sandwich."

"What?" she asked, her eyes wide.

"Oh, you haven't heard?" Cilla asked. "They like to share."

Yikes.

"Jeez, Cilla, you're terrifying the poor girl," Chardonnay said. "They like to share, Effie. But I've never known them to have a girlfriend."

Wow. Never?

"Effie, will you help me with a dance move later?" Cilla asked.

"Sure! Of course I will."

Chardonnay picked up a piece of brownie. "I gotta go. Thanks for the brownie, Effie."

"No problem."

They all left and she got back to work. That was until *he* walked into the office. She hadn't seen Damon Steele much since she'd started working here. But when he was around . . . he was there. Filling up space. Sucking out the air in the room.

But not in a bad way. In a way that meant she couldn't breathe . . . because he was Steele.

Dominant. Strong. Sexy.

It was pretty disappointing that she didn't have a lot to do with him. Or with Grady. Sure, she was his assistant, but many of his instructions came to her via email or text.

If she was insecure, she'd think they were avoiding her.

But that was just silly.

Wasn't it?

"Hello, Mr. Steele," she said with a smile, trying to hide the way he affected her.

He raised an eyebrow. "You know better, Miss Effie."

"Um, right. Steele, can I help you?" She attempted to sound professional while sitting on a seriously comfy chair in a dingy, dark office that had really seen better days, but which she'd tried to brighten up.

She'd bought a couple of throw cushions for the chesterfield. She'd wanted the ones with sequins that were in the shape of different animals. But instead, she'd gone for animal print. She figured that was safer. Even if one of them was pink, black, and yellow. So not exactly masculine.

She'd also put a really bright rug down on the floor and a few pictures on the walls. Grady had told her to make the office her own. He'd claimed he was hardly ever in there, so it was all hers.

So she'd done that.

"This place is . . . different."

"Do you like it?"

He stared at her for a long moment, then looked around. Oh, he didn't like it. Then she glanced again at everything. It was probably a bit pink. The pictures that she'd hung were cool, but maybe he didn't like images of different animals drinking tea with tutus on. Or he didn't appreciate the neon green rug.

Yeah, maybe he just wasn't into any of that.

"I can change it all," she said hastily. "If you don't like it."

"Is this your office?" he asked.

"Uh, well, Grady said it was. But it's your building. Which is why I didn't paint the walls. Even though I thought it would be cool to put blackboard paint on one wall so I could write all my notes to myself."

Maybe that way she wouldn't keep losing her notes. She'd written a note with her computer password on it, and she couldn't for the life of her find it. She'd had to change the password.

"Do it," he told her.

"W-what?"

"Do it."

"But that's not just furnishings. It's touching the walls."

"Effie, I don't like to repeat myself. Do. It."

"Got it," she whispered, excitement bubbling inside her. "Thanks, Steele."

"Damn. Cute."

"Sorry?"

He shook his head. "Nothing."

She frowned, unsure what was going on with him. "Did you need something?"

"New girl that started, she all set up?"

"Um, yes." At least on her end. She'd seen her on stage and she was a good dancer, if a bit uninspired.

But that had nothing to do with Effie. Not unless she asked for her help like Cilla.

"Good."

"Yep. Good." She still had no idea what was happening. What did he want? Was he checking up on her? Oh my God. Did he not think she was doing a good job? What could she do better? She was trying as hard as she could not to get lost in her head. To focus. But there were times she went into la-la land. However, she always got here early and worked late to make up for any time that she daydreamed.

"Effie? You listening?"

"I promise I'll do better!"

He rocked back slightly, eyeing her with confusion. "Do what better, Spitfire?"

"Um, whatever it was you were going to tell me that I wasn't doing good enough?"

He crossed his arms over his chest. "You thought I was coming in here to tell you that you weren't doing something well?"

"That's not why you're here?"

"No, babe," he told her gently. "That's not why I'm here."

"Oh. That's good then. So I'm doing a good job?"

"Now you're just fishing for compliments."

She totally was. But did that mean she wasn't going to get them? That was disappointing.

"Your landlord get that security light installed at your place?" he moved forward to open the container on her desk and drew out a piece of brownie.

"Um, yes." Technically, she'd done it. But he didn't need to know that.

"Good. You buy this?"

"Uh, no. I made it."

He took a bite. "Damn. That's good."

A flush of pleasure filled her. "Thank you."

His lips twitched. "Happy now?"

"What?"

"You got your compliment."

Shoot. So she had.

"Anything you need to tell me?" he asked.

Uh. Was there? She didn't think so. She searched through her brain. He didn't need to know that she'd gotten a couple of weird phone calls. From numbers with no caller IDs who'd just hung up.

Or that her period had started yesterday and the cramps were killing her.

Or that she'd eaten way too many jelly beans last night and given herself a tummy ache and a blue tongue. Since the blue and white ones were her favorites.

Or that her neighbor had a party last night and kept her awake. And that he'd been doing that nearly every night this last week and she was on her last nerve.

"Spitfire," he said firmly.

"Uh, yep."

"I can see I might need to come in and ask that more often."

"Huh?"

"Not sure of everything that's going on in your head, but is there a reason why you told Raul that he didn't need to keep picking you up for work?"

Oh. That's why he was here.

She shouldn't feel a hit of disappointment that he wasn't here just to see her. Nope. Because that would be silly.

Which she often was. Because she was forever hopeful. Which, given her life and the way things constantly went to shit, was extremely silly.

But here she was . . . being silly once more.

Silly and hopeful.

"It's a waste of time for him."

"Waste of time?"

"Yes, I can get myself to work. I don't need him to take me. So I told him that."

"He's picking you up for work, Spitfire."

"Really, it's not necessary." She gave him a big smile to ensure he knew she wasn't actually arguing with him.

He leaned his hands down on the desk and she had to fight hard not to lean back.

"Yeah, he is."

"I'm in charge of how I get into work, and I say he's not."

Shoot. What was she doing?

He's your boss.

"You work for me?" he asked weirdly.

"Uh, yes."

"Then you do what I say. If I say he picks you up, then he picks you up. Understand?"

"All right." She gave in because he was her boss and she didn't want to make him angry.

"All right?" he asked, looking surprised.

"Yes, all right," she said.

But she wasn't happy about it. So when Steele went to reach for another piece of brownie, she leaned over and snatched the container away from him.

He raised his eyebrows. "I don't get more brownie?"

"Nope."

Effie braced herself for anger because this wasn't a very nice thing to do. And Effie was always pleasant. Always good. Always bright and happy and cheerful.

Just like Nan taught her.

Except, apparently, when Damon Steele grew bossy with her. Which seemed to happen every time she saw him.

"Because you didn't get your way?"

All right. That made her sound slightly petty.

"Because you're being unreasonable."

"How'd you plan on getting to work if Raul didn't pick you up, Spitfire?"

"Um, on the bus."

"So you'd rather take the bus, walk in the cold from the bus stop to here, pay for a ticket, sit among strangers who could be anyone. One of them could have a weapon, a gun or a knife. They could be in a bad mood that day, see you and decide that you remind them of their ex-wife who has been jacking them around, and they'll take their anger out on you. Is that what you want?"

"Well, no," she said faintly. And now she was feeling somewhat terrified of the bus. Which was not good since it was her main mode of transport when she wasn't at work.

"So you're going to be mad at me for wanting to keep you safe from some knife-wielding madman with a vendetta against his ex-wife?"

"When you put it like that... although don't you think that's unlikely?"

"Always found it's best to plan for the worst. Means there's less chance of a nasty surprise."

Wow. Really? That was kind of a sad way to live.

Then again, she did the opposite. Always thought the best was going to happen... and was constantly let down.

"But what about everyone else here? Do you pick all of them up?"

"Most of them drive." Reaching over, he grabbed a piece of brownie. "Behave yourself."

Behave herself? She always behaved herself. She frowned as she watched him walk out of the door.

And then it occurred to her that he said that most of them drove here. What about the ones that didn't? Was Raul busy traveling all over the city, picking them up?

Somehow, she thought not. So why was she special?

14

Effie's phone rang as she rushed into the office. By the time she got to the desk, the phone had stopped, and so she set her stuff down before stretching her back.

It had been pretty good lately, but sometimes, it played up. Like right now.

She set down her treats for the day and pulled her phone out. Another unknown number.

What the heck?

She was damn sick of this.

That was the third time someone had called her and hung up in the last two weeks.

It rang again and anger filled her.

"Listen," she said into the phone. "I am sick of this. If you keep calling me and hanging up, I am going to the cops."

It was an empty threat. But the person on the other end didn't know that. And she was done. Those phone calls where no one was on the other line . . . they scared her.

Effie had spent too much time being scared. Scared to let Joe know how she felt. Afraid to let go of him when he died. Terrified she'd mess Brooks up for life. Petrified she'd lose Brooks too.

Worried all the time. About everything.

So she really didn't need some fucking asshole calling her and hanging up and making life harder for her.

However, the person on the other end didn't hang up. Nope, they cleared their throat. That was new. They never usually made a noise before hanging up.

"Ms. Stephenson?"

"Who is this?" she demanded. "And why do you keep calling me then hanging up? That's really rude."

"Um, I don't believe that I have done that."

Okay, she was beginning to think that perhaps the man on the other end of the line wasn't her prank caller.

"Oh, who're you?"

"My name is Jonas Real. I'm a lawyer."

"A lawyer?" she asked, frowning. Why would a lawyer be calling her?

"Yes, I represent Tanya Ford. I believe you currently have custody of her son, uh, Brooks Ford."

"His name isn't Brooks Ford." Stupid name. Something Tanya had given him because she thought it was funny. "It's Brooks Keaton." That was Joe's last name, and he'd made certain that Brooks had it after Tanya had gone nuts.

"Right. My apologies. You're correct."

"Why are you calling me?" Her heart was racing.

She's in jail. There's nothing she can do.

"Ms. Ford would like to get in touch with her son, Brooks."

"Excuse me?"

"She would like to get in touch with him. To call him. Perhaps arrange visitation."

"You . . . what . . . she . . . huh?" White noise was filling her head so she could barely hear him as he repeated himself.

Didn't matter how many times he said it. She still wouldn't believe it.

Why the hell did that bitch think she got to get in contact with Brooks? She wasn't getting anywhere near him. And was she completely bonkers? Did she really think it was a good idea for her sixteen-year-old to visit her in prison?

No. Nope.

"Ms. Stephenson? Are you still there?"

"I'm here."

"Do you think you could arrange for Brooks to take some calls from his mother?"

"No."

"No?"

"No." The word was fainter than she would have liked. She wished she'd sounded strong. Certain. But it was the best she could do when she couldn't . . . fucking . . . breathe.

This was what she got for thinking everything would be all right.

Maybe she should be more like Steele. Believe the worst.

"Shouldn't you talk to Brooks first? He's sixteen now, he might like to get to know his mother."

"No. I don't need to speak to him. Do not call me back." She ended the call and then placed her head down on the desk.

Breathe.

Just breathe.

Fear had hold of her, though. It made her tremble. Why . . . why was Tanya doing this now? She had never tried to get in contact with Brooks. Not once.

And now, out of the blue, she just decided she wanted to talk to him? What about all the birthdays and Christmases? Had she not thought to call then? What about when Joe died?

Her breath shuddered in and out of her lungs.

"Spitfire? What's wrong?"

Shit. Why hadn't she shut the door? And why did Steele have to turn up now?

He'd been in pretty much every day of the last week to try whatever treat she had with her.

Chocolate chip cookies. Lemon bars. Hedgehog slice. All of it.

She'd realized that he had a big sweet tooth. He must work all of it off at the gym because the man didn't look like he carried any fat on his chiselled body.

"My neighbor is loud," she said quickly. She had to come up with something to tell him.

"What?" he asked in a low voice.

She sat up. "My neighbor. He's a jerk. Always partying at night."

"You call the cops?"

"No, of course not."

He narrowed his eyes. "Why would you say of course not? You had problems with the cops?"

"Me? No." And that was the truth. "Just not necessary. It seems mean to call the police because of a bit of noise. I just have to work up the gumption to go upstairs and tell him to turn it down."

And she would. Maybe Tuesday next year.

Yep, that sounded as good a time as any.

"You're not doing that."

"E-excuse me?"

"You know this neighbor well?"

"Um, not really. He's lived above me for about three months. A guy in his early twenties. He likes to party. He also argues a lot with his sometimes-girlfriend. I don't really get it."

"Get what?"

"Why would you stay with someone you really didn't like? I mean . . . they don't just argue, they get really, really mean."

"Baby," he said in a soft voice.

She stared at him in surprise even as a warm glow filled her. Baby? He'd called her baby. No one had ever called her baby. And they definitely hadn't called her baby while staring at her with gentle eyes.

"You called me baby," she whispered.

"Sure did."

"You really shouldn't."

"That so?" Now he looked amused. Sometimes, it was difficult to keep up with his changing moods.

She really wondered if he should get someone to take a look at his head for him. Split personality was no laughing matter.

"I lost you, Spitfire?"

"Um, how can you lose me when I'm right here?" she asked.

"You'd be surprised," he muttered.

She would? What was he talking about?

"Now that I have you, I need you to listen to me. You listening?"

"Um, yes. I believe so."

"No."

She stared at him for a long moment. "No, what?"

"No. The answer is no. Are you going up to tell him to keep the noise down? No. When there is a party? No. When they're fighting? No. Now do you see how no is the answer?"

"That really makes no sense. What if the question is should I put my seatbelt on in a moving car? Is the answer no then?"

"Don't sass me."

Huh? Was she sassing him? Well, okay, maybe a little.

"So you think I should just put up with them keeping me awake all night? Well, I suppose I can deal. I've been watching some really interesting infomercials. I'm thinking about trying this piece of exercise equipment for free for thirty days. Apparently, it will tighten my butt." And her butt could use that.

"What's the answer?"

Huh?

Oh. Wait.

"No?"

"That's right. No."

"I can't buy the exercise equipment?"

"Baby, that stuff is a waste of time and money."

Aww, he was calling her baby again. She melted.

"You want to go to the gym? I'll take you to mine. But does your butt need any work?"

"Uh." Yep, plenty.

"What's the answer, Spitfire?"

Dear. Lord. He was out of control.

"No."

"You're getting it. I'll take care of your neighbor."

"Haha, sure you will."

He just shot her a look. Oh, crap. Maybe she should have told him about the lawyer calling her. That would have been the smarter play here, turning him on some scummy lawyer instead of her scummy-but-knew-where-she-lived neighbor.

"That's not necessary," she said hastily.

"Consider it done."

"I really don't want to consider it at all," she told him. "Because I don't want that to happen. You cannot talk to my neighbor."

"That's tough you don't want it." He reached into the container on her desk, pulling out a piece of chocolate cake.

That's all he said. What did that mean? Was he not going to do it? Crap.

"Steele," she started to say, but she was interrupted.

By him choking.

Well, not actually choking. But he was making a noise like he was going to vomit. Then he grabbed a tissue and spat out the piece of cake into it.

She stared at him in horror.

"What the hell is this?" he demanded.

"Uh, chocolate cake."

"This isn't chocolate cake."

"It is! It's just I'm trying to cut down on the sugar and bad fat, so I used avocado and dates. You don't like it?"

"Don't make this again." He grabbed another tissue and cleaned himself up.

Wow. Really.

She thought it was a pretty good creation. Although she'd noticed Chardonnay pulling a face earlier when she'd tried a bite too.

"That's not very nice," she muttered.

"Neither is this cake. And it shouldn't even be called cake. It's criminal that it looks so delicious and yet tastes so terrible."

Her mouth was open as she gaped at him.

She wanted to be angry. But the truth was that Steele was right. It was sad. That's what it was.

Sad-cake.

"If I have to deal with your neighbor, Spitfire, I'm going to need actual cake. With actual sugar. And actual fat."

"But I don't want you to deal with my neighbor."

"Why not? You worried about them?" He gave her a stern look.

"Why would I be worried about them? I'm worried about you."

His eyes widened. "Baby."

She would not melt at him calling her baby.

She. Was. Not.

"You do know who I am, right?"

Uh-oh. "I've heard rumors. I don't listen to rumors." Because those rumors were scary. But before she'd gone to the interview, April had told her a few things. Chardonnay had told her a few more.

"Good rule to live by, Spitfire. In this case, the rumors are probably wrong."

She knew it.

"I'm much, much worse."

He was just teasing, right? Hell. She wasn't sure. She tugged at her earring. Today, she was wearing long earrings with sloths climbing the end of them. They were adorable. Joe had given them to her years ago.

She sighed as her phone rang again.

Please do not be that dickhead lawyer.

Maybe she should sic Steele on him too. She could make him cupcakes. She was good at baking cupcakes. Effie frowned as she saw it was Brooks' school calling.

"I'm sorry, I have to take it. It's St. Augustine, Brooks' school."

When he didn't leave, she decided to answer anyway. If there was one thing she'd discovered, it was that Damon Steele was an immovable object.

15

Steele was half-listening as Effie answered her phone. He picked up the container of cake and opened the lid before throwing it in the bin. It landed with a heavy clunk.

That cake should be illegal.

"What? Yes! There must be a mistake. Is he all right? Yes . . . yes . . . all right, I'll be there soon."

He raised his gaze to her as she put her phone down. Then she suddenly stood, and her face grew pale as she swayed.

"Effie!" He jumped around the desk to grab her before she could fall over. "What's wrong?"

"Oh, nothing . . . nothing. I'm just . . . light-headed. Happens sometimes."

It happened sometimes? It shouldn't be happening anytime.

"I gots to go."

He narrowed his gaze. Did she mean to talk like that? Or was that her Little slipping through? Either way, he didn't like that she'd just looked like she was going to faint.

He liked even less that it 'happened sometimes'.

"Where do you have to go? Brooks' school?"

"Yes! Yes, I gots to go. I . . . I . . . I need to go. Where's my bag?"

Steele looked around and saw the bright pink monstrosity sitting by the desk. He picked it up and took hold of her hand. He didn't trust her to walk on her own while she was feeling dizzy.

And let's face it, he liked holding her hand. He liked that she was smaller than him, yet curvy and soft. He knew she'd feel good against him.

Naked.

Fucking Grady. He just had to go and hire her.

"Wait! Wait!"

She tugged at his hand, looking up at him anxiously. "Where's my phone? I need my phone."

"Baby," he said, trying to hold back his amusement. He didn't want her to think that he was laughing at her. She was obviously rattled and he wasn't sure what was going on. But if something had happened to her kid, then it wasn't a laughing matter.

"What? I need my phone, Steele!" she cried.

"Look at your hand."

"I don't have time."

"Look at your hand," he said in a sterner voice. Effie needed to learn to listen and obey.

Someone should teach her that.

He really wanted that someone to be him. And Grady.

Together, they'd take care of her.

She glanced down at her hand with a huff.

So much attitude. That suited him. It gave him a reason to punish her. Nothing too harsh. However, a few pops on the bottom never harmed anyone. If it kept her safe he was more than prepared to spank her. Or have her write lines while sitting with a plug up her bottom.

It was strange, though. He hadn't been a Daddy Dom in a long time. Hadn't intended to be again. But Effie brought out all of his Daddy instincts. Part of it was probably all those cute earrings she wore. And the confetti shoes that she hadn't taken off.

Part of it was just Effie herself.

Something about her screamed at him that she needed his protection. And Steele liked being needed. So did Grady.

In fact, he thought that his best friend might need it more.

He definitely functioned better with control. And he'd never have that with Steele.

Fuck. He needed to get this out of his head and get her to that school.

"Come along, Effie." He tugged her into him, wrapped an arm around her shoulders and rushed her out of there.

"What . . . what are you doing?"

"Getting you to the school. What's happened? Is your boy sick?"

"N-no."

He was texting as he walked, letting Raul know he needed him. He got to the back door and opened it.

"Wait there for my signal to move," he commanded.

"What?"

He ignored her question and leaned out, looking around. Only Raul was there.

"Come."

"Is there a problem? Danger?" she asked as she stepped out, looking around cautiously.

He shot her a surprised look. "No, of course not." He opened the door and ushered her in. "If there was any danger, I wouldn't allow you outside. Tell Raul where we're going."

She rattled off the address for the school and Raul nodded before raising the privacy screen.

Steele drew her seatbelt over her and then did his own. He still needed to look at a booster seat for her.

"But you acted like there was danger," she pointed out.

"Always pays to be cautious, Spitfire. Taking your safety for granted will get you killed."

"Do you always live like that?" she asked.

"Of course. Now, what's going on with your kid?"

"Um, the school said that he was caught fighting with another student. But I don't understand. That's just not Brooks. He's a really good kid. And I know that most people think their kids are the best kids out there. But with Brooks, it's true. He never gives me any problems. He's super smart. Never breaks the rules and is always home by curfew. He gets straight A's. I nearly flunked high school because all I was interested in was dancing."

"You wanted to be a dancer?"

"So badly," she whispered. "And I was good. But I just . . . it's hard to make a career out of dancing. So I worked a lot of different jobs after school, just whatever would allow me to have time to dance. And now, I just dance at home, where no one watches me."

Fuck. Now he was jealous that Grady had gotten to see her dance. He'd said she'd danced like a dream. Well, until she'd gotten to the pole that is.

"Thought stripping might have been the perfect career for me," she muttered. "Forgot about the stripping part, though. No one actually wants to see me naked."

"Baby girl, you're overwrought, which is why I'm going to ignore that. But say that again, and you and me? We're going to have trouble."

She gulped and looked over at him. "Trouble?"

"Uh-huh. The sort where you can't sit properly the next day."

"I don't . . . I don't think you're allowed to spank me."

"I am if you give consent."

"But Grady—"

"Grady will agree if he hears what you just said."

"Yikes," she whispered. Then she took in a deep breath. "I've got to be calm when I go in there. A grown-up. I know Brooks is still a teenager, but sometimes it feels like he's the mature one. What . . . what if they try to take his scholarship? Oh God. Oh God."

He could see her fear. Feel it. He had to get her to calm down. She was tugging at her ear so hard that he was worried she was going to rip the earring right out.

"It's going to be all right."

"Can I hold your hand?"

He was stunned for a moment and didn't reply.

"Never mind. Stupid Effie. I'm so sorry. What was I thinking? You're my boss and I'm asking you to hold my hand like a child. Jelly bean. I need a jelly bean or two or ten."

She picked up her handbag and was searching through it, muttering to herself. Things started flying out of the huge thing. Should she even be carrying something that enormous when she had a bad back?

Suddenly, something flew through the air and smacked him in the face. What the hell?

He picked it up and saw it was the same toy sloth that he'd seen in her handbag.

So it was likely hers.

Interesting.

"Here they are!" She held up a small bag of jelly beans triumphantly. As though she was holding a child she'd just given birth to.

He glanced around the back of the car. There was stuff everywhere. A hairbrush lay on the seat between them, as well as a pack of gum. On the floor, he spotted a compact mirror, three pens, two hair ties, and four tampons.

"Open, damn you, open."

He continued to gape at her as she tugged at the packet of jelly beans, her frustration clear.

Then the bag burst open and jelly beans rained down, filling the backseat of the car.

"Oh no."

"Effie," he said in a low voice, needing to head things off before she totally lost it.

Unfortunately, as she completely lost it, he realized that he'd reacted too late.

"They're everywhere! I l-lost all my j-jellybeans." Her lower lip started trembling.

Shit.

This was . . . unexpected. She was always so darn cheerful. Well, except when she was being bossy. Even then, that made him smile because she was so adorable.

Time you took control.

She might not appreciate it later, but this was what she needed right now.

"Effie, look at me."

"Oh no. I m-made a huge m-mess of your car. I'm s-sorry. So sorry." She bent down to pick up about fifty thousand jelly beans.

"Effie."

Jesus. She was going to make herself ill, bending over like that. He pushed the stuff off the seat and then leaned over to undo her seatbelt. Then he slid her across the seat toward him.

He quickly put the middle belt around her.

"Steele, what are you doing? I've got to tidy all of this mess up."

"Look at me."

She continued to ignore him. What the fuck? No one ignored him. Not even Grady.

"Effie. Look. At. Me."

To ensure that she did and that he didn't start losing his goddamned mind, he reached out and cupped the side of her face, turning her to look up at him.

"All the mess—"

"Stop." He placed his thumb over her mouth and her eyes widened. "You're going to stop talking now and listen to me, baby girl. Understand?"

Her eyes went even wider as he called her baby girl. Shit. Grady was going to kill him.

But he didn't care.

It was worth it to see the warmth in her eyes, the way she slid against him.

"I don't give a shit about the state of my car. That can be tidied up. I do give a shit about the state of you. You need to calm down, baby."

She shook her head, her eyes moving away.

"I didn't say you could move your eyes away," he warned in a low rumble. "Eyes back on me."

Her gaze shot back to him.

Good. So she could follow directions. Steele decided to try something else.

"That's a good girl."

Oh yeah. More softening. He liked that too.

He moved his thumb away from her mouth. "Now, you're going to listen to me. Give me your hand."

"W-what?"

"Give me your hand. You asked for it before and I was too slow to give it to you. So give me your hand."

He got impatient when she didn't move and reached out to grab her hand.

"Jesus, you're freezing. Why didn't you say something?" He bent down and adjusted the heat for her.

"Oh, it's okay. Just poor circulation."

He shot her a look. "Why haven't you told me about this before?"

She gave him a confused look. "Why would I?"

"Part of working for me, Effie."

"Does everyone who works for you tell you every little thing about them?"

"You're not everyone. And I spend more time with you than any of them. If you are feeling cold, I need to know. You don't do a good enough job of taking care of yourself."

She gasped, long and loud.

So dramatic.

He fought back a grin. Dramatic and cute.

"I see that you're not looking after yourself, then I have to step in."

"You're nuts."

"Call it what you like, baby girl. But it is what it is." He wrapped his hands around one of hers and started rubbing it briskly. "Does this have anything to do with your dizziness earlier?"

"My old back injury means that sometimes I have low-blood pressure and poor circulation."

"Then you should be wearing your gloves all the time."

"It would be hard to type while wearing my gloves. I really need to pick this stuff up."

"Effie, look at me."

She raised her gaze to him.

"Don't go borrowing trouble before it's happened."

"Right. You're right." She nodded. "There's no way they can suspend Brooks. Or take his scholarship. He's amazing. The principal will be reasonable. He's a school principal. I'm sure he's a very nice man."

16

"You are not a very nice man."

Yeah, she probably shouldn't have said it like that. Now, instead of thirty-five, she sounded as if she was five.

But that didn't make it any less the truth. He wasn't a nice man. At all.

He was a judgmental asshole.

When they arrived at the school, she'd been in such a panic that she couldn't even remember how to get to the admin building. Luckily, Steele was excellent in a crisis. She'd even told him he could put that on his CV if he ever needed to get another job.

Of course, then she'd realized he owned his own businesses. And there were rumors that he was also The Boss. But like she'd told him, she didn't listen to rumors.

When they'd gotten to the admin building the secretary had given her a sympathetic look before taking them through. She'd really expected Steele to leave. She was convinced he had far more important things to do than stick around a high school.

What she hadn't expected was for him to walk into the principal's office with her.

The principal was a wizened older man who looked like he should have retired about twenty years ago. He was wearing a suit two sizes too big, and obviously no one had told him that mud-brown was not his color.

She was uncertain that mud brown was anyone's color.

When they'd entered the room, he'd looked her up and down dismissively. Rude asshole. This school was the best in the city, and she'd been so happy when Brooks had won a scholarship to come here. But Effie hoped that he hadn't been putting up with this sort of attitude from teachers and other students.

Brooks had been sitting off to the side, holding an ice pack to his face. She'd gone straight to him, gasping in shock at his black eye and the blood under his nose and on his white shirt.

She'd immediately demanded to know what had happened. And that's when Mr. Cleary, the principal, told her Brooks was being expelled.

Like hell.

"Ms. Stephenson, this has nothing to do with being nice. He was caught fighting. That is against the rules of St. Augustine. And it is clearly laid out in the terms and conditions for his scholarship. We ask that he pack up his locker immediately and that you let us know where he is going so we can send his records there. Good day."

She just gaped at him. Inside, she was quailing; she wanted to run and hide. But this was Brooks. No one messed with her kid.

She felt Steele come up behind her and place his hand on her lower back.

"Maybe you want to tell us what happened before you start laying down judgment," Steele told him gruffly.

"What happened won't change the outcome," he said huffily. Although he was eyeing Steele nervously.

Steele's touch gave her the boost of courage she needed.

"Actually, I think we have the right to know what happened," she said. "Brooks? Were you fighting, honey?"

"I fought back when I was ambushed by three guys."

"You were ambushed?" she whispered. She tried to rush over to him again, but Steele grabbed her around the waist, squeezing with his hand.

Right. They needed to hear the rest of the story. Then she could fuss over him.

"I was walking along the hall after school when I heard these three guys picking on Stella. They were making fun of her. Calling her names. So I stepped in and told them to leave her alone. They got in my face. One of them reached out to touch her and I pushed him back. That's when Darrin, he's the leader of their little group, hit me. Then they all attacked."

"Three boys attacked you? And are they expelled?" she asked the principal.

"There is no evidence that they attacked him first. They said that he started it. He provoked them and threw the first punch. That he went crazy and they were just defending themselves. They also said they weren't bullying the young lady in question."

"What?" she said faintly. "Well, where are they? Where is she?" Her heart raced with fear and anger. How dare these boys lie? And why did the principal believe them over Brooks?

Actually . . . she knew exactly why.

"Effie, it's all right," Brooks said. Getting up, he came to her. "Everything will be all right."

"Actually, it's not all right," Steele said. "I'd like to see these boys and that girl. Get their side of the story."

"And who are you?" the principal asked snootily right before the door to the office slammed open and two boys walked in.

They were identical, but not. Oh, their features were the same, but one of them had his dark hair longer and messier. His blazer was open and so were half of his shirt buttons. She could see a T-shirt underneath. His shoes were scuffed and there was a wicked grin on his face.

Trouble. Total trouble.

His brother, on the other hand, was dressed impeccably. His hair was cut shorter and styled. He had his blazer buttoned, shirt done up with a tie, and there wasn't even one scuff mark on his shoes.

"What are the two of you doing barging in here?" the principal demanded. "Where is Ms. O'Ryan? Why isn't she at her desk?"

"I don't know. Where do you think she is, brother?" the well-put- together one said.

"Maybe she went to the bathroom, bro," the messier one replied.

"Yes, or maybe she ran off to Turks and Caicos to escape Dracula."

"Don't think he sucks blood, though, brother. Think he sucks souls."

"The souls of children just trying to learn." The one with the tie on shook his head. "Shameful. Just shameful."

The principal stood, glaring at the boys, clearly incensed. "The two of you are not supposed to be in here. And you need to leave."

"But we've got some information that you need, Donny," the one with the tie said. "We know you're big on gathering all evidence before making a judgment. Right? Because you wouldn't want the board to look into why you're trying to get rid of scholarship students. Why you're turning your back and ignoring the bad behavior of some students, yet coming down hard on others."

"Nope, bro, he wouldn't want the board to know about that." The one with longer hair turned to look at them with that grin. "Hello, I'm Baron and this is my brother, Royal."

"What are you guys doing?" Brooks asked, staring at them both with a hint of awe.

"Royal and Baron?" Steele said in a quiet rumble. "You're Ink's boys."

"That's us," Baron replied, not losing the grin. "And you're Damon Steele."

"Damon Steele?" Mr. Cleary whispered. "You're Damon Steele?"

"I can see my reputation precedes me," Steele said.

"That's because you're the shit, man," Baron said.

"Baron!" Mr. Cleary said. "You will not use that language."

"Oh, shove it, Donny," Baron replied. "No one is interested in your opinion."

"Would you like me to get your parents down here?" the principal asked.

"You can do that if you wish," Royal told him, brushing off some imaginary lint. "Ink might be interested in hearing what's going on here."

"I will call your stepmother. Don't think I won't."

Both boys stiffened.

Royal leaned forward and she tensed. Wow. For someone who was still in school, he had a commanding presence. Brooks pressed up close to her.

"Don't worry, Effie," Brooks whispered to her. "Baron and Royal are good guys. They always stick up for the underdog."

"They're friends of yours?" she asked.

"Nah, they're older than me. But I've seen them in action."

"Did you just say that you'd call our Ma?" Royal said.

The principal swallowed heavily, but then a gloating look filled his face. "Yes, I will unless the two of you leave."

"We're not leaving," Baron said. "Not until you get your head out of your ass and discipline those other assholes and apologize to Brooks for being a sad excuse of a principal."

"Then I can see I'm calling your mother."

"Even think about it and we will end your career. Got me, Donny?" Baron warned.

"We are not worried about you calling Ma," Royal said. "She will always have our backs. What we don't want is for her to be anywhere near you. She doesn't need to be exposed to your bullshit."

They were protecting their mother? That was crazy. And amazing.

"And you shouldn't have called Brooks' Mom down here, either. She doesn't need this stress. You dating her, Mr. Steele?" Baron asked.

"He's my boss," she said hoarsely.

Royal eyed her with interest. Then his gaze went to Brooks and his face hardened. "Why is Brooks in here while those other three idiots are free to go around terrorizing the school?"

"This is none of your business," the principal said.

"He's expelling me," Brooks said. "They told him I threw the first punch and that they weren't picking on Stella."

"Interesting. Isn't that interesting, brother?" Royal asked.

"It sure is," Baron asked. "Considering that Stella is the one that came and got us. Told us the full story of what happened. Brooks here is a hero, and those three assholes are bullies."

"Baron, there's a lady here," Royal said. "Language."

That was kind of funny considering Royal had said bullshit just a few moments ago.

Baron nodded. "Sorry, Brooks' Mom. That was rude of me. Although they are assholes."

She didn't know what to say, considering the principal had

just scolded Baron for swearing and he'd basically told him to shove his opinion.

"Um, well, that's all right." She agreed with him—they were assholes. But she guessed that she probably shouldn't call them assholes.

"So you've got the girl that these boys were harassing telling a different story than those boys," Steele said. "That changes things."

"I don't believe it does," Mr. Cleary said, giving Steele a nervous look. "It's still three against two."

"Oh, in case you're wondering why Donny here is sticking his feet in when he's clearly so scared of you he's about to piss himself, again sorry Brooks' Mom, it's because the dads of those three boys line his pockets," Baron told them all, as he leaned back against the wall.

"That is not true!" Mr. Cleary's face was growing a rather alarming shade of purple.

"It is," Royal said. "What's more, we have proof. Oh, and we also have proof that Stella and Brooks are telling the truth."

"How do you have that?" Mr. Cleary asked. "Were you there?"

"Nope," Baron said. "But my brother is great at surveillance and we have camera footage."

"You put cameras in my school?" Mr. Cleary gaped at them. "Tell me why I shouldn't expel the two of you!"

"Well, you might want to rethink that when we tell you that we've got a camera in here," Royal stated.

The principal suddenly went pale and sat back in his seat.

"I'm guessing you have something more on this idiot than him taking money from some of the parents?" Steele asked.

What was happening here? She didn't even know. She looked to Brooks, who was staring at Royal and Baron like they were gods.

"I . . . I . . ."

"Here's what is going to happen," Steele said calmly. "You're not going to expel Brooks. You are going to expel those three boys."

"I . . . I can't! I took their money."

Steele shrugged. "Far as I can see, that's your problem. Before these two came in, I was going to get nasty. You cause any problems for Brooks or Royal and Baron, you answer to me. And I can guarantee I am far scarier than those boys' dads. You understand me?"

His voice was cold and dark. Effie shivered, glad he was on her side. Because if that voice was ever aimed at her, she was pretty certain that she'd pee herself.

In fact, she thought that the principal might well have done that.

"I said, do you understand?" Steele barked.

Mr. Cleary jumped, then nodded frantically.

"Good. Let's go."

The three boys immediately headed out the door, but she stood there, glaring at the principal. She couldn't believe that he was taking bribes. That he was going to kick her kid out for doing the right thing simply because she didn't have the money to line this asshole's pockets.

That was so . . . unfair.

"Effie?" Steele asked gently. She was kind of shocked that a man that big could talk that quietly.

"You . . . you're a sad excuse for a human being," she finally said. She was so angry and upset that she could barely focus on the words running through her head.

"Come on, Effie. Time to leave. You don't want to be breathing the same air as him."

No, she didn't.

But she was still trembling with everything she needed to say to him. To tell him what a horrid person he was. How dare he treat children like this?

"You're supposed to protect the children in your care," she told him. "You're abusive and . . . and a terrible dresser. Mud-brown is not your color."

There! She got some of what she needed to say out. And she'd managed not to tell him that he looked like a giant poo. Which likely would have been a step too far.

Maybe.

17

As she stepped through the door into the waiting room, she wasn't sure why all three boys were smiling.

"Good call, Brooks' Mom," Baron said. "Never noticed it before, but that suit makes him look like a turd."

"He's definitely excrement," Royal added, his eyes narrowed as he took in Steele. "I know your reputation, Mr. Steele. I also know that you're related to Spike. So I thought you might've come down harder on him."

"You boys saved me from doing that," Steele replied.

Huh? What had he been planning on doing?

"I take it there is a reason why the two of you haven't used the evidence you have on him to oust him yet?" Steele asked as they all walked out to the parking lot.

Baron and Royal shared a look. Lord, they were trouble.

"We'd planned to oust him with a bang," Baron said.

"We weren't going to show our cards yet," Royal added. "Until Stella came and told us what was going down."

"We don't like bullies. And he's the worst sort of bully." Royal eyed Brooks. "Brooks, we're going to Mel's Diner. You want to come?"

"With you?" Brooks looked dumbfounded.

"Yep, bro, with us." Baron slapped his back.

She could see how much Brooks wanted to go with them. And she understood it. There was no way these boys weren't extremely popular. And the fact that they likely didn't care whether or not they were popular probably made them even more so. So she totally understood why her boy wanted to go hang with them.

So she was shocked as he shook his head. "I need to go see to Aunt Effie."

Shoot. What was he doing?

"I'm fine, Brooks. You go," she insisted.

"We like a guy that looks after his mom," Baron said. "You okay, Brooks' Mom? You look a bit pale."

"She might need sugar," Royal said.

"I think I've got some emergency chocolate in the car," Baron said.

"Oh, I don't need anything," she said quickly. "Thank you, though."

"You sure? It's the good stuff. We keep it for when Ma needs some," Baron told her.

"I'm okay, really. Thanks."

Although she kind of felt like crying. Happy tears. Because it was just so sweet the way these boys took care of their mom.

"Those are cute shoes," Royal said.

"They look like they have confetti on them. Do you like confetti?" Baron asked.

"Brother, who wouldn't like confetti?" Royal asked.

"True." Baron nodded.

"What about a cuddle? That helps our Ma. We could give you a twin cuddle," Royal offered.

"Um, that's very sweet. But really, I'm good."

"You sure, Brooks' Mom?" Baron asked. "Our cuddles are magic."

"I'm sure. I'm not actually his mom, though."

"Aren't you?" Royal asked. "Is she not your mom, Brooks?"

Brooks stared at her, and she gasped at the look of love on his face. She swayed and Steele fitted himself at her back, giving her strength. And holding her up.

"She is in all the ways that count," Brooks said.

She would not cry. She was not going to cry. A small sniffle might have escaped, but she didn't let her tears escape.

"You're not going to cry, are you, Spitfire?" Steele asked in a low voice.

"Certainly not," she replied huskily.

Damn it.

Do not cry. Do not.

"You see to your ma, man. We'll wait," Baron told him. "Stella's planning on meeting us there. And you know she'll want to give you a hero's welcome."

She saw a slash of red enter Brooks' cheeks.

The twins headed off to get into a car.

"Brooks, honey, I've got to go back to work. You go with your friends. They seem nice, if a little terrifying. Are you sure they're only teenagers?"

Brooks grinned, then grimaced as his face was obviously hurting him.

"Or maybe we should take you to the hospital to get checked out. You need to keep icing that. Actually, perhaps you need to come with me so I can check that it's taken care of."

"Effie," Steele said quietly, wrapping his arm around her waist.

"Yes?"

"Let the boy go get a hero's welcome. I bet his girl will take good care of him."

"She's not my girl." Brooks glanced away shyly. "She is cute, though."

Good. Something had happened with the last girl he'd been dating which he wouldn't tell her about. But she knew he hadn't been out with her again.

Hopefully, this Stella girl really was a sweetheart.

"All right then. You go off and let, uh, Stella take care of you. Just text me before you leave the diner and when you get home. Okay?"

Brooks didn't immediately leave. Instead, he looked from her to Steele. "You going to be okay, Effie?"

"Of course, honey. Why wouldn't I be?"

"Mr. Cleary didn't upset you?" Brooks asked.

"Nope. Not at all," she lied. "I knew it would all work out."

Brooks eyed her like he didn't believe her. "You're not lying to me, right, Aunt Effie?"

Uh-oh.

Steele stiffened behind her.

"Me?"

"Uh-huh. You." Brooks gave her a stern look.

Shoot.

"All right, I was a bit upset. But I wasn't scared. Not with you there. And Steele."

His gaze went up to the man behind her. "Right, Mr. Steele. Good to meet you."

And her too-grown-up-for-her-own-good nephew held out his hand. Steele reached around her to shake it.

"You too, Brooks."

Brooks cleared his throat. "You brought my aunt here?"

"Yeah. She was in a rush. Wanted to make sure she got here safe."

To her shock, something like relief filled Brooks face.

"Spitfire, can you go wait in the car while I talk to Brooks?" Steele asked.

"Um, what?"

He squeezed her around the waist again. "Car. Wait. Go."

She sent him a look. Was he seriously ordering her to the car so he could talk to her kid? What was he going to say to him?

Steele leaned in to whisper to her. "Trust me?"

Did she trust him? The guy who'd insisted on buying her slippers because her shoes were rubbing her feet? And had bought her gloves because hers had worn out? The guy who came in each day to eat her baking?

Yeah, she guessed she did.

"You okay, honey?" she asked Brooks. "I can take the rest of the day off if you need me to."

"I'm good, Aunt Effie. And I want a moment with Mr. Steele too."

"Just Steele," he said predictably.

She sighed and turned to walk off to where Raul was parked. Raul must have been watching because he got out and opened the door for her.

"Buckle up, Miss Effie," he reminded her.

She climbed into the back of the car, shocked to see it had been completely tidied. Shoot. She felt terrible that Raul had had to tidy up her mess.

He'd put all her things into a small basket he must have had stashed somewhere. Her hairbrush, mirror, tampons, gum, and Slowly the sloth were all in there.

Oh my God.

Had Steele seen Slowly? What must he think? Was he wondering why the heck she carried around a toy sloth?

With a groan, she stuffed everything back into her handbag, wishing she had a second emergency packet of jelly beans.

Her hand brushed against her phone and she drew it out, horror filling her as she took in the three missed calls.

All from Grady.

Shit. She might be in trouble.

～

STEELE WAITED until Effie was safely back in the car and out of earshot.

"You were gonna have her back in there." Brooks wasn't asking a question but rather making a statement.

"Of course."

The kid swallowed heavily, then brushed his hair off his face. It looked like he was about a month overdue for a haircut, his dark hair flopping around his face. Green-blue eyes peered up at Steele. "My aunt needs someone at her back. Looking out for her. She hasn't really had that since my dad died. That really upset her and she wasn't in a good way afterward. But she still went to bat for me. I had to go into foster care for a bit because she wasn't able to look after me straight away due to her back. And the people I was with were good to me, but they weren't her."

"I get that," he said quietly, letting Brooks talk.

"Aunt Effie, she's strong, but she always looks for the best in people. And she gets upset when they let her down. Which happens. A lot. So I appreciate you looking after her today. I didn't want them to call and upset her, but they insisted."

"You had a lot of problems with that principal?" Steele asked.

"A few."

"Those kids?"

"Yeah," he muttered.

Yeah, Steele thought that was likely the case. Little assholes probably thought he was an easy target. Steele might need to inform them that he wasn't without protection.

He wouldn't do that through the kids, though. Nope, he'd go straight to the source of their attitude.

The parents.

"I'm gonna give you my number. You have any problems with anyone, you call me."

"Really?" Brooks looked uncertain. "Not sure my aunt would like that."

"She doesn't have to know."

"You want me to lie to her?"

"Lie? No. But have you been telling her about the problems you've been having?"

"No. She has enough to worry about."

"Well, let's just keep making sure she has nothing to worry about. Get out your phone. I'm going to give you my number, you call me. Also want you to text me the names of those kids and their parents if you have them."

"What are you going to do?" Brooks asked, eyes wide.

"Nothing too bad." Yet.

Brooks put Steele's number into his phone, which looked so old it was a wonder that it was still supported. He needed a new phone. So did Effie since hers actually looked older.

He'd get on to that.

"Oh, and Brooks?"

"Yeah?"

"Seems to me that Effie has had someone at her back all these years."

The kid frowned in confusion.

"You."

"I can't do much to look after her."

"Course you can. And the best thing you can do if she has any trouble, is to call me. Got me?"

"I've got you." Brooks gave him a tentative smile. "Look after her. She's special. She needs someone to protect her from the bad so she can keep spreading around her good."

Damn. This kid was smart.

"Oh, and if she's already eaten her emergency jelly beans, you might want to get her some more. Jelly beans calm her. They make her happy. She especially likes the white and blue ones."

"Got it," he muttered.

With a chin lift that spoke of the man he would become, Brooks turned and strode off to where those deviants waited for him.

Christ.

What were the odds that Effie's nephew would go to the same school as the twin tornadoes that lived with Ink?

Steele turned to look at his car. Right, that was one issue dealt with. Now, to go deal with another.

18

Effie sat nervously as Steele folded his large frame into the back of the car. She turned to him immediately.

"What did the two of you just talk about?"

"Guy stuff."

"Guy stuff? How can you have guy stuff to talk about? You don't know Brooks."

"I'm a guy, so is he. We know the same woman and we both have an interest in that woman. Therefore, we have guy stuff to talk about."

"Did you just say, therefore?" she asked.

"Why would you fixate on that?"

Urgh. Get your mind focused, Effie.

"Never mind. It just doesn't seem like a very caveman, alpha man word to use. Wait ... interest in me? What interest?"

"I'm your boss."

"My old boss was a guy. The only time he ever paid attention to me was when he was yelling at me."

The energy in the back of the car changed suddenly. It grew

darker, more electric. She sucked in a breath as he turned toward her.

"He yelled at you?"

"Uh, did I say that? Why did I say that?" she muttered to herself.

"Maybe because it's true. And before you try to lie to me, Effie, you should know something."

"What's that?" she whispered.

"That you shouldn't ever fucking lie to me."

"Fair enough." Yikes. "But I still want to know what you said to Brooks."

"And I told you, Spitfire. Guy stuff. You ever grow a dick, you'll get it."

"Ew." She wrinkled her nose.

"Did you just say ew?"

"Um, yeah. Dicks are kind of ew."

He rolled his eyes heavenward, which she thought seemed overly dramatic. "Did you hear that? She thinks dicks are ew."

"Do you believe in God?" she asked.

"I believe in something. Maybe not God."

"You talk to him."

"Gotta pray for some patience. Maybe he'll grant me some."

"Are you saying you need patience to deal with me?" That seemed awfully rude.

"Yep."

"Hey! I'll have you know I'm a very sweet, nice person. I never rock the boat. I never make people angry or upset. Basically, I'm Switzerland."

"Switzerland?"

"Yeah, the peaceful spot in the middle."

"In the middle?" For some reason, his voice was strangled and he was pretty sure that she had that saying a bit wrong.

"Right. In the middle. Switzerland is landlocked, right? I wasn't very good at school, so maybe I'm wrong."

She was wrong a lot.

"Baby, I don't know who is telling you that you're like Switzerland, but they're lying to you. Because you're trouble. Pure and simple. But if you want to be in the middle . . . I'm down with that."

"In the middle of what?"

Her phone ringing interrupted him. "Uh-oh." Drat. She should have turned it to vibrate.

He stared down at her phone. "Uh-oh? What is uh-oh?"

"Um, well, it's Grady. And I think he might be mad. Because I've already had three missed calls on top of this one."

"Three missed calls? Really." He looked thoughtful. "We'll get to Grady in a moment. First, we've got to talk about a few things."

"Like what Brooks said to you? Has he been having trouble with the principal? Those boys? Are they bullying him? Oh my God! They're bullying him, aren't they? I'm going to have to call their mothers."

Shoot. Effie wasn't good at this sort of thing. But she had to do it. This was Brooks. He was hers and she had to protect him.

"You're not doing anything. I'm taking care of it. And you don't need to worry about Brooks. He's a good kid."

"You're taking care of it?" she asked with alarm.

"Yep."

"Uh, Steele, I really hope you won't take offense at this . . . but I'm not sure this needs your brand of taking care of things."

"Just what do you think I'm going to do? Order a hit?"

She sucked in a breath, feeling her eyes going wide. "That would be bad."

"Baby, I'm not going to do that. I'm just going to have a chat with those little assholes' dads. These kids weren't born being shitty humans, that's got to come from somewhere. I'm just going to let it be known that you and Brooks have someone at your backs. Well, in your case, I'm at your front."

"My front?" she asked, confused.

"Yeah, because if there's any trouble, you will be behind me. Understand?"

Not really.

But she just nodded. Because it seemed simpler.

"Now, we've got to go before Grady's head explodes." He reached over and did up her seatbelt. She should protest that she could do that herself.

But she didn't say anything. Because it felt good to let someone else take care of her. He'd had her back in there. He'd had Brooks' back. Even though he hadn't had to do much, hadn't really thrown his weight around, she knew he would have.

"You would've waded in, wouldn't you?" she asked.

"Hmm?" he asked after knocking on the privacy screen to let Raul know they were ready to go.

"You would've waded in to help Brooks. You didn't really have to because of those slightly terrifying boys. But you would've, right?"

"Of course I would have."

Of course he would have.

"I don't need to know what you said to Brooks. Or what he said to you."

"You don't?" Now, he gave her a curious look.

"Because you had my boy's back. Nobody . . . nobody since Joe has done that for us."

His face softened. "Baby."

"I'm gonna bake you a cake. A red velvet cake with cream cheese frosting."

"Baby."

"Might sound odd, but it's delicious. And it's all for you."

"I don't need a whole cake."

"Well, you get one when you have my boy's back," she told him.

"I've got your back too."

She sucked in a breath and barely held in her tears. "Right." She turned to look out the window, blinking away tears.

"Although I'm not happy with you."

"What?" She turned back to gape at him. "Why not?"

"What happened when we arrived at the school?"

Umm. She searched her brain for the answer to his question. What happened?

They'd arrived, left the car, and she'd forgotten where the admin building was, so he'd had to guide her there.

"Oh no, did I stand on your foot?" she asked.

"What?"

"Did I stand on your foot? Or did I not answer when you asked me something? That happens when I'm in a panic. I get caught up in my own head. I didn't mean to ignore you."

"Baby, that happens all the time, not just when you're in a panic. I'm used to it."

"It does?"

"You live in your head half the time. So yeah, it happens."

Great. She was a terrible person.

"I'm sorry."

"That's not the thing you should be apologizing for."

Oh. She searched her memory again.

"You've got no clue, have you? The car didn't even stop before you had the door open and were jumping out."

"It hadn't?"

"It hadn't."

She tugged at her sloth earring. "And that's why you're, uh, upset with me?"

"I'm more than upset," he countered. "This is the sort of

upset, that if you were mine, you'd be over my knee in the backseat of this car, getting your butt spanked. And even though you're not mine, you do that again, I'm tanning your ass. And that is not a joke. I do not care that I'm your boss. I'll fire you, spank you, then rehire you."

"You can't do that."

"I can't?"

She gulped.

"You put yourself in danger, Effie. I don't like that. I might not be your man, but I'm your boss. And when you're with me, I'm in charge of your safety. Which means when it comes to safety, you do as you're told."

"That's bonkers."

"That's fact."

"You can't be this way with everyone who works for you."

"Nope. But I don't spend as much time with them, so you get the full Steele protection."

"Lucky me," she grumbled.

"I know. I'll accept another cake in lieu of thanks."

She narrowed her gaze. "I'll get right on that."

Were his lips twitching? She was sure his lips were twitching.

"I don't want my bottom spanked." Yikes. Now she sounded like she was sulking.

"You think not?"

"I think not."

"You'd think wrong then."

"Excuse me? Are you telling me that I want a spanking? That I'd like it?" This was dangerous territory.

"Hmm, not a punishment one, baby girl. But that doesn't matter, because seems to me that you need one. Pure trouble. Sweet, sassy, and a little clueless."

"I don't think it's nice to call me clueless or trouble. And I'm definitely not sassy."

He just looked at her like she was full of shit. Maybe she was a bit sassy. When she forgot to be nervous.

You don't want to upset him too much, Effie. Be nice.

Crap, she wished Nan would get out of her head.

"I'm your employee."

"Right. Which is why you just got a warning and aren't sitting there now with a hot bottom and wet cheeks."

"I'm . . . you . . . we . . . dear Lord."

He was outrageous.

She knew she should tell him that she was horrified. Should make it clear this was incredibly inappropriate. But the trouble was . . . she liked it.

She wanted to know what it would be like to belong to his man. To have someone who cared enough to take her in hand when she did silly things.

Even though she couldn't actually remember jumping from the car, it sounded like something she would do.

And up until now, nobody would have given a shit if she had done that. Except for Brooks, of course.

But he did.

Damon Steele.

A man that should scare the living daylights out of her.

And there was another problem on top of that . . . he wasn't the only one she was attracted to.

Because there was something about the calm, cool Thomas Grady that made her want to ruffle him up, see him smile, have him touch her.

She wanted to belong to them both.

Lord, she'd been reading too many romance books.

"How about I just don't do that again," she muttered.

"Good call, baby." He tapped something on his phone. "Just got to make a stop."

"What for?"

"Will only take a moment." They pulled up outside a convenience store. "Stay here."

She was tempted to throw him a salute. But she figured that she liked this job and should probably show her boss some respect. So, instead, she gave him a big, cheesy grin. "No problem, Sir."

He eyed her for a moment. "I don't like that."

Huh?

Before she could question him, he left.

That was odd. What did he mean he didn't like that? Her being polite?

Sheesh. She felt like she couldn't win. When he returned, she couldn't see what he'd bought. And she bit her lip against asking him.

They took off again, approaching Pinkies five minutes later.

"Brace yourself," he told her.

"For what?"

"Grady."

She gulped. "Do you think he's going to fire me?"

"Fire you? What? Why?"

"Because I left my job without telling him. Technically, he could fire me."

"He's not going to fire you. Although he just might make good on that spanking."

She gaped at him. "Grady wouldn't do that."

He grinned. "Baby, don't you know that it's the quiet ones you have to look out for?"

The car came to a stop and her door was yanked open. She turned, letting out a startled squeal as she saw Grady glaring down at her. Reaching in, he undid her seatbelt.

"Out."

She attempted to climb out, accidentally stepping on his foot as she moved. But he didn't step back, so she decided not to say sorry.

When he took her hand and marched her into the building, she started to rethink that no apologizing stance.

Maybe if she got in quick, she could dissipate some of his anger. It wasn't that he looked mad. No, he looked like Grady. Just a more intense, somewhat scarier Grady. He didn't yell. Didn't hold on to her harshly.

But he definitely had a hold of her. They headed to their office, where he shut the door behind them.

Only for Steele to open it and walk in. "Forget about me?"

Grady locked the door.

And then he started pacing. This felt alarming. Effie didn't think Grady was a pacer. He always kept his energy locked down, unlike Steele whose energy could fill a room.

Steele was the bull. You could see him coming, but you would be hard-pressed to get out of his way. Pure fire and fury.

But Grady . . . he was the dark shadow. The hidden assassin. You would never see him coming. Not until it was too late.

So this pacing confused the heck out of her.

She thought Steele might be interested in her . . . but wasn't going to do anything about it because she worked for him.

Grady . . . well, she didn't think he was interested in her like that.

"Um, are you all right?" she asked.

"Is your phone broken?" he asked.

"Ugh, no."

He turned to Steele. "Yours?"

Steele just shrugged. What the heck? Didn't he see that Grady was upset?

Maybe she should apologize. Surely, that would help.

"I'm sorry!"

He turned back to her. Drat. Actually, the smart move would probably have been to let Steele handle Grady.

"Are you? And what are you sorry about, sweetheart?"

Yikes.

She loved being called sweetheart. But she wasn't sure she liked it while he was staring at her as though he was hungry and she was the prey.

"Um, well, I . . . I should have told you I was leaving!"

He stalked toward her. Oh, this wasn't good. She stepped back, but he kept moving forward.

Not good at all.

19

Effie glanced at Steele, who was leaning against the wall with his arms crossed over his chest. She shot him a desperate look.

He winked at her.

No help at all. Awesome.

"Should you have?" Grady asked.

"Yes."

"Why?" he asked.

"Um." By now, she was against the desk and she slid along it, thinking it might be prudent to put the desk between her and Grady.

But he just followed her around. She moved to the other side, keeping it between them.

"Because you're my boss!" Whew. She congratulated herself for remembering that.

"Am I?"

"Yes. Unless . . . am I fired?" Her heart raced, fear filling her. This was the best job she'd ever had. She never thought she'd like doing this sort of work, but she did. And it paid really well.

Plus, the people here were nice, for the most part. "Please don't fire me."

"Grady," Steele said in a low voice.

She glanced over to see he was no longer smiling. Grady turned to him, pointing. "Quiet. You didn't answer my calls either."

Steele sighed. "Didn't you know she was with me?"

"Only because Raul answers his fucking phone!" Grady didn't yell, but his voice held a definite snap and Effie jumped in reaction.

"You're scaring her," Steele pointed out.

"I'm giving her a warning so that maybe next time she just up and leaves, she'll remember to let me know."

"I really am sorry," she whispered.

But they didn't seem to hear her. Instead, they were glaring at each other. She moved her head back and forth between them.

"You knew she was with me, so you knew she was safe."

"But before I knew that, I had no idea where she was! Anyone could have taken her!" Grady snapped back.

Wait. What? Had he . . . had he been worried about her?

"Were you worried about me?"

Grady's gaze snapped back to her. "Of course I was worried about you. You left. Without a word. And I had no idea if you were safe. And you expect me not to worry?"

"I wasn't even sure you'd know I was gone," she admitted.

"You're going to wear a tracker," he said bizarrely.

"Uh, what?"

"A tracker. You're going to wear one."

She glanced over at Steele to find him grinning like a madman again. Was he even listening to Grady?

"Steele," she said in a low voice.

"Yeah?"

"I think something's wrong with Grady."

"Oh yeah, something is definitely wrong with Grady."

"Then could you not say something to help?" she asked desperately.

"Like what?"

"I don't know. Just something."

"All right." Steele nodded. "How do you want her to wear the tracker?"

She glared at Steele. "That's not what I meant!"

"Isn't it? Well, it's what I want to know. I'll get something created to hold the tracker. What are you thinking? A necklace?"

They were nuts. Completely and utterly nuts.

She wasn't even entirely sure what was happening right now.

"Too obvious," Grady replied. "I'm thinking an ankle bracelet. Or something to go in her shoes. She doesn't have many pairs."

"Hmm, we should buy her more shoes," Steele commented.

"Agreed. I saw some cute light-up ones I think she'd love."

What the heck was happening?

Did they realize she was still in the room with them? She needed to get things back under control.

Although she wasn't sure she'd ever had any control around these two.

"You aren't buying me a tracker. And you're not buying me light-up sneakers. Although I would like to know where you saw them because they sound adorable."

Maybe after a few more pay checks she could buy herself a pair. She did love cute shoes. And perhaps she could get some cute socks to go with her cute shoes.

That would be adorable.

"We've lost her," Steele said.

"That's all right she doesn't need to pay attention for us to get a tracker sorted for her."

Wait. What?

"No tracker."

Grady raised his eyebrows at her coolly. "Did you leave in the middle of the day without letting me know where you were?"

"Yes, but there was an emergency!"

"Was it so urgent that during the drive to Brooks' school, you couldn't text me to let me know where you were going?"

Shoot.

She could have done that.

But also . . . Raul was a big fat tattletale. And she was going to tell him that the minute she saw him. And she wouldn't be baking him any more of her pecan chocolate cookies that he loved.

Okay . . . that was a lie. She would totally keep baking those for him. Who was she to deny him his favorite cookies?

But they wouldn't be made with love.

All right . . . that was a big fat lie too.

Darn it.

She tugged at her earring, wincing slightly as it pulled too hard.

"Stop that," Grady commanded. "I'm going to take your silence as agreement."

"I'm sorry. You're right. I should have texted to let you know where I was."

"And you could have texted too." Grady turned to Steele.

"She was out of her mind with worry, man. When we got there, she undid her belt and opened her door before Raul even came to a stop. Jumped right on out of the car."

"What?" Grady turned back to her.

What. The. Hell?

Had Steele just thrown her under the bus? Or, in this case, thrown her in front of a rather irate-looking Grady?

"You did what? What were you thinking? You could have hurt yourself!"

"I'm taking the cake back." She pointed at Steele.

"You'll still make me the cake." He gave her an arrogant, knowing look.

Darn it. She totally would. Urgh.

"I didn't mean to. I don't even remember doing it. I just needed to get to Brooks."

"He's all right, isn't he?" Grady now looked alarmed.

"Came to a girl's aid when she was being picked on by three guys. Those guys jumped him. Principal tried to expel him because he's a scholarship student and those boys said he started it. Those boys' parents are also lining the principal's pockets."

Something changed in Grady then. The heat in his rage disappeared and he became chillingly cold. This Grady . . . he was absolutely terrifying.

"What?" he whispered.

Deadly. Furious. He would terrify her if he wasn't mad on behalf of her kid.

"I'm dealing with it," Steele said. He didn't even seem to notice that Grady had turned into an ice-cold warrior king.

"You need me to make him disappear?"

"I don't think we'll have to. Ink's kids go to that school."

"Ink's kids?"

"Yeah, remember that his woman has those twin stepsons?"

"I remember. They'd be what? Seventeen? Eighteen?"

"Think so," Steele replied. "Anyway, they must have cameras everywhere in that school. They handed the principal his ass and I think they plan to shove him out the door. Hard."

"Interesting."

Steele gave him a look. "I think Ink will have something to say if you recruit those kids."

"They sound like the sort of kids I'd like to know."

"So, am I good to go back to work now?" she asked.

When would she learn? If no one was paying her attention, she needed to keep quiet. But nooo, she had to go open her big mouth.

Both men were now staring at her.

"From now on, if you need to leave this building for any reason, you text me. Understand?" Grady said in a low, commanding voice.

"Ah, but what if I'm on a break?"

"You text me when you're leaving and when you get back. And where you're going."

"Um, just saying. I don't think you can do that." She knew he couldn't do that. Because it was nuts! She wasn't a prisoner.

"Look, I wasn't in any danger. And I'm really sorry I didn't tell you, but I'll make up the time. And I'm sure nothing like this will ever happen again."

"I'm not," Grady countered.

"Trouble magnet," Steele muttered.

There was a knock on the door before she could answer.

"Yes?" Grady snapped.

"Oh, um, I wanted to talk to Effie?" That sounded like Ana, one of the dancers.

"What do you want with her?" Grady asked, looking disgruntled.

"Oh, uh, I'll just come back later when she's in."

She opened her mouth to say something, but Grady shot her a look.

Effie huffed out a breath, but decided it was better not to upset him. She'd go check on Ana later. She was having some problems at home and might need someone to talk to.

"I don't care about the lost time," Grady told her. "You'll go home at your usual time tonight. But from now on, if you leave during work to go somewhere, you text me. Today, I had no idea where you were. I didn't know that you were with Steele, so it took me a while to call him. Then, to call Raul when he didn't answer. Do you know what I thought that entire time you were missing?"

"Umm."

"I thought some asshole had somehow got in here and kidnapped you."

Wow. That seemed really far-fetched.

"Why would anyone want to kidnap me?" she joked. "That's ludicrous."

"No," Steele growled.

Huh? What did he mean, no?

"That right there is not happening. No more talking badly about yourself." Grady started stalking her once more and she started backing up.

Bad idea, but once she started, she couldn't stop.

She hit the wall, and before she could slide away in a different direction, he was there.

Right there.

Right in front of her. And she could feel the heat coming off him. Funny, she hadn't expected him to be so warm.

Silly Effie.

He placed his hands on either side of her head. Although he didn't need to cage her in since she was incapable of moving.

Another knock on the door.

"Who is it?" he called out.

"Um, oh, it's Ryan." He was one of the bartenders. "Is Effie in?"

"No. Go away."

She sucked in a breath. "You shouldn't talk to your employees like that."

"They always bother you this much?" Steele asked.

"It's not a bother. It's my job to take care of them."

"No, your job is to schedule them," Grady corrected. "To make sure they get paid. It's not your job to look after them in any other way."

"Maybe not. But that's me being nice."

"Were you ever planning on being nice to me?" Grady asked her.

"I'm nice to you!" She stared up at him, aghast. How could he think that? She was lovely to everyone.

"Hmm, not sure you are. If you were being nice to me, you wouldn't run off in the middle of the day without telling me where you were."

Sheesh, he just wouldn't let this go.

"Steele didn't tell you either."

"I don't keep track of Steele's movements."

"You don't need to keep track of mine either!"

"That's where we'll have to disagree. Yeah, I think I do. Which is why I still think you need a GPS tracker."

"I don't think you can legally make me wear one."

"I'm not sure we've ever been that concerned with the law, have we, Steele?"

"Nope."

She glanced over to find the big man resting back on the couch, arms crossed behind his head, watching them both like they were his favorite TV show.

"This is the thing, sweetheart. We both have enemies. One of them could have gotten into Pinkies and taken you and we'd have no idea where you were."

"I think that's unlikely, right?" What kind of enemies was he talking about? And why would they kidnap her?

"It could still happen."

"But why take me? I mean, why wouldn't they take one of the dancers? Or the bar staff?"

"Why take you? Because you mean more to us than all of them combined." This came from Steele. But when she glanced up at Grady, she found him nodding in agreement.

Okay, that was unexpected. "I mean something to you?"

"Yes," Grady replied.

20

Grady was breaking all the rules right now.

This right here was part of the reason they'd made this rule. So that neither of them stepped over the line with an employee. Because they'd have to face them again and again. And because they might think they meant something more than they did.

Effie actually did mean something to him, and it wasn't right to lead her on. He knew that Steele didn't want a serious relationship.

"Grady?" Steele asked in a low voice.

He glanced over to see the other man staring at him curiously.

Grady stepped back, away from her, and straightened his clothes.

"I don't understand what's happening," she whispered. "How ... how do I mean more to you?"

"Because we want—"

"Because we work closely with you," Grady interrupted

Steele, knowing what he'd been about to say. "That's why you mean something to us."

Steele shot him a frown. If they were going to change the rules, they needed to discuss that first. Not jump in when feelings and emotions were heightened. That would just create a mess.

Grady didn't like messes. He liked things tidy and orderly.

"There are going to be some rules."

Steele groaned.

"Rules? What do you mean? For working here?" she asked.

"Yes."

"What sort of rules? And does everyone have these rules?"

"No."

"So, just me?"

"Yes," he replied.

"Because we work closely together?" There was a strange look on her face that he couldn't read. And he didn't like that. What was she thinking? "And you were worried about me. I don't really understand it. I thought you were upset because you were paying me and I disappeared. That I would understand. My old boss would have yelled. He likely would've fired me. But I don't think you're going to fire me."

Even though she sounded like she was speaking to him, it was more like she was talking to herself. She tilted her head to the side. "I don't like rules." She pouted.

"You need rules," Grady told her.

"What are these rules?" she asked.

"If you need to leave work, then you call or text me."

"All right. I can do that."

"Really?" he asked.

"Yes. That seems more than reasonable. What else?"

"You'll wear a tracker."

"No. Not happening."

He opened his mouth to argue, but she spoke up first.

"No. I don't buy your excuse that you have enemies. I'm just an employee."

He didn't like this at all. He glanced at Steele, who also didn't like it. But he also knew if he pushed too hard, she could run.

"Fine. No tracker," he said.

He was still buying her one. Maybe a couple. He might be able to slip one into that monster bag of hers.

"She already has a rule about undoing her seatbelt while a car is still moving," Steele added.

"Good. Also, no lying. Understand?"

She sighed, but nodded. "I guess I can agree to that. Anything else?"

Oh, there were plenty more rules he could give her. Plenty that he was dying to lay down. And enforce.

Spanking was generally Steele's thing. When they'd gone to the club to play, Grady had preferred other forms of punishment. Sensory deprivation while edging a partner. Nipple clamps. Taking away their ability to speak. Tying them down and doing whatever the fuck he wanted to them while they begged him to stop.

But with Effie . . . hmm, he could imagine bending her over his desk, pulling down her pants and panties, and scorching that plump ass of her.

"No more putting yourself down," Steele told her. "I don't like it. I don't want to hear it, and I really don't want you to think it or say it. So you'll stop."

She licked her dry lips. "And what happens if I break these rules? Am I fired?"

"No," Grady said, realizing he didn't really have a leg to stand on. What use were rules if there were no consequences for breaking them?

"Yes," Steele said.

"Steele," he snapped.

"He just wants to fire me so then he can spank me before he rehires me," she told him.

"I'm sure that's not what he's thinking," Grady said.

"Of course that's what I'm thinking," Steele said.

Good Lord.

He glared over at Steele, who gave him an unrepentant look back. His best friend was a man who was used to getting his own way and unapologetic about it.

"He's not going to do that."

She gave him a doubtful look.

Yeah, he shared those doubts. Most of the time, he was able to predict the other man's actions and thoughts. But right now, that was difficult. Because Steele didn't seem to have any issues changing things up with Effie.

"Just stick to the rules and we won't have to worry about consequences, all right?" Grady said.

"Yes, I suppose." She looked doubtful, though. Reaching up, she tugged at her earring.

Without thought, he grabbed her hand and gently drew it away.

She gave him a surprised look. Yeah, he was shocked himself. He didn't usually initiate touch like that.

Clearing his throat, he stepped back and adjusted his clothing, making sure they were straight and unwrinkled. He hated looking unkempt.

"We'll leave you to get on with work." Turning, he moved to the door and unlocked it.

Opening the door, he realized that Steele wasn't right behind him. Spinning, he saw him reach into his pocket and pull out a packet of jelly beans.

He held them out to Effie, who stared down at them like they held the secrets of the world.

"For me?"

"For you. However, you're not to eat them all at once, understand?"

"That doesn't seem very much fun." Another pout.

Adorable.

"Effie," Steele said sternly.

"Oh, fine. I like the blue and white ones best so I'll just eat them. Thank you." She took them, staring up at Steele with wonder.

Grady could tell the other man was taken aback. He probably hadn't expected that reaction over a bag of jelly beans.

But he recovered quickly. "Drink some water too. And no working late." Then he turned and walked toward Grady. "Let's go. There's work to be done."

Grady followed him out, resisting the urge to look behind him at Effie.

Steele led him through the club, where, surprisingly, no one attempted to get his attention.

In fact . . . in the last few weeks, he'd barely had to answer any questions about the club. His time had been freed up.

Those complaints and issues hadn't gone away . . . but he knew who was now fielding them.

That's her job.

Yeah . . . but it could be a lot. Had he even checked in to make sure she was coping all right?

Fuck. He needed to keep a closer eye on her.

He followed Steele upstairs to his private lounge. The other man headed over to pour himself a bourbon.

"A bit early, don't you think?"

Steele just stared at him before he slammed it back. He was going to get drunk quickly if he kept that up.

"Something you want to talk about?" Grady asked.

"She's a Little."

Grady blinked at him. That wasn't what he'd expected him to say.

"How do you know? Did she tell you?" He couldn't see how that conversation would come about.

"No. Of course not. But she still has that toy in her bag."

"You know that doesn't mean anything. Lots of adults have stuffed toys."

"That they bring to work with them?"

He had to admit . . . that wasn't terribly likely.

"It still doesn't mean anything."

Steele paced back and forth, clearly conflicted. "I want her."

"Yeah. I can see that."

"I basically told her that."

Grady sucked in a breath. "We have that rule for a reason."

"Know that. I made the damn rule. But when it comes to her . . . I don't much care."

"And what will that mean for her after you've finished fucking her?"

"After *I've* finished?" Steele asked. "Like you don't want her?"

"I don't need to fuck her."

"Grady, you might like to pretend you're a robot without feelings, desires, and needs. But we both know that's not fucking true."

Grady shot him a quelling look.

"You freaked the fuck out, man. I could see it. She could see it. You know it. And you never freak. Not unless someone means something to you. Didn't see it before. You kept it hidden well. But you like her."

"Pour me a drink," he commanded.

Steele threw him a look but poured him a bourbon.

He took a sip from it. No way was he slamming back bourbon that cost three thousand dollars a bottle.

"I don't know how this happened. But the first moment I saw her on that dance floor . . ."

"Wish I'd seen that," Steele said with genuine regret. "And now she's never allowed back near a pole."

"Agreed. But it was her dancing before she even got to the pole that was . . . it was beautiful. She's beautiful. And kind. Smart. Since she started, the only issues or complaints I've had to deal with have all come from Lucy. She's been dealing with them all."

"All of them? Do we pay her enough for that?"

"If it was anyone else, I'd say yes. But I don't want her stressed out." He didn't like how often her door had been knocked on in the short time they were together just before.

"Keep an eye on that," Steele commanded. "She's got a lot going on. She doesn't need extra stress."

"Her boy is good?"

"Sixteen going on forty. Seems like he tries to take care of her as much as she does him. Smart. Empathetic. Yeah, he's a good kid. But he shouldn't be putting up with shit from rich assholes at his school."

"Do you want me to take care of that?"

"I've got some names, I'll send them to you. You see what you can find out. All of this will likely be coming from their fathers."

"Want to send a warning?" Grady asked.

"Yeah. A warning to begin with. More if necessary."

"I'll get onto that." Nothing would give him more joy.

"We also need to do something about her upstairs neighbor. He's been keeping her up late at night. I'll send one of the guys around to give him a warning."

Grady nodded. "So what are we going to do about Effie?"

About their feelings for her. About their need for her.

Steele frowned off into the distance.

"We both want her," Grady said.

Still nothing.

"But she works for us and she's not a one-night stand, Steele. I won't risk hurting her. Or losing a damn good assistant."

Steele turned to look down at him. "Pretty sure she's Little. Definitely submissive. She needs help. Protecting. Guiding. She got dizzy when she stood up earlier."

Alarm filled him. "What?"

"Says she gets low blood pressure and poor circulation from her back injury. Doesn't take care of herself. Always smiling even when she doesn't mean it."

"I don't know about that last part. She doesn't smile all the time with us."

"That's a good thing."

Grady was startled for a moment, but then he realized that Effie's smiles weren't always genuine. They were a mask.

"She hides her true thoughts," he said.

"And only lets them out when she feels safe," Steele added.

"Since when are you more insightful than me?" he complained.

Steele grinned. And Grady realized this was the deepest conversation they'd had in a long time. For the last year, it had felt like Steele was pulling away. Not on purpose. Not because he didn't care. But because life had become a pit of nothing . . . and Grady understood that. He'd felt that for a long time.

But now Steele was coming back. He'd smiled more in the last few weeks than he had in the year before.

And that was because of Effie.

Grady could kiss her just because of that.

Steele turned to look at him. "We've shared women, but only for sex."

Fuck.

He grew tense. Was he going to warn Grady off? Say that he wanted her to himself?

"I don't want to lose someone else," Steele said suddenly. His voice was stark. "Not after Jacqui."

Was he going to give up before he'd tried?

"Haven't lost you, though," Steele murmured.

Okay, now it was getting hard to breathe.

"I can look after myself." Fuck, what was he doing? Was he trying to talk Steele out of this?

Steele eyed him. "Yeah. And she won't be able to do that."

"So we work harder to protect her. More rules."

Steele's lips turned up at that. "More rules. You think we can keep her safe?"

"If we work together. If you're willing to share."

Surprise filled the other man's face. "You think I'd take her for myself? Grady, you called me four times looking for her."

"And you didn't pick up once, asshole."

"You called her three times."

Grady swallowed heavily.

"You're telling me you'd walk away from her if I decided I wanted her for myself?"

Would he? He loved Steele. But he couldn't stand it if he was on the side-lines, looking in.

"If I walked, I'd keep walking."

Steele's eyes flared. He got what he was saying. He'd lose Grady for good.

"Good thing I don't want her all to myself then, isn't it?" Steele told him.

Relief filled him.

"But we both agree this is more than just sex."

"I want to fuck her," Steele said, sipping on his next drink. "But I want to pull her into my arms and cuddle her more. When I think about her, sure, I might think about how amazing her tits look or how much I want to squeeze that ass. Especially when she's riding my cock. But mostly, I want to make sure she's looked after. That she's got enough to eat, that she's warm and not in pain. And now, I also want to know what she's like when she enters Little space. What age she might regress to. If she's ever had a Daddy."

Fuck. His feelings were deeper for her than Grady had realized.

Which was both good and bad. Because if all of this turned to shit . . .

You just have to make sure that it won't.

"We probably shouldn't spring this on her too quickly," he warned.

Steele shot him a look. "What?"

"She's our employee. We already have a position of power. Especially as she needs this job. We don't want her saying yes, thinking that she has to in order to keep her job."

"One way of fixing that problem."

Grady pointed at him. "No. You cannot do that to her." He knew precisely how Steele thought he could get rid of that problem.

By firing her.

"Why should she have to work? We can take care of her."

"You are not that dense, so don't pretend that you are."

"I like to get my own way," Steele said.

"Believe me, I know. But if we start something with her, then we do it right. Take it slow. Ease her in. Think about it from her perspective. We're her bosses. We're both Dominants. And there are two of us. That's not normal to most people. We'll have to make sure we're on the same page when it comes to her."

"We're always on the same page," Steele said.

They were. There was a sense of safety in that.

"If she's important, then we should take it slow. Be careful. Make sure she really is it."

Steele was quiet for a long time. "Never thought I'd be in a relationship. Being in one with you . . . that feels right. She feels right. But yes, I'll be careful and go slow. Well, what's slow for me."

Grady thought that was likely the best he'd get.

"We're really doing this," he murmured. "Together."

"Did you really think we'd do it apart?"

Grady hadn't. Mostly because he'd never thought to find someone special to him. Someone who wasn't Steele.

And he never thought Steele would want someone after Jacqui died.

Poor Effie, she didn't know what the hell was headed her way with the two of them.

Steele could be extremely protective. And Grady . . . well, he liked his order and control.

So yeah . . . they'd both need to be careful and go slow.

While still moving forward and showing her that they wanted her.

21

Effie read the news report again.
Not April.
It wasn't April.

She didn't know why she'd felt so panicked when she'd heard the news report on the radio this morning. But a report of a woman being murdered near April's hometown had just freaked her out.

"What are you doing?"

She let out a huge squeal and jumped out of her seat, her knee banging into the desk.

"Effie!"

She stared up at Grady as he rushed into the room toward her.

"Um, morning, Grady."

Breathe through the pain. It was just a little bump.

"Shoot. I didn't mean to scare you. Are you all right?"

"Who me? Oh yeah, I'm fine. You look nice this morning. Is that a new shirt?"

He sent her a look like she wasn't fooling him.

Darn it. Normally, her acting skills were far better.

"Did you bang your knee?"

"Just a little bit." She held her finger and thumb apart an inch.

"I'll get you ice. Is it bruised? Do you need a doctor?"

She gaped up at him. Whoa. Way to overreact.

"Uh, no. I just banged it. It's fine."

He eyed her like he didn't believe her.

"Would you like a coffee? Let me get you a coffee." She wanted to get up, but he'd crouched right in front of her. So if she moved, she was going to brush up against him.

And she was pretty certain that Grady didn't like to be touched. That was the vibe she got from him after working here for seven weeks now.

Which was totally cool, of course.

She was soo cool with that. Like an ice cube.

Yep, she could live in Antarctica, she was just that damn cool.

Also, she was an idiot.

Because what she really wanted was for him to touch her. And part of her couldn't help but be upset that she wasn't likely to get that.

Still, maybe she could squeeze past him. So she started to stand.

"Freeze," he commanded.

She froze.

"Whoa, you could be in the army or something," she told him.

"What?"

"Maybe a marine. You bark, 'drop and give me twenty,' and everyone in earshot would do that. Although I never saw the point of dropping and giving twenty, you know?"

Sometimes, when she got nervous, she spoke too much.

"You okay, Effie?" he asked in a surprisingly gentle voice.

"I keep embarrassing myself around you. And Steele. It's just . . ."

"Are you scared of us? I know we're intimidating, but we won't hurt you."

Oh, she knew they wouldn't hurt her physically. But if she let herself start to think about having them in her life . . . fantasizing about what that would be like . . . then things were going to hurt.

Because she guessed men like the two of them didn't stay single for long. She wondered what it would be like to have them both? Chardonnay had told her they liked to share, but she guessed that was just for sex.

Nothing more.

She'd been reading way too many ménage and reverse harem romances. That sort of thing just didn't happen in real life and she knew it.

"Effie? Stay with me, sweetheart."

"I know you wouldn't hurt me," she blurted out. God, why couldn't she stay focused? "Sorry. I just . . . had my mind on other things."

She waved a hand over at the computer screen.

Frowning, he glanced at the screen. "Christ, why are you reading that?"

"It's news."

"So?"

"So . . . I should read the news, right? I need to know what's going on in the world."

"You need to know that some poor woman was murdered in Wyoming?"

"I have a friend in Wyoming. She's slight and has dark hair."

"Sweetheart," he murmured in a soft voice.

Damn. That soft voice could be her undoing. She felt it deep inside her. She wanted to keep listening to it. Wanted to hear him use her name in that voice.

But she had to guard herself against getting hurt. It happened to her a lot. She trusted the wrong people. She just wanted people to be nice. Was that such a terrible thing to hope for?

"Is she on her own?" he asked.

"No. She has a husband."

"He's a good man?"

"Yeah, he's the best," she replied, not understanding the sudden scowl that filled his face.

"Then, if he's any sort of man, he'll take care of her. So there's no reason to think that she's in danger, is there?"

"No. I just got freaked. I'm just being stupid. Right?"

"Effie," he growled. "You know better than to talk about yourself like that."

Right. She did.

"Are you worried for your safety?" he asked.

"No, I'm not scared for me. This murder happened in another state."

But he was still frowning. "You don't live in a good neighborhood."

"There's nothing wrong with my neighborhood."

Well, that wasn't entirely true.

He shot her a dark look. "No lying. That's a rule."

Right. Those rules.

She still didn't quite understand why she had them.

But Grady seemed really into them.

It had been two days since he'd laid down the rules, and it felt like something had changed between the three of them.

She just wasn't quite sure what that something was.

Which made her nervous.

"How do you feel about a dog?" he asked.

"A dog?" she repeated. "Are you getting a dog? I love dogs. If you want to bring him into work, I can help look after him. We could get him a bed for in the corner of the room. Oh, this is so exciting. What sort of dog are you getting?"

"Not me, sweetheart. You."

"Oh, I'm not getting a dog." Why would he think that?

"No, we should get you a dog. It's added security. People would be less likely to mess with you if they heard a dog barking. Something like a Rottweiler would work well."

She gaped at him. "Um, I can't have a dog."

"Why not? You clearly want one. If it's the landlord, I'll talk to him. Or better yet, we find a better place for you to live."

What was happening right now? Something weird was going on.

"Um, I don't want to move, and I'm not sure the landlord would like me having a dog. But the main reason I can't have a dog is because I can't look after one. Between Brooks and I, we're out of the house too much. It wouldn't be fair to the little guy."

"He could come here."

Great. He had an answer for everything, didn't he?

And he was going to force her to lay it all out.

"Grady, there have been times I've barely been able to keep myself and Brooks fed. I can't take on a dog. It's not just feeding them, it's vet bills, trainer bills. What if they get sick or hurt? I won't be able to afford to get them fixed, and that would break my heart."

Grady eyed her for a long moment. "I could pay for the dog."

Um, she so didn't think so.

"No," she said firmly.

Another thing she'd learned with these guys. That being firm was important.

Not that it seemed to get her far.

"You don't feel safe, Effie."

She puzzled those words out, not sure why he cared. And why he felt the need to do anything about her fear.

"I feel safe. Really," she insisted. "Sure, it's scary to think that some poor woman was murdered. But that sort of thing happens all the time. It just freaked me out because it was close to where April lives. That's all. Trent, her husband, would never let anything happen to her."

And as much as she might want that sort of relationship, she knew that wasn't in the cards for her.

She was too busy just trying to survive. Although that had become a lot easier with the money that went into her account each week.

She was getting close to splurging and buying herself a pair of shoes that lit up.

"You'll tell me if you feel different."

Wow. That was kind and really unexpected.

"I will."

"Good. Now, show me."

"Um, show you what?" she asked, confused.

"Show me your knee. I want to check that it's not bruised."

He was joking, right?

But this was Grady. He didn't seem to joke much.

"I've got pants on," she told him.

"If they don't roll up, then you can just take them off."

"No, I can't."

What the heck? Was he really expecting her to just take her pants off?

Sheesh.

Luckily, they rolled up and he inspected her leg. His hands felt so hot and firm against her skin.

She had to hold back a shiver of pleasure.

Lord, imagine how she would feel if he touched her with purpose? With affection, with caring. With the intent to actually cause her pleasure.

She might self-combust.

"Are you all right, sweetheart?" he asked quietly.

"Um, yes. Really, my knee is fine. I'm fine."

He gave a nod and then stared down at his hands before he stood abruptly and stepped back. "You're here early."

"Um, yes. I had some things to catch up on."

"If your workload is too heavy, then you should tell me."

Did Grady think she was complaining? She really wasn't. And it wasn't like she'd actually been working. She'd started off her day by looking through news reports online.

"Oh no, it's not. I just wanted to get a head start on a few things. But I haven't even really started. I heard that news report on the radio as Raul was driving me here. I suppose I shouldn't really be looking things up like that on a work computer. That's not grounds for dismissal, is it?"

"Effie."

"I mean, I wasn't looking up porn or anything. And I hadn't officially started work."

"Effie."

"But this isn't my computer, so I guess I shouldn't be doing things like that."

"Effie, stop," he commanded.

She stopped. But if he told her to drop and give him twenty, she was not going to be cool with that.

A girl had to draw a line. And push-ups were hers. Even if she could do them, which she doubted. Her arms would probably collapse underneath her and she'd go splat on the floor, squishing her boobs.

"Effie, what are you thinking about right now?"

"That squished boobs are no fun." She paused, horrified at what she'd just said. "Um. Ah. I . . . shit. I just said boobs in front of my boss."

"Sweetheart."

"And porn. I talked about watching porn in front of my boss!" she wailed.

"You watch porn?" The question came from the doorway.

She closed her eyes. She knew whose voice that was. But she couldn't look over at him.

"Effie? You okay?" Grady asked, sounding concerned.

"No."

"Is that why your eyes are closed?" Steele asked.

"I'm trying to pretend that neither of you are here. And if I can't see you, then you can't be here. Right?"

"Um, not sure that's the way it works, sweetheart," Grady told her gently.

"Is she embarrassed about watching porn?" Steele asked in that deep, loud voice of his.

Why had she never noticed how loud it was until just then?

Probably because he's never talked about you watching porn until just now.

This was really not awesome.

Find the happy.

There's got to be something good about this. Right?

Just smile. Everyone will like you better if you smile.

Sure, Nan. She'd get right on to that. After she stopped dying of embarrassment.

Why had she come into work early this morning?

"She's not embarrassed about watching porn," Grady started to say.

Nope.

Enough.

She opened her eyes to glare at them both.

There was no *happy* in any of this. Just pure embarrassment.

"Will you both stop talking about porn? I do not watch porn. I do not like porn. And I do not want to talk about porn anymore."

They both gaped at her.

Then Steele smiled. Usually, she liked his smile. It was a gorgeous smile. He was a handsome guy and he was even more attractive when he smiled.

But right then . . . nope, she didn't like it.

"Just suggesting, Spitfire, that if you don't want to talk about porn, you should probably stop saying the word porn."

"Urgh!" She needed to hide. That's what she was going to do. Hide until they were gone. Closing her eyes hadn't worked. So hiding would have to.

Only where to hide? She glanced around. There was just one place that she could get to that would work.

She pushed her chair back and stood.

"Uh, Effie? Are you all right?" Grady asked.

She crawled under the desk.

"What is she doing?" Steele asked.

"I think she's getting under the desk."

"Did she drop something?"

"Uh, no. She appears to be sitting under it." Grady peered down at her, so she buried her face in her knees. "And hiding."

"Hiding? Who's she hiding from?" Steele asked in that gruff voice of his.

"My thought would be us. Since we're the only people in here."

"Why would she need to hide from us?" Steele asked in an incredulous voice.

"I'm guessing she's embarrassed about the porn talk."

God. Would they just stop talking?

"That's ridiculous."

It was not ridiculous! It was not silly to be embarrassed and hide.

Of course it's silly. You're being an idiot and embarrassing yourself more. You're hiding under your desk.

While your bosses are in the room.

Shit. Shit. Shit.

Effie, don't let people know you're different.

They won't like you if you don't smile and pretend everything is all right.

She clasped her hands over her ears as though that would actually keep Nan's voice out of her head.

Crap. Thirty-five years old and she was still hearing her Nan give her life lessons.

Life lessons that she really didn't want or need.

Deep breath in. Let it out slowly.

"Effie? Effie, if you don't answer me soon, then I'm pulling you out of there," Grady said.

Get it together.

Another breath in, then she squealed as she felt the desk move. She glanced up to see that Grady had one end and Steele had the other.

"What are you doing?" she asked. "Be careful with the computer."

"Fuck the computer," Steele said gruffly. "Are you all right?"

Damn.

Those words shouldn't make her want to cry. They shouldn't reach around her heart and pump it full of warmth.

But they did . . . because when was the last time anyone had asked her that? Well, other than when she actually hurt herself physically that was.

"Do you think it's possible to die of embarrassment?" she whispered.

Nan was right.

She simply wasn't normal.

"No," Grady said bluntly. Which was typical for Grady. He wasn't a guy who sugar-coated things. Mostly, she appreciated that. Sometimes, like right now, she wished he'd make stuff up to make her feel better. "And you have no reason to be embarrassed."

"I talked about porn. And I hid under my desk. From my bosses."

"Up you come," Steele told her before reaching down and actually picking her up.

Wow. He was strong.

He set her down on her feet in front of him.

Right in front of him.

She went to step back only to feel Grady move in behind her, so she was sandwiched between them.

Something a woman could only dream of. And something she had on good authority that every woman who worked at Pinkies had likely dreamed of.

"Don't want you sitting on the floor," Steele told her. "That's not where you belong."

She liked sitting on the floor sometimes. But it did feel like the older she got, the harder it was to get up and down.

And you're only thirty-five.

Yes, but sometimes she felt worn down by life. Like she was aging faster than everyone else.

"You good?" Steele asked.

She smiled wide. "I made peanut butter cups today."

"Sounds delicious, but that's not what I asked. You okay?"

"Of course."

His eyes studied her, then narrowed. "You're not."

Yikes.

How did he know that?

"No lying, baby girl. We've talked about this."

Gulp.

"I've talked about it with her too. She might have a problem," Grady stated.

"I do not! I do not have a problem with lying!"

"You have a problem with following instructions?" Steele asked.

"Um. I don't think so."

"I think you do. What time is it?"

She glanced up at the clock. "Ten-forty-three."

"What time do you start work?" Steel asked.

Drat.

"Twelve."

"Good news for you, you're not on the clock, so we're not your bosses right now. Means you don't have to be embarrassed at watching porn."

"I wasn't watching porn!" she cried.

His eyes twinkled. Oh. He was teasing her? That was just plain mean.

She felt warmth enter her cheeks.

"Bad news for you. If we're not your bosses right now, we might need to punish you for lying."

"And coming in early," Grady added.

Steele gave him a look, then nodded.

"You can't punish me."

They couldn't, right? Lord, what was happening to her life? She didn't know when things had changed from them being strictly her bosses to this . . . where they teased her about spanking her.

It was just teasing, right?

"From now on, you don't start work early and you don't work late, understand?" Steele said. "If your workload is too big, then we lighten it."

"That's what I told her," Grady said.

"Good. Then it won't need said again. And if you need to watch porn, Spitfire, there are more private places to do it."

Effie groaned and placed her hands over her face.

"She was watching news reports about that murder in

Wyoming," Grady explained. "She heard it on the radio in the car. I'll talk to Raul about not having the radio on when she's in the car."

Good Lord.

"She was worried as she has a friend there who looks like that woman," Grady added.

"Your friend got a guy? One who'll protect her?" Steele asked.

"Yes," she whispered. "I was just being silly."

Steele cupped the side of her face. And God, his hand was so warm and steady. "I don't want you worrying about your safety, understand?"

Lord. She should not get used to this.

This wasn't going to be her life. Between the two of them. Having them hold her up, protect her, surround her in warmth.

It was never gonna be her life.

But God, did she want it.

Then she felt something even more surprising. Two hands on her hips, steadying her, and Grady leaning into her.

"You're safe, baby girl. We're going to make sure of that."

She gulped at Steele's words. Her neighbor hadn't had a loud party since she'd told him. She didn't know if he had something to do with that or if it was a coincidence.

And she was scared to ask.

A warm hand cupped the side of her neck, fingers reached around the back to squeeze. Opening her eyes, she stared up at Steele.

Her breath caught.

Yeah. Something had definitely changed.

"No more hiding from us. You got nothing to be embarrassed about. All right?"

She nodded because he seemed to be waiting for a reply.

"Let's get her stuff back in place," Steele said.

She watched as they shifted the desk, swaying slightly at the loss of their touch.

That could be addictive.

Steele moved like he always did, with a grace that belied his size. But Grady was more jerky. Working on instinct. Deep in his head. She knew all about that. Only, she worried that she was the one that had put him in his head.

Steele's phone rang as he reached into his pocket and pulled something out, placing it on her keyboard.

"Fingerless gloves. Wear them." Then he stepped out.

Grady moved to follow him.

"Grady?"

He stopped but didn't turn to her.

"I'm sorry."

She expected him to leave. But he turned, frowning down at her. "Why are you apologizing?"

"Um, well, I, uh . . . I think I did something to upset you, and I'm sorry about that."

"Who taught you that you always have to be the one to apologize?" he asked.

"No one."

Wait. Was that true?

Always say you're sorry, Effie. Even if you're not. People appreciate an apology, doesn't matter who is in the wrong.

Christ.

"Hey, look at me."

She raised her gaze to Grady's.

"Where did you go just then?"

She didn't want to tell him. So she just stared up at him.

He sighed and nodded. As though he understood. Then he reached out. His hand kind of stopped in mid-air, though. As though he didn't quite know what to do next.

Acting on instinct, without even thinking about it, she grabbed his hand.

He jolted and she let go. "Sorry." Crap. She was messing up all over the place.

But to her shock, he reached out and took her hand. "You don't have to keep saying sorry. You have nothing to apologize for. And you didn't upset me. Sometimes, I . . . sometimes I get so involved in the details that I forget about the emotions. My childhood, well, it was all about emotion. And not the good kinds. As a result, I became rather detached from all of that. I'm trying to find a way to be more in-tune with my emotions. But it's not easy."

Her heart melted for him. She squeezed his hand. "It's all right. I understand."

"Just be patient with me." Letting go of her hand, he walked out.

Yeah, things had definitely changed. Because no boss acted that way with their employee. They might be friendly, they might tease. But they didn't sandwich them between them.

Or cup the side of their neck with their big hand.

Or hold their hand and ask them to be patient.

The thing is . . . she didn't know whether to be terrified or excited.

Maybe a bit of both.

Returning to the desk, she glanced down at the gloves, running her finger over them. Expensive and pretty.

Lord. She was in trouble.

∽

THE NEXT DAY, Grady bought her Mace.

Steele bought her fluffy socks and ate half of the peppermint mocha brownie she'd made.

The day after that, Grady bought her a Taser.

Steele bought her a new scarf and ate several apple cinnamon muffins.

And then Grady bought her a rape whistle.

Steele bought her a woollen hat.

She knew she had to find a way to make them stop.

The thing is . . . she just didn't want to.

22

Damn Vanessa.

So freaking unreliable.

Effie was supposed to have gone home three hours ago. She was exhausted, hungry, and her back was really starting to ache. She wasn't used to being on her feet for hours on end. Let alone carting drinks around.

She'd never waitressed before and she'd spent the first hour messing it up. But now she'd kind of gotten the hang of it. However, she didn't think she'd be making much in tips. Especially as she wasn't dressed like the other servers.

"Hey, girlie. This isn't what I ordered," an older man with a long gray beard yelled at her.

She gritted her teeth.

Smile, Effie.

It was really hard to see the good side of anything when she was hurting and hungry.

But she forced a big smile onto her face and walked over to where the grumpy old fart was. "What seems to be the problem?"

"I ordered a Jack and Coke."

She still couldn't see the problem. "That is a Jack and Coke."

"There's too much Coke, girlie. You shafted me on the Jack."

Like she'd freaking made it. Nate, the head bartenders had. But she didn't argue with the jerk. Instead, she took the glass back. "I'll go talk to Nate about that."

"And hurry it up, will ya? I don't have all day to wait. Man needs a drink."

Right. Because it was thirsty work just sitting there. Effie couldn't remember the last time she'd had a drink of water. She was dying of thirst. And she'd kill to sit down. But tonight was busy and there were no breaks coming her way until things quieted down.

Fucking Vanessa.

The next time she saw her, she was going to . . . well, she didn't know what she was going to do. But she certainly wasn't going to be nice to her.

As she reached the bar, she leaned against it, trying to ease some of her weight off her back.

It didn't really work, unfortunately.

"Yo, Nate," she called out.

"Yeah?" Nate was a good-looking man. Broad-shouldered with dark hair. He filled out the tight black T-shirt of his Pinkies uniform nicely. Walking over, he looked down at her. "Darlin', you don't look so good. You need to get yourself home. How many hours have you worked today?"

"About ten. But only three waitressing."

A frown took over his face. "Go home. We'll be fine without you."

No way. She was the one who'd rostered Vanessa on, so this was her responsibility.

"There's a gentleman without a drink over there, Effie," Lucy said with a sneer as she walked up to them. "And you're just standing here talking."

Nate turned his gaze to Lucy, and while he'd never been anything but kind and friendly to her, there was nothing but chill when he looked at Lucy.

"Then how about you grab a tray and start serving drinks, huh?" Nate asked in a dark voice.

Lucy gave him an affronted look. "It's not my job."

"More your job than it is Effie's. She's been working ten hours straight and she's dead on her feet. Seems to me, you should be picking up the slack, not her."

"I am not serving drinks. And it's her schedule. Her fault." Lucy strode away, leaving an icy wind in her wake.

Or maybe that was just Effie's overactive imagination. What she wouldn't give to have some snappy reply to wipe the smug look off her face.

"Effie? Effie, you still with me, darlin'?"

She jolted and looked over at him tiredly. "Sorry, I was thinking."

"Yeah. Here's the drink, but you stay there. I'm going to take it to that ass. There was plenty of Jack in his Coke."

She glanced around at the number of people waiting at the bar for him to serve them and shook her head. She smiled big. "I got this, Nate. But thanks, that's really sweet of you."

"Never been called sweet before, darlin'."

"Well, I think you are. Everyone here is so nice. Except for Satan's mistress."

Nate just winked at her as she took the drink as well as a couple more drinks for her other tables.

Serving was hard work. She was going to do something nice for all the servers.

She walked toward the crotchety old man first, putting his drink down with a smile but not saying anything. She didn't trust herself not to tell him that he was a nasty old man who needed to learn to use his manners.

Then she moved to her other tables, giving them more sweetness. One of them even tipped her big. Bonus.

"Hey, girlie!" the man yelled over the music again.

Smile, Effie.

You look prettier when you smile.

With a sigh and without glancing over at Nate, she made her way to the old man.

"Yes, sir?" she asked politely.

"I told you, more Jack in my Coke!" He reached out and grabbed her arm.

Effie froze. She wasn't used to being grabbed. He shook her arm, making her jolt. A stab of pain went through her back. It probably would have been all right if she wasn't already in pain from lugging drinks around for three hours. Those trays got heavy after a while.

A squeak of pain escaped her. Damn. He was strong for an old guy.

"Let me go!" she said quietly, trying not to draw attention to herself.

Suddenly, someone stepped between her and the old guy, grabbing his arm.

"Let Effie go. Now."

She looked up, surprised to see Lex standing there. She hadn't even seen him move over here.

"Everything all right here?"

She glanced over to see Nate standing there, scowling at the crotchety old guy. Had he come over to help her as well?

"This asshole had his hand on Effie," Lex said.

"You okay, darlin'?" Nate asked.

"Yes, thanks."

"No, you're not," he countered.

Um. She didn't know what to say to that. Especially since he was right.

"She cheated me! There was barely any booze in that drink!"

"Asshole, I made that drink," Nate said. "There was plenty of whiskey in it. You wanted a triple, then you should have asked for it. Now, you don't get anything since you're banned."

"Banned? Nate, you don't have the ability to ban anyone," Lucy said, coming up to them.

Great.

"Actually, I do," Nate replied quietly. "I'm in charge of the bar, you're in charge of the servers, even if you think you rule the whole place. Lex, get rid of him."

"With pleasure," the bouncer replied.

"Effie, you come sit down," Nate ordered. "You're off shift."

Whoa. Was every guy that worked here so dominant and bossy?

"She can't go off shift," Lucy said with frustration.

Nate just shot Lucy a look and gestured toward the bar. Effie moved slowly behind him. Sitting was probably the last thing she should do with the way her back felt.

Moving was likely better for it. Although she wasn't sure she was capable of doing much of that. What she really wanted was to take some of her heavy duty painkillers and lie down.

And sleep.

But she dragged herself over to the bar.

"What do you need, darlin'?" Nate asked.

"My handbag. It's in the office."

"Lucy, go and get her handbag," he ordered.

Lucy scowled. Effie opened her mouth to say she'd get it. She really didn't want to be beholden to Lucy. But when she tried to move, her legs nearly gave in on her.

"Sit," Nate ordered. "I'll get you some water. Lucy."

"I'm going. But I will be speaking to Damon about this."

Great. She was probably going to get fired. Vanessa hadn't turned up and Effie had made a mess of serving drinks. Then she'd made a scene.

She sipped at her water as she waited for Lucy. What the heck was taking her so long?

Finally, the other woman returned with her handbag. There was a look of sympathy on her face.

Yeah, she wasn't going to trust that look.

She'd worked here for over eight weeks now. And what she knew without a doubt was that everyone detested Lucy. And the feeling seemed to be mutual, since Lucy seemed to think she was better than all of them.

"Here you are, Effie." Lucy handed her bag over.

"Thanks," Effie muttered, searching through her bag for her pills.

"I'm sorry about before," Lucy apologized. "I've got a bit of a headache and it's making me a bit sharp."

A bit sharp? She was always sharp.

"Do you want another drink? You look a bit pale. Vodka?" Lucy moved behind the bar.

"No, thanks."

Lucy's face kind of dropped. Was she actually trying to be nice? Now Effie felt terrible. But she couldn't drink with these pills. It would make her go loopy.

"Perhaps orange juice?" she asked.

"Sure. I'll get that for you."

Effie found the pills and shook two out. Then Lucy placed a glass of orange juice in front of her.

"Thank you." She drank it down with the pills. There was a bit of a strange taste to the orange juice, but she shook it off. Just a bit sour, she guessed.

"Hey, I make a great Virgin Pina Colada," Lucy said. "Want one?"

"No alcohol?" she asked.

"Nope."

"Um, I don't know. I should get back to work."

"No more working for you, darlin'," Nate said, coming up. He eyed Lucy suspiciously, but she went away to deal with something.

Effie pushed the juice to one side.

"She manage to fuck up pouring orange juice?" Nate asked, dumping it out into the sink behind him.

"Something like that. I need to get back to the tables. The other servers are slammed. I took some pain pills. They'll help soon."

The only problem was that they'd probably start making her sleepy soon. But it was that, or she wouldn't be able to move from the pain.

"I texted Olivia," Nate told her. "She'll be in soon."

Relief filled her. "Really?"

"Yep."

"You didn't have to do that." Guilt filled her. That was her job.

"Darlin', you look like you're about to collapse, so yeah, I did. Did you take care of him?"

That last sentence was aimed over her head and she turned carefully to see Lex standing there.

"Yeah, he's gone. Are you all right, Effie?"

Lex was quiet. Watchful. Tall and muscular. She liked him.

"I'm good. Thanks for saving me, Lex." She patted his arm. "Now, I'm going to work until Olivia gets here."

"Are you sure you should?" Lex asked.

"You're both so sweet and kind. But I promise, I'm fine."

"Darlin', you're gonna need to stop calling me sweet. I've got a reputation to protect."

She just grinned at Nate.

"You sure, Effie?" Lex asked.

"I promise, I'm good." She patted his arm and moved over to her next table. About five minutes later, a woozy feeling came over her and she went back to the bar.

"Here, Effie. Drink this. You look a bit strange." Lucy handed her a glass of something.

"Um, thanks." She took the drink without noticing what it was. "No alcohol?"

"Of course not."

Effie drank it down. Wow, she hadn't realized she was that thirsty.

"Thanks."

She walked back to another table. But the world was tilting, and for some reason, she found that hilarious. A giggle escaped her and she nearly tripped. But when she glanced down at her feet, there was nothing there.

That was even funnier. She banged a drink down on a table.

"Hey, that's not mine."

"Just enjoy . . . enjoy it all," she said as she made her way back to the bar.

"Here's another drink, Effie," Lucy said.

"You know, Lucy," she said, gulping it down. "I was wrong, you're not such a bitch."

"Thanks," Lucy replied. Although there seemed to be something wrong with her voice.

"Can you make a drink that tastes like jelly beans? I loveeee jelly beans."

"Sure, Effie. Anything for you."

"Yeah, you're not a bitch at all. You're so sweet."

"Effie, are you all right?" Nate asked.

"Nate!" She threw her arms up in the air. "You're the best too!"

"What's wrong with her? What did you do?" Nate demanded.

"I didn't do anything. But I think . . . I think she might have taken something," Lucy whispered.

"Did you put something in her drinks?" Nate asked.

"No! How dare you suggest that!" Lucy said.

"I want to dance! I want to get up on the stage and dance! Where's Chardonnay? I'm sure she'll dance with me! Come on, Lucy, let's dance!"

"Shit. We need to get her out the back." Suddenly, Nate was in front of her. He wrapped an arm around her. "Come on, Effie. Let's get you out back so you can lie down."

"But I want to dance!"

"What the fuck is going on here?"

23

Grady watched as Effie spun, smiling wide at him. There was something different about this smile.

She actually looked happy. Really happy.

And he thought it would never be a bad thing to see that smile on her face . . . for the rest of his life.

As she spun, she tripped and he reached out to grab her.

"Stupid air. Keeps tripping me up!"

He held her against him, breathing her in. Fuck. She felt so good in his arms.

"You smell so good."

"Do I?" he asked.

She snuggled into him as though she belonged there. Then she tilted her head back to smile up at him. "You are sooo pretty."

Fuck. She was beautiful.

Even though he and Steele had had a conversation a week and a half ago about moving things forward with her, they hadn't had much time to actually do anything.

Well, Steele seemed to find time each day to stop by and eat some of her baked goods. And Grady knew that she'd baked him an entire cake of his own. He knew that because Steele had guarded that thing like it held the crown jewels and hadn't even shared one piece.

Greedy bastard.

However, they hadn't figured out how to move forward with showing her that they wanted more than a boss-employee relationship with her. Then he caught sight of her eyes. Her pupils were enlarged.

"Has she been drinking?" he asked, looking over at Nate. "What is she even doing here?"

She should have gone home hours ago. Shit. Why hadn't he checked in with Raul that she'd gotten home? He'd been running around doing shit all night at some of Steele's other businesses and had barely had a minute to spare.

Steele was talking to his lieutenants about some stuff that had been going on around the city lately. In particular, he wanted to warn them that Wolfe and a few of the Rykers were still around and to watch out.

So he hadn't checked to make sure she'd gotten home safe.

A mistake.

"She's been filling in," Nate told him. "Vanessa didn't turn up."

Grady frowned. "Lucy, call her. Tell her she's fired."

"All right, Mr. Grady. But what do we do about Effie? She's been acting strange for the last half hour."

"Hey, Grady? Tell you a seecit," Effie whispered loudly.

A seecit?

She gestured to him and he leaned down. Did she mean a secret?

"Lucy isn't such a bitch," she told him.

He was fairly certain that she'd meant to whisper it. Unfortunately, she'd ended up yelling it.

"I think she's delusional," Nate said dryly.

"Shut up, Nate," Lucy snarled.

"She's been filling in for Vanessa? You mean she was serving drinks?" Grady asked.

"Yeah, I tried to send her home," Nate told him. "But she reckoned it was her job to fill in for Vanessa."

Fucking bullshit. And he'd need to ensure that she got over that sort of thinking quick. There was no way she should be on her feet serving after having worked a full day. And he'd be telling her that as soon as she was in her right mind.

Grady wrapped his arm around her waist as she swayed.

"Will you dance with me?" she asked.

He tightened his hold on her, worried she might fall.

"No dancing."

She pouted. "Meanie."

"Has she been drinking?" he asked Nate.

"I poured her a water. But Lucy got her an orange juice." Nate frowned. "What's this?" He picked up an empty glass.

"I made her a Virgin Pina Colada," Lucy defended. "And it was just an orange juice. She kept saying she was thirsty. Do you think she's taken something?"

Grady narrowed his gaze at Lucy. He didn't trust her as far as he could throw her. Then he turned back to his girl.

"Effie? Can you look at me?" he asked.

"Aren't all the lights pretty? And the dancers? I love to dance. Will you dance with me, Grady?"

"Effie. Look at me."

She gaped up at him. Then her lower lip trembled again. "Are yous mad at me?"

Fuck. He had to get her out of there. It was like her defenses were blown and her Little was coming out. Something he was certain she wouldn't want everyone in Pinkies to know about.

"No, Twinkletoes, I'm not," he whispered to her. "But I do

need you to stay with me. Okay? I'm going to get you somewhere safe."

"Safe?" Her head moved back and forth and she clung tighter to him.

Fuck if that didn't make him feel a hundred feet tall. Women were always drawn toward Steele, not him. They didn't search him out for protection. Or to look after them.

So yeah, he was going to ride the high of her turning to him for protection for a while.

"Are we not safe? Are there boogie men around?" she asked,.

"Boogie men?"

"Bad mens. Come to get you. Never fear, I will protect you. Brooks used to get scared of the dark. And of people hiding under his bed and stuff. So I hads to check under the bed and in the closet. And behind the curtains. That's a good hiding place for those boogie men."

Did she mean the bogeyman?

"That was scary," she told him. "I didn't like having to search for them. I had to be brave for Brooks, though."

Poor baby. He couldn't imagine how hard it was trying to raise Brooks by herself. And having to do things that she was scared of but pretending she wasn't.

"Who would be scared of checking a closet?" Lucy scoffed. "Obviously, she's taken something. Maybe you should search her bag."

The way she said that struck him as wrong.

"Why would you say that?" Nate asked, obviously thinking the same.

"Just a suggestion," Lucy said, sticking her nose up in the air. "She's obviously taken something. And while she was working. That's grounds for dismissal."

"She shouldn't even be working. And this is none of your business," Grady said. "Go deal with the tables in Effie's section."

"Me? Wait tables?" Lucy gaped at him.

"You did it for years. You should know what you're doing."

Lucy glared at him before she seemed to recall who he was.

"Such a bitch," Nate muttered as she stormed off. His gaze grew concerned as he stared down at Effie. Grady stiffened, not liking that look. "Think she's all right? I can get her some more water."

"She'll be fine. I'll take care of her. Come on, sweetheart. Let's get you to my office."

"But I don't wanna work. I wanna play."

"You can play in the office," he promised. He wasn't used to taking care of a Little. He should probably call Steele.

Only, there was a part of him that wanted to know how to look after her. That wanted her to look to him for everything.

Strange.

Steele should get there soon. He could help with her.

"When Steele gets here, tell him where we are," he ordered Nate.

Nate raised his chin in acknowledgment.

Grady kept his arm wrapped around Effie as he led her across the room.

She tripped and he tightened his hold.

"Oopsie. My feet keep tripping over something, but I can'ts tell what. Can you?"

"Air," he told her.

"That's silly. Why would they trip over air?"

She tripped again, and when they were out of sight, he bent down and lifted her onto his hip.

"Ooh, this is fun. Can I go on your back like a horsie?"

"No. But do you know who would make a great horse?"

"Who?" She leaned back and he had to grab her tighter to keep her from falling backward.

"Whoa, no. Put your arms around my neck."

"Huh?"

"Effie. Arms around my neck."

"You're very bossy."

"And you're not very good at listening," he said as they reached his office.

Well, their office now.

"I knows. I just start thinking about things and I forget to listen. Listening ears, Effie. Listening ears are activated." She cupped the back of her ears with her hands.

Damn. Adorable.

He'd never understood it before. The desire to take care of a Little. He'd always liked to have clear boundaries and rules. Having a Little to care for . . . sure, you could have rules. But Littles could be unpredictable and often sensitive. They always seemed to need more emotionally than Grady would or could give. He'd never been very good with emotions.

Giving aftercare wasn't as bad because he had a routine. Things he knew how to do. Chocolate, water, blanket. Holding them if necessary. Although at the club, he'd always gone for submissives who didn't need as much aftercare.

But a Little would likely need not just one cuddle, but a whole lot of them. And more support for their needs than he could deal with.

"Steele," he told her as he sat her down on the sofa.

"Huh? Where's Steele?"

"No, he's not here. He'd make a good horse."

"Ooh, he'd make a great horsie!" She clapped her hands, then slid back against the sofa. "I's tired."

"Are you? That could be because you've worked over ten hours today."

"Mores than that. I came to work early to gets things done. And I hads to stay. Vanessa didn't turn up."

"It's not your job to cover for the servers." He could tell that this wasn't the time to have this conversation, though. She wasn't going to take any of this in.

And he still needed to find out what was going on. If she hadn't been drinking, then what had she taken?

Moving over to the mini-fridge, he drew out a bottle of water. Then he sat on the coffee table in front of her.

"Effie, what are you doing?"

She was moving her fingers together, up and down.

"Incy-Bitsy spider. Do you know it?"

"Um, yeah, Twinkletoes. I know it."

"I like that nickname. And when you call me sweetheart. Makes me feel special."

"You are special, Effie."

"Nuh-uh, silly. I's just Effie." Suddenly, she sniffled. "I wanna go home."

"We'll go home soon, all right? I want you to tell me if you drank or took anything, though."

"I drunks lots of stuff."

"Did you see anyone put anything into those drinks?"

"Yeah."

"Yeah? What? Who?"

"Lucy. She put drinks in the drinks. Silly." She grinned at him.

"All right, smart-ass. I'm going to take it that you didn't actually see anything. What about pills? Did you take any pills?"

"Just painkillers. My back hurt. Do you likes spiders, Grady? I reckon they get a bad rep."

"You do?"

"Uh-huh, they're just misunderstood. Like me."

"How are you misunderstood?" he asked.

"Everyone thinks I'm brave. But can I tells you another seecit?"

"Sure, sweetheart."

"I'm scared. All the time. Terrified that I'm going to do something wrong with Brooks and scar him for life. Worried I'll lose my job again and not be able to house and feed him. Scared people will know that it's all a lie."

"What's all a lie?"

"The happy. It's all a lie, Grady."

Okay, he wasn't sure what the hell she was talking about.

A knock on the door made her scream and she jumped into his lap. He wrapped his arms around her in shock.

"Effie, be careful with your back."

"I can't feel it."

"At all?" he asked.

"No, I had to take something 'cause it was sore from all the walking."

Okay.

"The pills in your handbag?"

"Uh-huh. Nots my magic beans, though. I wish my magic beans helped with my sore back."

"Um, what are your magic beans?" he asked.

"Jelly beans, silly!" She started giggling.

Strange. Those pills hadn't had this effect on her last time. It was like she was drunk or high.

"Come in," he called out.

Nate poked his head in, his eyebrows rising as he took in Effie on his lap. But Grady didn't care. He could think whatever he liked.

Steele and Grady intended to claim Effie. Perhaps it was time they actually did that instead of tiptoeing around things the way they had for the last week and a half.

If Nate knew she was his and Steele's, he'd never have allowed her to work as a server out in the bar.

No fucking way.

And he would have called him straight away to let him know something was going on with her.

Yeah, he wanted everyone to know she was theirs.

"What is it?" he asked more sharply than he intended to.

"I brought Effie's handbag in."

"Thanks." He held out his hand.

Effie leaned back against him and looked up at Nate. "Hi, Nate."

"Hey, honey. You feeling any better?"

"I feels great. I'm not in any pain and that is always amazing."

"No pain?" Nate asked, looking worried.

"She has an old back injury. Sometimes it flares up."

"Was it hurting earlier, Effie?" Nate asked. "You looked like you were in pain."

"Yeah. But it would've been okay if that guy hadn't grabbed me." She wrinkled her nose.

"Who the fuck grabbed you?"

Grady felt relief as Steele entered the room. Maybe he could work out what was going on with her. Surely her pain killers wouldn't be enough to make her go like this? But that seemed to have been the only thing she ingested.

Effie reached up her arms. "Horsie! Giddy-up!"

24

That wasn't exactly the greeting he'd expected.

Steele gaped down at Effie. Although that wasn't his biggest surprise.

Nope, that was the fact that Effie was sitting in Grady's lap.

Grady's. Lap.

The man who didn't really give affection unless it was expected of him, and then it didn't mean anything as he was only going through the motions.

The man who didn't cuddle, didn't hold hands, or didn't even kiss a woman he was fucking or dominating.

The man who most certainly would never engage in PDA was just sitting there with Effie on his lap.

And he didn't even look that awkward about it. In fact, his arms were tight around her.

Holding her.

Had Steele entered some sort of alternate universe and he didn't know it?

He'd been prepared to give Effie all the affection in their relationship. He knew what Grady was like and he was used to him.

But women often didn't understand him. So he'd figured he'd have to overcompensate for the lack of physical affection from Grady.

Now, it seemed that he might not have that issue.

After all these years, it appeared they might have found a woman who could break down those walls. Steele was inside the walls. But he didn't want to hold Grady's hand.

But you are attracted to him.

Yeah. There were times they'd crossed swords when they'd been with the same woman. When he'd found himself admiring the other man's cut body. And yeah, he liked it. But he had no idea if Grady felt the same way, even though he thought sometimes it seemed that he might. Besides, there was also the fact that he'd never been attracted to another man before and was confused by it. As well as worried that any move he made might mean the end of their relationship.

And he couldn't live without Grady.

Would Effie really get behind Grady's walls? It seemed like she might already have.

He'd known she was at least part way there when Grady had suggested that they start a relationship with her. Grady had never been interested in a relationship with anyone before.

Which was why Steele had agreed to take it slow when he didn't really want to. Nope, what he wanted was to take Effie home with him and ensure she was taken care of. Protected.

He studied Effie closely. Something wasn't right.

"What's wrong with her?" he demanded.

"Not sure," Grady replied grimly. "I think it might be the painkillers she took. They might have made her a bit loopy."

Steele frowned. "The ones in her handbag? She's taken them before."

"I know," Grady replied. "Which is what is concerning."

"I's not loopy," she said. "I don'ts take them much because they make me sleepy and a bit loopy."

"But you just said you're not loopy." Steele walked forward and sat on the sofa, facing them both. Then he grasped her chin. "She's definitely taken something. Maybe they were different pills."

"Would they be in her handbag?" Nate asked.

Steele looked from him to the handbag he was holding. He took it with a nod of thanks.

"You best get back out there, but before you do, you need to explain who the fuck touched our girl," Steele demanded.

"Our girl?" Nate repeated.

"Our girl," Steele said firmly.

He knew he'd agreed to take things slow, and he wouldn't rush Effie. But he didn't like everyone not knowing that he was making a claim.

So he was going to fix that by making a claim.

Grady would just have to deal. And considering Grady always did, Steele knew he would this time too.

Nate moved his gaze back and forth between them. "I'm gonna say something that might get me fired. But I figure that Effie doesn't have many people watching out for her."

"Might be best you don't say it then," Grady suggested, his eyes narrowing.

Fuck. Nate didn't want to get on Grady's bad side.

"Might be. However, I've still gotta look in the mirror at myself after tonight and like what I see. So I'm gonna say it. Effie isn't a girl looking for a good time. She's not the type you fuck and leave. She's the type you hold on tight to. And you don't let go."

Yep, that really fucked him off. No matter if he did admire that Nate was saying it to the two men who could fire him.

Steele stood, unable to curb the anger.

"Are you really going to stand there and insult us like that?" Grady asked in a low, deadly whisper.

Oh fuck. Things were bad if Grady was close to the edge.

"I like Effie," Nate defended. "Someone has to look out for her."

"No one has to look out for me. I can look out for myself." She pointed at her face. Except she moved her finger too much and managed to poke herself in the eye.

"Ow! Owie!"

"Did you hurt yourself?" Grady asked, sounding alarmed. "Let me see."

"It hurts," she sobbed, holding her hand over her eye.

"It's all right," Grady soothed. "Just let me see, sweetheart."

Steele moved back to her. He knew this wasn't Grady's strong suit.

Loyalty, he had in spades. Intelligence, definitely.

But empathy. Not so much.

"You . . . you won't touch my eye? I don'ts like things touching my eyeball. Those sorts of balls should never be touched. Other balls, yes. Eyeballs, no."

"All right, Twinkletoes. I won't touch your eyeball." She removed her hand slowly and Grady checked her eye. "It looks okay."

"It doesn't feel okay."

Grady stared up at him, clearly looking for guidance.

Steele felt an unusual warmth unfurl in his chest. Was this the way it could be? The two of them feeding off each other? Using their strengths to help their girl?

He sat beside them, the coffee table creaking.

"Maybe we should move." Grady carried her to the sofa, sitting again with her on his lap.

It was telling that he didn't want to let her go. Steele leaned forward to grasp Effie's chin.

"Do you want the good news or the good news?" he asked.

"Hmm, let me think about that for a moment. I don'ts want to make the wrong decision."

Steele grinned.

"I want . . . the good news!"

"Good news is that your eyeball is still in your eye socket."

She heaved out a breath. "Whew. That is a big relief to me."

"Thought it might be," he said dryly. Damn, she was funny. Usually, she tried to keep her true thoughts and feelings tamped down. But he'd seen her let go of that control a few times.

And he preferred this Effie. The one who felt safe enough to be herself.

"The other good news is that I have a way to fix your eyeball."

"You do?" She stared at him in wonder.

He wanted that for the rest of his life. Her, staring at him like he could fix everything.

"I do. Close your eyes."

She eyed him suspiciously. "You're not gonna do something gross, are you?"

"Never."

"Okay, I trusts you."

Surprise filled him and he glanced at Grady. To his shock, Grady was staring at her with something like softness in his face.

She closed her eyes and waited.

Steele leaned forward and lightly kissed her closed eye. "Better, baby girl?"

"All better." She opened her eyes and stared up at him.

"Good girl. Now, you just rest, understand me? I'm not even sure why you are still here this late."

"Vanessa bailed," Grady told him in a grim voice. "Effie decided it was her job to fill in for her."

"We'll be making sure she knows better once she feels more

like herself," Steele dictated. What the fuck was she thinking? She'd already worked a full day. She didn't need to be serving drinks on top of that.

And walking around, carrying drinks with an old back injury that sometimes flared up?

No. Not happening.

She should be home resting.

He had half a mind to make her cut her hours. And he probably would if he thought she'd let him cover her bills.

When Steele wanted something, he tended to bulldoze straight ahead. And he always got what he wanted.

But Grady was right.

Effie would likely run if he went too fast. And while he wouldn't allow her to run far, things would go smoother if he could go slow.

Grady's face filled with shock as Effie let out a contented moan as she snuggled her face into his neck.

"What is she doing?"

"Snuggling you." Steele had to bite back a grin. "Seems our girl is a cuddler."

Which was fucking great for him. That's what he missed most about not having a woman of his own. Cuddling. Especially at night. Steele liked to hold on to his woman.

Grady liked to sleep alone. Or he usually did.

"I take it back," Nate said suddenly.

Fuck, he'd forgotten the other man was even in the room.

"I can see it now. She's not a one-night stand, is she?" he asked them.

"No, she's not." Steele turned to give him a firm look.

"Does she even know that? I mean, you guys haven't made it obvious. I would've called you as soon as she turned up for Vanessa's shift if I'd known."

"We were going slow," Steele told him.

"This is slow?" Nate asked.

"Things are a bit different now," Grady said. "She needs some care, don't you, Twinkletoes?"

She grinned up at Grady. "I like that nickname. But I like sweetheart too. And Baby girl. Not Spitfire, though." She glared up at Steele.

"That's too bad, Spitfire."

"Never had so many nicknames. Does it mean you like me?"

"That's exactly what it means," Steele told her.

"Goodie. That means you can be my horsie."

He shot Grady a look as the other man snorted.

"I'll explain it later," Grady told him as he stood.

"Right. Tell us about this fucker that touched her," Steele demanded.

Nate ran his hand over his face. "Uh, yeah. This old guy got grouchy with her over the drink she served him. Grabbed her arm. I was making my way over, but Lex got to him first and threw him out."

Anger filled Steele. "What the fuck!" He swung to Grady. "She should never have been in that position."

"No argument from me," Grady replied.

Effie was doing something with her fingers that he couldn't figure out.

"Anything like this happens again, you call us. Immediately," Steele told him.

"Got it." Nate nodded. "But I'm guessing nothing like will happen again."

"Damn straight," Steele muttered, furious at the thought that some asshole had put his hands on her. "And that's when her back really started to hurt?"

"Yeah, I think so. Lucy came in here and got her handbag. I think Effie took some painkillers. Didn't realize they would do this to her, though, or I would have found someone to take her home."

Steele searched through her handbag and drew out the same bottle of pills from the other night. That was odd, though.

"The bottle says not to take them with alcohol. She definitely didn't drink any alcohol?" he asked Nate.

"Not that I gave her," Nate said. "However, fuckin' Lucy poured her some drinks. She said they were free of alcohol, but I wouldn't trust that bitch."

"Wait," Grady said. "You said that Lucy got her handbag for her?"

Nate nodded. "Yeah. Shocked me. Nicest thing she's ever done."

"She could have gone through it," Grady said. "Found the bottle, read the label, and snuck some alcohol into Effie's drinks."

"It can't have been much alcohol," Steele said.

"I don'ts like alcamahol," Effie said. "Icky. Makes me feel funny. Don'ts drink it."

"So she's a lightweight as well," Grady said.

"Do you really think Lucy would do that? Why?" Steele asked.

"She's probably seen that you're interested in her," Nate said. "Jealous bitch wants to get into your pants, Boss."

Steele gritted his teeth. Motherfucking bitch. "If she put something in Effie's drink, I'll fucking kill her."

"Not if I get to her first," Grady added. "I'll get the camera footage up as soon as Effie is taken care of."

"But Lucy knows where the cameras are," Nate said. "She would have hidden what she was doing."

Not all of them.

Steele knew Grady had put in extra cameras that he'd told

no one about. They were there to ensure that no one could steal from them. Or do anything else they shouldn't.

"Nate, you can go back to work now," Steele said dismissively.

Nate gave him a knowing look, but nodded and left.

"He knows about the extra cameras now," Grady pointed out.

"He suspects, he doesn't know," Steele said. "And I don't think it matters. Nate has worked for us for years." Although he'd learned not to trust anyone too much. No one but Grady.

And maybe someday, the girl in his arms.

"We been moving too slow?" he asked.

"Perhaps," Grady allowed.

"She asleep?"

"I think so. Effie?" Grady asked.

She let out a small snort, then she sat up. "I gots another seecit."

"Do you just?" Amusement filled Grady's face.

Who was this man? Steele hadn't seen him look this happy and carefree in . . . well, maybe never.

"What is it?" Grady asked.

"I've got magic beans!"

"You do?" Grady asked.

"Yep! You want some. I can give you some of my magic beans."

"You keep them, sweetheart."

"Okie-dokie. Ooh, I has got another seecit."

"What is it?"

"I think Grady's pretty."

Steele's eyes widened.

"I'm not pretty. I'm a man." Grady gave her a stern look.

"Men can be pretty. He's pretty. But, shh, don'ts tell him that I think of kissing him."

"You think of kissing me? Um, him?" Grady asked, appearing shocked.

"Uh-huh, but it's very naughty. Cause you know what? Do you?"

"What?" Grady asked

"I thinks of kissing Steele too. Isn't that so bad?"

"Why is that bad?" Steele asked.

"Because I can't have two men. That's silly. G-greedy. Nan said it's bad to be greedy. She said I'd get fat if I ate too much. Guess . . . guess Nan was right. She said that no man would want me if I frowned or got mad or complained."

Jesus.

Steele met Grady's gaze with his own. Nan had a lot to answer for.

"My bosses are a bit scary, but at least they're pretty to look at."

"Effie, eyes on me." Steele sat again, leaning forward to take her chin in his. "Fuck, it's like she's totally drunk."

"Yep." Grady had to catch her as she nearly slid out of his lap. "It's like trying to hold on to slime."

"I like slime. It's so slimy. Can I haves some of your slime?" she asked.

"No," Steele told her.

Her lower lip trembled.

Dear. God.

He had experience with Littles. With women crying. But he'd never felt like he'd been hit in the gut like this when faced with a trembling lip.

That lip . . . it could well be his fucking kryptonite.

No. Be strong.

"No slime?" she asked.

"No slime," Steele told her. "It will make a mess. Get into everything. No slime."

"That's so sad!" she wailed.

"Effie." He couldn't give her an inch or she'd take a mile. He had to stay firm. Set boundaries.

Even if that was difficult as hell.

"You should have a badge," she said.

"What?"

"Like a warning sign that says you are so mean."

Grady snorted.

"Give her to me." Steele held out his arms.

Grady's face tightened. "No."

Steele eyed him. "We're going to share her. Remember? Sharing her means you need to actually fucking share her."

"Fuck." Grady closed his eyes, then breathed in and out slowly. "I don't know what's wrong with me, but I don't want to let her go."

Steele understood that. That didn't mean he wasn't going to push the other man to let her go. He finally lifted her over to Steele.

Christ. He loved holding her. She fit perfectly in his arms. She wasn't too small or too big.

Just. Fucking. Right.

And what was he? Fucking Goldilocks?

"Effie, listen to me."

"You gots pretty eyes. Like a clear sky with no clouds."

He did?

"I want you to listen to me, Effie. Grady and I might be scary. We might be dangerous. But you never have to fear us. Tell me you understand me."

She opened her mouth and he waited for her agreement.

"I'm going to be sick."

25

Grady wiped Effie's face while Steele held her against him as they sat on the floor. She made a pitiful noise. "I don't feel so good."

"I know, Twinkletoes," he said soothingly. "I'm sorry you don't feel good. But we're going to make you feel better."

"I needs to go home. Brooks is all alone. I need to go to him."

Grady shared a look with Steele. The last thing he wanted was to take her home. But she was right, Brooks was on his own. And at sixteen he could probably handle it. But they couldn't just call him and tell him they were stealing his aunt for the night.

"We'll take you home," Steele said.

"Good. I want my bed." She moved her feet back and forth. "Why aren't I moving?"

"Because you're not standing, baby," Steele told her with a grin.

Grady stood and then helped her up, holding her steady against his chest.

"You smell so good."

"Is that another seecit?" Grady asked.

"Why would it be a secret? Don'ts you know how you smell? Silly man. Lucky you're so cute."

"Cute and pretty?" Grady said in a mock growl. "I ought to spank you just for that."

"Promises, promises."

He gave Steele a surprised look, to find the other man was grinning.

"Come on," Steele said. "Let's get Sleeping Beauty home to her bed."

"I's not Sleeping Beauty! I don't want to sleep for a hundred years, then be awakened with a kiss! Could you imagine that morning breath?"

Grady grinned.

"Oh, I'm sorry. Who are you then?" Steele asked in a serious voice.

"I's Belle. I tame monsters."

"You certainly do," Steele told her, staring at her like he'd never seen her before. "The monster-tamer."

Grady knew that Steele often saw himself that way. He'd been called the Beast when he was cage fighting. And with what he did for a living, sometimes he thought himself a monster.

And if he was, then Grady was too. And perhaps that wasn't a bad thing. Because to keep yourself safe sometimes you needed to be a monster.

Besides, if it meant keeping Effie safe, he'd be whatever he needed to be.

"Come on. Let's get you home." Steele stood before taking her back into his arms.

He held her cradled against his chest like a baby with his arm under her ass.

"I puked," she said miserably.

"I know, baby," Steele soothed. "We'll get you some water, all right?"

"It's gross."

"I know. Shh, don't worry about that. Nobody cares that you were vomiting."

"What's wrong with me? Why do I feel so funny? I don'ts like it. My pills have never made everything go so weird."

"I don't know. But we'll find out. That I promise you."

They managed to get a few sips of water into her before she snuggled her face into Steele's neck. He rocked her back and forth as Grady gathered her stuff up and a blanket to wrap around her.

Grady gave him a surprised look. "You rocking her to sleep?"

"It's working, isn't it? She's fallen asleep."

Grady gave him a small smile. "The two of you look good together."

Maybe they didn't need him.

"Three of us would look fucking better," Steele told him gruffly.

Grady felt his doubt leave him. The three of them. It had always been the two of them. But perhaps it had never felt completely right because something had been missing.

And now . . . it was the three of them.

Grady moved toward them. Taking care of someone still didn't come naturally. He wasn't sure it ever would.

Although it had come naturally before. When he'd cradled her close.

So maybe things came more easily when it was Effie.

He pressed his chest to her back and breathed in her scent. Bubblegum.

So Effie.

"She's gorgeous, isn't she?" Steele said.

"Precious," he murmured.

"I want to keep her, Grady."

Grady nodded. That's what he wanted too.

"Come on, let's go. Raul is waiting outside," Steele said. "We can check the cameras later."

Steele turned away and Grady followed, carrying her handbag. They were nearly at the back entrance when he heard someone yell out to them. Turning, Steele saw Lex walking toward them.

"Is she all right? Is Effie okay? I didn't have time to check on her again after I threw that guy out."

Fuck. They'd forgotten about the asshole who'd grabbed her.

"She's fine," Grady told him. "She took some painkillers and they reacted badly."

"That's not good. Should she be taking them?"

"We think someone might have given her something that reacted with them," Steele told him grimly. "We're going to get her home now."

"She's a good girl."

"That guy, he's banned for life," Steele stated firmly. "You get any identification?"

"No, but I'd know him if I saw him again. He won't be getting back in here."

"Good man." Steele nodded to him.

They headed out to the car, where Raul already had the door open for them, and got her seated between them with her belt on. She was slumped against Steele, but her hand rested on his thigh.

And he didn't feel the urge to move it.

Strange.

He wasn't one for casual touch. A handshake wasn't a problem. Touching a sub to bring them pleasure or pain was not really an issue either. Sex. He did it because he felt the urges, same as anyone else. But often, his hand did just as good a job. If not better, since he didn't have to engage in interactions after.

Steele usually took care of that part for him.

However, keeping detached from Effie was damn near impossible.

To distract himself, Grady looked out the window at the neighborhood Effie lived in. "I don't like bringing her back here. It doesn't feel safe."

"She's been living here for a long time."

Grady didn't take offense at Steele's words because he knew that he wasn't saying that he thought she'd be fine.

He was saying that because he wanted to point out to Grady how his thinking had changed about her.

"I know, but it doesn't feel good enough for her now."

"You know I don't like it that she's here either. I'd take her home with us, if it wasn't for a couple of things."

Right. And he knew what one of those things was. "Brooks."

"We can't take her home with us and leave him on his own. And we can't uproot him suddenly. He's a smart kid, but he's still only sixteen."

Yes. Grady understood that.

"I want her in our house," Steele replied. "That's what will happen eventually. But tonight, we take her home."

He didn't like it. But he understood it.

As Raul pulled up outside her house, he exited the car and held the door open for Steele. He'd already found her keys in her handbag. As well as her stuffed toy sloth.

He wondered if the sloth had a name. No doubt it did.

After unlocking the door to her apartment, he held that door open too.

Fuck. This place was smaller than he'd thought.

"See if Brooks is home," Steele ordered, carrying Effie inside.

But he didn't need to go looking for him as one of the internal doors opened and Brooks stood there, staring at them both, wide-eyed. "What's going on? Mr. Steele? What are you both doing here? Shit. Effie! What happened to Aunt Effie?"

"Shh, man," Steele told him in a gruff voice. "Everything is fine. Your aunt is fine. And call me Steele. None of that mister shit. This is Grady, Effie's other boss."

Brooks nodded to him. "Right. Aunt Effie texted earlier and said she had to work late. That's not good for her, having to work long hours. The doctors said . . . "

"What did the doctors say?" Grady asked as he trailed off.

"It . . . it doesn't matter. That's Aunt Effie's business. I wasn't supposed to overhear them. But I don't like her working late." He glared at them both. "Why did you make her stay?"

"Brooks, calm down," Steele said firmly, standing there with her in his arms like she didn't weigh a thing. "We didn't know she'd decided to work to cover a server's shift. Or we would have brought her home ourselves earlier."

Brooks visibly relaxed. "Oh. Sorry. I just . . ."

"You're protective of her," Grady said. "You shouldn't have to apologize for that."

"Uh, yeah. She's all I've got. She's always taken care of me. And she needs the same in return." Brooks frowned. "She passed out after taking her painkillers? The prescription ones in the bottle?"

"Yeah. Does that happen often?" Steele asked.

Brooks shook his head. "No, but she doesn't take them often. And usually, she waits until she's home and safe to take them. She must have been really hurting."

"Or she took them hoping she could keep working for a bit longer," Steele said.

"She needs to go to bed," Grady said firmly. "Where is her bedroom?"

To his surprise, Brooks went red.

"It's all right," Grady told him. "Steele will just carry her in and put her to bed. That's all."

"Um, no, that's not it," Brooks said. "Put her in my bed."

Grady stared at him, not understanding. "She sleeps in your bed?"

"No! Jeez. That's her bed." He pointed at the couch.

Steele looked at the couch, then at Brooks. "She sleeps on the couch?"

Grady knew that tone of voice. He was only keeping it together because he held something precious in his arms.

"Yeah . . . I keep telling her to take the bedroom. But she always says that teenage boys need their privacy and that she's shorter so it's better for her to take the couch."

Now he understood the red on Brooks' cheeks. He wasn't worried that they intended to do something to his aunt. He was embarrassed because he was sleeping in a bed while she slept on a sofa bed in the fucking living room.

And he understood why Steele was close to the edge.

Because it wasn't good enough.

Effie was right. Brooks needed his own space. He needed good sleep. But she wasn't right in thinking that she needed to sleep on the couch.

What about her back?

"This isn't good enough," he said.

Brooks' shoulders drooped. "I know. But whenever I offer to quit school and get a job, Aunt Effie says over her dead body. She always said we were close to getting a better place. But then she lost her job and had to use her savings to keep us going. Really. Put her in my bed. I'll take the couch tonight."

Steele glanced over at Grady. He nodded. It would have to do. For tonight, at least.

Fuck. He'd intended on sleeping on the couch tonight, wanting to ensure she was all right. He guessed the floor would be all right. But he wasn't sure how Brooks would feel about him sleeping on the floor of his bedroom.

"We should stay," Steele said. "Make sure she's okay."

Brooks gave him an alarmed look. Glancing back and forth between them, he straightened his shoulders. "I have this. I can take care of my aunt."

"She was pretty out of it," Grady told him. "Almost like she was drunk."

Brooks frowned. "Really? The pills aren't usually that bad."

"Has she ever drunk any alcohol while taking them?" Grady asked him.

Brooks jerked. "No! She doesn't even like alcohol. I've only seen her take a few sips of Baileys during the holidays. Aunt Effie doesn't drink or use drugs. She would never abuse drugs either. She hates taking painkillers."

"Nobody is accusing her of anything, kid," Steele said gruffly. "Let's get her resting, yeah? Then we can talk about her care."

Brooks led them into a large bedroom with a queen-sized bed, a desk with a few books on it, plus a nightstand with a lamp.

Not a typical teenage boy's room. He couldn't even see any dirty socks on the floor.

"I just changed my sheets today," Brooks said, gathering up some pillows to make them into a U-shape.

"What are you doing?" Grady asked.

"Aunt Effie likes to feel surrounded when she sleeps. And it will stop her rolling around. She's been known to roll out of bed before."

Hmm. That wouldn't be good with her sore back. He wondered if she needed one of those beds with sides on them.

Steele laid her down in the middle of the U-shape, then Grady reached down to tug off her confetti shoes. He needed to get her those light-up shoes. He drew off her shoes, noting that her feet were swollen.

Was that due to poor circulation?

"Her feet are swollen," he commented to Steele.

"Oh, they often are," Brooks said. "She likes to sit with them up. They're not as bad when she's not on her feet all day like she was at her last job. When they used to get bad, she'd go to the mall and get a foot massage. When we had the money."

Good to know.

Steele drew the covers over her. And Grady wondered if he'd kiss her good night. But they both sensed Brooks was on edge, so they tucked her in and walked with Brooks out to the living room.

"I need to get her a glass of water. She always gets thirsty in the night." Brooks rushed to the small kitchenette, giving them another wary glance on his way past.

"He's not going to be okay with us staying the night," Grady told Steele.

"I know."

"I don't want to leave, though."

"I know," Steele repeated with a sigh.

Brooks came back. "Um, well, thanks for bringing her home. You guys aren't like her last boss. He'd have yelled at her, upset her, then expected her to keep working."

"Yeah, I'm going to need the name of that jerk."

Brooks eyed Steele with not a small amount of hero worship.

Grady understood that look. It was the same one that had likely been on his face when he'd first met Steele. Even though they were both thirty-nine, sometimes Grady still felt that hint of hero worship.

Steele took no shit from anyone. He was a hard man.

But when you were in with him . . . then you were all the way in. Sometimes, that wasn't always a great thing because they were both men who liked to be in control.

But most of the time, it was.

Because he was family.

The only family Grady had. The only one he claimed, anyway.

And he was Steele's family.

"Those boys that attacked me that day . . . they all apologized."

Steele crossed his arms over his chest. "Did they?"

"Yep. One of them looked like he was gonna piss himself while he did it. You did that, didn't you?"

Steele didn't reply.

"I looked into you. You were a cage fighter for years. And you were good at it." Brooks cleared his throat. "And you own a stripper bar. Where my aunt works."

Fuck. Had he heard about everything else?

Brooks looked off into the distance. "And I've heard that you don't always operate on the right side of the law."

Yep. Fuck.

"And you think that makes me a bad person?" Steele asked calmly.

"My aunt works for you both. I want her to be safe. I have to keep her safe. She's all I have. I'm all she has."

"No," Steele said quietly. "You were all she had. She was all you had. Now, you have us too."

"Why?"

"We care about your aunt. We want to look after her. And you."

"Steele, this might be too much," Grady warned. "He's only a kid."

Brooks frowned at him. "I've got to protect my aunt. He gets that." He pointed at Steele.

"Here's the thing, Brooks," Steele said. "Yeah, I operate outside the law sometimes. But I care about your aunt. A lot. I've only known her a short time, so I'm trying not to overload her. But she has my protection."

"What if your other *work* comes back on Effie? What if you're putting her in danger?"

"I won't allow that to happen." Steele kept his gaze steady on Brooks.

The kid nodded.

"Your aunt only deals with our legal operations," Grady said carefully. He still wasn't certain that this was a good conversation to have with him.

"Aunt Effie seems like she's naive, she's always trying to see the good in people. And she doesn't like to upset anyone. But don't think she's stupid," Brooks warned. "She's not. I'm sure she knows something."

Steele nodded. "She said she's heard rumors."

"Right. So this, whatever it going on between you guys, this isn't just . . . fuck, it's not about sex, is it?"

It was clear Brooks was uncomfortable asking that.

Grady was going to let Steele do the talking as he felt uncomfortable as hell too.

"We like your aunt, Brooks," Steele said firmly.

"We?" He looked between Grady and Steele. "Right. Yeah. Fuck. Aunt Effie has never had a boyfriend. I mean, maybe when I was young and can't remember it. I don't know if she's ready for two."

"Your aunt is special," Grady told him. "And she needs

people who will look after her. Having both of us . . . it means another person to protect her."

"I won't have her used or ridiculed. I know you think I'm just a kid, but one day I will be someone. So you hurt her, I will come for you both."

Fuck. The kid had balls.

Huge fucking balls. Bigger than most guys he knew.

"I have no doubt about that," Steele said. "But we're going to try our best not to hurt Effie. I'm having this conversation with you out of respect to you as her protector. You need to know that that's going to become our job, though. And that means that soon you guys won't be living here. It means that soon, Effie won't have to sleep on a couch. You won't be in a neighborhood that neither of us likes for you. And you won't have to worry about bullies at school or neighbors upstairs being loud, and Effie won't have to worry about a fucking thing."

Brooks stared at Steele with wide eyes.

Okay, that might have been too much. Even for a mature kid like Brooks.

"I get that we might seem like we have nothing, but we have each other. And I'm still gonna protect her. Which means I won't let you push her into anything she doesn't want. I'm not sure how she's going to react to both of you wanting her."

"We're prepared to move slowly so as not to spook Effie," Steele told him.

"How long do you think she'll need in order to agree to move out of here?" Grady said. He hated that she lived in this dump. Even if it was better than where he'd grown up. But not by much.

Effie was a good guardian to this kid though. Because there had been no way his parents would have given up a bed for him. He'd slept on a mattress on the floor.

"I don't know."

Grady turned to Steele. "If it's going to be longer than a few days, we should get her some sort of orthopedic topper for the sofa bed. And a security system. Maybe a guard."

"Guard?" Brooks asked. "I thought you said she wouldn't be in danger?"

"She won't be," Steele said firmly. "But that's because we intend to make her as safe as we can. That might seem overwhelming, but we both protect those who belong to us. And that includes you too."

"I don't need protection."

Grady thought about reminding him about those boys who attacked him. And how Steele had taken care of them, by scaring the living shit out of their parents.

But he decided not to.

He understood pride. A bit too much.

"Got that," Steele said. "Still going to protect you. Because that's what a man does. That means I'm going to have a guy watching this place. Not because Effie is in danger but because we're claiming her. And it's something we should have already done."

"That's not necessary." Brooks gave him a wary look.

"It's called taking care of you both," Steele replied. "We're going to be back first thing in the morning with breakfast. Unless you need us to stay."

Grady wanted to insist they stay, but when he shot a look at Steele, he gave him a firm look back.

Fuck it.

"No. She'll just sleep. I'll keep an eye on her."

"You need your sleep, kid," Steele said. "Make sure you get it."

Brooks threw his shoulders back. He wasn't ready for them to look out for him. Probably a good thing since Grady didn't have a clue about looking after a sixteen-year-old kid.

"I can take care of myself."

"Sorry. Meant no disrespect. You have my number, use it if you need to."

Brooks just nodded.

"Lock up behind us," Grady urged.

"I always lock up."

26

After making sure that Brooks had locked up, they walked to the car and got in. But Steele didn't tell Raul to leave yet.

"That went better than I thought," Steele said.

"It did?" How was he expecting it to go?

"Kid is protective of his aunt. But I think he knows I'll look out for her since I looked out for him with those little assholes who were bullying him. He's a good kid, and Effie had a big hand in raising him. And that's despite the fact that she's obviously had a lot of struggles. She's strong."

Good. Effie was going to need to be strong in order to be with them.

"I don't want to leave her," Grady said. "Not when she's . . . vulnerable."

"I don't either. But the kid was going to freak if we said we were staying."

"Never known you to care so much about someone else's feelings when you want something," Grady commented.

"He means a lot to her. She freaked the fuck out when she

thought he was in trouble at that school. The kid is her kid, even if she didn't give birth to him. That means we have to tread carefully with both of them. I'm not real good at treading carefully, we both know that. So I'm going to need your help."

Ordinarily, he'd give Steele whatever he asked for. But in this instance, he wasn't sure that he could help Steele hold back.

"I'll try. It won't be easy, though. I want her out of there. Both of them."

Steele grunted, but he was clearly deep in thought. He hit the privacy screen button, lowering it. "Take us back to Pinkies, Raul."

"You bet," Raul replied.

He raised the screen again before turning to Grady. "She's definitely a Little."

"Yes, she is."

"You're not a Daddy Dom."

Grady frowned.

"I wasn't going to say anything bad about that. Just feeling you out . . . are you all right with her Little side? You know I'll take care of her. You don't have to do any of that."

Grady tapped his fingers against his thigh, thinking. "I know that. But if this happens again. Or if she needs to regress . . . I want to know how to take care of her."

Steele shot him a startled look. "Yeah?"

"Yes. Perhaps there is some Daddy Dom in me after all. I'm not sure how it will go, though. Perhaps I'll fail at it."

"Thomas, you've never failed at anything in your life."

Steele using his first name hit him hard. Like a dart aimed at his heart. Which had long ago been surrounded by a fence of concrete and barbed wire.

Which only Steele could ever infiltrate.

"That's not true," he murmured. "There was that algebra test in sophomore year."

"Fuck, all of us failed that. That asshole teacher had it in for us."

Yes, and Grady had arranged a small surprise for Mr. Ryland later on that week. When his wife had gotten a letter at her work, containing images of Mr. Ryland . . . taking a strap-on up the ass.

One attached to his girlfriend.

He smiled to himself. He might not be obvious when he threw his weight around. Or intimidate and scare like Steele did just by being Damon Steele.

But he had his own way of getting even.

"We need to move forward," he said. "With Effie. This can't be allowed to happen again."

"And we start with lunch tomorrow." Steele grinned at him.

Right.

When they got back to Pinkies, he immediately went to his computer to check the cameras. Steele followed him into the room.

It didn't take him long to find what he was looking for since he had the time frame already.

"That. Mother. Fucking. Bitch."

"Show me." Steele watched the feed, and Grady could feel the anger emanating from him.

Fuck.

"I'm going to fucking kill that bitch! She knew. And she gave her vodka? What the fuck was she hoping to achieve?"

"To make a fool out of Effie? To make it seem like she was drunk on the job? Maybe to get her fired?" he guessed. "Likely all three is my guess."

"I'll teach her to mess with our girl." Steele straightened.

"Wait." Grady grabbed his arm. Christ. He liked touching the other man.

He liked it far too much.

"For fucking what?"

"To calm down."

"Why would I want to do that?" Steele demanded.

"Because if you go out there and confront that bitch right now, things could get carried away. Let's get someone there with us. I'll call Lex in. Get him to bring her."

"Fuck it. Fine."

Ten minutes later, Lex arrived with Lucy. She smiled at them both. Christ, did she think that smile was sexy?

It was the sort of smile that would give you nightmares. With lots of teeth and little soul.

Lex planted himself at the door, giving nothing away. But he was there as a witness and to get rid of the bitch if she went psychotic.

"You want to tell us why you put vodka in Effie's drinks?" Grady demanded. He wasn't in a mood to play with her, as gratifying as that might be.

That smile dropped. Although she didn't keep the shocked look for long. Smart. She was intelligent. Even if she was a bitch.

"I don't know what you're talking about. I didn't put any vodka in her drinks."

"No?" Grady asked, leaning back in his chair. He didn't have to look behind him to know that Steele was there.

Backing him up.

Always backing him up.

"No. And if that's what she said then she's a liar as well as a pill pusher."

"What makes you think she's a pill pusher?" Steele asked.

She turned her gaze to him, obviously liking his attention.

Okay, he was going to revise that thought about her being intelligent.

"When I got her handbag, a bottle of pills fell out. I picked them up. They looked like some strong painkillers."

"They are," Grady confirmed. "She has an old injury that she sometimes has to take painkillers for."

"Well, maybe she got addicted to them. That happens." She gave them a look of fake sympathy. "Poor Effie."

"Effie isn't addicted to her painkillers," Grady told her. "And she knows better than to drink alcohol with them. Because it says on the bottle not to and Effie is a rule follower." Mostly. "Actually, Effie doesn't drink at all beyond some Baileys at Christmas."

"If that's what she told you—"

"She didn't tell us jack shit, woman," Steele snarled.

Okay, Steele was about to lose it.

"You set her up," Grady accused her. "You saw those pills in her handbag, read the label. Then you saw her take them, and when she told you that she didn't want any alcohol in her drinks, you put some in them anyway."

"You have no proof of that."

Now the bitch had smartened up. Her face was pale.

"Actually, we do. Got Nate, who witnessed Effie telling you no booze, and we have you on camera, putting fucking booze in her drinks!" Steele thundered.

She jumped with a squeal. Yeah, she'd never encountered Steele like this. Mostly because Steele had never had much to do with her.

How she ever thought she was going to catch Steele's eye, Grady had no idea.

"But . . . how?"

"I had other cameras installed," Grady told her. "I'm just not very trusting."

"Thank fuck," Steele said. "Now, go gather whatever shit you have here because you ain't never coming back. Lex is gonna go with you to make sure you don't grab anything you're not supposed to. And to make sure you fucking leave. Don't ever let me see you here again."

That's when a calculating look came over her face.

And the real Lucy appeared.

"Are you threatening me?" she asked. "Because that would be a very bad thing."

Turning, he took in Steele's smile. Which wasn't a smile at all, but a promise. And if the stupid bitch didn't realize that . . .

"Go. Now," Grady snarled.

"I can make things difficult for you . . . for this place . . . all it would take is a word in the wrong people's ears."

"Get . . . out . . . now!" Steele thundered.

She jumped again and Lex took hold of her arm. She shook his hand off her. "Get your filthy hand off me." She stormed out.

"Don't worry, I'll make sure she goes," Lex said.

"Make sure she goes quietly. And not out the front," Grady said. "She's likely to try and make a scene."

"Oh, I know. That bitch is all about the drama." Lex turned and walked away.

"Think she'll be trouble?" Grady asked.

"Her? No. What's the worst she can do?"

Hmm. A woman scorned? Probably more than they thought.

27

Effie woke with a thumping headache.

Opening her eyes, she glanced around, unsure where she was.

She was in a bed. In a dark room. Her heart raced until her brain fully understood that this room was familiar.

This was Brooks' bedroom.

But why was she in his bedroom and not her own bed? And where was Brooks? And why did she have a bad feeling in her stomach?

There was a knock on the door.

"Come in."

She sat up as Brooks entered the bedroom, carrying a tray. On it was a plate of buttery toast. Yum. And coffee.

"You made me breakfast in bed? You didn't need to do that. You're too good to me." She reached for the coffee as he set the tray down on the nightstand and took a sip.

Ahh. That was perfection. Brooks knew exactly how she liked her coffee.

"Um, actually, I figured you'd probably need coffee this morning," he said hesitantly.

She watched him closely. "Does whatever you're about to tell me have something to do with why I'm in your bed? And why I have a bit of memory blank about how I got here?"

"Ah, yeah."

"Oh God, just tell me." The dread was almost too much to bear.

"You don't remember getting into my bed because, uh, you were asleep."

"Asleep?" How could she get into bed if she was asleep?

"Uh-huh, and, uh, Mr. Steele carried you to bed."

"Oh my God, no," she breathed out.

"Yes."

"No."

"Uh, yeah, Aunt Effie."

"Fuck. Sorry, shouldn't have said that."

Brooks' lips twitched. "I've heard the word fuck before."

"But not from me."

"What about that time you stubbed your toe against the coffee table? Or when you spilled spaghetti all down your shirt? Or when you saw a mouse in the pantry?"

"All right, I get it. How come you have to have such a good memory? Why couldn't you be one of those unobservant kids?"

Brooks just grinned as he sat on the side of the bed, watching her.

"You want to do me a favor and forget all those times?" she asked.

"Sure, Auntie, I'll get right on that."

She sighed and ran her hand over her face. "What the hell happened?"

"They said you took some of your pain pills."

"They?" she asked.

"Um, Mr. Steele and Mr. Grady. Your bosses."

"Holy crap." They'd both been here? "Shit. I don't usually drop into a coma like that." Sure, the pills made her tired. Maybe a bit loopy if she took them on an empty tummy. But she was never completely out of it.

And she felt like there was more to it. What wasn't she remembering?

"They didn't like that you sleep on the couch."

"What?" She froze. Fuck. They'd been in the apartment?

Of course they have. Steele carried you to bed.

"Yeah. They didn't like it at all. And when I told them I had offered to sleep on the couch, they didn't like that either. Effie . . ."

"Yeah?"

"They said they were leaving someone out the front of the building to make sure we were safe."

"What?" she whispered. "Why? Are we not safe?"

"I think . . . I kind of think they wanted to stay. To make sure that you were all right. But they didn't want to push me, and so they, um, they said to call them if you needed them and that someone would be sitting in a car out front all night."

What the heck?

"That seems . . . intense." Kind of scary. And kind of, well, caring? Was she nuts to think that?

"Aunt Effie? I don't know any other bosses who act like they do. They seem . . . they really seem to care about you."

"I don't . . . I don't really know what's going on. But they have a rule about getting involved with any of their employees."

"Right. Well, I'm just saying . . . they might be breaking their own rule. And I guess if you make the rule, you get to change it."

"I guess." She probably shouldn't be having his conversation with her sixteen-year-old nephew.

"Did they . . . did I . . . ?" She cleared her throat.

Be the adult, Effie.

"I'm sorry if I embarrassed you."

Brooks scowled. "How would you do that?"

"By passing out and getting carried into bed. And I'm sorry you had to sleep on the couch. I hope you weren't scared."

"Aunt Effie, I wish you'd sleep in the bed. I've told you that lots of times. It should be me sleeping out there. And not just because you have a bad back. But because I should be between you and the front door."

"What?"

"Royal and Baron say that a man is no man if he doesn't do his best to protect the women in his life."

Yikes.

"But it's my job to protect you." She was the adult.

"I'm getting older, Aunt Effie," he said gently. "I'm not a kid anymore."

She sighed and nodded. "I know. Truth is, I'm not sure you were ever a kid. Well, except when I was changing your diapers."

He groaned. "Let's not go there."

"Your dad used to hold his breath while he was doing it. I swear he nearly passed out several times."

"Aunt Effie! Shut up!"

"Sorry." She held back her grin. Sure, it was her job to embarrass him. But it was also her job to acknowledge that he wasn't her little boy anymore. He was a young man. "Baron and Royal seem to have some, um, interesting opinions."

"They're good guys."

"I'm sure they are."

"They look after their stepmom. And they say her boyfriend is a good guy too. They told me he's going to propose soon. He showed them the ring and asked their permission first."

"Really? That's so sweet."

"You're not going to cry, are you?" Brooks gave her a horrified look and she smiled at him. There was still some teenage boy in there.

"I'm good."

"They also said that they know about Steele and Grady because Ink, their stepmom's boyfriend, is good friends with Steele's brother-in-law."

His brother-in-law?

"So they've heard things and they said that we might hear things too. Some of them good, some of them not."

"What?" she whispered.

"Do you know anything about what Steele does?"

Shit.

Yeah, she knew. Because she wasn't an idiot. And because she'd been warned.

But she hadn't intended to tell Brooks. Because she didn't want him to know how desperate she'd become.

Desperate enough to work for a man who had a . . . reputation. The thing was, the thing that Chardonnay had made clear was that Steele was a good boss. And that nothing bad ever touched the people who worked for him.

"I know."

Relief filled Brooks' face, which confused her.

Then she got it. He was worried he'd have to tell her.

"And you're okay with that?" he asked.

"Kind of? I mean . . . I've heard things, but they're rumors. You know I don't like to judge or make assumptions about people. And the thing is . . . sometimes good people do bad things. Or they get in trouble for good reasons. And sometimes, the world isn't black and white. There's gray in there."

"I know, Aunt Effie. It's all right."

She tugged at her sloth earring. "I'm not sure if your dad would approve of me working for a guy who . . . who doesn't always operate on the right side of the law. I'm not sure he'd like them around you."

Especially not after what Brooks' mother had done.

"Dad isn't here," Brooks told her. "And this is different from the woman who birthed me."

"Brooks,"

"I was worried in the beginning that you might get hurt. That they might hurt you or someone close to them. But . . . the way they were with you last night. Having a guy sitting in a car outside our place all night . . . those aren't the actions of guys who would hurt you."

"Yeah, I don't think so either." She took another sip of coffee. Damn, she felt like crap this morning. What had happened? Why did she basically pass out? And what else happened?

"I'm gonna meet up with Baron, Royal, and some other friends soon. Are you all right on your own?" Brooks asked her.

"Yes, of course. Is Stella one of those friends?" she asked.

His cheeks went red. "Uh, yeah."

She didn't push him any further. "I'm glad you're friends with those boys. Are you . . . are those boys at school . . . they're not bullying you anymore?"

To her shock, Brooks grinned. "Nah, Auntie. You don't have to worry about them. Every time they see me coming, they basically run the other way. And not just because I'm friends with Royal and Baron. But because of who *you're* friends with."

"Huh?" she asked.

"Steele told me he was going to take care of things, and he did. Another reason I'm cool if you want to, you know, get involved with him. Or with Grady. Or with both of them."

"Both of them?"

"Don't act so shocked. I see the smut you read."

"Brooks Keaton!" She gave him a shocked look. "What are you doing looking at what I read?"

"Can't help it if you leave the books out." He stood as she mock-glared at him.

"You shouldn't be looking! And it is not smut." She crossed her arms over her chest.

"Oh, yeah." He grinned. "Should I tell my English teacher that we should study one of your books instead of Othello?"

"Don't you dare!" He turned and raced out of the room as she grabbed a pillow to throw at him. "Brat! Someone obviously didn't raise you right!"

He peeked around the edge of the door. "Are you forgetting that you raised me?"

She huffed. But she smiled after he left. Then she lay back on the bed.

What the heck happened last night?

∽

An hour later, Effie was brushing her hair when a loud knocking on the door made her jump.

"What the heck?"

Who would that be? It was midday on a Sunday. Pinkies was closed on Sundays and Mondays. She'd intended to spend the day cleaning the apartment, grocery shopping, then watching a movie. Brooks was at Baron and Royal's place and wasn't coming back until dinnertime.

Putting down the brush, she let out an irritated sigh as the knocking continued.

"All right, I'm coming. I'm coming." She opened the door with a slam. "What do you want?"

"Good morning," Grady replied.

"More like afternoon," Steele added, looking her up and down. His lips quirked.

She glanced down at herself, blanching as she realized she

had on her house-cleaning outfit. Which consisted of a slightly ratty T-shirt with a picture of a sloth on it, which said: Not to brag, but I got out of bed today.

It was oversized and faded from being washed so much.

Underneath, she wore a pair of tights that had pictures of dancing pigs on them.

Shit.

"Sorry, I didn't know it was you guys. I'm not . . . I, uh . . . I was about to clean the apartment," she said lamely.

Don't just stand there, blathering on, Effie, or they're going to think you're not normal.

She plastered a smile on her face. "Good morning. This is a lovely surprise."

"Don't," Steele warned.

"Um, don't what?"

"Fake smile. I don't like it."

"She does it a lot," Grady said, walking inside. Well, pushing his way in, since she didn't invite him. "Especially when she's embarrassed or thinks she's been rude."

Steele followed but paused in the doorway to stare down at her intently. "Fucking adorable."

What?

Did he . . . he didn't really think that, right? She was a mess.

Although at least she'd had a shower and brushed her teeth.

"Close the door before you let all the heat out," Steele ordered. He glanced around. "Fuck."

"What?"

"Thought it might look better in the daylight. Think it looks worse."

"Hey! That's not very nice." Although this place was kind of a dump, at least it was clean. And she was doing the best she could.

"Fuck," Steele muttered again. Then he was in front of her, cupping the side of her neck again.

Damn. So warm.

"Sorry, baby. Nothing against you. Just don't like you living here. All the light and beauty that is you shouldn't live here in the dark."

She just stared up at him, mouth open.

She waited for Nan to give her some unwanted advice. But there was nothing. Even Nan didn't know how to reply to a big bruiser of a man, who didn't always operate on the right side of the law, being so damn sweet it was shocking.

He ran his thumb over her cheek and her legs gave out. She would have fallen to the floor if Grady hadn't moved in behind her.

Damn.

She closed her eyes, wanting to savor this feeling.

Because being between the two of them? It kind of felt like heaven. She'd experienced it once. And like the greedy person she was. She wanted more and more.

Being between the two of them made her feel so warm. As though she had someone she could lean on and into because they could take the weight of her life and lessen it for her.

Make it so she could conquer anything.

"Baby, you need to turn the heating up in here," Steele lightly scolded. "You're cold."

"I'm always kind of cold. I turn it up much more and poor Brooks roasts to death."

"Then you should have socks on," Grady said.

"Or her slippers. Put thick socks on the list."

"List? What list?" she asked.

"The 'things we need to provide for Effie' list," Steele told her.

"You do not have any such list," she said, glaring up at him.

He just looked down at her. His face was serious.

Lord help her.

"You guys don't need to keep buying me stuff."

"Gonna disagree with you about that, baby girl," Steele replied.

Then he stepped back and she stumbled forward. But he grasped her around her hips, steadying her.

Then he turned her to face Grady, who studied her intently. "How are you feeling this morning?"

Was that why they were here on a Sunday? To check in on her?

What the heck had happened last night that they thought they had to come today and check on her in person?

"I'm good."

"Is your back sore?" Grady asked.

"No, it's fine. Thank you for asking."

Grady's face softened, growing warm. "You're welcome, Twinkletoes." He didn't touch her. But that look on his face . . . yeah, her legs were growing weak again.

"How about your stomach? Any nausea? Chills? Headaches?" he asked.

"Um, no. Is there a reason I would have those things?"

"You ever drunk alcohol while taking those pain pills of yours?" Steele asked gruffly.

She turned so fast that the room spun. An arm wrapped around her middle. That was something that Steele would do if he saw her growing dizzy. But Steele was in front of her.

Which meant that it was Grady who'd wrapped an arm around her. Trapped her to him. Holding her steady. And it was Grady who slid an arm under her legs and lifted her into his arms, carrying her to the sofa to set her down.

Brooks had put away the blankets and pillows and pushed the sofa together. Grady sat her down, then sat across from her on the coffee table. His knees were on either side of hers, trapping her.

"I didn't drink any alcohol," she told him. "I promise. I wouldn't do that with those pills. And I don't even like drinking."

"We know, baby girl," Steele reassured her.

"Then why would you ask that? What . . . what's going on? And what happened last night?"

"You don't remember it?" Grady asked.

"No. The last thing I really remember is Lucy getting me my handbag. And taking some painkillers. I wish I hadn't done that. But I've never reacted badly to them before."

"Don't worry about that right now," Grady told her. "Do you want to get changed?"

"Changed?" she asked. What was he talking about? Why would she need to change?

"Your clothes," he said. "Do you need to change your clothes?"

"I was just . . . these are my cleaning clothes. I wasn't expecting company." If they expected her to dress better, then they should have called first.

"She needs to put on a sweater, socks, shoes, a jacket, scarf, and gloves," Steele dictated, moving around the room. "Is that . . . does the floor go down right here?"

"Yeah, I think the foundation is sinking slightly."

Steele just stared at her for a long moment. "Why hasn't that been fixed?"

"Um, well, the landlord is kind of elderly. And I'm not sure that he could fix it." Other than bulldozing the place. And she would rather have somewhere to live than a house that was level.

"At least he put in security lights," Steele commented.

"Uh-huh."

Grady eyed her steadily. "Did he pay someone to install those lights?"

"Uh, no."

"So he got up on a ladder and did it?" Steele asked.

Shit.

"Coffee!" She jumped to her feet. "I need to get you coffee! And cookies! I must have cookies somewhere. Would you like cake?"

"You have cake?" Steele asked.

"Not yet. But give me an hour and I'll have cake. Not that you want to stay for an hour. I'll bring you one on Tuesday. What do you want?"

"Red velvet with cream cheese frosting," Grady demanded.

"Oh, you liked the last one?" she asked.

"Didn't even get a crumb. The big guy hogged it all."

"Whoa. That's a lot of cake to eat."

They both stared at Steele, who crossed his arms over his chest. "I'm a big guy."

That he was. He really was. And she had a thing for that. All those muscles . . . pinning her down . . . holding her tight while Grady lashed her pussy with his tongue. Was it wrong that she liked the idea of being held down? Of being . . . forced?

One of her previous lovers had tried to give her what she wanted in bed. But the other three had been kind of horrified. And she'd learned never to mention it again. And it wasn't like she'd had any sex in the last seven years.

Not since Joe died.

So maybe she wouldn't really be into that. She could only do it with someone she fully trusted anyway. So getting to where she was comfortable with being restrained . . . yeah, that took a bit.

And needless to say, she'd never mentioned the fact that she was a Little to any of them. That she liked to regress. That she enjoyed having someone look after her in pretty much all ways.

Only one person had ever given her a safe space to be herself.

And he was dead.

He was also the only man she'd ever loved. And he'd never known exactly how she'd felt about him.

And fuck, that still hurt.

"Effie? Have we lost you again?" Grady asked.

"Um, yeah, sorry." She smiled at them both. "Red velvet with cream cheese, I can do that. So if there's nothing else, I'll let you both get on with your day."

They didn't move.

Big surprise there.

Grady stood and got in her way. She swallowed heavily at the intense look on his face.

"These windows are so fucking old, you're losing heat constantly."

She glanced over at Steele. "What?"

"Place is falling down."

"No, it's not. It's fine."

Steele shot her a gaze. "Even you can't Pollyanna this place, baby."

Pollyanna this place?

"What does that mean?"

"Means you've got a habit of trying to make the best out of a bad situation. You look for the positive in everything."

"Is that bad?"

"Nope." Steele shook his head. "Not as long as you have someone who'll protect you if shit does go bad. Who'll make sure that no one takes advantage of your sweetness."

"Um, I don't really have that."

"You do now."

Holy. Crap. What was happening right now?

28

Grady stared down at Effie for a long moment.

He could tell she was freaking out. And he needed to do something to help her not freak out. But the problem was reassuring freaked out women wasn't a skill he really had.

"We're taking you for lunch," Grady stated.

"I don't understand what's going on," she whispered.

"What's happening is that we're going for lunch. Now, you have five minutes to get changed. If you want to."

"Or what?"

"Or you go as you are."

She glanced down at herself. "I can't go like this."

"Why not?" Grady thought she looked cute. He'd noticed she liked sloths. And cute earrings. He added those to the list of things they needed to buy for Effie. He also noticed that they didn't have a lot of stuff. It would make moving them to their place easier when the time came. But he wondered if there were things Brooks needed as well.

"I . . . I . . . these are my cleaning clothes."

He just stared down at her, still not seeing the problem.

"Go get changed, Effie," Steele told her in a low voice that held a hint of hardness. "We'll wait for you. You don't want to walk, I carry you. Got to get you in your coat first, though. And shoes. But we're taking you out for lunch. Now, off you go."

She just stared at him some more.

Then Steele made the next move. He drew her over to the bedroom door, then he gently but very deliberately patted her ass. "Go."

And she went. Which Grady was surprised at. Because he felt for sure that she might freak out. Start talking about sexual harassment. Or just plain harassment.

He let out a breath he hadn't known he was holding.

Steele gazed over at him, then back to the bedroom door. "Think she's getting dressed or sneaking out the window?"

"I have no clue."

A grin twisted up the ends of Steele's lips. "That's half the fun."

For him, maybe.

Grady liked a bit more predictability in his life. Well, not that every aspect of his life was predictable. It couldn't be with the job he had and the life they led. But what he could keep the same, he did.

"Should I go around and check she isn't climbing out the window?"

Steele shook his head. "Nah, Effie is a good girl. She won't sneak out. It wouldn't be polite."

"How do we get her past that?"

"Over being polite all the time?"

"Yeah. It's like she thinks she always has to be polite, and smile, and not make waves." That seemed a stressful way to live.

"We just need to get her barriers down," Steele said. "They were down last night. We need to keep them that way."

"You're saying she was the real Effie last night?"

"In part. She's taking a while." Steele moved closer to the door and knocked on it.

They both heard her squeal.

Wait. Did she keep her clothes in Brooks' bedroom? Grady guessed she had to, it wasn't like she had a closet out here.

Fuck, he hated this life for her.

He'd lived this life. And he'd had it worse. But he still really, really hated it for Effie.

"Effie? You getting changed? You need some help?" Steele asked.

"Yes!"

"Yes, you need some help?"

"No!" she cried out. Then the door opened and she glared up at Steele. "I'm getting dressed. I don't need help."

She slammed the door in his face. Something Steele wasn't used to. The other man turned and winked at Grady. "And that's how we get to the real Effie."

"By annoying her until she starts getting sassy?"

"Nothing wrong with throwing a bit of sass. Means she feels safe to do so. And if she throws too much sass at us or she's not doing what she's told when it comes to the important stuff, well, that's just a reason to tan her hide, isn't it?"

Hmm, the idea of turning Effie over his knee . . . of pulling up the T-shirt she was wearing and pulling down her pants and panties before spanking that round, heart-shaped ass. Yeah, he could actually totally get behind that.

Especially if she started getting too sassy for her own good.

She could give them some lip. But she wasn't allowed to put herself at risk. Or speak badly about herself. Or lie.

"By not leaving her alone with her own thoughts for too long. We can't let her get into her head. Nothing good comes from that."

All right. Grady could agree with that.

~

Steele did up the last buttons on her coat.

"Do you really think this is necessary?" she asked.

She could barely move.

"Got to keep you warm."

"We're going out for lunch. I'm going to walk from the apartment to your car. Then from the car to the place where we're eating. I'm not going out to traipse across Antarctica."

"You're going to wear the jacket and you're going to stop throwing sass at me."

"I am not throwing sass at you," she replied indignantly. "I'm just telling you that dying via suffocation because I have too many clothes on is not the way I want to go."

"Definitely getting sassy." He was grinning as he said this, which seemed in exact opposition to his words and the gruffness of his voice.

So she couldn't tell if he thought that was a good thing or not.

She was so confused by these guys. They were supposed to be her bosses.

But that wasn't the vibe they were giving her.

Steele was upset about the state of her apartment and overly concerned about how much clothing she wore. While Grady just watched her with an attentiveness that was both worrying and thrilling.

So confusing.

"Noted. If you start suffocating, I'll give you mouth-to-mouth."

She sucked in a breath.

Joking. He was joking.

Or was he?

Because she wouldn't object to some mouth-to-mouth.

Grady held out his hand to her. She looked down at him in confusion. Then she slapped her hand against his.

He stared at her for a long moment before his lips twitched. "Key, Effie."

Oh. My. God.

Why? Why did she keep doing that? What was wrong with her?

"Oh. Um. I . . . sure." She handed over her key. She wasn't even going to try and lock her door herself. No doubt, she'd drop her keys or make a complete idiot of herself.

Steele guided her out the door with his arm around her shoulders.

Another thing about looking like the abominable snowman while wearing about ten layers of clothing? She couldn't feel his arm around her.

And she liked feeling him. Knowing that he was anchoring her to him.

But there was one thing missing. And that thing was Grady.

She looked back at him, worried that he was feeling left out. But if she held out her hand to him . . . would he reject her?

Effie had an issue with rejection. No matter how nicely it was packaged, it would still be a rejection. And she wasn't sure that her heart could handle that.

And then Grady did something he rarely did . . . he offered her a small smile.

She gave one back.

And that . . . that felt more monumental than any touch.

Steele led down the path toward a huge, black truck.

"Where's Raul?" she asked.

"Day off," Steele replied.

"What?"

Steele's lips twitched. "We give him days off, you know. He's not in servitude to us or anything."

"Oh, I didn't mean. I just . . . I've ever seen you drive yourself before. Or this vehicle."

He just shrugged.

Grady moved ahead of them and opened the back door. Before she could even figure out how she was going to get up into the cab of the truck without making an idiot of herself, Steele wrapped his hands around her waist and lifted her into the air, settling her into the seat.

She squealed and turned back to glare at him. "You could've warned me."

"Seatbelt," was all he replied.

Jeez.

"I was going to do up my seatbelt," she muttered. "I don't have a death wish."

He froze and stared down at her.

Shit. She wished she hadn't said that. She bit her lip, looking away. Gently, he grabbed her chin and twisted her head back around.

"Baby, we'd never risk you. Never. Not by driving recklessly. Not by acting stupidly. Never."

She looked from him to Grady, who was already in the front passenger seat but had turned to look at her.

"I think I told you that's how Joe died. Brooks' dad and my best friend."

"You did," Steele said gently, brushing her hair off her face. "And that's how you injured your back."

"Yeah," she whispered. "The thing is, Joe, he . . . he would have . . . he likely would have survived if he'd been wearing his seatbelt. But he . . . um, well, I guess he thought he was invincible. No one is invincible."

"No, baby. No one is." Steele cupped her cheek. "I'm really sorry that happened to you."

"I survived. I wasn't sure I'd walk again. But I did it. I got custody of Brooks. Joe's will was clear. He had full custody and he didn't have any family, so Brooks became mine. His mother's family has never had anything to do with him." Should she mention the call from the lawyer? No, she hadn't heard anything more from him. "We survived. We did it. But without Joe . . . it was hard."

"You loved him?" Grady asked.

"Yeah. I loved him." She didn't try to deny it or justify it by saying he was her best friend. She just laid it out there.

Both men stared at her for a long moment. Then something sweet happened. Something so sweet that she knew she'd savor it for a long time.

Steele leaned in and pressed his lips to her forehead. Nothing else. Just that soft touch before he drew back and shut the door, walking around to the driver's door.

She let out a shuddering breath before an even sweeter thing happened as she did her seatbelt up.

Gardy reached back and squeezed her leg. "Sorry about your best friend, Twinkletoes."

"Me too."

They were silent as they drove and she knew it was her fault. She'd ruined things by getting too real.

People don't want to know your problems, Effie.

Be a good girl. Be happy. Smile.

"So? Where are we going?" she asked with a smile. "It's a nice day, isn't it?"

They stared at each other.

"Baby, it's gray and cold as fuck," Steele replied.

"Um, yes. But at least it's not raining or snowing, right? It can always be worse. This is a really nice truck. You take excellent care of it."

There wasn't even any dust. Or trash. Yikes, when she'd owned a car, that thing had been trashed.

"Gets us from point a to b," Steele said.

"Ah, right. So, what do you guys like to do on your days off?"

"You mean besides kidnapping our assistant?" Grady asked.

She stilled. "Um."

Grady turned to her. "Joking."

"You know how to do that?" she asked before she thought better of it.

"What?" Grady asked.

"Joke?"

His eyes widened as he stared at her.

"Forget I said that. Sorry, it was rude."

All of a sudden, Steele's laughter filled the cab of the truck. Grady glared at him. Crap, she needed a change of subject. But only one thing popped into her head.

"So, I, um, never did thank you for taking me home last night and putting me to bed. And, uh, Brooks said you had someone watching over the apartment all night? That's, uh, really sweet of you guys, but totally unnecessary."

They were silent and she saw them glance at one another. They did that a lot. Had these silent conversations.

"First, we're going to have a talk over lunch," Steele told her. "And part of that chat is going to be about you disobeying us and working longer hours than you are allowed to."

Allowed to?

Dear. Lord.

"Part of that chat is also going to be about your protection and how that's going to play out," he added.

"What do you mean, how it's going to play out?" she asked.

"It means that things might need to change a bit," Grady said. "We don't like your neighborhood or your apartment. We've made some safety changes, but if you insist on staying there, we need to make more."

"What? What changes? And why wouldn't I insist on living there? I have nowhere else to live."

"Sure, you do," Steele continued. "Eventually, you'll move in with us. Sooner rather than later, I'm thinking."

29

Was this a dream?

It had to be, right? Because Steele had not just said what she thought he'd said.

Eventually, you'll move in with us.

That had her more than a bit freaked out.

This was nuts.

More nuts than her usual nuts. Which was saying something.

"She's gone silent. That's not a good sign," Grady said.

"We need to get her out of her head."

Huh?

"I'm not in my head."

"Baby, you're totally in your head," Steele replied. "Perhaps, you should have ridden in the back with her. Kept her from overthinking."

"How would he have done that?" she asked curiously. Because she'd tried a lot of things. None of them worked.

"Well, I'd do it by kissing you," Steele said. "Not sure what Grady would do."

She couldn't breathe. Was he . . . was he serious?

She barely noticed him parking in front of a diner.

"I'm not . . . I don't understand what's happening," she whispered.

"I'm just going to lay it out there as we both like honesty," Steele said.

"All right." She braced herself.

"We both want you, Effie."

That . . . that was it?

They wanted to have sex with her?

There was no denying she wanted that too. But more than she wanted sex with them, she needed her job.

"I . . . I can't."

Grady turned to look at her. "This isn't a good place for this conversation."

Steele grunted. Was that a yes or a no grunt?

"You don't want us both?" Grady asked in a tight voice. She wasn't sure exactly what he was thinking. But she was still too busy reeling from what they'd said. It shouldn't be a complete surprise. She'd often wondered if Steele wanted her. But she hadn't thought he'd bring it up. And she hadn't been sure that Grady felt the same.

What about their rule about fucking employees?

Did that mean she was fired?

"This is . . . I can't even think . . ." Crap.

"This really comes as such a surprise?" Steele asked.

She shook her head. "Not exactly. You don't act like ordinary bosses. You call me baby and Twinkletoes. And you care about me. And help me. But I didn't think . . . you've got that rule about sleeping with your employees. Does that mean I'm fired?"

"No, Effie," Grady said firmly. "That's not what this is about."

"We don't want to fuck you, baby."

"I don't understand," she whispered.

"So much for blunt and to the point," Grady said dryly.

"What we are trying to say is that we want more with you, Effie," Steele told her. "We don't want a quick fuck. Baby, we want you. All of you."

They *wanted* her.

Wanted *her*.

"Both of you?" she managed to ask. She forced herself to look at them both as they turned to her.

"I want you, Effie," Steele said. "I want you in my bed. But more than that, I want the right to protect and take care of you, to nurture your dreams. Hug you when you're down and discipline you when you break your rules. I haven't felt this way about a woman. Ever. I . . . I lost my sister a long time ago and she was my world. She and Grady. After that, I decided I never wanted to be with anyone that I might risk losing. But you're in my head. You've snuck your way through my barriers. And now . . . I don't see my life without you in it."

"But we barely know each other." She licked her dry lips.

"That's why we're going to date. That's why we decided to take things slow. To get to know each other. But I think we've gone too slow. I want the right to take care of you. And I need people to know you're ours. So you have our protection. I also want to spank that delicious ass of yours, and taste your mouth whenever I feel like it. Along with other parts of you."

Holy. Crap.

Steele was raw, powerful sexuality. Way too much man for her. But Lord help her because she didn't have the power to say no to him.

That could be an issue. But only if he took advantage of her inability to turn him down. Which she was sure he wouldn't.

"You want to get to know me?"

"Yep."

"Because you want to fuck me and spank my ass?"

"Among other things." His lips twitched. "I was fucking bored with life, baby. Going through the routine without feeling much. In fact, the only thing that's really kept me going is Grady. Until you came into our life. You make me smile. Best part of my day is going in to see you, eating whatever you've baked, and seeing your smile light up the room. And I'm a greedy fucking bastard. Always have been. Because I want more of that. I want your light to be the first thing I see when I wake up and the last thing when I go to sleep at night."

It was too fast. Way too fast.

And yet, Effie knew better than most how precious life was. How someone you loved could be taken from you in the blink of an eye. Obviously, Steele had experienced that too.

"I'm sorry about your sister."

"Thank you, baby. I'll tell you about her one day."

She gathered up her courage. Because Steele was the easier one to read. Grady was far trickier. But that didn't mean he was any less important. And she didn't want to come between the two of them. She didn't want him to think that he had to be with her because Steele was into her.

And she didn't want him to think that she wanted him any less, if he truly wanted her.

"Grady?" she whispered. "Are you . . . do you . . . what do you want?"

He stared at her for a moment. "Part of the reason I wanted to hire you is because of that rule. Because I knew Steele wanted you. And the truth is, I wanted you too."

He'd hired her so she'd be off-limits?

"I don't understand. You didn't want to want me?" she asked.

"No. Because I knew you weren't a one-night stand kind of girl and, at the time . . . well, at the time I didn't think a relationship was something I wanted. Nor Steele. And more than you needed a night in our bed, you needed a job."

It hit her hard and fast. "You pitied me? That's why you gave me a job? Was there even a job?"

She needed out of here. Now. She reached for the door handle, opening the door. She tried to jump out, but her seatbelt caught her.

Fuck. She couldn't even make a proper getaway.

"Urgh, such an idiot!"

"That's five," Steele rumbled.

She froze. "Five what?"

"Five spanks. Once you agree to be ours and we're ready to move to that step, you're over my knee for five smacks to your ass. Not putting up with you putting yourself down anymore, baby girl."

Holy. Heck.

"Listen to me," Grady said in a low, commanding voice that had her eyes shooting to his. It was getting cold with the door open, but she didn't move to close it. "I knew you needed the job. I could tell you were down on your luck. But I would not have hired you if I didn't need help. And you've been an amazing assistant."

"I . . . I have?"

"Yes. You've made my life so much easier. Even if I think you're taking too much on and working too hard."

"I didn't want you to regret hiring me."

"I don't." It was said so firmly and with such certainty that the tightness in her chest eased.

She licked her lips. "What do you want?"

"You," he replied instantly. "I'm not good at this. At talking about emotions. At telling you what you mean to me or even showing it. But know this. I've never felt like breaking that rule. Until you."

Effie took several breaths, trying to soak in all of that information. She wished she could just say yes. But there were so many more things to think about. And now she could see why they'd made that rule.

"If this doesn't work... my job..."

"Your job is safe," Steele told her firmly. "If this doesn't work, and you can't stay working for us then we will help you find a new job."

"And pay your wages until you do," Grady asked. "We'll put that in writing."

Steele nodded.

Okay. That was... that actually took care of her biggest fear. Well, there was something else.

"Both of you?" she whispered.

"Both of us," Steele repeated, watching her steadily. He probably thought she was going to freak out. She had to admit... she was close to losing it.

"That's not... normal. I mean, I know that the two of you like to share. But you said yourself that you've never been in a relationship... what about what people will think? What if someone gets jealous? I don't... I don't want to come between you both."

"You won't," Steele said. "If we have problems, we'll talk to each other. Grady and I have been best friends since we were ten."

"Steele saved me from a bully," Grady added. "I was living in a foster home at the time. They were good people, but they weren't family. When I met Steele, that's who he became."

"So we know how to deal with each other. And we won't involve you in any arguments."

"That doesn't seem right." She frowned.

"No, that's us protecting you," Steele told her. "Which is our right as your men. We make your life easier, not harder. We're both men who like to be in charge in varying ways. I'm likely going to be extremely overprotective. Grady has a fixation on rules and control. You'll have enough to deal with. You don't deal with our shit too. Understand me? And I can safely say that as many of your worries, fears, and burdens that you want to give us, we want to take."

Lord.

Good Lord.

It was like they were made for her. Not having any worries or fears seemed like an impossibility. But if anyone could shoulder them it was the two of them.

"Brooks." It was all she could say, but she knew they'd get where she was coming from.

They shared a glance. "Baby, your kid is sixteen going on forty," Steele told her. "If I scared easily, it might scare me how mature he is."

"I know. But he's still a kid, and I need to look out for him. He's my responsibility."

"We understand that," Grady said. "And you've done an excellent job with him. What I can tell you is that he already has more than a bit of an idea about us. And he did not in any way seem concerned about both of us wanting you. Although he did tell us that if we hurt you, he would find a way to get revenge on us."

"He did?" she whispered. That was such a Brooks thing to do. "He's such a good kid."

"So if that's all the worries you've got at the moment, how about we go feed our baby?" Steele suggested.

Their baby.

She liked that.

But what would they think when they learned that she actually liked regressing? That she was a Little?

Part of her knew she had to tell them.

And part of her was scared too.

30

Effie had the look of someone who was going to bolt.

Grady understood that feeling. When it came to speaking about his emotions, acknowledging that he had them... yeah, he'd rather run.

Her eyes were wide, and she looked slightly ill as Steele took her hand to lead her into the diner. That could be why Steele had taken hold of her hand—to ensure she didn't bolt.

Although Steele was also far more demonstrative than Grady.

Not hard since Grady wasn't really touchy-feely at all.

But when it came to Effie, he wanted to touch her. He hung back, trying to regain his control, which also gave him the chance to watch the two of them.

God, they looked good together. Grady wasn't a small guy, but compared to Steele, he was. The other man was wide and tall. And while Effie wasn't tiny, she looked petite next to him.

Beautiful.

Suddenly, he was regretting hanging back. He wanted to be a part of the two of them. But how?

Then Effie turned and gave him a worried look. And she did something unexpected. She held out her hand to him.

As she did, she bit her lip. Steele turned to look at him, glanced down at her hand and grimaced.

No doubt he thought Grady would reject her. He leaned in to say something to Effie. Her face dropped. She tried to hide it by plastering on one of those fake smiles that Grady fucking hated.

Nope. Not on his watch.

As she dropped her hand, he stepped forward and took it, grasping it in his far bigger one.

"You don't have to if it makes you uncomfortable," she whispered up to him, trying to tug her hand free.

"Stop," he told her firmly. "You try to pull away from me and I'll be adding another five to Steele's."

He glanced over at Steele to check his reaction. The other man nodded at him.

When Grady looked down at Effie, he kind of expected her to be frowning or objecting. But her face had gone soft, filled with a sort of wonder.

Because he was touching her?

He needed to make an effort to do that more often then.

"People might stare," she said quietly.

"Do you really care?" Steele asked.

She looked from one to the other. Then a twinkle of adventure filled her eyes. "No. I don't think so. Most of them will probably just be jealous that I have two gorgeous hunks with me."

"Hunks?" Grady asked. "Do people still use that word?"

"Effie uses that word," she replied.

"And does Effie usually talk about Effie in the third person?" Steele asked, staring down at her like she was the most interesting person he'd ever met.

As though he wouldn't mind putting her in his pocket and carrying her around.

"Effie does when Effie feels like it." Then she started giggling.

Christ. He'd never heard her giggle like that. And he wanted to listen to it more often.

"Sorry." She sobered. "I, uh, maybe I need some lunch."

"Don't apologize for that," Grady said sharply.

She glanced up at him in surprise.

"If I could hear you laugh every day for the rest of my life, then I would've lived a rich life."

He heard her suck in a breath, but he didn't glance down at her. Instead, he headed into the diner. That might be the end of his mushiness for the day. Maybe the week.

Or, you know, the century.

∽

Effie barely even noticed entering the diner. Or if anyone stared at her being led inside by two stunning men. She was too busy reeling from Grady's words. Not only were they beautiful words. But they'd come from Grady, who clearly had issues expressing himself most of the time.

If I could hear you laugh every day for the rest of my life, then I would've lived a rich life.

She knew she'd treasure those words for the rest of her life.

Grady let go of her hand and she felt a stab of disappointment. But he simply turned and started to unravel her from all of her layers of clothes. Then he slid into a circular booth. Steele placed a hand on the small of her back to push her into the booth. She soon found herself sandwiched between the two men. And they were close. So close she could feel their thighs brushing against hers.

Arousal filled her.

She was in real trouble here.

"You all right, Miss Effie?" Steele said to her quietly. He placed an arm over the back of the booth and she instinctively leaned into him.

Grady glanced over at them and she worried about giving him the same affection. But it was harder with him. She'd felt sure he was going to refuse to hold her hand before, and the disappointment had hurt.

But he hadn't.

So she risked reaching over to brush her hand over his as it sat on the table.

He gave her a look filled with warmth. Which was like a long hug from Grady.

"I'm fine," she said huskily.

"Are we overwhelming you?" Grady asked.

She held up a thumb and forefinger. "Little bit."

"Good," Steele said.

"That's good?" she asked, surprised.

"If you're busy thinking about us and what we're going to do or say next, then you're not going into your head and worrying about shit you don't have to concern yourself with."

"How do you know it's stuff I don't have to worry about?" She turned to him and he ran a finger along her lower lip.

"Because anything that you truly have to worry about, you'll tell us and we'll take care of it for you."

Holy heck.

She knew he'd said that earlier in the truck, but it still sounded magical.

"You'd really want to do that?"

"We wouldn't just want to do it," Grady replied, pulling a piece of paper from his pocket. "We need to do it."

"Because you like to be in charge?"

"Yes," Grady replied. "And because we want to take care of

you. Now, if you're going to be with us, there are a few things to discuss."

She glanced up at Steele in alarm, but he seemed unworried. He just winked at her.

The server approached and Grady ordered coffee for them all.

"What is there to discuss?" she asked.

"The rules are still in place but will change slightly."

"How?"

Grady started to write things down and she glanced over to see it was a list titled: Effie's Rules.

Holy heck.

"These are your rules so far: One: No putting yourself down. Two: No leaving work without texting me. Three: No lying. Four: You must always wear your seatbelt when a car is moving."

Right.

"The next rule is that if you get into any trouble, if you hurt yourself, feel ill, or need something, then you will tell us immediately. Understand?"

"Yes. I understand." That was actually a really sweet rule.

"Six is that you will do your best to keep yourself safe. That means things like not walking around alone at night. Or texting while driving. Jaywalking. That sort of thing."

"I'm not allowed to jaywalk?" she asked.

"No," Grady replied.

She looked at Steele again. He just raised his eyebrows back. He seemed in complete agreement with his best friend.

Yeah, she was definitely in trouble here.

"The next rule is around gossip."

"Gossip?" she asked.

"Yes," Grady replied. "Gossip. I don't like it."

"You don't like any gossip?" That was kind of odd.

"He means gossip about us," Steele explained. His fingers brushed against the tender skin of her neck and she shivered.

How could that be so arousing?

Definitely. In. Trouble.

Then he leaned in and kissed the spot right behind her ear.

"Steele," she whispered.

"Damon," he whispered back.

"What?" She turned to give him a startled look.

"I want you to call me Damon. Especially when we're in bed together."

"Really?" Oh God. The idea of being in bed with him was going to make her brain explode.

"I like the idea of hearing my name from your lips."

"All right," she replied. Yeah, she liked that idea a lot.

"All right, Damon."

"All right, Damon," she repeated.

He smiled at her. "That's my good girl. My baby is being so good, isn't she, Grady?"

"She's being a very good girl. She might need a reward." Grady stared down at her intently.

"I think you're right. Perhaps later, when we're alone."

"I . . . I . . ." Shit. She had to say something before things got along any further. "There might be things about me that you don't know and that maybe won't like."

She didn't want them to stop. But she didn't want to keep anything from them, either.

"That's why we're going to get to know each other better," Grady told her. "Starting with lunch."

"And moving on to more," Steele said. "After lunch, we want you to come home to our place."

"I . . . I can't." Disappointment filled her. "Sunday afternoons are mine and Brooks'. He'll be home at four. We'll watch a movie and get take-out. I . . . I'm sorry." They had to know that Brooks would always be her priority.

"That's fine," Steele said, surprising her. "Tomorrow. After Brooks has gone to school, we'll pick you up and you can spend the day at our place. Bring your bathing suit. Or not."

"You have a pool?"

"Yes," Grady replied. "But it's too cold for the pool."

"Not too cold for the hot tub, though," Steele told her.

Wow. A hot tub with these two? That might just kill her.

"Back to the rules," Grady said. "Are they agreeable? Is there anything you want to add?"

"I just . . . um, no gossiping about the two of you?"

Steele gave her a serious look, nodding at the server as he delivered their coffees. "Give us a few more moments?"

The server gave them all a curious look, but nodded and left.

"Gossip isn't just silly fun. In my line of work, it can be dangerous," Steele explained, removing his arm from around her. She immediately felt the lack of warmth. But then his hand landed on her thigh. "You've heard things about what I do. And that's as much as I want you involved, understand me? There are things I cannot and will discuss with you to protect you. And I don't want you talking about us to your friends. Even anything innocent, all right?"

"All right. I don't have many friends anyway."

"Really?" Grady drawled. "I'm pretty sure all the dancers and servers at Pinkies have adopted you. They spend enough time in your office."

"I . . . it doesn't stop me from getting my work done!"

He raised his eyebrows. "Did I say it did?"

She tugged at her earring. "Sorry."

Steele removed her hand from her earring. "Stop that."

"I do it when I'm nervous," she explained.

"We've noticed," Grady told her. "But you will stop. You could harm yourself and that's unacceptable."

Jeez. They were so bossy and intense.

"Let's order lunch," Steele suggested, picking up a couple of menus and handing them over to them both. "I'm starving."

Effie took a quick glance around the diner. This wasn't the sort of place she expected them to eat. But they looked as at home here as they had in the restaurant they took her to for dinner.

"You have the other list?" Steele asked Grady.

"Another list?" she asked. How many lists did one man need?

Grady drew out another list. "I've been researching the foods that can help with inflammation."

"What?" she asked. He'd looked into food that might help with her back pain?

Warmth flooded her. Just when she thought they couldn't get any more amazing, they shocked her.

"Fortunately for you, there weren't many S foods. But let's see what's on the menu that might work. The foods mentioned are avocados, ginger, berries, garlic, and veggies like broccoli, cauliflower, and brussels sprouts."

"I'm not eating brussels sprouts," she said. "That's just wrong. I'm going to have the pancakes."

"Pancakes aren't on the list," Grady said. "Fatty fish is. Is there any fatty fish?"

"There's smoked salmon," Steele said.

"Salmon is an S food," she protested. "I'm not eating that."

"You'll eat what is good for you," Grady said firmly. "How about toast with avocado and poached eggs, along with a bowl of fruit salad?"

That sounded . . . well, okay, not awful. But she still wasn't eating it.

"I'd rather have the pancakes with maple syrup and whipped cream. But I'll compromise."

"Yeah?" Steele drawled. "How are you going to compromise?"

"I'll have blueberries in the pancakes."

There. Done.

"How about a small serving of pancakes," Grady said. "And a large bowl of fruit salad?"

They drove a hard bargain. She sighed. "Okay."

The server returned and they both ordered. To her surprise, Grady ordered for her. But that wasn't a big deal. If it was what he wanted, she could give him that.

When the server was gone, she put her hands on the table, fidgeting.

Steele rested his hand on the back of her neck, and immediately, she felt calmer. "You okay, Spitfire?"

"Yeah, my brain is spinning a bit."

"I want you to promise me something."

"Um, what is it?" She knew better than to promise something before she found out what it was.

"Promise you'll spend tomorrow with us."

She was nervous, but she wanted that. So she immediately nodded. "Yes."

"Such a good baby." Steele leaned forward and kissed the tip of her nose. "I also want you to promise to text or call us if you start getting too worried. This will only work if you share your concerns and burdens with us, all right? If you start to think this won't work or you doubt our feelings for you, call us. Promise me that."

She looked between him and Grady. Sucking in a breath, she let it out slowly. "I promise."

"Damn, our baby is such a good girl. Isn't she, Grady?"

"Like I said before, she definitely needs a reward."

"Hmm. Tomorrow."

Was Steele going to kiss her? She didn't know whether she was more nervous or excited at the thought. But he drew slowly back, staring down at her intently. "You were made for us, Effie. I know this seems to be moving fast, but Grady and I have already talked about this. We were trying to go slow. However, we decided that after last night, it was time that people knew you were ours. Including you."

Holy. Heck.

"If you were ours, Nate would have known to call us the instant you tried to fill in for Vanessa," Grady told her.

"That really wasn't a big deal."

Both of them stared down at her. From the look on their faces, she took it that they disagreed.

"It was a big deal and it won't happen again, understand me?" Steele said firmly. "You push us on that, and you'll spend the next day on your feet or stomach because you won't be able to sit."

Holy. Hell.

She wanted to ask them if they were Doms and what they were into. But that didn't seem like a conversation to have in a freaking diner.

"She looks a bit like a deer in headlights," Grady said.

"Effie, if you need us to take things slower, we can. As long as we move forward. Understand?" Steele asked.

Not exactly. But she nodded anyway.

"We don't want to scare you. We know we're not easy men," Grady explained.

Steele ran a finger over her lips again. "Why don't we save the deep and meaningful stuff until we're alone at our place tomorrow?"

She nodded in relief. That sounded like something she could do.

31

"Could you tell me what happened last night? I can only remember bits and pieces. I'm not . . . I'm really not sure what happened. My pills have never caused me to lose my memory. And I keep getting these weird flashes. Like I was tripping over air. And people were telling me secrets. Bizarre, right?"

"Not quite as bizarre as you think," Grady said. "There were some secrets being shared, only you were the one sharing them."

"What? I was sharing secrets? Oh my God, what did I say?"

"Nothing bad," Grady soothed. "Actually, you were quite funny."

"I was?" Funny haha or funny weird? She wasn't sure she wanted to know. "I just can't understand why I'd act like that. I'm so sorry."

"You don't have to apologize," Steele told her gruffly. "It wasn't you who poured vodka into your drinks."

"Someone . . . someone put alcohol into my drinks?" she

asked. "Who would do that? Oh my God. It was Lucy, wasn't it? That . . . that bitch."

"That bitch," Grady agreed, his face dark. "But don't worry. She's going to get what is coming to her."

"What do you mean?" she asked. "What is going to come to her?"

"Nothing that you have to worry about," Grady told her. "She's been fired. Lex escorted her out of Pinkies and she won't be returning."

Okay, good.

Although she felt a bit bad too. She tugged at her earring. Steele reached up to free her hand.

"Will she be all right?" she asked.

Steele cupped her chin, tilting her head back. "Spitfire, she put booze in your drinks when you said no booze. And she did this because she found those pills in your handbag and saw that you weren't supposed to drink with them. And she did that because she wanted to get rid of you."

"Because she's obsessed with you." She nodded.

"What?" Steele asked.

"Oh." She looked at Grady. "He didn't know?"

"I think he's in denial."

"Wow. Dude, she was obsessed with you, like stalker-obsessed. She's probably got a shrine to Steele in her bedroom. Gets out her vibrator and comes thinking about you. Maybe she even writes your names together with little love hearts in her diary."

Okay. Effie probably should have tried to think before speaking. Because they were both staring at her like she'd lost her marbles.

"You really think that she was so into me that she'd have a shrine to me in her bedroom? One she'd masturbate to?" Steele asked, showing no embarrassment as he said the word masturbate.

Didn't matter, she'd gone red enough to impersonate a stop light.

Oh God.

What had she just said? And in the middle of a freaking diner?

Knowing she needed to hide, she slid under the table. Maybe she could just crawl out of here. Make a run for it. Sure, she didn't have a car or anything but she could take the bus home.

Right?

"She's trying to hide again," Grady said.

"It's cute."

"I don't like her sitting on the floor in a public place where I can't be sure that the floor is clean enough," Grady stated.

"Come here, baby girl. You're upsetting Grady." Steele reached down for her.

She was upsetting Grady? She didn't want to do that. Also, Grady got upset? She knew he got angry which was a scary sight. But upset?

"Watch your head." Steele put one hand on top of her head to protect her as he drew her up into the booth.

"Perhaps we need to look into some sort of restraint when she is sitting," Grady suggested.

"I don't need to be restrained!"

Of course she said this just as the server returned with their food. He paused and looked at them all.

"Um. Uh."

She attempted to slide down off the seat again. She was just going to hide down here forever.

"Oh no, you don't," Steele said, placing a large arm firmly over her stomach. "And you can put the food down."

"I, um, ah, are you all right, ma'am?" the young guy asked.

"No," she cried.

He gaped at her as he set the food down.

"You just ma'amed me. That means I'm old. I'm officially old."

"I, uh, it . . ."

"We're fine," Grady said firmly. "So is Effie. Effie, you want to put this guy at ease before he calls the cops on us?"

Which they definitely wouldn't like. Since they didn't like gossip. She was also guessing they wouldn't want the attention of the police.

"Sorry," she said, smiling brightly at the server, who continued to blink down at her. "I haven't had any coffee. I'm loopy without my coffee."

The server glanced down at her mug. She looked to see it was half empty. Shoot. There went that excuse. But she just widened her smile. "So nice of you to be concerned. I really am okay. Do you like working here? Seems like a nice diner."

"Um, yeah. It's fine. I've got to get back to work."

"I feel like he didn't believe me," she muttered as Grady placed her small plate of pancakes in front of her. As well as her big bowl of fruit.

She liked some fruit. But she liked pancakes more. She dug into the pancakes, taking a bite. "Yummy."

Steele used another fork to pick up some berries and held them to her mouth. "For each mouthful of pancake, I want you to eat some fruit as well."

So not cool. But she took the fruit. Then had a sip of coffee.

"So good."

When she was finished, she sat back and rubbed her tummy.

"Feeling good, baby girl?" Steele asked.

"Uh-huh. I love pancakes." She bit her lip. "I didn't mean that stuff I said earlier about Lucy. I was being mean."

You need to do better, Effie. People don't like it when you're angry or sad or grumpy. They want happy Effie.

She sucked in a breath, feeling herself growing tense.

"No, you weren't," Grady countered. "Lucy was nuts. And she was definitely the sort to have a masturbation shrine in her bedroom to Steele."

She groaned. "Can we please stop saying the word masturbate?"

"You don't like the word masturbate either? No porn. No masturbation." Steele shook his head. "I don't know. Seems boring, taking those words out of the English language."

"You don't have to take them out of the English language. Just out of my language and any language around me." And she was acting like a crazy person.

"You're a bit nutty," Steele told her.

"Um, yeah." She winced. Nan would not be happy with her.

"I like that."

He... he what?

"We're all a bit crazy here," Grady murmured.

She wasn't sure she believed him. They seemed pretty normal to her. She was the loopy one.

And while she thought Lucy was a total bitch, she also couldn't help but feel a bit sorry for her.

Because becoming infatuated with Damon Steele wasn't a hard thing to do.

And when you added Grady to that...

Irresistible.

"Effie? What are you thinking?" Grady asked.

Yeah, there was no way she was telling him what she was thinking. Her brain scrambled.

"Um, I was thinking that it's my turn to pay since you guys paid last time."

Instantly, she knew it was the wrong thing to say. They both stiffened. Then Steele turned to her. She swallowed heavily.

"Would you like to make that five, ten?" he asked.

Uh. What?

"The five spanks you're owed," Grady said almost casually. "Would you like it to be ten?"

"No." What kind of question was that?

"Then you won't mention paying for anything, but especially anything for us, ever again," Steele told her darkly.

Definitely in trouble.

But the very delicious kind.

After they paid for the meal, they'd driven her back to her apartment and stayed with her until Brooks returned home. Only leaving after they'd given orders to her to not eat too much junk food, drink plenty of water, and go to bed early.

So darn bossy.

And part of her loved that.

32

Effie, you aren't in your crummy apartment anymore.

She looked around Grady and Steele's house. Only, it wasn't a house.

It was a freaking mansion.

She'd guessed they had money. They dressed nicely, had a driver, and an expensive-looking truck. Plus, they owned several businesses.

But this was still next-level. This place was immense. There were security gates at the front and a long, tree-lined cobblestone driveway that led to the most stunning house she'd ever seen.

It was enormous with two floors. A wide porch wrapped around three sides and on both levels. The bottom half was stone, while the top was timber boards. It looked like the most luxurious ski chalet she'd ever seen.

And the inside was even more spectacular. Huge high ceilings. Rooms that were big but not cold. A sunken living room with an enormous stone fireplace and a big, comfortable-looking sectional in front of it.

Curling up in front of that fire with a blanket, a book, and hot chocolate was her idea of heaven.

"You okay, Effie?" Steele came up behind her, wrapping his arm around her.

He'd picked her up on his own today, explaining that Grady was working on something but would meet them at their place.

She still hadn't seen Grady. Then again, she was barely in the door.

"This place is amazing." Ahead of her were wall-to-ceiling windows that offered peeks of the backyard and the wall of trees that surrounded them. "It's magical."

"Glad you think so, baby girl. You and Brooks are welcome to come stay whenever you like. In fact, I think we should have a sleepover soon."

Oh, she liked that idea. A lot.

"Brooks would love it here, but I'm not sure I'm ready to bring him."

"Understood."

"However, he did mention staying over at a friend's place on Saturday..."

Whoa. That was forward for her.

Don't push yourself on people, Effie. No man will respect a girl who just gives it away.

She clenched her hands into fists. Damn it. She was getting super tired of Nan's voice in her head.

"Baby girl? You all right?" Steele turned her, cupping her chin in his hand.

"Yeah, sorry. I just... was that too forward?"

"Spitfire, I want to make something clear."

She sucked in a breath. Whatever he told her, she could take it. Even if he was telling her to back off a bit.

"If I thought you'd agree, I'd have had you living in my house yesterday."

"W-what?"

"I'd have you living with us by now, baby. I want you. Grady wants you. The only one who has to get that is you. But don't worry, we're prepared to do what's needed to show you how much we want you." He moved his hand around to her neck, cupping the side of it. His thumb remained under her chin, keeping her face tilted back.

"Starting with this," he murmured. Bending down, he kissed her lightly.

She let out a small gasp and he took total advantage, pressing his tongue inside her, kissing her deeply.

And the man could kiss.

She leaned into him, gripping him to keep herself steady. When he drew back, she was panting, her body floating.

Steele's gaze was hot. His hunger for her clear.

"That was so fucking hot."

She jumped with a gasp, turning to see Grady leaning against the wall, watching them.

What did it say about her that she found the idea of him watching her hot?

She didn't know. But a shiver of arousal ran through her. Steele turned her around so her back was pressed to his chest.

"Like what you saw?" he asked huskily.

"Yes," Grady replied.

"Grady likes to watch," Steele told her.

Grady's eyes narrowed. Was he upset with Steele for telling her that? Not wanting him to feel bad or get angry, she spoke up.

"I like it too."

Grady's eyebrows rose. "You like being watched, sweetheart?"

"Y-yes."

"You've had that before with a boyfriend?" Steele asked. "You had someone watch as you fucked?"

Lord.

Nan would roll over in her grave at how blunt he was. She definitely wouldn't approve of Steele. Grady, possibly.

Both of them . . . yeah, she would have had a heart attack on the spot.

"No."

"You've thought about it, though?" Steele asked.

She didn't say anything. She was too busy staring at Grady, who kept watching her as Steele cupped the front of her throat, holding her head up. He didn't put pressure on her throat, but the threat was there.

And it just made her hotter.

"I've thought about a lot of things," she blurted out.

"That right?" Steele murmured. "You have some desires, some wants that are going unfulfilled, baby girl?"

"I . . . I . . ."

"Answer him," Grady said firmly.

"I guess so," she whispered.

"You only guess so?" Steele asked. "Here's the thing, baby. We're not mind readers. We'll try our best to meet your needs, but we might miss something, and you need to tell us if we do."

"She needs a safeword in case we go too far."

"Safeword?" she asked in a strangled voice.

"Yep," Steele said, his hand moving down her chest and over her breast. She shuddered. "You know we both like to be in control. It's not just a game in the bedroom. For us, it's part of our life."

"Y-yes," she replied, sucking in her stomach as he placed his hand there. Could he feel her rolls? How rounded her tummy was?

Shit. She really needed to start doing crunches or something. That was it, she was going back on a diet tomorrow. Maybe by Saturday, she could tone things up a bit? Was that possible?

"You've gone all tense," he murmured. "We never want to push you too far."

Shoot. He thought she'd tensed because of their conversation.

"Which is why you'll have a safeword," Grady said. "And you'll use it if we push you too much, scare you, hurt you."

She sucked in her breath.

"We don't want to hurt you," Steele told her. "But sometimes pain can bring pleasure. And we don't know how you'll react to that. Other times, when you're punished, pain just might be pain. But we never want to harm you. Understand?"

Sort of.

Steele tugged her head to one side so he could kiss his way down her neck. She groaned.

"She needs to concentrate for this conversation, Steele," Grady warned.

"Hmm, you're right. Problem is, she's just so delicious. And she's still tense."

Because he had one hand on her stomach. But if he hadn't felt her stomach rolls, then she wasn't going to point them out.

Suddenly, Steele spun her away from him and somehow situated her in a chair. She stared up at him as he breathed heavily.

"Fuck. You're like an aphrodisiac. Can't get enough."

Pleasure filled her and she tried to stand, to go to him. But Grady was suddenly there, crouching in front of her and filling her eyesight.

"Good morning," she said, shocked at how breathless she sounded.

"Good morning, sweetheart. Have you had breakfast?"

"I, um, yes." Breakfast? Why were they talking about breakfast when she wanted other things?

"And what did you have?"

"Uhh . . . I'm not sure I should tell you."

"No?"

"I think I'm going to plead the fifth." Shoot. Her Little was close to the surface. They had her off-guard. It was the kissing and the bossiness and the kinkiness.

She didn't know whether she was up or down.

"The fifth?" Grady repeated. "I don't think you can plead the fifth with us. Can she, Steele?"

"Definitely not." Steele leaned against the side of the fireplace. "What did you have for breakfast, Little girl?"

"I'm not a Little girl," she replied, her heart racing.

"Aren't you?" Steele asked.

She licked her dry lips. "Are the . . . are the two of you Doms?"

∽

GRADY KNEW SHE WAS NERVOUS.

Nervous and brave.

He hadn't gone to pick her up this morning because he'd wanted to get a few things done. Namely, setting into motion some plans to ruin Lucy's life, ensuring that Brooks' former bullies were behaving themselves by sending someone out to check in with their parents. Oh, and doing some more research into back injuries caused by car accidents.

All in a morning's work.

Still, he regretted not going to pick her up after Steele left. It was ridiculous, but he felt this pull toward her. Wanted her around him all the time.

Once they convinced her to move in here with them, he might order her to strip, then have her sit next to him while he worked. Perhaps he'd even like to touch her. Or have her touch him.

Yes . . . he could imagine having her kneeling between his legs, sucking his cock. But even more, he wanted to tie her to his desk. Secure her with her legs spread, her pussy on display so he could pet and play with her at will.

That wasn't a fantasy he'd ever had before. But this was Effie everything was different with Effie.

Standing, he drew over a stool to sit on in front of her.

Now wasn't the time to play with her. It was the time for some talk.

"What did you have for breakfast?" Grady asked.

She groaned. "You're like a dog with a bone."

"Best answer him, baby girl. Before he ties you up and tortures the answer out of you."

Her eyes widened as she stared from him to Steele. Grady sent Steele a quelling look. He didn't need to fucking terrify her.

"You like doing that? Um, bondage, I mean?"

Grady studied her. She didn't appear freaked out. Maybe she liked the idea of being tied up.

And perhaps that's why Steele mentioned it. Sometimes, he forgot that the other man was very intuitive.

"I do. Do you like that?" he asked.

"I think I would. I've never had much opportunity to explore . . . well, to explore anything."

She tugged at her earring. Today they were little bumblebees. So cute. Reaching up, he drew her hand free. A zing of pleasure rushed through his body.

And her face grew soft. The tension in her body eased.

Pliant.

He liked that.

"I want you to know that you can tell us anything, sweetheart," Grady told her. "We won't judge. Truth is, we've probably seen or done most things."

"So you are Doms?"

"Tell us what you ate for breakfast first," Steele said. "Then we'll talk about this."

She huffed out a breath. "I still think pleading the fifth should be a thing."

"It is a thing," Steele replied. "Just not for you, baby girl."

"A cookie and some coffee."

It was worse than he'd expected. She really did need someone watching after her. Steele could do that for her. Ensure that she ate properly, got enough rest, and took care of herself.

But she might need more . . . she might need that from you too.

Can you be there for her Little?

Before, he would have said no. He would have left that part to Steele.

But everything was different with Effie.

33

"Right. That means you need a proper breakfast, young lady," Steele said firmly.

"But it was a healthy cookie with nuts in it!" She dropped her lower lip out on a pout.

"That doesn't make it any better," Steele told her. "A cookie is not proper food. A cookie is a treat."

"Hey! Don't be mean to the cookies of the world! I'm pretty sure they think they are proper food. You might hurt their feelings."

"Cookies don't have feelings. And if they did, they'd know that they weren't an acceptable breakfast food. Grady is going to make you breakfast and you're going to eat it, even if I have to feed it to you."

"But I'm not hungry."

"You can't be full from just a cookie," Grady said.

"It was one of those protein cookies. So I really don't need more food."

A protein cookie?

Yeah. Still unacceptable.

"Grady," Steele prompted.

"I'll make some scrambled eggs. I've got some avocados too. And berries."

"I really can't eat."

"Keep protesting, baby girl, and he'll make you a Brussels sprout and spinach omelet," Steele warned.

"Now that's just plain cruel. I can't believe you'd be so mean, Daddy."

Steele's entire body froze. She had already guessed they were Doms, even though they hadn't answered her yet. But he hadn't thought she'd realized he was a Daddy Dom.

Steele hadn't even been certain that she knew she was a Little.

Well . . . he guessed he had his answer.

Suddenly, she stood and looked around her. Grady was already heading toward the kitchen, when he paused after he heard Effie call Steele Daddy.

So, neither of them was close enough to catch her as she took off.

"Fuck." Grady stared over at him. "We should have explained."

"I wanted to spend some more time with her first. To get her used to the idea."

"I'm guessing she knows something about Daddy Doms and Littles," Grady said.

Steele ran his hand over his face. "Yep. Want to split up to try and find her?" If she tried to go outside, the alarm would go off. He'd set it again when they'd entered the house. He wasn't taking chances with his girl.

"I'll take upstairs," Grady said. "You look down here."

Steele set off. Fuck it. He messed that all up.

~

You need to act normal, Effie.

People won't like you if you're different, dear.

Just try to fit in.

Nan would definitely be horrified if she could see her right now. She was curled up under a desk, with her face buried in her knees.

Why had she done that?

She couldn't believe she'd called Steele Daddy.

Was she losing her freaking mind? Sure, there were definite signs of him being a Dom. But that didn't mean that he was a Daddy Dom. Or that he wanted a Little.

Everything had been going so well and she just had to go and fuck it up. Did she have a self-destruct button?

"Idiot. Idiot. Idiot."

"You're not allowed to call yourself names." The voice wasn't scolding. It wasn't horrified. Instead, it was soft, gentle. "And if anyone is the idiot, baby girl. It's me."

Great. She'd totally given away her hiding place. She couldn't even get that right.

"Idiot."

"Was that aimed at you or me?" The chair she'd dragged into place to cover her hiding place, was moved away and Steele appeared next to her.

Well, she didn't move her head to look, but she could tell he was there. She could feel his warmth, his presence.

"Baby girl, I know that you're upset and want to hide, but I need you to look at me. I'm worried about you, I need to know you're all right."

He was worried about her?

"Baby," he said warningly. "Look. At. Me."

Right. He was at the end of his patience.

So she turned her head to look at him as he sat on the floor next to her. Then she realized her eyes were blurry.

"Crap. I'm leaking."

He raised his eyebrows. "Leaking?"

"Yeah. Stupid eyes."

"Baby." That was all he said. But that one word conveyed plenty. Affection. Desire. And possibly that he thought she was slightly bonkers.

"We have to stop you from hiding when you're scared or embarrassed, baby girl. Instead of running away from us, you should run to us. We want to be your safe place. The place where you can hide. Where you can be yourself."

Lord, she wanted that too. So much.

"I made a dick of myself."

"Nope."

That was all he said. Just nope?

"I did," she insisted. "I called you Daddy."

"And I liked it."

It took a moment for those words to sink in. Then she turned her head to him more fully.

"What?"

"And I'm gonna insist you do it more often."

"Are you . . . are you saying that to make me feel better?"

"Thought you'd know me by now. I don't say stuff to make people feel better. I know what I want and I go after it. And I want you. Now, I have you. You're sweet, adorable, and sassy. Amazing. You're also gorgeous, loyal, and smart. All fucking good. And the fact that you're a Little. Icing on the fucking cake, baby."

Icing on the cake?

"You knew already?"

"Yeah." He said it without apology. As though he hadn't just rocked her world.

She wiped at her eyes and he moved, reaching up to grab a

box of tissues. But when she reached out a hand to take some, he drew the box away.

"Come here, baby."

She shook her head. She wasn't ready for that yet.

"Baby, come here."

She shook her head.

A stern look filled his face. He patted his thigh. "Here. Now."

Okay, she figured she was going there. She slid out of her hiding spot and climbed into his lap.

"Baby, when you're told to come. You come."

She gaped up at him. Was he for real? "What?"

"You heard me. If I have to keep repeating myself, your ass is getting turned red."

Holy. Heck.

He drew out a tissue and started to gently wipe her face. Then he pressed a kiss to her temple.

Okay, so maybe it wouldn't be a bad thing to go to him when he asked. Well, not that he asked.

He then drew his phone from his pocket and sent a text. "Letting Grady know where you are."

Oh. Oops.

"Effie, I'm a Daddy Dom."

Right. She got that now.

"You're a Little."

She nodded.

"Going to want some verbal answers, Spitfire."

"Um, yes. I am."

"Have you ever had a Daddy Dom?" he asked.

"Urgh, sort of?"

"How do you sort of have one?" he asked.

"Well, uh, I've never had a boyfriend who was a Daddy Dom. Not that I'm saying you're my boyfriend, we didn't talk about labels. Oh, shit."

His chest was moving and she glanced up at him suspiciously. "Are you laughing at me?"

"Baby, we don't have to talk about labels, because I don't care about that shit. Call me what you like to your friends. You're mine. I'm yours. You're Grady's. He's yours. Got me?"

"I think I've got you."

"You need any more clarification on something?"

"Just the whole, uh, Daddy Dom stuff, I guess."

"Right. I'm a Daddy Dom. Have been for a long time, but after my sister died, I just didn't feel it anymore. Or I didn't want to get involved with Littles. I had sex. I dominated the women I had sex with if they were good with that. But that's all it was. I didn't want a *girlfriend*. I didn't want a Little."

"And now?" she whispered.

"And now, there's you. My sweet, sassy, sexy Effie. All I see is you. You're who I think about when I go to sleep and when I wake up with morning wood, you're who I think about as I jack off."

"Steele!" She gaped up at him. "I don't think you should tell me things like that when you're my boss."

He let out a bark of laughter. "Think we're past worrying about proper boss-employee behavior, don't you?"

Considering she was sitting on his lap after he'd just wiped her nose, yeah, maybe.

"Grady?"

"That's for you and him to talk about. Grady is definitely a Dom. He's played at clubs. But he's never had a Little to take care of before."

"Oh." So she could only be Little with Steele?

"Doesn't mean he doesn't want to look after you when you're Little. Might just mean you have to be a bit more patient with him. I'm the easy one."

Haha. Good one.

"There's nothing easy about you, Damon Steele."

He grinned down at her. Then his smile faded. "Grady cares a lot about you. But he might not always know how to say it. So look for the signs, okay?"

"I can do that. It can be hard to talk about things like this."

"Yeah? Did you ever try to talk about things with someone and they hurt you? Rejected you? That why you have a tendency to hide?"

She bit her lip.

"Everything all right?" Grady asked, entering the room.

"Yeah," Steele replied. "I've told her I'm a Daddy Dom and that not only do I not have a problem with her calling me Daddy, but I want her to call me that."

Grady nodded.

"Told her you're a Dom too. That you've played at clubs before. But we haven't discussed limits or desires."

Grady came around to lean against the desk. She stared up at him.

"I was just asking our girl whether she'd told anyone about her needs before. She said she's sort of had a Daddy Dom."

"Sort of?" Grady raised his eyebrows.

"I, um . . . Joe was a Daddy Dom. He's the one who helped me realize I was a Little. But he wasn't *my* Daddy Dom, if that makes sense. Still, sometimes, if I needed to go into Little headspace, he'd help me get there." She shrugged. It was painful to remember if she was honest. Because it was something she'd wanted from him but only partially got.

Steele's hand came to the back of her neck. "That can't have been easy, baby."

"It was good and bad. I had a couple of boyfriends that I tried to ask . . . well, to explain what I wanted. One of them was game to try things, but it just didn't work. After Joe died, well, I was recovering both physically and mentally. And then with

Brooks . . . sometimes it just felt like all my energy went into getting by. And there wasn't anything left for dating. Plus, I just didn't feel safe revealing that part of myself to people. Not after being rejected before."

"Baby," Steele said soothingly, rocking her back and forth. "You don't have to worry about being rejected by us. You can tell us anything. Any desires, any needs, you tell us. Understand?"

She nodded, although she was still somewhat unsure.

Grady crouched down and reached out to touch her chin. A shock of surprise and pleasure filled her.

"There might be things we want. Things that you might not have tried before and might be nervous about. This doesn't just go one way. There's always give and take. And communication. Something I'm not always good at, but I'll try if you will."

"Yes," she said quietly. She cleared her throat. "I'll try."

"That's my good girl," Grady told her huskily. "You definitely need a reward."

"Even though I ran away and hid?"

"Do you do that often? You used to do that with Joe? Those other idiots?" Steele asked.

"Idiots?" She turned her head to look at Steele. "Why do you call them that?"

"They let you go, didn't they? Idiots."

Oh. That was sweet. Even if untrue.

"You didn't answer the question," Grady pointed out.

She tugged at her earring.

"Uh-uh. No more of that." Steele drew her hand away and lightly slapped it.

Okay. Whoa.

"Not really," she said. "The hiding thing is kind of new."

"We need to make it so she comes to us," Grady said, looking at Steele.

"That's exactly what I said. Running away from us isn't acceptable." Steele squeezed her, then let her go.

Grady reached down and lifted her onto her feet. But instead of immediately letting her go, he took hold of her hand and led her from the room.

"No, from now on, you come to us. If you run and hide, when we catch you, you'll need to be punished."

"Maybe it's time we talked about this safeword. Because it sounds like I'm gonna get punished a lot."

Steele let out a bark of laughter and she couldn't help but turn to grin at him.

Even though she hadn't been joking.

34

Grady led her into the most gorgeous kitchen. There were light marble countertops and dark gray cabinets. And it had the most enormous island she'd ever seen.

"This is beautiful."

He didn't reply. Instead, he just lifted her onto the counter.

It seemed like Grady wasn't as reserved anymore. Perhaps because they'd loosened the no-employee rule? Or maybe it was something else.

Whatever it was, she liked it.

"What would you like your safeword to be?" he asked her as he started whipping up some eggs.

"Um, I don't know." She reached for a grape that he held out to her, but he drew it back.

"No. Open."

With a blush, she opened her mouth and let him pop the grape into her mouth. She glanced around as Steele moved into the room and sat at the small dining table.

"Maybe spinach?" she suggested.

"Bit long, but all right," Steele agreed. "Grady, Effie is having Saturday off."

"I am?" she asked.

"Done," Grady agreed as he whipped up some eggs.

"Why do I need Saturday off?" she asked.

"Because you're going to have a nap in the afternoon. Then Raul will pick you up at five. You'll have dinner at Pinkies with us and then spend the evening in our area. Then come home with us for the night."

"Oh. I don't need a nap, though. I can still work."

"You need the nap." Steele gave her a firm look that made her shiver. "You won't be sleeping much."

Dear. Lord.

"What . . . what exactly do you want from me?" She congratulated herself on asking that question. It seemed a sensible one to ask. One that would help set up rules and boundaries.

Grady turned to her, his face serious. "Everything."

Steele walked over and leaned a hip against the counter next to her leg. "Think I should stand here in case you feel the need to run."

Grady eyed her. "If I put you somewhere, that's where you stay."

"Hmm. Good rule." Steele nodded.

Grady pulled out that darn list and a pen and added it.

"Do you carry that thing everywhere?" she asked.

"Yes."

Good Lord.

He started cooking the eggs, then turned to slice up an avocado. She wouldn't lie, it smelled delicious.

"When you say everything . . . do you really mean, everything?"

"Yes," Steele said. "Doesn't mean you have to give it all to us right now. As long as there are no threats to you, physical or emotional. Those things we need to know now. There are things about us we might not give to you yet. But when the time is right, we will. Yeah?"

"Okay, yeah." She got it.

"But we're all in with you. And eventually, we want you to be completely in too. Understand?"

She thought so. Eventually, they'd want to know all of her. And have all of her. And she'd have the same from them. But if there were things she couldn't tell them right now, as long as they weren't a risk to her, she could keep them to herself.

Shoot. She was learning to speak alpha male. That was scary.

There wasn't much she was holding back anymore, but she wasn't positive she could say the same for them.

"Food is ready," Grady told them. "I'll get coffee."

"Let's get you over to the table." Steele lifted her off the counter, cradling her against his chest.

"I can walk."

"I like to carry you. And I'm used to getting what I want. So expect me to carry you a lot."

"Anyone ever tell you that you're very arrogant?"

"Sure, they didn't live long, though."

"What?" she asked.

He sat in a chair with her in his lap. "Joking, baby girl."

Jeez.

"I can also sit on my own chair."

"Hmm. I don't know. I was thinking that you might need a high chair. So you'll stay where you're put."

"W-what?" She stumbled over the word as Grady put a huge plate of eggs, toast, and avocado slices on the table. Whoa. That wasn't all for her, right?

He went back to the kitchen and returned with three mugs of coffee.

Then he sat in the chair next to them. "Agreed."

Her eyes widened. "I didn't think you were a Daddy Dom, Grady?"

"I've never had much to do with Littles beyond spending time with Millie. That's Spike's Little. Spike is Steele's brother-in-law. I didn't think I had it in me to give a Little what they needed. My nurturing side is a bit . . . stunted. Growing up, my parents didn't show me or each other affection. I've learned to fake it over the years with others. With you, I don't want to do that anymore."

She sucked in a breath, not knowing what to say.

"I might pretend with others, but I won't with you. I'll give you all of me and hope that's enough."

"It will be more than enough."

His face softened. "So sweet. I didn't think we were good enough for you. I still don't. But you are ours. If sweet lands in your life, you grab hold and do whatever is necessary to protect it."

There was her fierce Grady. Mostly, he gave off a refined air. But there was a definite edge to him. Something that told her it would be dangerous to mess with him or come between him and something he wanted.

"So I agree you need a high chair," Grady said.

"I don't!" She leaned forward, nearly falling into his lap. Steele had to tighten his hold on her to keep her pressed against him.

"You nearly fell off your chair," Grady pointed out.

"I did not. I just leaned over too far."

"Uh-huh." Grady picked up the knife and fork and started cutting up her food.

She gaped at him. No one had ever cut up her food that she could remember. Maybe when she was very young.

Then Grady held some up to his mouth and blew on it

before pressing it to his lips. "Perfect. Open up."

"I . . . you . . . you don't have to feed me."

"But I want to." It was said simply, without arrogance. As though he knew he would get exactly what he wanted.

Whoa. These guys were something else.

"Do you want me to do choo-choo noises?" Grady asked.

"No!" She squirmed.

"I think that might be a lie," Steele said. "Bad baby. We might need to punish you for lying."

"It's not a lie! Grady doesn't have to do them!"

"That's not the same as not wanting them," Grady pointed out.

"I don't want you to do anything you're not comfortable with."

"A bit of knowledge for you," Grady replied. "I very rarely do anything I don't want to do. Now, open up for the choo-choo train."

"That's a good girl," Steele praised as she ate the mouthful. "What a good girl you're being for Daddy."

She flushed with pride even though she hadn't done anything remarkable. Damn, these scrambled eggs were good though. She reached out for her coffee mug, but Grady lightly slapped her hand away, then he held the cup up to her lips. Wow. It was perfect. He'd remembered from the diner yesterday how she liked her coffee?

Of course he had. Grady had a definite eye for detail. While Steele seemed like the big picture guy. Together . . . they were a fine-tuned machine.

She just hoped she kept that machine running smoothly, rather than putting a cog in it.

"What's wrong, baby?" Steele asked. "You've gone all stiff."

"I just . . . don't want to do anything to ruin this. Us. Or the two of you. Please don't let me do that."

"Hey," Grady said firmly. "I don't know who taught you to think that way, that you could possibly mess anything up, but that's not going to happen. There are three of us in this relationship. It's not all on you. And there's nothing you could do to ruin this except leave us. Understand?"

"Yes."

"And we won't let you do that," Steele added. "Our job is to look after you, support you, hold you up when you're feeling down. Cheer you on when you need it. Got me?"

"And my job?"

"To do as you're told," Grady told her.

She gaped at Grady, looking for a lip twitch.

Not. A. One.

These guys would be the death of her.

Grady fed her some more food.

"How young do you regress in Little headspace?" Steele asked.

"I, um, well, I've only sort of gone as young as three before."

"Ever felt like you wanted to go younger?"

Shoot. How to answer?

Be honest.

She squirmed. "Sometimes. I just didn't feel . . . comfortable doing that with Joe."

"You should know that no matter what you need as a Little, I'm here to give it to you," Steele told her. "I want to."

Lord. This man.

Grady watched them steadily.

"What about . . . what about what you want, Grady?" she asked.

"I like control. You know that. Rules. I especially like bondage. There are some things . . . I won't mention them yet. But later. You also know I like to watch."

She squirmed. She liked that too.

"I haven't been in a relationship with a woman since college. I'm not always good at showing or telling people how I feel. You'll need patience."

"I can do that."

Steele squeezed her waist with his arm. She understood. With Grady, she'd have to look for the signs.

Like him making her breakfast and feeding it to her.

Like him carrying around those lists.

Knowing how she liked her coffee.

Looking up how to help her back injury.

Even making choo-choo noises.

Yeah. Signs.

"When you're comfortable with it, I might tie you to my bed and torture you with pleasure without letting you come. When I'm working, I might secure your arms in a way that won't harm you, but leave your legs free, so I can eat that pussy whenever I get hungry."

Dear Lord.

"When Steele is fucking you, I might sit in the corner of the room and watch, jacking myself. And then, when he's done with you, I might order you to crawl to me and suck me off."

Oh God.

She wanted that. All. Of. That.

He studied her, surprise filling his face. "None of that scares you away?"

"No."

"From the way she keeps squirming, I'd say it all turns her the fuck on," Steele added. "Reckon you could lay it all on her."

"There's more?" she asked. Good Lord. More might actually kill her.

"Yes, but that part you'll get later." Grady gave her a heated look.

Okay, then.

35

Steele carried his girl into their living room.

He hadn't been lying when he said he liked to carry her. And the way she snuggled in against him . . . well, he thought she liked that too.

"Did you bring a bathing suit?" he asked as he settled them into the corner seat of the sectional. He put her between his spread legs and then grabbed a blanket from the back to cover them.

"Yes."

"Disappointing."

"What?" she asked, looking back at him.

"I'd rather you went naked."

"Oh, you really don't want me to be naked in the hot tub. There's nothing good about my naked body."

She really, really should have thought before she said that. And the way he instantly stiffened behind her told her she was in trouble.

"Um, I think I'll go see if Grady needs help with the dishes." She tried to move away from him, but he tightened his hold on her.

"He doesn't need help and he wouldn't save you. He'd simply hold you down for me."

"Hold me down?" she asked. "For what?"

"For the spanking you just earned. And that's on top of the spankings you're owed."

"What? What spankings? And why is this darn blanket trying to suffocate me?" She was trying to work her way free, but she wasn't going anywhere fast.

Steele grabbed the blanket and threw it down on the floor.

Stupid blanket.

It needed a good talking to.

He turned them both so that he was sitting with his feet on the floor. He settled her on her feet between his legs.

"What's going on?" Grady walked in. Well, he didn't simply walk. He strolled.

Honest to God, both of them were so freaking sexy that sometimes it hurt to look at them.

"Do you want to repeat what you just said?" Steele said.

"Nah, you know what. I'm good."

Why did she have to go pointing out that she was flawed?

Like they wouldn't have noticed?

You shouldn't eat too many sweet things, Effie. It's not good to be so . . . rounded.

"Urgh, shut up, Nan."

The silence in the room and the way both of them stared at her clued her in to the fact that she'd just said that out loud.

"I'm not nuts! Honestly!"

"No one said you were, baby girl," Steele said. He tilted his head to the side. "You were talking to your nan?"

She puffed out a breath. "I know it sounds nuts, but my nan, well, she raised me from when I was young. My mom didn't know who my dad was. At school, she was bullied pretty badly and I think that affected Nan as well as her. My nan could be pretty strict. She wanted my mom to act a certain way, so Mom left as soon as she could and I think she went a bit wild. Anyway, she got pregnant with me and then moved home for a while. Nan said that one day she woke up and Mom was gone, leaving Nan with me to raise."

"Fuck. How old were you?" Grady asked, coming closer.

"I was three. I don't really remember my mom. Just photos I saw of her."

"She never came back?" Steele asked.

"No. When I was ten, a policeman came to the house to tell Nan that she'd died in a house fire in Utah. She, uh, she died along with her husband and child."

"That bitch."

She jumped at Steele's words. "It . . . she died, Steele."

"So? That doesn't make her a bitch? She can still be a bitch. She went off and made another family and left you with your nan, who didn't seem that great of a person to be left with."

"Nan really wasn't that bad. I mean, she was strict and had a lot of advice. Some of it . . . wasn't that great. I think she was trying to stop me from becoming like my mom. And she . . . I don't know, I think she believed that she was helping me."

"How was she helping you?" Grady asked. "What kind of advice did she give you?"

She tugged at her earring.

"No," Steele said firmly, pulling her hand away and giving it a light slap. She stared down at him.

"I'm going to need to come up with another way of stopping you from doing that."

"If her hands were tied, she couldn't do that," Grady said.

"Good point. Next time you tug on your earring like that, you don't get to use your hands for an hour."

She huffed out a laugh. "Yeah, right."

They gave her serious looks back.

Holy. Heck.

"What sort of advice, Effie?" Steele asked. "What did you hear her say just before?"

"Um, it's just stuff about how I shouldn't eat too much or I might get too round and then I won't be attractive. Or, you know, how I should be agreeable and happy so that people like me. Stuff like that," she whispered as she saw the way Steele's face filled with thunder.

She turned to Grady and saw him standing still as a statue.

"That . . . you hear that sort of poison in your head?" Grady whispered.

"Um. It's not that bad."

"That's why you smile so much even when you clearly aren't happy?" Steele asked. "Because that bitch is poisoning your mind."

"This isn't acceptable. She can't live with that sort of shit in her head," Grady said fiercely.

Whoa. Effie didn't think she'd ever seen him look this upset.

"Agreed."

"It's really okay," she said, hastily. "I've heard it for a long time."

"And you haven't done anything to stop it? Joe didn't help you stop it?" Steele asked.

"He . . . I . . . I never told him."

Steele straightened his shoulders.

"But you told us," Grady said.

"Of course she told us," Steele said. "Because she trusts us to help her with this."

Um, also because they were super pushy and likely wouldn't let it go. But she decided not to mention that.

"Every time that Nan speaks to you, I want you to tell us," Steele told her.

"I, um, every time?" Or did he just mean whenever they were around?

"Every. Time."

Holy heck.

"Grady, add it to the list," Steele demanded.

"On it already."

"She says something in your head, you call one of us. Understand me?" Steele gave her a firm look.

"But what if you're working?" she asked.

"You call. We don't answer, leave a message and we'll call you back."

"What if you're asleep?"

"Well, considering the hours we work, it's unlikely that we'll be asleep while you're awake, but if Nan's voice is there in a dream and you wake up, you call. Hear me?"

"I hear you," she replied. Even though she thought they were crazy.

"Good," Steele said firmly. "Because Nan is messing with your view of yourself. You're fucking beautiful. So stunning that I can't believe you've said yes to being with us."

She gaped down at him. "What?"

Grady came around to sit next to Steele. "She doesn't believe you."

"I can see that. Effie, in this relationship, we're the lucky ones. Grady and I."

She shook her head. Grady had said something about not being good enough for her before, but she hadn't really taken it in. Because it was preposterous. "Okay, have you two been smoking something? Don't you look in the mirror? You're gorgeous. Sexy. Successful. Smart. And you smell really good, like leather and the sea."

"Yeah, baby, we're all those things. And we're still the lucky ones." Steele shook her lightly. "Because you're all of that and more."

"I'm not," she whispered.

Steele narrowed his eyes. "Yeah. You are. And we'll say it until you believe it. Until you know it."

"Until Nan is gone from your head forever," Grady added.

Lord. That sounded amazing. Even if she still didn't believe it.

"Time for your spanking," Steele said.

"You don't need to spank me. I've learned my lesson," she said quickly.

"Effie said that we wouldn't want to see her naked. That there was nothing good about her naked body."

She glared at Steele. "Tattletale."

He just stared back at her steadily. "Excuse me?"

"Nothing!" she blurted out.

"Sounds like someone needs to spend the day naked," Grady mused.

What? No!

"I'll take the spanking!" she said quickly.

Both of them eyed her.

"This time, it's a spanking. Next time, you spend the day naked. I think Grady will have some fun tying you up and playing with you. You ever been edged?" Steele asked.

Her eyes widened.

"Even if she hasn't, I'd say she knows what it is," Grady commented.

"I . . . um, I've never experienced it. But I've read books with it, and I really don't think I want to experience it."

Grady just smiled.

That smile was pure evil. And she felt it in her pussy.

Yikes.

"I don't think I like that smile." She pointed at Grady.

"You like this smile."

Damn him. She so did.

"Just like you really want to know what it's like to be edged. Or you'd be using your safeword. Or telling us no."

"You know it's no fun when you're all logical and stuff." She pouted.

Grady let out a chuckle that had her melting.

Shoot. All these guys had to do was laugh or smile or say something sweet, and she was putty in their hands.

"Not fair. I wish I had that ability."

"What ability is that, baby?" Steele asked.

"To make you putty in my hands."

They shared a look.

"You don't think we're putty in your hands?" Steele asked gruffly. "Do fucking anything for you, baby. Anything."

"All I think about is you. What is Effie doing? Is she safe? Warm? Is her back hurting?" Grady said.

"Is she eating properly? Getting enough water to drink," Steele added. "Is she happy? Sad?"

She sucked in a breath at their words.

"There's nothing we wouldn't do for you, Effie, except hurt you or stay away from you. Get me?" Steele demanded.

Yeah. She thought she was starting to get them.

"You're both my putty."

"Total putty," Grady agreed.

Of course, that didn't make them pushovers, they wouldn't just start giving in to everything she wanted. Otherwise, she'd be able to demand no spankings.

Only you don't really want that, do you?

"Now we've got that settled, you're still getting a spanking,"

Steele told her. "Five for yesterday. Five for lying earlier. And now ten for talking badly about yourself."

"I don't think Putty spanks."

"Oh, Putty definitely spanks," Steele replied firmly. "Putty knows he has the world in his arms and he makes sure that world knows she's fucking everything. Putty also protects that world with everything he has."

"You know, Putty is an interesting name."

"Don't even think about it," Grady warned. "If we have children, one of them will not be called Putty."

What a party pooper.

She was thinking it could be a whole thing. Putty, Slimy, Doughy.

Hmm, maybe not slimy. They might get called Slimy Wimy.

Wait . . . kids. They had thought about kids?

"You guys want kids?"

"Probably too soon for this conversation, but yeah. Down the track, we might want kids. If you'd want that?" Steele said carefully.

"Yeah," she said huskily. "I'd want that."

"Sweetheart?" Grady queried. "That wasn't supposed to make you cry."

She sniffled. "Everything makes me leak at the moment. It's awful."

"Poor baby," Steele crooned.

Something else he just said occurred to her.

"Wait. Twenty spanks? Are you kidding me?"

He had to be kidding, right? Had he seen the size of his hands? They were like paddles. There was no way she could handle a spanking from him.

Steele let go of her hips and patted his lap. "Nope. Now, over you go."

She couldn't just climb over his lap . . . right?

But the way he was staring at her told her that he expected just that.

"Let me help you." Grady held out a hand to her.

"So kind," she said sarcastically.

"I thought so."

Jesus.

Nerves filled her, but there was also an edge of excitement. This was what she'd wanted for so long. Someone to surrender to. Who would love her as she was, quirks and all. Someone to protect and cherish her. Who would help ease the load.

Someone who'd care for her enough to correct her when she disobeyed.

Only, it seemed she didn't do things by halves and she had two someones.

So she took Grady's hand, who stood to help her over Steele's lap.

"I'm going to bare your bottom," Steele told her.

She stiffened. "What?"

"I only give spankings on the bare. Unless we're talking about warning taps."

Warning taps?

"On the bare?" she squealed.

"Yep. That a problem?" Steele asked.

Only because of the cellulite on her thighs. But she didn't think it would be wise to mention that.

"I need to make up a list of her limits," Grady commented.

"Now would be a good time to talk about that," Steele said.

What? Right now?

"I don't think we need to do that right now," she said, trying to sit up.

Steele pressed a firm hand on the small of her back. "Stay where you are, baby girl."

Shit.

He raised up the back of her dress.

"I'll write up a proper list for all of us," Grady said as Steele lowered her tights to her knees.

Shit. Shit.

"Relax, baby," Steele commanded.

"Relax? How am I supposed to relax when you're going to see my bare butt? And spank it?"

"Point taken," Steele said. "But tensing will only make the pain worse."

Crap.

He started to lower her panties. "These are cute, baby girl. Although I think we should have a no-panties rule in the house. Unless you're in Little headspace or you have your period."

"We'll need to buy some things for here," Grady said. "I'll need another list for that. Things for her Little and period supplies. Can you make me a list of the things you prefer?"

"I can buy my own period stuff!"

Smack!

Holy. Shit.

That stung!

"Ouch! Daddy! That hurt!"

"It's meant to," Steele replied.

"But why? Effie didn't do nothing!" She pouted, her Little peeking out.

"If we want to buy you things to make you more comfortable when you're staying here, then we will."

Sheesh.

"But I don't expect you guys to buy me stuff. I know I don't have that much money, but I can still buy my own personal items. I don't want you to think I'm using you."

Grady cupped the back of her neck with his hand, massaging lightly. "Neither of us think you're using us. The fact is, Steele and I are being selfish in wanting to buy you things as it makes us feel good."

She wasn't so sure about that. But she nodded. She'd make sure they didn't get out of control.

"I still want to buy my own period things."

"Periods are nothing to be embarrassed about," Grady told her. "Everything, remember?"

"Yes, but I didn't think everything included bodily functions!"

"Well, now you know differently." Steele ran his fingers over her bottom. "Her ass looks so pretty pink."

"It does," Grady agreed huskily. "Right, limits, sweetheart."

"I . . . buying me period things!"

Smack!

"Not a proper limit," Steele warned her.

Fine.

"No blood. No humiliation. No name-calling."

"What about bondage? Gags? Blindfolds? Whips? Paddles? Canes?" Grady asked.

"I don't . . . I don't know about the cane or a whip. That seems scary."

"Don't worry," Steele told her. "It's not something either of us is really into. Paddles, yes. Are paddles all right?"

"I . . . maybe. I've never tried anything like that."

"We can ease into it," Grady told her.

"All right," she whispered. "I'm all right with the rest. But I don't think I could be gagged and blindfolded and bound at the same time. It's not that I don't trust you, it's just . . ."

"Shh," Steele told her, rubbing her bottom. She realized that since taking down her panties, he hadn't removed his hand from her bottom unless he was smacking it. None of this is happening right now. We'll work our way up to things."

"But you're okay with just one of those at a time? Or perhaps being bound and blindfolded?" Grady asked.

"Yes, I, um . . . I like the idea of being bound in particular."

"How do you feel about parts of you being bound while other parts are not?" Grady asked.

"I'm not sure I understand."

"What if I was to wrap up your top half and leave your bottom half free? Then I could play whenever I liked and you wouldn't be able to stop me."

Holy. Crap.

These guys were killing her.

"I could . . . I could be good with that."

"I'd say she's more than good with that," Steele added. He slid his hand down between her legs. "She's getting wet."

"Good girl," Grady murmured. "Getting wet for your Daddies."

Did he realize he'd just said Daddies? She stilled and she felt Steele stiffen, then relax.

Okay, she wasn't going to point it out. She didn't care what Grady wanted to be. . . as long as he wanted to be with her.

Steele ran a finger along her slit. "Yes, definitely wet."

She found herself squirming on his lap, wanting more. "Please."

"Stay still," Steele warned.

"Is our good girl being naughty?" Grady murmured. "Not sure she deserves her reward after her spanking."

"Hmm, you're right. Naughty girls don't usually get to come after a spanking."

Shit. Shit. Shit.

"I bet she tastes delicious though," Grady mused.

"Let's see."

Holy. Heck.

Steele's long, thick finger went back between her lower lips again.

"Part for me, Effie," he commanded.

With a whimper, she widened her legs.

"Wider," he ordered.

Holy heck. A shiver washed through her.

"Damon," she whispered.

"Like my name on your lips, baby girl. But you're not doing as I told you, which doesn't make me happy."

She widened her legs as far as she could.

"That's my girl." His finger pushed into her pussy, thrusting deep.

She let out a small cry, arching back as he pumped it in and out of her pussy.

"What a good baby you're being. That's it. Get nice and wet for me."

Fuck.

His finger drew out and she immediately missed it, wanting it back inside her. She was panting heavily as she looked up. Then she stilled.

He was sucking on his finger, his eyes closed. "Fuck. Me. Delicious."

Then she moved her gaze to Grady. And saw something unexpected. But not unwanted. There was hunger on Grady's face. Pure, undiluted need.

But she didn't think it was because he wanted to be the one tasting her arousal.

Or not entirely.

She thought he was imagining himself licking it from Steele's finger.

Definitely not the first time she'd wondered whether Grady was into Steele.

She just wasn't sure if Damon knew or not. Or even if he was into men.

Was she . . . was she coming between them? But then again, they'd been best friends for a long time and it didn't appear that Grady had ever made a move. She knew they liked to share. But did they ever touch each other?

"Want to taste?" Steele asked Grady.

"Yeah, but I want to eat from the source. After."

What . . . what did he mean? That he wanted to, uh, eat her?

Fuck. Fuck. Fuck.

She wanted that so badly that she swore she nearly came there and then.

"I think our baby likes that idea," Steele said, dropping his hand to rub her bottom again. "I forgot to ask if there is any position that hurts your back? Are you all right like this?"

"Um, I think it would only be a problem if I was in the same position for a while, I think."

"If there is ever anything that hurts your back, you tell us," Grady said sternly. "I'll add that to the rules."

"I will."

"That's our good baby. Right, the count is twenty. Say your safeword if you need to."

36

Grady swore he was close to coming in his pants just from watching Damon spank Effie's naughty bottom. He reached down to adjust himself.

Steele caught the movement and sent him a knowing look as he paused to rub the warmth into her skin.

"How are you doing, Spitfire?" Steele asked.

"It hurts," she said pitifully.

Worry filled Steele's face and he paused. "It's too much?"

She was silent for a moment, sniffling. "No, Daddy."

"Your back?" Grady asked. He made a mental note to look into the best spanking positions for someone with back issues.

"It's all right. My back is pretty good most of the time."

He wasn't sure that he agreed. He thought that Effie liked to make light of it but that it gave her more issues than she let on.

Steele moved his arm to her lower back and she let out a moan of pleasure.

Grady was going to add massages to the list of things they needed to ensure she got.

"Last ten," Steele said.

He moved quickly, not giving her much time to think. His hand landed again and again until she was kicking her feet. Until her bottom was red and hot, jiggling with each slap, and she let out small sobs.

Poor baby.

But she'd brought this on herself. She needed to learn that they wouldn't put up with her talking badly about herself.

When he was finished, Steele turned her over so she sat sideways on his lap. He cuddled her in close, speaking to her quietly.

Fuck. They looked so good together.

Then she turned her face toward him. Poor sweetheart. She was crying again. He knew she hated doing that. She held out her hand to him and he immediately took hold, letting her draw him in close. He brushed his lips over her cheeks and she let out a small, satisfied sigh.

"Good baby, you're being so good for Daddy," Steele murmured to her. "What a precious Little baby. Our baby."

Grady ran his hand up and down her thigh until she calmed.

Then he grabbed a couple of tissues and Steele turned her so she was facing away from him but still on his lap. She winced as her ass obviously brushed up against him, but otherwise didn't complain.

Grady thought about just handing her the tissues but decided against it. He had to do what felt right . . . even if it wasn't what he was used to. And he felt curious. What it would feel like to take care of her in all ways?

So he lightly grasped her chin and wiped her face clean. Then he held the tissue to her nose. "Blow."

Her eyes widened.

"Effie. Blow."

She blew her nose and he felt surprisingly satisfied. Uh, it seemed he liked doing this. He'd enjoyed feeding her before. And now, cleaning her up.

"That's my good girl. Definitely being so good for us."

"Isn't she?" Steele murmured. "She's earned that reward."

"Indeed." Grabbing hold of her tights and panties, he slowly drew them down her legs.

Her eyes widened, but she didn't protest as he dropped them to one side.

"This is what you're going to do," he told her. "You're going to put your hands on your thighs and keep them there. If you move your hands without permission, then I'll play with you for far longer without allowing you any release. Be our good girl and you'll get to come sooner, understand me?"

She nodded.

"Words, Effie," Steele told her.

"Yes, I understand."

"Good girl." Grady thought about removing her dress, but knew she wasn't quite there yet. Although she'd have to get there soon because he wanted to see her naked.

Her warped view she had of her body needed to change. And he'd do whatever was necessary to help her see what they saw.

"Place your legs on either side of Damon's and keep them there."

"Yes, Sir." She stiffened. "Um, sorry. I don't know what to call you."

"I prefer my name on your lips." For the moment, anyhow.

"Yes, Grady."

"That's a good girl. So damn precious. We're going to take good care of you, aren't we, Damon?"

"Yes," Steele replied huskily as he tilted her head to the side and kissed up her neck.

It occurred to Grady that he hadn't even kissed her yet. But he'd get there. A first kiss was special.

So, instead, he made his way up the inside of her legs. Steele widened his legs to accommodate Grady's wide body.

She let out a small whimper as he moved up her inner thighs, raising the bottom of her dress.

"Grady," she murmured.

"You can always use your safeword," he told her.

"I . . . I . . . oh."

He glanced up to see that Steele had one of her breasts in his hand. He was playing with it over the material of her dress.

Fuck. He wanted to see her breasts badly. He was so hard it was painful.

He moved closer to her pussy. So damn pretty. Parting her lips, he studied her.

"Is . . . is something wrong?" she asked.

"Nothing is wrong," Steele told her gruffly. "You're fucking perfect. Isn't she, Grady?"

Fuck. He realized he'd been still and silent for too long.

"So fucking perfect," he murmured. "I've never seen such beauty."

"It . . . I . . . it's not beautiful."

Smack!

He slapped his hand down on her inner thigh, making her jolt with a cry.

"Have you ever had your pussy slapped, sweetheart?" Grady asked.

"N-no."

"If you want to find out how it feels, keep saying bad things about this pretty, perfect pussy."

She sucked in a breath, but he didn't want to give her too much time to think. That's when stupid shit came out of her mouth. And he didn't want to punish her right now . . . he wanted to reward them both.

So he ran his tongue along her pussy lips, making her moan.

Fuck, yes.

He pressed it in deeper, pushing it inside her passage. Fuck, she tasted good. Like nothing he'd tasted before.

And he could get addicted to the sounds coming from her mouth. Her thighs were tightening around his head.

Was she close already?

He knew it had been a long dry spell for her, but surely she'd been seeing to things herself?

Then again, maybe not.

He drew back, glancing up at her as he pushed two fingers inside her.

"Oh. Ohhh."

"Fuck me, I think she's close," Steele said.

"Yeah. How many times do you think we can make her come?"

Her eyes shot open and she stared down at him. "W-what? I can't come more than once."

"Challenge accepted."

Challenge accepted?

Was he kidding her? There was no way she could come more than once. Even when she made herself come, she was too sensitive afterward to come again.

Then again, it had been a while since she'd had the opportunity. She could only play with herself when Brooks wasn't around. And, to be honest, she hadn't felt like it lately.

But God, with how Grady could use his tongue—if anyone could make her come twice, it would be him.

And then there was Steele. He was playing with her nipples, kissing her neck, driving her higher and higher.

Grady's tongue returned to her clit, flicking it firmly as his fingers drove in and out of her.

"Fuck, baby," Steele groaned. "Give it to him. Give him all of it. Come for us."

It washed over her. So sweet and sharp that it made her gasp. But before she could come down from it properly, they were pushing her higher, into a deeper, stronger orgasm that made her scream.

Fuck. Fuck.

That was amazing.

She was floating. Her mind was dazed, her lips curling up into a smile. She felt them moving, then she opened her eyes to find Grady had shifted and was sitting beside Steele once again. His gaze was on her as his fingers continued to thrust in and out of her.

"What a good girl you are. So sweet and precious," he murmured. "Are you going to come for us again?"

"I can't," she cried.

Even if she thought she could have a third orgasm, there was no way she could do it while he was looking at her.

He flicked her clit with his thumb and she jolted with a whimper.

"I want you to come again. And you will."

"I can't!"

"Too sensitive?" Steele asked.

"Yes."

"We'll get you past that."

"But . . . but . . . I can't do it with you watching."

Grady grinned. That wicked, hot grin that made her insides melt. "We'll get you past that too."

Holy. Crap.

"Close your eyes if you need to, sweetheart," Grady told her. "But you're going to come again. I want to feel you come all over my hand, understand?"

Oh Lord.

Yeah, she thought she understood. A whimper escaped and she closed her eyes.

"I'm going to allow you that for now," Grady whispered. "But there's going to come a time when I'll order you to watch me as I make you come."

Fuck.

To her surprise, she came instantly. It wasn't as intense as the second orgasm, but it was softer and slower than the first.

And by the time she'd finished, she was exhausted. A spanking, a cry, and three orgasms?

She was so done.

"Think our baby needs a snuggle and a nap," Damon said into her ear.

Opening her eyes, she stared into Grady's satisfied face. Would he kiss her now?

But he simply drew his hand up to his mouth and licked it clean.

And Lord, she might have just come a fourth time.

As he moved back, Steele turned her to face him. Grasping her chin, he kissed her. It was a kiss of ownership. Possession. Heat and fire.

"So fucking hot. Do you know what you do to me? To us?" Steele asked.

She gasped dramatically.

Holy. Crap.

"I've been so selfish! I, um, can I . . . oh heck. Help you guys out?"

Steele looked at her for a moment before he threw his head back and laughed. She smiled, loving the sound of his laughter. Although she wasn't certain if he was laughing at her.

Bending forward, he kissed the tip of her nose. "Do I want your mouth around my dick and soon? Fuck, yes. But right now, it's nap time for my baby. She needs some care and attention. Some time with Daddy taking care of her."

Damn. These guys. Just damn.

Steele picked her up, cradling her against his chest.

"I don'ts need a nap. Really." She ruined that by yawning.

"I think you do. And Daddy is in charge, so what he says goes."

"That doesn't seem fair. Does Effie get to be in charge sometimes?" she asked.

"Effie does not," Grady said firmly.

That sucked.

"What would our good girl like? Some milk? Water?" Grady asked.

"Strawberry milk," she said. Then she buried her face in Steele's chest, not wanting to see their reaction.

"Hmm, I'm not sure we have strawberry milk," Grady said, running a hand down her back.

She shivered, knowing what those hands were now capable of.

"And doesn't that start with an S?" he asked.

"Doesn't count . . . it's a drink not a food and not having any strawberry milk is a crime."

"Indeed," Grady said with clear amusement.

"Not sure she should have sugar just before a nap anyway," Steele added. "Maybe some plain milk. In a travel mug since we don't have sippy cups or bottles."

Bottles?

Yikes.

She liked the idea of that. A lot.

"We'll have to get some of those, won't we? I'll get onto that," Grady said.

Steele turned away, carrying her up the stairs without even getting winded.

That was some strength.

They entered a masculine-looking room and she glanced around, feeling nervous. She moved her thumb up to her mouth without thinking.

Steele set her down on the bed, gazing down at her. "Fucking adorable."

Suddenly, she drew her thumb from her mouth. "Oh. Sorry."

"Nothing to be sorry about. I want you to feel safe enough to be yourself. Big or Little. Okay?"

She nodded. "Okay, Daddy."

"What do you need?"

"Not to nap."

"Nice try. If you don't know what you need, Daddy will take the lead."

Relief had her shoulders dropping. Steele observed her carefully. "I can see you like that idea. My girl doesn't want to have to think at all, does she? She wants us to make the decisions for her. I think that for so long she's been the one in charge that it's time for her to relax and let someone else take the reins."

Dear Lord.

It sounded like freaking heaven.

But almost impossible to believe. Although Steele and Grady seemed to naturally take charge of any situation. So, if anyone could do that, it was them.

"Right, let's get you to the toilet then. You must need to pee."

"Um, I do. But I can walk!"

"I think we've already had this conversation. Not a fan of repeating myself, which I've told you."

Holy heck.

Steele carried her into the bathroom and set her down in front of the toilet. Was he . . . was he going to stay? And shoot . . . she didn't have her panties.

"I'm gonna let you pee on your own today because you're still getting used to me. But eventually ... everything."

Something to look forward to. Not.

But true to his word, he turned to leave.

"Can I go get my panties?"

"You can have them back when you leave. Call out when you're finished."

Right. After she peed and cleaned up, she tried to peek at her bottom in the mirror, but it was too high for her to get a look.

"Trying to see how red your bottom is?"

She squealed and looked up to find Grady staring at her in amusement. She pushed her dress down.

That wasn't embarrassing or anything.

"I, um, yep."

Grady stepped forward. "It looks pink and beautiful. Come on, your milk is ready. Did you pee?"

She groaned and covered her face with her hands. "Yes."

"Good girl."

Reaching out, he took her hands from her face and then tugged her toward him. Grasping hold of her chin, he tilted her head back. "Damon said you want us to take control."

"I ... I ..."

"That's good, since that's what I planned on doing." Then he cupped the sides of her face with his hands.

Would he kiss her now?

He leaned in and kissed the tip of her nose. Her forehead.

That was sweet. So sweet she closed her eyes to savor it.

"Come. Nap time. Daddy is waiting."

He led her out to the bedroom, where she saw that the massive bed had some pillows in a U-shape in the middle. She gave Damon a surprised look.

"Brooks told us that you like to be surrounded when you sleep. So you don't fall out of bed."

Did he just?

"Crawl up into your nest, Twinkletoes," Grady ordered before he lifted her onto the bed. "Have you ever been swaddled while you sleep?"

"Um, no."

"We could try that," Steele mused.

Holy heck. That sounded good. But she wasn't quite ready for it.

Steele moved in beside her, pulling her up so she was resting against his chest. Then Grady handed him a travel mug. He held it to her lips while Grady sat down at her feet. He drew one into his lap and started massaging it.

Heaven.

"Her feet are slightly swollen," Grady commented. "We need to watch for that."

Steele grunted. "We will."

She drew her mouth away.

"Done, baby?" Steele asked.

She nodded and slid down into the bed as Grady got up so Steele could pull up the covers. The drapes were already pulled. They were a dark gray. The whole room was done in tones of gray and cream.

It was gorgeous and understated.

Suddenly, she remembered something. "I needs Slowly!"

"Slowly?" Steele asked.

"My sloth. He's in my handbag. I can'ts sleep without him!"

"I'll get him for you," Grady told her.

"Snuggle down, baby. Grady will be back with him in a moment. Shall I tell you a story about a princess and her knight?"

"What's about a princess and the ogre?" she teased.

"I do not look like an ogre, brat."

"But you sounds like one." She giggled as he tickled her.

"I can see I should have spanked you harder," he grumbled.

"No, Daddy! That would be mean. You shouldn't be mean to Effie. She's far too cute to be spanked."

"Effie is adorable. But there is no such thing as being too cute to be spanked."

"Bummer," she sighed.

"Here you are."

She glanced over as Grady walked into the room, holding her handbag and Slowly.

"Slowly!" She reached for him, tucking him in against her. Suddenly, her Big brain interfered. "I needs my phone. In case Brooks calls."

Grady nodded and handed it to Steele. He set it beside her. "You can answer it if it's Brooks. But no going online or playing games without Daddy or Grady's permission."

Grady frowned slightly but didn't say anything. She slid her thumb into her mouth with a sigh. She really was tired.

"What's this?" Steele asked, grabbing her arm. Drat, her sleeve had moved up at some stage.

He was studying the bruise on her arm. "What's this bruise from?"

"Oh, that's nothing." She tried to lower her sleeve.

"Effie," Steele said in a commanding voice. "Who gave you that bruise?"

"Nobody gave it to me."

"Do I need to remind you that you're not to lie to us?" Grady said in a stern voice. "Tell us. Now."

"I gave it to myself, all right?"

They both stiffened, looking at each other.

"Not like that!" she said. "I don't hurt myself. It was just . . . I was pinching myself because this job seemed too good to be true. A dream. So I would pinch myself to make sure I was awake. That's all."

"You will not do that anymore," Steele said sternly. "I mean it. I will check your arm in a week's time, and if that bruise isn't fading, you'll be in trouble."

Sheesh. They were so . . . intense.

"If you need to make sure that you're awake, we'll be happy to oblige," Grady told her in a smooth voice.

She wasn't even sure exactly what he meant. But part of her really wanted to find out.

"Sleep, my baby." Damon kissed her forehead. "Stay in bed until one of us gets you up, understand? Little girls aren't to get out of bed on their own."

"Be a good Little girl for us," Grady added, kissing her forehead as well. "Sleep tight."

Yeah. She was totally a good girl.

37

Grady glanced up from his laptop as Steele entered the kitchen. "You were in the shower awhile." His lips quirked with amusement.

"You saying that you didn't go into your shower to jack off?" Damon grumbled as he moved to the fridge to take out a bottle of water.

Yeah, Grady couldn't deny that at all.

Although it hadn't taken him long to blow his load. Fuck, just the memory of her spread legs as she sat on Steele's lap was enough to get him hard again.

"Just when I thought I was done, it's like I could feel her again squirming against me as you ate her out, and I'd get fucking hard all over again."

I could've helped you with that.

Fuck. This had been building for years. Yet, he wasn't brave enough to say the words. The one thing he was terrified of losing in this life was Damon. And so that was the one thing where he wasn't willing to take a risk.

"Maybe you should have some Gatorade. Replace all those

lost electrolytes. I don't want you getting dizzy on me and fainting from dehydration. I also don't want to have to tell the first responder that you passed out because your balls were empty."

"Fuck you." Steele was grinning as he came over to sit next to him. "What are you doing?"

"Buying things for a nursery. There's a new store in Billings that has things for Littles. I'm gonna order most of it online, but I'm thinking of going in there just in case there's something I miss."

Steele straightened. "Yeah?"

"Yes. I'm researching the best things. What do you think about buying her a crib? You can get them with padding around the sides so she won't hurt herself if she rolls around too much."

"I think that's a fucking great idea." Steele studied him carefully. "You researching this stuff because that's a Grady thing to do or for another reason?"

"A Grady thing to do?" he questioned.

"Yeah, you know what I mean. You do the research. You're the organizer. The brains. I'm the muscle."

"You're the muscle?" Grady asked. "I have fucking muscle."

Steele ran his gaze over him. "Yeah, you do."

Grady swallowed. Did he imagine that heat in the other man's gaze? He had to have, right?

Fuck. He was hard again. Maybe he should have spent longer in the shower.

"I'm doing this because I want Effie to have everything she needs," Grady said. "Do we need to talk about it beyond that?"

"Not now. But at some stage you might want to think about what you really want. Or she might start to get confused. All I'm saying."

A beep sounded on Grady's computer and he brought up the app for the camera he had in her room. "She's on the move."

"What? It hasn't even been an hour. And I told her to stay put if she woke up."

"Seems she's in a mood to be naughty," Grady said.

"Is she just? Little brat. Where is she?" Steele asked.

"Moving down the stairs."

"Coming this way?" Steele asked.

"No, she's headed into your study." Grady looked up at Damon. "She's looking at the photos."

"Um, time to do some explaining." Steele squeezed his shoulder as he moved past.

He pretended he didn't feel that in other parts of his body.

But it was hard.

Very hard.

∽

Steele in the doorway of his home office and watched as his baby moved along the wall of photos. Most of them were of him and Jacqui or him and Grady. Some of the three of them. A few with Spike. And a couple of Spike and Millie.

She stopped at one of him, Grady, and Jacqui from years ago.

"My sister," he said quietly.

She gasped, turning to him. "I'm sorry. I didn't mean to pry."

She had Slowly in one hand. He walked over to her and took her hand in his.

"It's not being nosy if I offer up the information." He pointed to another photo. "That's Spike. He was married to my sister before she died. His real name is Quillon, but no one else calls him that. That's his girl, Millie. You'll meet them at some stage."

"You kept in contact with him."

"Yep. He's quiet. Doesn't say much. Might scare you to begin with. But you'll love Millie, though. She's . . . quirky. Fun. They're good people."

"I've been called quirky. Nan used to say that I should act more normal."

He leaned back against the desk and drew her between his legs. "Nan didn't know everything. Nothing wrong with being quirky."

"I guess not. You were close to Jacqui, weren't you?"

"Yeah. She was my world. She and Grady. Our parents weren't the best. Not abusive, just neglectful and shitty. I basically raised Jacqui. She was mine, you know?"

"I'm so sorry."

"She was so beautiful. Quiet. Reserved. She and Spike lived in Chicago at the time. They'd just flown home after visiting me. A couple of guys carjacked them. Nearly killed Spike, and they shot my darling sister in the head."

"Oh God!" she cried. Turning, she hugged him tight. He felt her body shake and heard her sob.

"You're leaking, baby."

"I'm so sorry. I don't know what else to say."

He sat on the desk and lifted her onto his lap so she was sitting sideways.

"Not gonna lie, baby. Was the fucking worst day of my life. Didn't think I was going to keep going. Didn't want to keep going. Not without my light. Only thing that kept me going was Grady."

"Does he know that?" she asked.

"He knows what he means to me," he said with certainty. Although a part of him wasn't so sure.

"Maybe you should tell him anyway. And that's why you didn't think you'd ever be in a relationship?"

"Couldn't imagine ever falling in love. Risking losing someone again seemed impossible."

"But you've always had someone. Grady."

He tightened his arms around her. "Smart, aren't you? You're right. I've always had someone to lose. And I never have." He stared off into the distance. "Guess I always thought he was strong enough to survive."

"Or maybe you've still been holding a piece of yourself back. To make sure it doesn't hurt you as badly again if something were to happen to him."

He stood in shock, setting her on her feet. "What are you saying?"

"I don't know." She turned away, then turned back with a big smile. "Didn't you say we were going in the hot tub?"

It was her fake smile. The one he hated.

"Don't do that, baby. You don't have to be scared that you've upset me and hide. Either behind a fake smile or by actually hiding under something."

She bit her lip and raised her hand to her earring. Then she seemed to think better of it and dropped it.

"Good girl," he murmured, leaning forward to kiss her forehead. "You're such a good baby."

"And you're a good Daddy. And an amazing brother and friend. We'd all be lost without you, Damon Steele. So don't you ever talk about not being able to carry on, understand me?" She gave him a fierce look.

"I understand you. You want to tell me what you meant by me holding back with Grady?"

"Not right now."

"Hmm. Now, how about instead of that hot tub, we make some playdough?"

Her eyes widened. "You can make playdough?"

"Yep. I sure can."

She clapped her hands. "Let's do this."

"Good. Why you're being punished, I'll make you some lunch and some playdough."

"What? Why? I didn't do nothing wrong, Daddy!" Her hands crept to cover her bottom just in case.

"Did you stay where you were put? What did I tell you?" he asked sternly.

"Oh, shoot."

"Fifty lines, baby girl. Saying you will stay where you're put."

Well, bummer.

∼

Jeez, lines sucked.

They sucked sooo bad.

By the time she finished them, her hand was ready to drop off.

"Daddy, my hand hurts!" she called out from the kitchen table where she was sitting.

Steele and Grady were working in the kitchen, making lunch and playdough.

"You do the crime, then you have to do the time, baby girl," Steele replied.

She let her lower lip slip out.

"Poor Twinkletoes. Want me to kiss it better?" Grady asked, unexpectedly.

"I don'ts think that kisses will help," she told him with a pathetic sniffle. "I thinks it's gonna drop off."

"We can't have that." Grady sat in the chair next to her, then picked up her hand and kissed it lightly.

Okay, that seemed quite a Daddy thing to do.

And she loved it. Even if he didn't want to be her Daddy, it seemed like he didn't shy away from looking after her Little.

"There. How does that feel?"

"I thinks it's all better. It's a miracle!" She raised her hands up in the air. "Although I thinks that I should have magic beans. Just to make sure."

"No jelly beans before lunch," Steele decreed.

"Gosh, Daddy. You are such a meanie."

"Sometimes, a Daddy just has to be mean." Steele walked over and set a plate of green things in front of her. Then he picked up the pad and read over it.

Sheesh, didn't he trust her?

"What's this stuff, Daddy? Is it your lunch?"

"And yours," he replied.

"Nuh-uh, this is green."

"Don't tell me you don't eat green things?" Grady asked with amusement as he walked back to the kitchen and drew something out of the oven. Now, that smelled good.

"Is that lasagna?" she asked.

"Sure is," Grady replied.

"Yummy!" She threw her hands in the air again.

Steele put the pad down. "That's cute, but you need to try a kale chip."

"I don't think I do, Daddy."

"You do if you want to play with some playdough after lunch."

"Daddy! That's not nice."

Steele just gave her a stern look.

"What if it makes me sick?"

"You think I would give you something that made you sick?" Steele gave her a shocked look.

"It might. I might get the sickies from it."

"If you do, then you never have to try it again," Steele told her.

She sighed. Long and loud.

This was a huge imposition. But she guessed if Daddy really

wanted her to risk her health to try something this yucky, then she had to be a good girl.

Picking up a chip, she took a delicate bite.

Oh God.

It was delicious.

"Daddy! Why haven't you given this to me before?" She ate that one, then another. "These are sooo good. It's a crime I haven't eaten them before."

"Is it?" Steele said with amusement.

"Uh-huh, Daddy."

Grady walked over and set the lasagna down on the table. Then he reached for a kale chip.

Big. Mistake.

She smacked his hand away. "No!"

"Excuse me?" Grady asked.

"Not yours. Effie's."

"Effie has to share," Grady told her.

"No!" She picked up the plate and held it to her chest. "Effie doesn't wanna share."

"Baby girl," Steele said sternly. Although she thought she saw his lips twitch. "That's not the way things work in this house. Be a good girl and let Grady have a chip."

She gave Grady a disgruntled look. "One chip."

"Effie, share," Grady told her firmly.

She sighed. Long and loud. Very dramatically. She had to make her point.

But she let Grady have a kale chip.

Then she ate all the rest. And by the time she finished, she didn't really feel like the lasagna. But Steele insisted on feeding her some.

And he made the choo-choo noises. So that was pretty funny.

Grady stood when they were finished and started to clear plates.

"Effie help."

She stood, but both of them gave her a firm look.

"Effie will not help," Steele said firmly. "You're not allowed to carry around heavy things."

"Plates aren't heavy, Daddy."

"They are for Little girls."

So she had to sit and watch while they cleared up. But then Steele bought over several lumps of playdough. There was a red one, a blue one and a green one.

"Daddy! I loves it." She started playing with the different colors, rolling them into shapes.

To her shock, both men sat at the table and started creating things.

She made a snail and held it up. "Look at my snail!"

"Wow, baby girl. That's amazing," Steele told her as he put the finishing touches on his snowman.

"Best snail I've ever seen." Grady finished his house. Which looked awesome.

But not as awesome as this day.

Or her snail. Because it was the bomb.

38

Effie was expecting the knock on the door.
But she still jumped. Nerves filled her as she rushed over to open the door. There stood Grady, looking as dapper as he always did. Tonight, he wore a white shirt with navy blue pants and a vest.

"Delicious," she murmured.

He grinned. "I think that's my line." He ran his gaze up and down her. "Sweetheart, you look absolutely edible."

Her heart leaped in her throat at the memory of him eating her. And at the thought of everything they might do tonight.

It had been a long few days waiting for Saturday. And she'd spent far too much time thinking about what she was going to wear. She'd finally found this gorgeous, vibrant red dress at a store. It had been marked down and just within her budget. It had a sweetheart neckline and was tight around her breasts before flaring out slightly.

"Lord, baby. Damon is going to cream himself." She flushed bright red as he stepped farther into her apartment. "Too bad for him, he isn't here right now." Then he grabbed her around her hips and drew her into him. "But lucky for me, I am."

His hand went around the back of her head, holding her steady as he devoured her.

And it was amazing.

The man could kiss. Holy crap. If he hadn't been holding her up, she'd have collapsed onto the floor in a heap.

When he drew back, she stared up at him in shock.

"Might need to fix your lipstick now, sweetheart."

"Eek!" She moved out of his hold and into the bathroom. When she returned, he was leaning against the wall, holding on to her coat with one hand and staring at her hungrily.

How was it possible for one man to be that gorgeous?

And how was it possible for her to be this darn lucky?

"Come here," he murmured. It was said softly, but it was an order all the same.

When she got there, he spun his finger in the air. "Turn."

She spun around and he helped her put on her coat.

"I don't think anyone has helped me put a coat on before the two of you," she said. "It's very gentlemanly."

He huffed out a laugh. "Think Steele would object to being called a gentleman, but I'll take it."

"There's nothing wrong with being a gentleman."

"Course there isn't."

She turned back and he grasped hold of her chin. "You're going to be our good girl tonight?"

"Yes," she whispered.

He smiled. "You going to let us both fuck you? However we want? However we demand?"

She moaned. "Yes."

"If I want to take your mouth while Damon takes that pussy, you're going to let us?"

"Yes." Her heart raced.

"We didn't discuss anal play the other day. I was . . . distracted. You good with anal sex?"

"I . . . it's been a long time, but yes."

"Don't worry, sweetheart. We're not going to just start fucking you. Part of the fun is the preparation. But I got a set of butt plugs just for you. Along with some other gifts."

Butt plugs? Her asshole clenched at that.

And other gifts? Were they similar to butt plugs?

Holy heck.

"They're at Pinkies. But just so you know, we like our naughty girl too. We like you whichever way you come to us."

Damn. These guys.

They were kind of mobsters. They looked like sin. Yet, they said the sweetest things. The sort of things she'd always read in books or seen in movies, or wished for in her dreams.

"Brooks got away okay?" he asked.

And he just kept getting better.

"Yeah, sometimes it feels sad that he doesn't need me like he used to. And other times . . . well, it has its benefits." She gave him a shy look.

"It definitely does, Twinkletoes. You packed a bag?"

"Yep." She picked up the duffel bag she'd set by the door.

Grady held out his hand.

Huh. Effie thought they were past this but slapped her hand down on his. "Let's do this."

He looked at her for a moment. Then he threw his head back and laughed. He laughed until he had to wipe away his tears. Then, shaking his head, he reached out and took the bag from her.

"Precious," he muttered.

Oh. Right.

Lord, she was an idiot.

She knew she was blushing bright red as he took her hand to lead her outside.

But how much did she love that he was holding her hand?

A lot. She loved it a lot.

As they moved down the walkway, Roddy, her upstairs neighbor, strode toward them. He glanced up and grew pale at the sight of Grady.

"Hi, Roddy," she called out.

He grunted and skirted around them, giving Grady nervous looks.

"What did you do to him?" she asked as they approached the town car where Raul waited.

"Me? Nothing. But Steele sent a few boys to chat to him about his late-night parties. He hasn't been having them anymore, right? You would tell me if he was, wouldn't you, Effie?" He grasped hold of her chin, tilting her head back.

Finally, an epiphany hit her.

Was he more at ease touching her when he controlled it? When he'd played at clubs, presumably, he'd touched the subs. But he'd completely controlled the narrative.

That made sense.

Grady liked complete control. Always. He might never be all cuddly and affectionate in front of others, but he was definitely more at ease when it was just the three of them.

"Effie?"

"Yes, I'd tell you," she blurted out. "And no, he hasn't been having his late-night parties."

"What a good girl you are, gifting me your submission. You like that, don't you? Having us take charge?"

"Like might not be the right word," she whispered. "I think I could get addicted to it."

He grinned. Then he opened the door and helped her into the car. She slid along as he climbed in, putting her duffel at his feet. But instead of sitting by the door, he slid into the middle seat. Then he buckled her seat belt before doing up his own.

He knocked on the privacy screen and the car took off.

Then he grasped hold of her chin. "Now, to say a proper hello to my girl."

And oh my God. The kiss was off the charts. It started soft, then grew harder, more demanding. By the time he drew back, she was in a daze, just trying to remember to breathe.

By the time they got to Pinkies, she knew she'd likely have to redo her makeup. That her lips were probably swollen and her eyes were glazed.

And she didn't give a fuck about any of that.

All she wanted was to ease the arousal rushing through her. But what she most wanted to do was touch him. To make him feel as good as he did her.

"Grady," she moaned.

"Shh, be a good girl for me a bit longer. I'll get you inside and we'll do something to ease your need."

"You . . . I want you."

"I know. I want that too. But we're not fucking until I get you home and can take my time. Not fucking you for the first time here at a strip bar."

"How do you feel about getting head at a strip bar?" Then she realized what she'd just said. "I meant from me! From me! No one else better be giving you head!"

"I don't mind if you wanna give me head, honey," a man called out. "Titties and an ass like that, you can do whatever the fuck you want to me. Bet you suck like a hoover and those tits will bounce so pretty."

She froze and then looked around, seeing that they were in the main bar area of Pinkies.

Fucking hell.

She hadn't even noticed.

But she didn't even have to think how to react. Grady was all over it. He drew her even closer to him, pressing her face into his chest.

Then she heard another voice.

Oh, fuck.

"What the fuck did you just say?" a deep voice roared.

Oh, shit.

"Let me go, Grady." She tried to fight her way free.

"No, let Steele handle this. Stop, Effie. Keep fighting me, and as soon as we're upstairs, you're going over my lap to get your ass tanned."

She froze.

"Good girl."

"Lex, get this motherfucker out of here. And you listen to me, asshole. You don't speak to any woman like that in my club. Not if they're a stripper or a server, and certainly not if they're my. Fucking. Woman!"

Oh Lord.

Steele wasn't happy.

"I didn't know she was yours, man! Hey, I'm a paying customer! Get your hands off me!"

"Be thankful it's Lex touching you. If I touched you, you'd be eating through a straw."

Grady started moving her along and she had to turn away so she could see where she was going.

Grady stopped them at a door, which Trev opened with a respectful nod. She forced a smile for him, even though her stomach was in knots. "Hey, Trev, how are your girls?"

"They sure keep life interesting. Alice reckons she's old enough to date now. She's fucking thirteen. Not fucking happening. And Julia has decided that she's a vegan. Honest to God, Effie. I need some backup in my house."

His girls kept him on his toes, and they were only thirteen

and eleven. Wait until they were older.

"Upstairs, Effie," Grady said firmly.

"See ya, Trev."

"Later, Effie." He gave Grady a respectful nod.

Grady led her up the stairs, and when they reached the top he led her over to the sofa and quickly took off her jacket, before taking her handbag. She'd left her duffel in the car. Then he sat back, drawing her down with him.

"Is Damon all right? Maybe I should go to him. That really wasn't necessary."

"It fucking was. Now sit here and prepare yourself."

"For what?"

"Hurricane Steele."

39

Steele wasn't happy.

Nothing had gone his way today and he'd wasted way too much time on shit that was fucking annoying.

Which meant he didn't have time to go pick up their girl. Maybe he needed to get an assistant like Grady.

Then, he needed to fire Grady's assistant so she could spend more time with him.

He grinned at the thought. Grady might complain. Then again, it would free her up to give Grady head while he was working.

So he might not.

Steele had seen her during the week, but a few minutes here and there, along with some phone calls, just wasn't enough.

Steele wanted all of Effie.

He was all in.

He paused on the stairs leading up to his private area.

Did he love Effie?

That was impossible, right? He hadn't known her long

enough. But was there a specific length of time you had to know someone to know they were yours?

Fucked if he knew. But he wanted her in his life.

Forever.

So maybe he did know.

Shaking off his thoughts and needing to see them both, he took off up the stairs.

When he reached the top, he saw Effie snuggled into Grady on the sofa.

She studied him with wide eyes. Was she scared of him? He'd let Lex deal with the asshole. He'd held back. Which had been fucking hard when all he'd wanted was to rip the jerk's head off.

No one messed with his girl.

He stopped and crossed his arms over his chest. He was going to shelter her as much as he could from the more dangerous parts of his life. The areas where he was the Boss. But she still had to take him as he was.

There was no way he could change that. And part of who he was, was a man who would always lay down his life for his woman.

He held out a finger to her, then crooked it.

She stared at him.

"Come. Here. Effie."

She got up slowly, moving toward him. And he wished he could take a moment to study how gorgeous she looked in that killer dress. But then she started running, throwing herself at him. He took a tight hold of her, pressing her to him.

"New rule," he said. "I tell you to come to me, then you do, understand me?"

"Sorry," she whispered. "You just . . . you sounded so mad down there."

"Wasn't mad at you, baby girl." He'd have thought that was

obvious. But maybe to Effie, it wasn't. "And I'd never be so angry that I would harm you. Understand?"

"I was the one talking about blow jobs," she said. "And I wasn't that upset by what he said. I can deal with that sort of stuff."

"I thought we'd made this obvious, but it seems we've got to make it more obvious."

"What?" she asked as he picked her up and carried her over to where Grady was sitting, watching them closely.

Steele sat and settled her on his lap so she was straddling him. "You need to get this right now, Effie. We have your back. Maybe you've been doing it alone for a long time, but that stopped the minute you became ours. That means that if someone comes at you, bothers you, or upsets you, we take care of it. Even better, we fucking stop it before it can get that far. So no, you do not get some fucker saying shit like that to you without us doing something about it. Now. Do. You. Get. Me?"

"I get you," she whispered.

And this time, he thought she did. About time.

Wrapping his hand around the back of her head, he brought her in for a kiss. A kiss he should have had a while ago if he hadn't been busy fucking throwing some asshole out.

Grady tried to move and Steele grabbed his arm. "Where do you think you're going?" He was not in the mood for anyone to push him right now.

"Just going to check that guy is gone."

"You are not chasing him down."

"Chasing him down?" Effie looked at Grady in surprise.

"No jumping anyone in a dark alley," Steele warned.

"What?" she whispered.

"No, Grady," he repeated as the other man narrowed his gaze at him.

"You don't get to tell me no."

"Our girl is here in a shit-hot dress, looking like a dream. That guy is an idiot and a prick, but he's gone. And we both know that if you want to track him down and ruin him, you can do that later. Right now, are you really choosing to fuck him up over being with our baby?"

Grady looked down at Effie and his face softened. "I was promised a blow job. And there's the gifts we have for her."

"We better get on with giving her those, then."

"I don't need gifts," she said. But her tension had eased and she looked curious.

"That's tough, baby girl," he told her. "Because you're getting them."

A knock and the sound of Trev calling out his name made him groan. "Christ."

"That's what you get when you're The Boss," Grady said.

Fuck. Him.

"What is it, Trev?" he barked, setting Effie down next to him.

Trev walked in, giving him a nervous glance. "There's a guy here to see you. Said his name is Wolfe."

Motherfucking bastard.

"Fucking Wolfe. I'm over his fucking shit. Where is he?"

"Downstairs in the foyer."

"Take him to Grady's office," Steele ordered. "Stay there with him. I'll be there in a minute to make shit very clear."

Trev's eyes widened. "Uh, sure. Okay." Trev turned and took off.

"Damon, I think you intimidate him."

He glanced over at his girl as she stared at him worriedly. "Good. That's what I was aiming for."

She wiggled a finger at him. "It's not nice to intimidate people, especially if you're their boss. What if Trev has a problem? He won't think he can come to you."

"He better not come to me," he grumbled. "If he starts

coming to me with his fucking problems just shoot me in the fucking head. I am not here for them to off-load their problems onto me. I have enough of my own."

"Oh no, what's wrong? Is there something I can do?"

He stared down at her for some time before his eyes filled with heat. "Fuck, my girl. So damn sweet. You were right, Grady."

"I usually am," Grady drawled, making her giggle. "But what was I right about this time?"

"When you find sweet, you hold on tight, and you don't let it go."

"You need to learn to listen to me more," Grady said. "I'm as smart as I am handsome. Which means I'm really fucking smart."

She giggled again.

Christ. He loved listening to her giggling. And he also loved the carefree look on Grady's face. He didn't know when the man had grown so serious. Maybe it had been happening slowly over the past few years.

But Effie was bringing the old Grady back. And Steele wanted that with a hunger that surprised him.

"I'll be back soon."

"Hurry," she whispered. "I miss you already."

So fucking sweet.

~

Fucking Wolfe.

He hoped he got the message now. Steele wasn't calling his guys back. Wolfe should've had a better hold on his men in the first place, then they wouldn't have caused Steele a headache, coming into Pinkies and upsetting his girls.

And he wouldn't be looking to teach them a lesson.

He stomped up the stairs after talking to Wolfe and thought he'd died and gone to fucking heaven. Grady was sitting back on the sofa with his arms along the back while Effie was on her knees between his legs, sucking his fat cock into her mouth.

"Fuck me. How long did I take?"

"Too long," Grady replied. "I had to start giving Effie her gifts."

"Yeah. Which one did you start with?"

"Why don't you go exploring and find out?" Grady wrapped his hand up in Effie's hair as she tried to slide off his cock. "Uh-uh, no one said you could stop, sweetheart. You keep sucking my dick like the good girl I know you can be. Your mouth is so fucking hot. Feels so damn sweet. That's it. Suck on my dick. You like it, don't you?"

"Fuck. Does she?"

"Oh yeah. Our girl really gets into sucking dick. Our dicks."

Damn. She was fucking perfect for them. Steele moved in behind her. She had her legs pressed together, which wouldn't do at all.

He looked at her feet and noticed that she wasn't wearing an ankle bracelet. So Grady hadn't given her all of their gifts.

He raised her skirt up over her ass. She paused and he slapped her ass.

"Don't you stop sucking Grady's dick. You stop and you'll get your bottom spanked."

A low moan escaped her and Steele glanced up to find Grady was holding a small remote up.

Steele grinned. Ah, that present.

When he had her dress up, he could see that she wasn't wearing panties. "What a good girl for not wearing panties."

"So good," Grady said. "She needs a reward."

Fuck, yes.

"Part your legs, baby girl. As wide as they'll go."

She moaned but did as she was ordered.

He ran his hands up her thighs to her ass.

Christ. What an ass. Plump. Round. Fucking perfect. And it was time they started training it. He parted her ass cheeks, watching her hole clench.

Nervous. Excited.

Grady groaned. "Fuck, man. Will you hurry up? You have no idea how good she is with her mouth."

No, but he wanted to find out.

"Hand it to me."

Grady leaned over and grabbed the box sitting on the side table. Steele opened it up, retrieving the lube.

"Baby girl, Daddy is going to open up your ass."

She let out a protesting noise.

"I won't hurt you. And if you're worrying about anything else, like someone coming in here and seeing, you need to stop. Because I would never let that happen."

She relaxed and he knew that was what she'd been thinking. But he wasn't going to take offense because she'd soon learn.

He wouldn't allow anyone to touch her or see her. No one but them.

He placed some lube on her backhole and on his fingers. Then, slowly pressed his finger inside her as his other hand traveled south to her pussy. A small cord was hanging out that was attached to the egg Grady was controlling. He pressed his palm against her mound and could feel the vibrations.

He pushed his finger in and out of her ass as he ran his other fingers through her drenched pussy.

"Fuck me," he murmured. "She either really loves sucking you off, or she's enjoying the fuck out of having that vibrating egg inside her."

"Both," Grady grunted. His jaw was clenched tight. He was having trouble holding back his orgasm.

Steele knew how that felt. His own dick was pressing against his pants, demanding release. But he didn't want to take her here.

Nope. As soon as Effie and Grady finished work, they were taking her home. He didn't care if he was needed here.

People would have to fucking deal.

He moved up to two fingers in her ass as he flicked at her clit. She moaned and tightened.

"She's so close."

"Fuck, so am I. Get that fucking plug inside her."

Steele drew his fingers from her ass, loving the way she whimpered in protest.

His poor girl.

After he got the plug ready, he pushed it slowly into her.

"Push out, baby. That's it. Good girl. Look at your little asshole stretching to take the plug. That's it. Now that it's in, you get your reward."

"Fuck. Fuck. Hurry the fuck up, man. Make her come."

Steele moved his finger back to her clit as Grady hit the remote. It didn't take her long until she was screaming her release. As soon as she started to come, Grady grabbed hold of her head and surged deep.

And she fucking didn't even blink. Just swallowed him down.

"Fuck, baby. Fuck me," Steele whispered as Grady carefully drew himself out. "Fucking made for us."

Grady brushed his finger over her cheek. "Amazing. I've never had better head."

"Really?" She gave him a pleased look.

"Not ever."

Fuck. Now Steele needed to feel her mouth on his dick. "Time to go home."

"Bit early isn't it?" Grady asked with a knowing look on his face.

"Been waiting for this moment for far too fucking long. I try to take her now and some fucker will probably interrupt us. So we're leaving. Baby girl, the plug and egg stay in, understand me?"

She looked back at him and nodded.

Yeah. She was fucking perfect.

40

Effie looked up at Steele as he began stripping.

She barely remembered the drive back to their place. She was just a bundle of arousal and heat.

Need.

They'd sat in the back of the car with her between them, one of her legs over each of theirs as they'd continued torturing her.

Playing with her clit, cupping her breasts, and pressing the button so that damn egg vibrated.

Killing her.

And now they were in Steele's bedroom. She was lying on his bed where he'd tossed her and was about to see him naked.

Lord have mercy.

The man was huge. Muscular and strong and gorgeous.

Off went his shirt, revealing a tattoo that went down one side of his chest and an arm.

Holy. Heck.

How was it even possible to be that gorgeous? Tanned with a light spattering of hair on his chest and down his stomach . . . leading her down to where she really wanted to go.

She licked her lips.

"You want my cock, baby? Want it in your mouth? Your pussy? Your ass?"

She clenched down around the plug in her ass. Part of her wasn't sure she was ready for that.

But a bigger part of her knew that he'd make it good for her.

"Yes."

"Yes, what?" he asked.

"All of it. I want all of it."

"Say, please. Be a good baby and ask Daddy for it nicely."

"Please, Daddy. Please give me your thick cock. I need it so bad."

She watched as a pleased look filled his face.

"That's my baby." He moved to his pants, stripping them off. Even his legs were thick with muscle.

Powerful. Protective.

Hers.

"You're mine," she whispered.

"All yours, baby."

Her gaze slid to where Grady sat. He'd moved to the corner. It was darker there, in the shadows. But she could see he'd taken off his vest and undone the buttons on his shirt. He had one arm bent, the elbow on the arm of the chair, his chin in his hand.

Every inch the sexy Alpha. The king in his throne.

About to watch.

A shiver ran through her.

"And you're mine. And I'm yours," Effie said.

Grady nodded his head. That was enough. He didn't have to say anything.

They were both hers.

Wasn't she lucky?

"Time to strip, baby."

"Can we turn off the light?" she asked nervously. Only the

table lamp was on, but it was still enough for them to see all of her.

"Turn off the light?" Steele asked.

"Um. Yeah."

"Fuck, no." Reaching down, he removed her shoes, before he lifted her from the bed and set her on her feet. Then he turned her so she was facing Grady and he started pulling the zipper of her dress down.

This was really happening.

"I'd prefer to do this in the dark!"

"You had no trouble sucking Grady off with the light on. Or being eaten out during the day."

"I got caught up in the moment." And she hadn't been fully naked.

"You sure did. And you will again. So just fucking relax and let us see this beautiful body. Let us worship it the way it was supposed to be worshipped."

She couldn't help but suck in as he took her dress off, leaving her in her sexiest bra and nothing else. She slid her arm around over her tummy.

"No. If you can't keep from covering yourself up, you're getting your hands tied," he warned.

Crap.

She moved her arm back to her side. Grady watched them intensely. She could practically feel the heat coming off him. Did he like what he saw?

Then Steele took her bra off. Reaching around, he cupped her breasts, holding them up. Almost as though offering them up to the man in the chair.

Fuck. That was hot.

Then he tweaked her nipples and she moaned. The orgasm they'd given her in the club had made her hungrier for more. The second orgasm in the car just took the edge off.

More. She needed more.

"My baby is so hot. So fucking beautiful, isn't she, Grady?"

"Like a dream come to life," Grady replied. "Couldn't have made someone better for us."

Oh Lord. They were killing her.

"I like being watched," Steele told her. "But I'd only ever allow Grady to watch. Understand?"

"Yes, Daddy." He was so protective that he'd never allow anyone else to see her.

And she loved that.

Steele turned her to face him. "Want your mouth on my cock, baby girl. Can't wait any longer. Sit on the side of the bed."

She sat. Shoot. It really wasn't her best angle. One arm slid over her tummy. Then, suddenly, the egg inside her began to vibrate, making her moan. Her arm slid away as arousal rushed through her.

"I see we've just got to keep your mind off your worries and on how much you need to come," Steele muttered.

Christ. The plug in her ass shifted, sending more need through her. Then Steele stripped off his boxers.

Lord have mercy.

His dick was wider than Grady's and maybe as long. Either way, neither man was small, and she couldn't see how she would ever take one of them in her ass and in her pussy at the same time.

No way in hell.

"Baby. Suck. Now."

Oops. Her man was getting impatient. She wrapped her hand around the base of him and licked her way along the head.

"Do not play with me."

Effie smiled as she slid her mouth down on him, moaning with pleasure. She loved this and wanted to make him come like she had Grady.

"Fuck me, she really likes this, doesn't she?" Steele murmured, brushing his fingers through her thick hair. "That's it, my baby is so hot. Such a precious girl, sucking on her Daddy's dick. Take a bit more. How clever you are."

Damn. She lapped up his praise, preening.

He wrapped her hair around his fist and tugged it slightly. The sting of pain only made her hotter. She groaned.

"That's my girl. You like a bit of pain, don't you? I bet you're so wet right now."

The vibrations stopped just as she was about to reach that peak again. He drew her away so she could take a couple of breaths, then pushed his dick back into her mouth.

"Fuck. Fuck. Enough."

He stepped back, and she stared up at him curiously.

"Not a young guy anymore, Spitfire. If I come in your mouth, it's gonna take me a while to recover. And the place I really want to be is in that pussy. But first, I need to taste that pussy. So lay down on the bed, ass facing Grady. I'm gonna take out the plug and egg, then I'm eating you. And then I'm fucking you. Reckon after that, Grady is gonna want to fuck you too. Think you're up for that?"

What the heck?

Did she think she was up for that? Well, she knew she'd give it a go or die trying.

"I'm up for it."

"Good girl. Lie back, bend your legs with your feet flat on the mattress, and spread."

She hadn't realized exactly how much she would enjoy a bossy man. Especially a dominant man in bed.

But she liked that it took away her concerns over what to do next, how to move, and what to say or do.

She just followed instructions.

"That's it," Steele murmured, moving between her legs. He

leaned over her with his hands on either side of her head and kissed her.

Shit.

What a kiss. She didn't want to lose his mouth, so when he drew back, she chased after it, but he shook his head.

"No, baby. I need to taste you." His mouth moved down her body and he took her nipples into his mouth one after the other, sucking eagerly.

Fuck. Yes.

Her moan of pleasure filled the room. Then Steele kept going lower until he was kneeling on the floor, looking up at her.

That's when Grady drew close, sitting on the bed next to her.

"You undressed," she said with a pout as she took in his broad chest. Unlike Steele, he was completely smooth, without any chest hair. But equally as gorgeous.

Steele carefully slid the plug from her ass and then removed the egg.

"Keep her ready while I take these into the bathroom."

Grady smiled. "My pleasure." His mouth went to hers as his fingers played with her nipples. It was too much and not enough at the same time. She didn't even know that Steele had returned until she felt his tongue slide along her pussy.

"Oh. Ohhh."

Grady's mouth was now on her nipple, sucking fiercely as Steele drove her higher and higher.

He drew back to look at her. "Beg me, baby. Beg me to let you come."

"Please, Daddy. Please make me come. Please. I need it so bad," she cried as he pressed one leg back firmly against her body and then tongue-fucked her. His tongue moved to flick her clit, and that was it.

She was done.

As she was shaking her way through that orgasm, he loomed

over her, kneeling on the bed. "Do you need me to use a condom?"

"I . . . I have an implant, and I haven't had sex in a long time."

"We've always used condoms," Grady told her. "We always get tested every three months and both of us are clean. Are you okay with both of us to go bare with you?"

"God, yes," she said. "Please."

"That's a good girl." Grady kissed her as Steele started pushing his cock inside her.

Fuck.

That felt amazing. He was so big it was a stretch. But the best fucking kind.

"What a good girl you're being. Look at you taking his fat cock. It's stretching your pussy, isn't it? Just a bit further, you can take a bit more, can't you?" Grady asked as he watched Steele enter her.

Oh Lord. His words alone were almost enough to have her coming.

Once Steele was fully inside her, he took a moment to check in.

"Okay, baby?"

"God, yes, or I will be if you just move."

He grinned down at her. Then, without losing her, he stood back on the floor, and holding her up by her hips so they were in the air while her back was on the bed, he started fucking her.

Christ. So strong.

Grady stole her attention by feasting on her nipples.

"Oh. Oh. Please!" she cried out.

"Not yet, sweetheart," Grady told her. "You have to earn your orgasm. And you haven't begged enough."

Then Steele drew out of her, and she sobbed with disappointment. "Please, please, please. I need your dick. Please!"

"You sound so beautiful when you beg," Grady told her.

Steele turned her over. "Hands and knees."

She scrambled into place as Grady moved as well, sitting in front of her, his perfect, delicious dick just there for the taking. So she slid him into her mouth as Steele pounded into her from behind.

Her orgasm washed through her, making her gasp as Grady slipped from her mouth.

Steele groaned as he came, leaning over her and giving her some of his weight. Damn, she liked that.

Loved being pinned down.

Then he rolled over onto his back and grabbed her, pulling her on top of him. He placed his hand on the back of her neck, drawing her down for a kiss. "You good, baby?"

"Better than that," she whispered.

"Good." He slid his hand away while another hand moved up her back to wrap around her hair, turning her face to where Grady lay on his side beside them.

Yummy.

She was naked in bed with two extremely hot, naked men. And she'd just come. Spectacularly.

"You up for more, sweetheart?" Grady asked.

"Yeah. Just let me go clean up."

"No need to clean up," Steele told her. "You're just going to get messy again."

Oh hell.

"You can mess me up anytime." She grimaced after saying that. Especially when Steele threw back his head and laughed. "That sounded way better in my head."

"Did it? Poor baby. You up for some play?"

"Yes." She could barely breathe from wondering what sort of play he was talking about.

"Christ. Made for us," Steele muttered.

"My good girl. Always willing to try anything." Grady slid off the bed and she turned her head to watch him move to the nightstand.

"We keep some toys in there," Steele said.

She wondered if Grady kept toys in his room. And when she would get to see his room.

All in good time.

He returned with some rope and she sucked in a breath.

"I'm going to tie you to the headboard, then fuck you hard, sweetheart. Are you all right with that?"

Hell's bells.

She was so here for that. "Yes."

He gave her a smile. Lord, she'd say yes to pretty much anything for that smile.

Grady tied her wrists together and then secured the end of the rope to the headboard. This meant she could be rolled around but couldn't get free.

And then he set about torturing her. Both of them did.

She swore she could feel their lips everywhere. Their tongues. Their mouths. Even with their hands. And just when she thought they might be close to letting her come, they'd pull back.

She started begging, she didn't even know what she was saying, but she would do anything to get them to give her what she wanted.

Then, finally, Grady slid her onto her stomach. "Up on your knees. I need to get inside that pussy."

As soon as she was on her knees, he was entering her. She threw her head back before Steele caught her mouth in a kiss.

Grady drove into her with measured, powerful thrusts. Even in this, he seemed to want the ultimate control. It was only toward the end, when she knew he was close that his thrusts grew erratic. That's when Steele drove her into another orgasm with his finger at her clit.

Right before Grady let out a low moan, pressing deep.

Breathing heavily, she leaned against the bed, her arms out in front of her.

Stick a fork in her . . . she was done.

She wasn't sure she had the energy to move. But it turned out that she didn't have to. Grady untied her hands while Steele turned on the shower. They held her between them in the large, double-head shower.

Then Steele dressed her in one of his T-shirts and settled her on top of him as he lay on his back in the bed.

He held her tight as she tried to climb off him.

"I can't sleep like this."

"Why not?" he rumbled.

"Because I'll squish you."

"You've about zapped all my energy, baby. But I've got enough energy for this."

Before she could ask him what he meant, he was sitting with her over his lap and his T-shirt was up over her ass.

"No, wait, Damon!"

She squealed as he spanked her. It was hard and fast and it freaking hurt.

And after he was finished, she found herself back in the same position.

"That was not nice," she told him

"Neither is you saying bad things about yourself. You're gonna stop."

It was just the truth. But she knew not to say that.

"I'm gonna go do a few things before I sleep." Grady sat on the side of the bed and kissed her forehead.

"Wait. You're not staying?" she asked.

"Not tonight, sweetheart. You have time with Steele." He walked out of the room and she tried to stifle her stab of disappointment. She really did. But it sliced into her, thick and hard, settling in her stomach.

"Remember, baby. Watch for the signs."

Well, all signs pointed to the fact that Grady didn't want to sleep with her.

"This is about him. Not you. He never sleeps in the bed with me when . . . well, you know when."

When other women slept with them.

"So I'm just like those other women?" She grew tense.

"You want another spanking?"

"No!" she cried.

"Well, you're about to get one if you don't stop that. You know you're not like those other women. You're ours. Grady just has to wrap his head around what you need and how he wants to give that to you. He'll come around. He's not a snuggler. Never has been. But if you need that, baby, he'll give it to you. You just got to let him know."

She could do that.

She hoped.

41

Effie practically floated as she entered the kitchen. Or at least that's what it felt like. Grady was already at the stove, yawning. Had he even slept?

She felt weirdly shy. The two orgasms that Steele had given her this morning were now wearing off as she stood looking at the other half of her heart.

Because Effie was certain that she loved them. Both of them. There was no way she could imagine her life without them in it. She didn't care if it was too soon or what people would say.

When you knew. You knew.

They were the one.

Well, the two.

Grady turned to her, eyeing her for a moment. "Come here, Effie."

It wasn't quite said in the same tone Steele liked to use. But it was still a command.

"I don't want a pity cuddle."

His eyes flared before his face hardened. He reached over to turn off the stove.

"Excuse me? Why would you think it would be a pity cuddle?"

"I'm sorry," she blurted out. "I didn't mean for that to come out just like that. What's for breakfast?" She gave him her best smile.

Don't rock the boat, Effie

Be grateful for whatever anyone will give you.

"Your nan is talking to you in your head, isn't she?" Grady asked.

"I . . . I . . ." She dropped her gaze away from him. She didn't want to tell him. Didn't know if she could make herself that vulnerable.

"Fuck. Fuck."

She jumped, looking up with shock as something slammed against the wall. She stared down at the mug of coffee that he'd thrown against the wall.

That was . . . unexpected. Grady was the calm one. Steele had shown he had a temper, although she knew he'd never harm her. But Grady was usually tied down tight, his emotions under wraps . . . but not right now.

Right now, he seemed tortured.

He leaned his hands on the counter, bending his head down.

Fuck. Had she done that to him?

She rushed toward him, uncaring that she was barefoot and there were sharp shards of crockery on the ground. She wrapped her arms around him, pressing herself against his back.

"I'm so sorry. I didn't mean it. I didn't mean to hurt you."

He was so still that she was convinced he hadn't heard her. Then he suddenly straightened and reached around to grab her, pulling her to his front and then lifting her so she sat on the counter.

He still looked rough. Haunted. Effie wished she could do something to help. This wasn't her Grady.

She had to fix this.

"What can I do? I'm so sorry. I didn't mean any of it." She reached up to touch his face but pulled back at the last moment.

He grabbed her hand and drew it to his cheek, then he turned his mouth, kissing her palm.

"I fucked up last night."

"What? No, you didn't. If anyone fucked up, it's me this morning."

He shook his head and placed his hands on either side of her. "Sweetheart, I have my demons."

She nodded, eyes wide. "I guess we all do."

"Yes, but not all of us let those demons dictate their every fucking action."

She sucked in a breath at his savage-sounding words. Then she straightened her shoulders. "We're all nuts here, remember?" She threw his words back at him.

"Some of us more than others."

"Well, I hear my dead nan's voice in my head berating me constantly. So I guess you're right, some more than others."

His gaze narrowed. "I wasn't talking about you."

She raised her chin. "I'm nuts, crazy, loopy—"

"Stop that right now," he commanded. "One more word, and I will turn you over my knee."

Was she going to do it? She was operating on pure instinct here. But that instinct was telling her to push.

That it might be the only way to reach him.

"Promises. Promises."

Heat filled his eyes. "Is my good girl feeling naughty today?"

"Your good girl doesn't think you have it in you to spank her. She thinks you might be all talk and no action."

Suddenly, she was lifted off the counter and spun to face the island. His hand went to the back of her neck, pressing her down so her chest was against the cool countertop.

Then, his other hand went to Steele's T-shirt that she was still wearing. She'd snuck down here when Steele had gotten a phone call he'd had to take.

And sure, he might have told her to stay put. But since when did she listen?

"What's your safeword, Little girl?"

"Spinach."

Oh shit. She might be in trouble here.

"You'll use it if you need to. Now part your legs as far as you can."

She pressed her legs apart, swallowing heavily. Then, the hand around the back of her neck shifted, drifting down her back. She relaxed slightly. Maybe he was thinking better of this.

"Stick that ass out. Right out. That's a good girl. Still being good even when you're naughty."

She wasn't really naughty. Was she?

"You're a naughty girl trying to goad me into giving what you want from me and for not telling me what the fuck that bitch is saying in your head."

She jolted at that. "My nan wasn't a bitch."

"She makes you feel like you can't be you. She says things that make you feel small. I don't like that. And the deal was that you purge that stuff from your head, wasn't it? By telling us. Did you do that when I asked you what she said?"

"No," she whispered.

"No. You didn't. Which is naughty. And naughty girls get punished." He slid a hand between her legs, cupping her mound before running fingers along her slick lips. "God, you're totally wet. So beautiful."

"Grady."

"Are you going to take your spanking for me? Be my good girl again?"

"Yes," she cried.

"Yes, you are. Because you are my good girl." He slid his hand away and smacked it down on her ass.

She jumped, more at the noise than the pain. His hand kept spanking her, not touching the same spot twice. Soon, her breath was coming fast and she was close to tears.

That's when he stopped and rubbed the heat into her bottom.

"God, this ass. There are men who would give everything to touch this ass. To have you. To possess you. And you thought it was going to be a pity cuddle?"

"Grady." She tried to move, but he put a heavy hand down on her upper back.

"Stay still. You don't have permission to move."

She'd definitely bitten off more than she could chew. Now, she was bent over the counter, her stinging ass on display, and her feet were also strangely sore. Although she didn't give them much thought.

"I have to tell you something."

"You don't have to if it makes you uncomfortable."

"I owe you this. I can't expect you to open up and share with me if I'm not willing to do the same. But, fuck, no one knows all of this except Steele and it's fucking hard to talk about."

She tried to move again, and this time, he let her. She turned to look up at him. Reaching up, she cupped his cheek, not pulling away again.

"I don't want you to hesitate to touch me. I don't want you to hesitate when it comes to anything about me. But mostly, I don't want you to regret letting me be a part of this."

She frowned, confused by that. "No one is letting you be a part of this. You just *are* a part of this."

He glanced away.

"I don't know much about being in a relationship, let alone one with two men. But I figure that nothing works without clear communication. And we said we'd try. So here goes . . . we aren't just letting you be a part of this, Grady. Without you, there is no *this*. Because I don't want to be without you. I want you in my life, Thomas Grady. Forever."

He gaped down at her.

"And I know it's probably too soon. And you might think you need to run for the hills because this crazy woman just said she wants you forever. But you know what? I'm going to run after you, Thomas Grady! And then when I catch you, I'm going to tackle you. And then I'm gonna be really mad because I don't like to run! This body wasn't made for running. These boobs need a heavy-duty, super-strength sports bra before they even think about running. So when I tackle you, I'll likely have poked myself in the eye with one of my tits by then. But I don't care. Because you are a part of this. So deep in that you're woven into the fabric . . . and are you ever gonna shut me up? Because I really think you should."

He drew her to him, one arm around her lower back, the other around the back of her neck. Then, dipping her slightly, he kissed her. It was a vulnerable position, if he let go, he could drop her. But she just held on and kissed him too.

When he drew away, his lips were twitching.

"Poked yourself in the eye?"

"Shut up," she muttered.

Effie!

Shut up, Nan!

"Your tits need a heavy-duty, super-strength sports bra?" A chuckle escaped him.

"Shut up!" She pushed at his chest.

"You'd chase me down and tackle me?" This was said in a quieter voice, his face soft. Gentle.

"Shut up," she whispered back. Darn it. She wiped at her eyes. "Leaking."

"Little one." He cupped her cheeks. "I messed up last night. And then I thought I'd messed everything up just before when I lost my temper. And now, you're giving me so much sweetness I don't even know what to do with it."

"Well, you're doing the same," she defended.

"I just spanked your ass red."

"I shouldn't push. It's all right if you don't want to sleep with me. I might kick in my sleep. Damon didn't say anything, but then again, he kept me plastered to his chest for most of the night, his hands on my ass so I couldn't move. Maybe he was worried I'd kick. Or I could get all sweaty and stinky between the two of you. That would be gross. Or I might drool. No one likes sleeping with a drooler. Or a snorer. Brooks has never said that I snore, but I might. Oh God. What if I snore?"

He drew her into his chest, kissing the top of her head. "Little one, me not wanting to sleep with you both had nothing to do with you and everything to do with me. You know I struggle with intimacy. And there's nothing more intimate than cuddling a woman all night."

"So you've got no problem with sticking your tongue in my pussy, but you draw the line at cuddling?"

He let out a small bark of laughter. "Yep."

"And they say that women can be illogical. Sheesh."

"I'm a bit messed up."

"We're all messed up."

"What did Nan say to you before?"

Well. Hell.

Effie should have realized he'd ask her that. She cleared her throat. "She said to not rock the boat and that I should be grateful for what anyone would give me."

His hold on her tightened. "Fuck. Fuck that shit, Effie. I know I've already said it, but we need to get her out of your head."

"Know anyone who can perform an exorcism?" She winced at the poor joke.

"No, and I'm thinking that more than an exorcism, perhaps you need to talk to someone about this. Someone who has the tools to help you extricate her from your brain."

"I can't afford therapy."

"Well, good news for you, I can."

"Grady—"

"No, Little one. We're getting her out of your head for good."

"And what about you? Will you talk to someone about your shit?" she asked.

"Yes."

Surprise filled her. "Really?"

"Yeah. You. Or if I can't talk about it, I'll hold on to you, eat your pussy, feed you my cock, and fuck you until I forget."

"Not sure that is proper therapy," she muttered.

"It's the sort of therapy I want."

She opened her mouth.

"But it's not for you," he said quickly.

She frowned. "How did you know what I was thinking?"

"I'm as smart as I am handsome, remember?"

"Hmm, too smart for my good, I think."

He ran his hand over her hair. "I didn't mean to hurt you."

"I know. It just . . . it felt like a rejection."

He closed his eyes, looking pained. "Fuck, Twinkletoes. I really hate that I made you feel that way."

"It's okay."

Suddenly, his eyes opened, piercing her with his gaze. "It's not okay and you shouldn't say it is."

"But you're not in charge of how I react to things. You didn't mean it as a rejection, but I took it as one. So I kind of think that's on me and my fear of rejection."

"I think that most people likely have a fear of rejection. And I also think that it is very much on me if I made you feel that way. And now it's up to me to remedy that."

"Pretty sure you have."

"No, sweetheart. The way I remedy that is to tell you a bit about why I am the way I am."

"Oh. Should we finish cooking breakfast first?"

He shook his head. "No, this is the sort of stuff you get out quick."

"In case you chicken out." She nodded. "I do that a lot."

"Are you calling me a chicken?"

"What? Noooo. Me? I'd never call you a chicken."

He gave her a small grin. He was teasing.

Jerk.

He brushed her hair behind her ear. "So pretty. Even in the morning, no make-up, hair all a mess, with mascara smudges."

"Oh my God!" She put her hands over her face. "I didn't check to make sure that I looked all right before coming down here. Don't look!"

He chuckled. "Sweetheart, I've already looked my fill, spanked your ass, and had my fingers in your pussy. I think you're past hiding."

Bloody hell.

He was right.

She peeked at him through her fingers. "You sure that you don't have any magical memory-erasing abilities? Ooh, maybe I should try eating some magic beans and see if that helps."

"No jelly beans first thing in the morning," he ordered.

Such a party pooper.

"And I'm sorry. I seem to be all out of magical memory erasing abilities this morning."

"Drat. Typical."

He lifted her onto the counter, which was both a good thing and a bad one. Good, because it got her weight off her stinging feet. Bad, because now she had her weight on her stinging ass.

"I didn't have the best childhood," he told her.

Shoot. They were just getting straight into this? All right then.

"Okay."

"I know many people didn't have great childhoods, but mine was pretty much bereft of any sort of nurturing. My parents cared about two things, getting wasted and beating each other up. Occasionally, they'd remember I was there, and they'd hit me too."

Oh God. Oh no.

She could imagine little Thomas. How cute he must have been. And how awful his parents were to treat him that way.

"Grady," she said.

"I don't like my first name, because back then I was Thomas. That's the name they gave me. The name they used to scream at me. That's who I was at school, to all the kids that didn't want to be friends with me, to the parents who screwed up their noses when they saw me and wouldn't allow their kids to invite me to their parties. I was the kid with ripped clothes that were too small for him. Bruises I had to hide. Far smaller than everyone else."

That was hard to imagine now.

"Don't cry for me, sweetheart." He wiped his thumbs over her cheeks.

"I don't think I have any control over my leaking," she replied. "It has a mind of its own. I'm so sorry you had that childhood."

"I withdrew into myself. If I didn't have emotions, I couldn't get hurt. I didn't really think it all out, I was too young. But that's what happened. I was touch-starved, emotionally-stunted, and physically, I was a pure runt. And then my life changed."

"How?"

"My father nearly beat me to death."

"No," she said, horrified.

"He thought I'd stolen some money from his wallet. The thing is, I knew it was Ma. I saw her do it earlier that morning. But he was mad and I was closer, and I wasn't going to tell him it was her. Usually, he'd stop after a few slaps, but he was in a horrible mood that day and I ended up in the hospital for three weeks, recovering."

"Grady." She wanted to reach for him, to hug him.

But he shook his head.

"Don't. Not yet. You can't hug me yet. I've got to get this out."

She nodded and curled her hands around the edge of the counter.

"I got sent to a foster home. New town. New school. But I was still a small kid for my age. Still skinny. And strange. I didn't talk much. When I did, I sounded like a robot. I couldn't connect with my foster family, even though they were nice people. I didn't know how. And when they went to touch me, well, all I saw was my old man coming at me, hurting me. So they soon stopped trying."

Shit. Shit.

She wiped at her eyes.

"Then, one day, these three boys surrounded me as I was walking home. They started pushing me around and there wasn't much I could do about it. So I disassociated. Figured I'd let them get in their kicks. I'd survived worse, right? And that's when he came barreling in. He's always had a damn white knight complex. He has to be the protector."

The last two bits were said with clear affection and she knew who he was talking about.

"Damon."

"Damon. He ran those boys off, picked up my bag, and

walked me home. The next morning, he was outside my house, waiting to walk me to school. He was my age, but really big. He had friends, he was popular. Had this cute little sister who thought he hung the moon and for some reason, he wanted to be friends with the new weird kid. I still don't get it."

"I don't like bullies."

She startled as Steele spoke up from behind her. She turned to see him standing in the doorway, staring at them both. He wore a pair of gray sweatpants and a tight white, T-shirt. She'd never seen him in casual wear, even the day they'd eaten lunch at the diner, he'd dressed in a shirt and jeans.

And he'd looked incredible.

But this outfit . . . it was next-level amazing.

"That call lasted a while," Grady mused.

"I had a shower."

"That was the longest shower ever. And you've been taking some long ones," Grady said to him.

"Asshole," Steele muttered back. "I wasn't in the shower that long. Didn't have to . . . I'm completely spent."

"I've never known you to be spent," Grady replied.

"Me neither. It could be worrying. Could be just Effie." Steele stared at her with a heated gaze.

"I don't know what you two are talking about."

Grady grinned. "I like that, Twinkletoes."

"Um, good, then?" She was so confused.

"I had to take a call. Then I saw Effie wasn't in bed, where I left her," he said as he sent her a stern look. "But I heard you guys in here, so I figured I'd have a shower."

"Uh-oh, someone is in trouble for moving without permission," Grady murmured.

"But you left to take a call! And I needed coffee."

"I was coming back." Steele frowned at her. "I would have

gotten you coffee. I don't like you leaving my bed without me knowing."

"There are a lot of rules to keep track of," she said with a sigh.

"Poor sweetheart," Grady told her. "Don't worry, I'm going to write them up on a big board for you so you don't forget."

She gaped at Grady in horror. "You aren't."

He just smiled.

Darn it. She had a feeling he was being serious.

"You two talk?" Steele walked toward them.

"Yeah, we did," Grady said.

"You tell Effie that you want to play with her while she's asleep?"

What?

She turned back to Grady who was glaring at Steele. "I hadn't told her that part yet."

"Oops." Steele stared at them both calmly. "My bad."

"You fucker. You did that on purpose."

Had he? Steele's face didn't change expression. But yeah, she had a feeling that he'd done it deliberately.

"It was an accident."

"You know things that you'll go to your grave not telling anyone. It was not an accident."

Steele didn't say anything.

"Umm," she said, trying to disperse the tension. "So if you're allowed to lie, why can't I?"

Steele turned to look at her. "Different rules when you have a dick, baby."

"No, there's not."

"Totally are. Also, I'm The Boss."

"And that means you don't have to follow the rules?" she asked.

"Yep. Also, I'm your Daddy."

Lord, she got a thrill when he said that.

"Which means I make the rules. Also, that I won't always follow them. Not when I have your best interests at heart." His gaze caught on something on the floor. "Did someone drop a mug?"

That was a strange change of topic. And she hadn't even let herself think about the titbit of information he'd just dropped.

You tell Effie that you want to play with her while she's asleep?

Holy. Shit.

Holy. Fucking. Shit.

That made her so freaking hot.

She squirmed on the counter.

"I threw it," Grady explained.

The mood in the kitchen, which hadn't been all that great, grew more tense.

"You what?" Steele whispered.

Uh-oh.

These guys loved each other and she wasn't sure how deep that ran. She was pretty sure they both wanted more, but neither wanted to risk losing the other. She got that.

But right then, they weren't happy with each other.

"Guys," she whispered.

"She better not have been anywhere close when you threw that," Steele said.

Oh. He was worried about her?

"Grady wouldn't hurt me," she said with full confidence.

They both turned to look at her.

"He wouldn't. And you shouldn't get angry at him. That's not nice." She wiggled a finger at Steele.

"Not nice?"

"Neither is sharing seecits." Oops. She hadn't meant to say it like that. "I mean, secrets."

Steele's face warmed. Really. His moods definitely changed on a dime.

"Seecits?" he queried.

"I didn't mean to say it like that."

"I think my baby needs some time in Little headspace today," Steele mused.

Oh boy. She wanted that. Badly. But she didn't want Grady to feel left out. This was a strange balancing act in some ways. She glanced at Grady. He looked contemplative.

"That would be nice," she said.

"It would be nice." Steele's lips twitched. Then his gaze went over the floor again. "Is that blood?"

"What?" Grady's gaze shot to the floor, then up to her. He grabbed one of her feet, turning it over. "You've got cuts on your feet because you stepped on the shards of that mug. Why didn't you say anything? Why didn't I notice?"

"I'm fine. Really."

His face was filled with self-loathing.

"Why didn't you tell Grady you'd injured your feet?" Steele said, moving to the cupboard under the sink and drawing out a First-Aid kit.

Then he lifted and carried her over to the sink to wash her feet.

Grady was tidying up the mess on the floor.

"Because it was fine. They don't even hurt."

Steele shot her a look. Right. No lying.

"Fine, they hurt a bit. But no more than my butt."

"You got your butt spanked?" Steele asked, raising an eyebrow as he doctored her feet.

"Yeah, he spanks as hard as you do." She pouted.

"Nan was in her head again," Grady said. "Effie wouldn't tell me what she was saying."

Steele grabbed her chin, tilting her face back. "We have to get rid of that bitch."

"Will you two stop calling her a bitch!" she protested.

"You know, I've got some work to do. I'll see you both later." Grady's gaze was on her feet and she knew he was blaming himself.

She had to stop him from withdrawing. Now.

"Wait!" she cried out as he turned away. But he didn't pause. So she gathered herself up and threw herself at his back.

"Grady! Fuck, Effie!" Steele roared.

She landed on his back. He stumbled slightly but didn't fall. Yeah, maybe she should have thought this through better.

Especially as she glanced back at Steele to see his face was full of thunder.

"What the fuck was that?"

42

Fucking hell.

Just fuck. Fuck.

Grady knew he was messing up all over the place. Not sleeping in bed with them last night had been a mistake. He hadn't even given her a good cuddle before he left.

All because he had fucking intimacy issues. Born from a terrible childhood.

Well, fuck that.

He needed to work that shit out. Because his job now was to give Effie whatever she needed.

And he couldn't do that if his brain was so whacked that he was throwing around mugs and not noticing that she'd sliced her feet up.

He'd known he needed a minute to wrap his head around everything. His behavior. Steele's. Because he'd dropped that other bomb on purpose.

Steele wanted them to move forward, for all of them to get what they needed. And in his usual bulldozer way, he'd gone ahead and done that.

But some things needed a bit of finesse.

However, in turning away, the last thing Grady had expected was for her to throw herself at him.

"Um, I didn't want Grady to leave," she said in reply to Steele's furious bellow.

He tried to pull her off, to tug her around to his front. But she wrapped her arms around him like a monkey.

Christ.

"You could have fucking well hurt yourself! You will not do that again!" Steele commanded.

"Yeah, maybe I should have thought that through more. I just acted."

"Is your back all right?" Grady asked.

"Ah, yeah, it seems to be."

"Ten spanks. Corner time. And fifty lines. All after breakfast," Steele told her.

"Yikes. I think I'm in trouble," she whispered. "Horsie, giddy-up!"

"Excuse me?" Grady asked.

"Giddy-up! You need to save me from the ogre!"

"Being cute will not save you from the ogre," Grady informed her.

"I am not an ogre." Steele moved toward them.

Slap!

His hand must have landed on Effie's ass because she jumped and let out a small squeal.

"You are spending time with Daddy today. And Daddy is in a strict mood, so beware. You try to hide anything from me. and I will tan your hide until you can't sit for a week. And you." Steele turned to Grady. "I'm sorry for dropping your secret like that. It wasn't cool. I'll make breakfast."

Grady carried her on his back to the small dining table. Then he crouched. "Off."

She let go.

He turned to her, pointing at the chair behind her. "Sit."

She sat. He drew a chair over and sat facing her. "I apologize for losing my shit, throwing that mug, and not seeing that you were hurting. But sometimes, I'm going to need time to process stuff. All right?"

"Oh. All right. I'm sorry I jumped on you. I didn't hurt you, did I?"

"No, sweetheart. But *you* could have hurt you. And that is unacceptable. Understand?" He cupped her chin lightly with his hand.

"I understand. It was spur of the moment."

"Well, maybe next time, think first. Or you're going to give the ogre a heart attack."

"Yeah. He bellows like a lion when he's mad."

"He sure does."

"I can hear you both," Steele told them.

"You should have told me your feet were hurting." Grady gave her a stern look.

"I'm sorry." She bit her lip. "Are we good?"

"You tell me." He gave her a steady look.

"We're good. And, uh, about that other stuff . . ."

He raised an eyebrow.

"I . . . you want to, uh, do stuff while I'm sleeping?"

He shot his gaze up to Steele, then back to her. "It's not a deal-breaker, sweetheart. If you don't want that, then we won't do it."

"But you like doing that?"

"Most women aren't into it. So I haven't done it much. But yeah, I like it. I like waking a woman up with my tongue in her pussy. I like being able to touch and explore while she's sleeping. I like having my cock buried in a part of her body while she sleeps."

"Holy heck."

"But it is just a want. Not a need."

She swallowed heavily. "And if it's something I want too?"

Shock filled him.

"Consensual non-consent," Steele said.

"Huh?" she asked, screwing up her nose. "That sounds like one of those tongue twisters. Consensual non-consent. Consensual non-consent. Consensual non-consent. Definitely a tongue twister."

"Means that he won't wake you to ask for your consent because he already has it to do what he wants," Steele explained.

"I'd always stay within your limits, though," Grady swiftly told her. "And you always have your safeword."

"I give my consent."

Grady's eyes widened.

"Perfect for us," Steele called out.

Yeah. She certainly was.

"Then that's something we'll explore," he told her.

She smiled at him widely. A genuine smile. "Goody."

43

"Daddy, I'm tired of standing in the corner."

They were in Steele's office. He'd already spanked her, and now she was sitting in the corner on her hot and throbbing bare ass. While her cuts were shallow, Steele didn't want her standing on her feet for too long.

But none of that had been worse than having to write fifty lines about how she would not throw herself at someone or get out of bed without permission.

Sheesh.

"Your ten minutes starts all over again. You're meant to be quiet in the corner."

That. Just. Sucked.

"Is your back all right?" he called out.

She wasn't going to fall for that trick. Nuh-uh.

"Effie? Is your back okay?" he asked, sounding worried. "Effie. Why aren't you answering?"

"I am not answering on the grounds that if I do, you're going to start corner time all over again."

"Baby girl, if I ask you a question, I want an answer. Immediately. And I won't start corner time over again if I require you to answer me. Understand?"

Yeah. Sort of.

"My back is fine." Well, it had kind of gotten a twinge earlier when she'd thrown herself at Grady in the kitchen. Since then, they'd eaten breakfast. Actually, Steele had fed her breakfast. Then he'd helped her shower, only to put her back in another of his T-shirts. All the while, he'd been grumbling about getting her appropriate clothes.

Whatever that meant.

Grady had disappeared. But she wasn't worried about that. Well, not much. He said he needed processing time. And the truth was, she was kind of processing too.

He was kinky. Really kinky.

And, it seemed, she might be really kinky too.

Who knew?

Nan would probably die of shock if she knew. But Effie had to start living her life. Not living the life that Nan thought she should.

"Fine doesn't mean good in Effie-speak."

Effie-speak?

"Come here, baby girl."

Standing, she dropped the T-shirt and walked over to where Steele was sitting behind his desk.

Lord, he was hot. Gorgeous.

He lifted her so she was straddling his lap, then drew her into his chest. He rubbed her lower back.

Wow.

She melted into him.

"Yeah, just what I thought. Not fine. What am I going to do with you?"

"Well, you could show me that hot tub of yours. Or let me suck on your cock. Maybe both?"

He chuckled. "Right. I could do that. Or we could discuss you telling me when you're in pain."

"I feel that we've already had this discussion."

"I feel we have too. Which is why I'm not happy to be having it again."

"I just . . . I still find it hard to believe that you guys want me. All of me."

"I'll tell you as often as you need to hear it. We are the ones who are lucky to have you."

She didn't believe it. But she liked hearing it.

"What does your Little like?" he asked suddenly. "Grady is buying you a whole heap of stuff, but we haven't even asked you what you want."

"I . . . I don't really know," she said shyly. "Well, I like sloths."

"Got that, baby."

"And cute sneakers."

"Got that too."

"Animal earrings."

"Yeah, baby. I'm going to buy you all the pretty animal earrings and sneakers that you need and want. But what else?"

"I'm really not sure."

"Maybe it's a good thing that Grady is buying you a shitload of stuff, then."

She leaned back. "You guys don't have to do that. I'm just happy to be with you."

His face softened as he ran a finger along her cheek. "So sweet. You still look tired. How would my baby like a bottle and a nap?"

"How about ice cream and a blow job?"

He threw back his head and laughed. Then, picking her up, he carried her into the kitchen and set her on a stool with a stern order not to move.

Then he heated her up a bottle of milk. Unfortunately, it was regular milk, not strawberry milk.

Which she thought was a travesty.

Picking her back up, he carried her on his hip to the big sectional. He settled them both in the corner with her leaning back against his chest.

Steele chose a movie, putting it on before he placed the nipple of the bottle to her mouth. As the movie played, she started to relax as she sucked.

It was surprisingly soothing.

Her eyes even drifted shut. At some stage, she felt herself being shifted so her head was cushioned on a firm thigh and her feet were being gently rubbed.

Opening her eyes, she saw Grady had her feet in his lap.

And now everything was right in Effie's world.

44

Crap.

She was in trouble.

She glanced down at the bracelet around her ankle. This was all its fault. When Steele had snapped it around her ankle last Sunday afternoon before driving her home, she hadn't thought much about it.

Until he'd told her that she was never to take it off . . . because there was a fucking tracking device in it!

She was of two minds about it. On the one hand, she knew it was the two of them being protective. It was their way of taking care of her. Both of them seemed to need to know where she was at all times.

She guessed that might be due to Steele losing his sister. That must have been devastating. And she thought that Grady seemed to like the feeling of being in control. So she'd decided to wear the bracelet without a fuss.

However, it meant they knew her every movement. Like right now.

She drew out her ringing phone, groaning out loud as she saw the name on the screen.

Fuck.

Taking a deep breath, she answered the call. "Hello!"

"Where are you?"

"I'm good. Thanks for asking. There's peanut brittle in my office today if you're after something sweet."

"Effie. Where. Are. You?" Steele demanded.

Shoot. Sweet wasn't working.

"You know where I am." Because of the darn tracker.

"I know where you should be. Your ass should be sitting in your chair at your office in Pinkies. But where you are is at a pharmacy three blocks away."

"So you didn't need to ask where I was then, did you?"

Effie, you need to be nice. This handsome man wants you, but he doesn't want a shrew.

"Effie? Effie?"

"Sorry, Nan was telling me not to be a shrew."

"Not happy about that," he told her. "But thank you for telling me."

Whoa. Her legs weakened at his words.

"Effie, if you need to leave work in the middle of the day, what are you supposed to do?"

"Text Grady. Which I did!"

There was a beat of silence. Then another one.

"Didn't Grady tell you that he was out today?"

"Um. Yes."

"And that he couldn't check his phone?"

"Um. Yes."

"So what would be the logical thing for you to do if you knew he wouldn't see your text?"

"I'm guessing it's not sending up smoke signals?" she asked.

"Text me, Effie."

"You weren't even at Pinkies. It's only a quick errand."

"And what do you need on this quick errand?"

"Steele," she groaned.

"Tell me."

"It's personal."

"Tell. Me."

"Period stuff. All right? I've got my period."

Around her, a couple of people stopped to stare. She closed her eyes. Fan-fucking-tastic.

"Baby."

There was a lot in that one word. It was said softly, with care and attention. She let out a deep breath.

"Sorry, I can get a bit, uh, snappy when I'm cramping," she whispered.

"You got your period while at work?"

"Uh, yeah."

"You know we keep that shit out the back for the girls, right?" he asked.

"Well, yeah. Since I'm the one who keeps it stocked up. But that's for them, not me."

"Baby." This was said in a sterner tone. Which meant he didn't like what she was saying.

"Damon," she said quietly. "I can get my own stuff. I'm three blocks away. If you hadn't called me, I'd probably be back already."

"Right. We've got to have a talk. Soon as you get back. Hurry."

Lord, he was frustrating.

She grabbed what she needed and, shoving it in a basket, headed to the check-out.

With her head down, she walked outside.

And banged straight into something solid. Unmovable.

Her arms wind-milled, and the bag flew from her hand as

she attempted to regain her balance.

"Whoa, you all right there, doll?" Hands wrapped around her waist before she could fall flat on her ass.

Shit.

She glanced up at the handsome, if a bit rough-looking man she'd banged into. There was something strangely familiar looking about him. Perhaps she'd seen him at Pinkies or something.

"I'm so sorry! I didn't see you! My apologies."

"It's all right, doll. Let me help you pick up all your stuff."

Her stuff? She glanced around. Holy fuck!

"Oh my God!" She went on her hands and knees, scrambling to pick things up off the sidewalk.

"Whoa, doll. Get off your hands and knees. The sidewalk is dirty. Let me get the stuff." He hauled her up and brushed off her clothing before picking up the last items. One of which was a pair of period panties, the other a bar of no-sugar chocolate.

"No-sugar chocolate? Is that a thing?"

"Um, yep. It is. Thank you!" She snatched the things away from him.

"No problem."

She shoved everything in her shopping bag and then turned back to him, knowing she needed to use her manners. "So sorry for bumping into you."

"No problem, Twinkletoes."

When she turned away, she realized that he'd called her Twinkletoes. But that had to be a coincidence.

He was probably using it ironically because you banged into him.

With a groan, she headed back to Pinkies.

And to the ogre she had waiting there.

As soon as she walked into her office, she saw him.

Drat.

Maybe she should have tried to hide.

It wasn't too late. She eyed the desk he was sitting on. She could run around and hide in there. Of course, he'd know she was there. But there were probably plenty of other places she could hide in Pinkies. It wasn't open yet. She could hide somewhere and sneak out later.

Great plan.

It was the Thursday after she'd spent the weekend at their place. When Grady had opened up to her and she'd learned a bit more about what he needed.

She wished she could say he'd instantly become more open with her, but he was still somewhat guarded. But she understood that it would take time for him to become more at ease.

They hadn't had an opportunity to put any of his needs into play. Maybe this weekend since Brooks was spending Saturday night with the twins. And apparently, they were all going to the movies with some girls. Including Stella, the girl he'd stood up for at school.

She still hadn't met their stepmom, Betsy. But she did talk to her on the phone yesterday, so she felt good about him going there.

Sort of.

"Don't even think about it," Steele warned.

"Think about what?"

"Running or hiding. You're coming with me."

"Oh, um. I just need to . . ."

"To what?" he asked as he walked toward her and held out his hand. Right. This time, she knew what he wanted. But she didn't want to give it to him. She needed the stuff in this bag.

"To go to the bathroom." She didn't actually have to go yet, but it sounded like a good excuse.

"Got a private bathroom upstairs, you can use that." He reached out to take the bag.

She held on tight.

He tugged.

She held on tighter.

"Baby, give me the bag."

"I'll just be a few minutes."

With a sigh, he reached for her and picked her up, cradling her against his chest.

"Steele!"

"Daddy."

She froze. "Here? But I'm working."

"You've got the rest of the day off." He walked through the main area of Pinkies. Lulu, one of the dancers, was practicing on stage.

"Oh, she's using the moves I taught her. Looking good, Lulu!"

"You too, darling," she called back.

Oh yeah. Right. She'd forgotten she was being carried in Damon's arms like a toddler.

Yikes.

"Put me down."

"No."

"Please, Damon. Put me down. Please." There, two pleases, and she rubbed her hand over his chest for good measure.

"No."

Fuck it.

"Steele."

"Hush."

"Steele. Effie. How's it going?" That was Nate. She closed her eyes. Great. Seemed everyone was going to see her.

"Fine," Steele replied.

"Effie?"

"Hey, Nate. You good?" She turned to smile at him.

He was grinning widely. "Oh yeah, I'm real good."

Great. Just great.

Steele got to the door that led toward his upstairs area.

"Trev, I don't want to be disturbed. The only person who comes up is Grady."

"You got it. Hey, Effie."

"Trev," she muttered, still holding the bag of supplies. A cramp hit her and she hissed in pain.

Steele paused on the stairs. "You all right, baby girl?"

"Just a cramp."

"I'll take care of you. Don't worry."

"I'm supposed to be working."

"And I told you that you have the afternoon off."

"But I need the money."

He set her down on her feet when they were in his upstairs area. She glanced around at the large sectional sofa, the small bar area, and the two doors, one leading to a bedroom with a private bathroom and the other to a powder room.

It was comfortable.

But she had stuff to do.

"Jesus, Effie, I'm still going to pay you, baby."

"That doesn't seem fair."

His head rocked back. "What?"

"To you. You shouldn't pay me for work that I'm not doing."

"Baby, I don't give a shit about the work."

"I'll come in early tomorrow to make up for it."

"Effie. You. Will. Not." He grasped her chin. "You work far too much as it is. And I'm beginning to think I need to keep a closer eye on that."

"You don't."

"Yeah, I think I do. Because I don't want you to be so exhausted from working that you don't have time for other things. And I just want more of you. You've got to have time for

Brooks, that's non-negotiable. But I also want you to have time for me and Grady. So the thing that can give is work."

"I need the money."

"You got two men who are more than willing to take care of you, baby girl."

She flushed. "I can't do that."

"You can. We want that. Everything, remember? I have your back. So does Grady. In all ways."

She thought that maybe they should shelf this conversation for another day. Like maybe Tuesday next year.

"I should go use the bathroom."

His face darkened. Uh-oh.

"You left without letting me know you were leaving."

"Um, I let Grady know."

His face grew darker and he started moving toward her. She backed away. It seemed the prudent thing to do.

"And you know that Grady is out of town for the day. So you should have told me."

"It seems like a silly rule."

"That's not for you to decide."

She hit the wall and he put his hands on the wall on either side of her head.

"I'm in trouble, aren't I?"

"Yep."

"The kind where I'm not going to sit comfortably for the rest of the afternoon?"

"Do you usually get bad period pain?" he asked.

She didn't need a mirror to know she'd gone bright red. "What?"

Why would he ask her that? That wasn't a normal question for a guy to ask a girl.

Was it?

Shit.

"Effie, focus. I need your attention here."

Shoot.

"Um, yes. Sometimes. Most of the time."

"Right. That's something that you should have told us at some stage before you got your period."

"It is? Why?"

"So we know how to take care of you. You didn't have shit with you?"

"Uh, no." Hence why she had to go out and get some things. "Well, I mean, I had my emergency tampon."

"Your emergency tampon?"

"Every woman has an emergency tampon," she told him huffily. "If not two or three."

"Yeah. So you got more tampons in that bag?"

"Uh, no."

"No?" He frowned.

"I don't like tampons."

"You don't like tampons?"

"They feel icky inside me."

"Icky?"

"Are you just going to repeat everything I say?" she cried.

"Is that why you wouldn't use the stuff here, baby?" he asked.

"Well, yeah. Plus, that's not mine."

He frowned. "It is yours. You're a woman, that shit is here for the women who work here to use. So next time you need it, use it. Don't you keep track of your periods?"

"I cannot believe we're having this conversation." She stared up at the ceiling.

"Effie," he growled.

She dropped her gaze to him. "No, I'm not very good at that sort of thing. That's why I stopped taking the birth control pill and got an implant. I couldn't remember to take the pills."

"The implant didn't help make your periods less painful?"

"Uh, no." Lord, he was curious, wasn't he? And he didn't seem embarrassed. "Can we stop talking about this? Please?"

"Baby, I had two shit parents and a baby sister I adored. Who do you think helped her with all of this?"

"Oh." She hadn't even thought of that.

"So you use pads?"

"Sometimes."

"Effie."

"I use period panties." She went bright red. "I know it seems odd for a thirty-five-year-old woman to wear period panties, but it's so much easier."

"Baby, don't give a fuck how old you are. You wear what you want. They're in the bag?"

"Yeah."

"Right. Before we put those on you, we've got a punishment to get out of the way."

"A spanking?" she asked.

"Not while you've got period pain."

That was kind of sweet, but it also made her wonder what she had coming her way.

"Oh God, not lines," she groaned.

"Nope."

Hmm.

"Corner time?"

"Nope."

"What then?"

"You'll see."

He stepped back, then took hold of her hand. "Course, I owe you a couple of smacks for not letting go of that bag when I clearly wanted to carry it."

That was the only warning she got as he moved, putting his foot up on the sectional next to them, then tipping her over his thigh to smack her ass four times.

"Ow! I thought I wasn't getting a spanking."

"That wasn't a spanking. That was a couple of love taps."

"With hands like yours, there's no such thing as love taps. Those things are lethal weapons."

He grinned as he righted her. "I love it when you're sweet, baby. And when you're shy. Also love it when you're a bit of a smart-ass. Sassy. So cute."

"I wasn't trying to be cute."

"I know, you're just always cute," he told her as he drew her into the bedroom.

She looked at the bed where he'd laid out a few items. He took her handbag and the pharmacy bag from her. Searching through her handbag, he brought out Slowly.

He'd never mentioned the fact that she carried the soft toy everywhere.

"Your sloth is getting a bit worn."

"I can't throw him out!" she cried, reaching for the toy to hold him tightly against her.

"Baby, I'd never suggest that. I just thought that he might need a few stitches to keep him together." He eyed her strangely. Shit. She forgot that with Damon, if you gave him a few inches, he'd take a whole lot more. As in, he understood far more than she ever expected him to.

"Where did you get Slowly?"

She heaved out a sigh. "You won't be upset?"

He frowned. Then his face cleared. "Joe."

"Yeah. I carry him with me because it's like having a piece of Joe. But it also means I'm never alone. I know that seems silly . . ."

He tilted her face back. "It doesn't seem silly at all. And I don't care that Joe gave him to you. Why would I?"

Relief filled her.

"You know that I'm going to buy you things too. Grady, as well. There's a few of those things on the bed behind you."

She went back to the items on the bed.

The first thing she saw was the lube. Yikes.

Then a butt plug. Double yikes. But also, yippee!

And then there was a baby bottle. Also yay.

And a pacifier with a sloth's face on the front. Which made her smile. She wanted that right now.

Next to that was a onesie. An adult-sized onesie that also had sloths all over it. And beside it were a few coloring books and pens.

"Want some time with my baby girl. To give her what she needs from her Daddy. And we're having trouble carving out that time. You've got your period, it's hurting you, and you need some care. So I'm going to give you that while also giving you time with Daddy."

"Here?"

"I have to be here. But you'll stay in here while you're in Little headspace. I know it's not much, but there's a place for a nap. A television. Room to play."

"And the butt plug?"

"That's your punishment."

It was? Yikes.

"Undo your pants, bend over and touch your feet. Don't move."

Oh hell.

Her eyes grew wide. Really? "I have my period."

"I don't care about some blood. At all."

Whoa.

There shouldn't be any blood, but still . . . whoa.

"Really?"

"Baby. Really. Now, do as you were told."

She turned and bent over, touching her feet. Then she felt him pulling down her pants. Then, her panties.

Holy heck.

Holy. Heck.

"Widen your legs. Don't lose your balance."

She pushed them farther apart.

"Good girl. Look at you, being so obedient. Now, reach back and part your butt cheeks."

"What?" she squeaked out.

"Do as you were told, Spitfire," he said sternly.

Oh hell. Oh hell.

Reaching back, she held her ass cheeks apart.

"I can't believe I'm doing this," she muttered.

"This is punishment. It's not supposed to be comfortable." She heard the squirt of lube and then his finger slid into her bottom. She breathed out, trying to relax herself. A second finger joined the first, stretching her.

"Good girl." He slid his fingers free. "Now the butt plug."

The plug was more of a stretch, but once she got used to the burn, it started to feel good.

"Stand. I'm going to help you."

She stood, and he steadied her before he moved to the bed and put a pillow in the middle. "You're going to lie on the bed with a pillow under your stomach to raise your bottom up. Or do you need the bathroom first?"

Oh crap. She should have known that wouldn't be all of it. She shook her head and he took her hand to help her onto the bed.

"Five minutes, baby girl."

Five minutes. Okay, she could do five minutes.

Easy-peasy.

45

She should have known it wouldn't be that simple.
Being still and silent was just sooo hard.
And Daddy was really mean.
"Right. Your five minutes is up."
She breathed out a sigh of relief as he helped her climb off the bed.
"Can you take the plug out?" she asked as he grabbed hold of her hand and led her to the bathroom.
"Yep. Bathroom."
Crap.
"Lean over and grab hold of the sink," he ordered once they were in the bathroom.
Knowing it was pointless to argue, she did as instructed.
When the plug slid out, she breathed a sigh of relief. She watched him clean up, then he turned to her.
"Go use the toilet. Take out the tampon and then come back into the bedroom."
At least she had that much privacy. Maybe because she was on her period?

"I need my bag of stuff."

"No."

"No?" Urgh, he was infuriating sometimes.

"No."

"Yes, I do. I need to put those panties on." She hated talking about this sort of stuff. So she was shifting from side to side and she knew her face was red.

"I just plugged your ass. Gonna fuck it one day. And you're embarrassed over your period." He cocked his head to the side. "Let me guess, Nan didn't talk about periods."

"People don't talk about periods, Steele," she informed him primly.

"Uh, yeah they do, Spitfire." He trapped her against the counter with his hands on either side of her. "They talk about them because they're a natural bodily function. Nothing to be embarrassed about."

"Then why am I embarrassed?"

"Maybe because your nan taught you to be that way. But, baby, you need to get this. *Everything.*"

Right. Everything.

"If I thought it wouldn't freak you out, I'd fuck you while you had your period."

"Um. Oh. Uh. Wouldn't that be messy?"

"That's why they invented shower sex." He winked at her.

Shower sex.

Holy. Moly.

"I can see that idea intrigues you. We'll try that sometime." He stood back and then turned her to the toilet, smacking her ass. "Toilet. Go."

When she left the bathroom, he was laying out a small rubber mat on the bed and had her supplies on the bed with the other things.

"Is that . . . is that a changing mat?"

"Yep. One of the things Grady bought."

"But . . . you're not . . . I mean, I don't wear diapers, Daddy!"

"Just protecting the bed in case of accidents." He looked at her and she saw the amusement on his face.

She stomped her foot down. "I don't have accidents."

"Baby girl, it's nothing to be embarrassed about." Turning, he cupped her face between his hands. "Sometimes, Littles have accidents. But Daddy is always here to help them. That's his job."

Darn it. Effie wanted to be mad, but he was being sweet.

"You're not playing fair, Daddy," she told him as he stripped off her shirt and bra, then lifted her onto the change mat.

"How is that?"

"Because you can't be crazy and nice at the same time."

"I can't?" Steele grinned at her as he slid the period panties up her legs.

She thought about being embarrassed. But decided that she wasn't going to be. Well, her cheeks did grow a bit heated. Especially when he got them situated, then patted her mound.

"Daddy, did you just pat my pussy as though it had done a good job?"

"Of course."

"Daddy!"

"What? I give credit where credit is due. It's a very good pussy. I'm going to pet it and tell it that."

Lord help her.

"Now, let's get this onesie on you, some painkillers into you, and then you can have a nap."

"I don'ts need a nap." The large yawn she'd just finished might have made that a lie.

"Nap, yes," he said firmly. "Onesie. Painkillers. Bottle. Nap."

"I don'ts want milk."

"Water, then. Or I have some protein drinks. Hmm, maybe those would be good. We need to get some iron into you."

"Why? I don'ts like iron."

"Baby, you're bleeding," he explained as he got her into the onesie. She instantly fell further into Little headspace. It was just so cozy and soft.

"So?"

"Is it heavy?"

"What?"

"Your period? Is it heavy?" he asked.

"You ask lots of questions for someone with a pogo stick," she muttered.

"Spitfire, you're adorable when you're cute, but not when I'm asking you a serious question."

"Yes, it's heavy."

"So you need more iron. You don't eat much meat. You steer clear of S foods. So we need to find more iron for you. Maybe beans."

"Beans, beans, they're good for your heart. The more you eat, the more you—" He put his hand over her mouth.

"Hush." He moved his hand.

"Daddy, you can't stop the song once it's started. That's just wrong."

"Can and did." He grabbed something off the bed and held it up. "What's this?"

"My chocolate! Gimme!" She made grabby hands at him.

"No-sugar chocolate? What even is this crap?"

"I thought it would be better than sugar chocolate. And they didn't have any jelly beans. Hey! I do eat beans! See?"

He just shook his head. "You don't need sugar-free chocolate. I'll get you some real chocolate. After your nap."

Oh, goody.

"I'm going to go fill your bot-bot. And then you can have some painkillers."

When he was gone, she finished the rhyme. Because it was a crime to stop halfway through.

Plus, it was funny as heck.

So she was smiling as he returned. He gave her a suspicious look, then shook his head. "I don't think I wanna know."

He arranged everything on the nightstand, then sat on the bed, positioning her on his lap so she leaned back against one arm. He popped some painkillers into her mouth, holding the bottle up for her so she could swallow them down.

She pulled back, staring up at him, then over to the door. "What if someone needs you?"

"Not for you to worry about."

She bit her lip.

"It's for Daddy to worry about."

She reached for her earring, only to realize that the onesie had built-in mittens.

"No one will dare come in here except Grady."

She nodded and dropped her hand. He held the nipple up and she took it eagerly. She kind of liked her bot-bot.

Then, despite her protests, Steele put her down for a nap, with her new sloth pacifier in her mouth.

It was the best nap of her life.

∽

When she woke up, she noticed she was surrounded by pillows.

Huh.

When had that happened? Shrugging, she sat up and a light cramp hit her. Darn it. The painkillers had taken the sharper edge off but she was still sore.

Pushing off the covers, she knocked over a pillow and Slowly onto the floor.

"Oh no, Slowly!" She reached down and picked him up, brushing him off gently. "Are you okay?"

Hmm. Seemed she was still in Little space then. She shrugged, too uncomfortable to care.

Moving to the bathroom, she took care of business. Which meant taking off the onesie to pee. It was only after she had it off, that she realized it had an opening in the back. But she wouldn't be able to reach that anyway.

Putting the onesie back on, she washed her hands and studied herself in the mirror. Yikes! Her hair was a bit of a fright. How had it gotten that messy? She tried to calm it down, but she just seemed to make it worse. Then her tummy grumbled and she sighed with frustration.

"Effie? Where are you?" Steele called out.

Oops. He didn't sound pleased. But she couldn't imagine why. Oh, unless he'd thought she'd left?

"In here, Daddy!" she called out as she opened the door and stepped into the bedroom.

He turned, frowning at her.

"Where did you think I was?" She was still in the onesie, her clothes on a chair in the corner.

"Well, I knew you weren't where I'd put you. In the bed. Where you should have stayed." He pointed at the bed.

"I hads to pee."

"Then you should have called me. I need a baby monitor for in here. In fact, we should make this room more baby girl friendly."

She wasn't quite sure what he meant by that. "I have to ask to use the bathroom?"

"You stay where I put you." He waggled a finger at her. Rude.

"Daddy, I don't has to stay where you put me."

"Yes, baby girl. You do. Especially in Little headspace. I wonder if we can fit a crib in here."

He was crazy.

Although she wasn't completely opposed to the crib. So she decided the best idea was to change the subject.

"I should get changed and go back to work."

"Didn't I tell you that you're taking the afternoon off?"

She bit her lip. "Yes, well, but that doesn't feel right."

"Who is the boss?" he demanded.

"Grady," she replied instantly. Because, technically, he was her boss. Even though Steele was The Boss.

His eyes narrowed. "I'm rethinking my views on spanking you while you have your period."

"You're The Boss, Daddy!" she said quickly. "The big boss. Biggest, bossiest boss of all the bosses."

He stared at her for a moment. Probably wondering why she was acting like an idiot. Then, to her shock, he gave an arrogant nod.

"That's better."

Good. Lord.

"Now, how is your period pain?" His face and eyes had grown warm. He was a hard man to keep up with.

"I'm fine."

And just like that, the warmth was gone. See? It was impossible to keep up with this man's moods.

"You're very moody," she informed him.

His eyebrows rose. "Sorry?"

"I'm the one with my period and you're the one who is being moody. Maybe we're synced."

"Synced?" he asked in a low, warning voice.

But she didn't take any notice of the warning in his voice.

More fool her.

"Yeah, maybe you have IMS."

"IMS?" Suddenly he was in front of her. And she had to crane her neck to look up at him.

"Yep. Like PMS but for men. Irritable Man Syndrome."

"Irritable Man Syndrome?"

"Umm . . ." Her eyes tried to search for an escape route. But there was no way she was getting around him.

Did he have to be so darn big?

"Definitely rethinking my stance on spanking you right now, baby girl."

Uh-oh.

"Maybe it's time Effie stopped talking."

"Perhaps it's time Effie was honest with her Daddy. Because a baby girl doesn't lie to her Daddy."

"I didn't lie exactly. I feel better than I did. A bit crampy." She rubbed her tummy which grumbled. "Little bit hungry. I need chocolate."

"You need proper food. Something with iron in it. Not sugar."

"Daddy, that's just mean. And you got to admit, you have all the symptoms of IMS. Grouchy with mood swings. Maybe you need some chocolate. And not the sugar-free kind. The real stuff."

"No."

That was all he said. Just no.

Sheesh.

"Did you go potty while in the bathroom?" he asked, taking her hand.

Her eyes bugged out of her head. "What?"

"I asked if you went potty."

"You can't call it that."

"Can call it whatever I like, baby girl." His eyes were back to dancing.

Mood. Swings.

"I used the toilet, yes. Thank you for asking." Urgh, why did she just thank him for that?

Idiot.

Now his lips were twitching. "You're a nut."

She was a nut? *He* just said the word potty and wanted her to stay where he put her.

He started tugging her toward the door that led out to the main room. She tugged back.

He turned, eyeing her. Then, without a word, he swept her up and held her on his hip.

"Daddy, what are you doing?"

She wriggled, trying to free herself.

"Stop moving around," he commanded, smacking the side of her thigh. "I don't want you to slip."

"That would never happen, Daddy," she said confidently.

"You think not?"

"No, cause you'd never let me fall."

He stilled at the doorway and glanced down at her. "You're right. I never would." He carried her out into the main room.

"Damon," she whispered nervously.

"I'd never let you fall, baby girl. I'd also never let you be in a position where you might be embarrassed or humiliated. Trust me?"

"Always," she replied. And she knew he meant it. He'd never do anything that might hurt her. Physically or emotionally.

"Your trust means everything."

As they entered the room, she saw he'd moved the coffee table over slightly. Sitting on top were a laptop and cup of coffee. Then just behind the coffee table, he'd set a fluffy rug down on the floor in front of the sectional.

Sitting on the fluffy rug were some coloring books and pens, along with a pile of blocks and a set of wooden dolls with outfits that you could change out.

"Ooh, Daddy! I love those dollies!"

"That's good, baby girl. Because I need you to do some playing while Daddy works for a bit, all right?"

"You shouldn't work so much, Daddy! You should play with me."

"Maybe in a while." He set her down on the floor just as her tummy grumbled. "But let's get you some food first."

She stiffened, wondering how he was going to get the food. Would he have someone send something up from the kitchen?

"Relax, Spitfire. Daddy has it all sorted." He moved behind the bar and shifted things around.

She decided to let go of her worries and grabbed one of the wooden dolls, setting it up on a stand and then sorting through the outfits. She even distracted herself from her hunger and her cramps.

Ooh, this outfit was so cute!

"Baby girl, here is your snack. I want your water all gone within the next thirty minutes."

She glanced over to see he had a sloth plate filled with cut-up vegetables and pieces of fruit. There was ranch dressing for dipping and slices of cheese with crackers. And some chocolate! Yum. As well as a sippy cup with a sloth on it.

"You bought all this for me, Daddy?"

"Grady did. Now, drink and eat."

She ate the chocolate first. Then a few pieces of cheese and nearly all of the crackers. But left everything else.

Yucky.

A few sips of water, then she forgot all about drinking the rest as she created a few buildings from the blocks and colored in a picture before going back to the wooden dolls.

"Baby girl," Steele interrupted her.

Ooh, he must want to see what she created.

"Look, Daddy!" She held up her doll. "Isn't she pretty?" She gave the doll an admiring look. She had a bright green skirt, a purple crop top, and some kickass boots.

"Umm. She looks interesting."

"Daddy! She does not! She looks hot. I wish I could wear this."

"You can wear whatever you like," he said. "Although you won't be wearing that for anyone but me or Grady."

She rolled her eyes. Silly Daddy. But he didn't have to worry, she wasn't actually going to buy that outfit.

"It's been forty minutes, baby girl."

"Really? I is having such a good time that it's flying. Whoosh!" She ran her hand through the air.

"That's good. But not what I meant. What did I tell you to do?"

"I don't know, Daddy. Did you tell me to have a good time? Good news! I is." She grinned up at him.

"Good to know," he said dryly. "But Daddy wanted you to eat more than just the crackers and cheese. And to drink your water, didn't he?"

"That's so boring, Daddy. I is busy."

"Right now, you're in trouble." He pulled her up onto her feet and walked her over to the corner. "Five minutes corner time. Daddy is going to put some water in your bot-bot. Seems the only way to make sure that you eat and drink is to feed you myself."

Well, she wasn't going to argue with that.

But she really didn't think it was necessary for her to spend time in the corner.

"Daddy, I don'ts want to be in the corner," she grumbled as he positioned her with her hands on her head.

"Is your tummy cramping?" he asked with concern.

She thought about lying.

Then thought again.

"It's a bit sore but not too bad," she admitted.

"We need a heating pad for you. Grady should be on his way here, I'll get him to pick one up for you."

"Daddy no!" She turned to give him a firm look.

"Excuse me?" He gave her a frosty look back. "Are you allowed to say no to Daddy?"

She pouted. "But, Daddy, I don'ts need it."

"I say you do. And what I say goes." He cupped the side of her face. "I'm always going to give you what you need, my baby."

Darn it.

He knew just how to make her insides go all gooey.

"Corner time," he ordered.

With a sigh, she turned around. Unfortunately, because she seemed unable to stay silent or quiet, those five minutes turned into about forty hours.

Slight exaggeration, but that's what it felt like.

"Come here, baby girl."

Turning, she moved toward where Steele was sitting on the sofa, shaking his head. "You're terrible at corner time."

Well, she didn't know why she'd want to be good at corner time. That seemed silly.

"Sorry, Daddy!" she told him, trying to actually look sorry.

She wasn't sure she succeeded.

"You're a brat. But you're my brat. And you're adorable." He drew her onto his lap, settling her back against his arm before reaching for her bot-bot.

She opened her mouth and eagerly sucked it into her mouth. She played with her fingers as she drank down the water, moving them up and down.

Effie loved about being held like this and having her Daddy feed her a bottle. It was soothing. It made her feel safe.

Cared for.

When the bottle was empty, he helped her sit and rubbed

her back.

"What a good girl you are for drinking all your water," he told her.

"I knows!" she crowed, clapping her hands. "Effie is a good girl. Effie deserves a treat! Jelly beans!"

"No jelly beans," he told her.

She pouted. "Mean. Magic beans!"

"Isn't that the same thing?" he asked.

"Nooo, silly Daddy. Magic beans are jelly beans that are . . . magic!" She moved her hands in a wide arc, flicking her fingers back and forth.

"Still no."

"You're such a party pooper sometimes, Daddy."

"I am?" he asked, raising an eyebrow.

"Yeah, it's a real problem. We should probably get that seen to. They likely have party pooper doctors."

"Really?"

"Yep. We'll get them to have the party pooperiness pulled out of you."

"Good to know. I feel so relieved now," he said dryly.

"Me too, Daddy. Me too."

"Well, until that happens. I guess we'll just have to make do with me being a party pooper. Which means you now get to eat some fruit and vegetables."

"Noooo! It should be illegal!"

"Illegal?" he asked.

"Yep. Should be illegal to be made to eat vegetables when you have your period." She wrinkled her nose.

"Well," he said, tapping her nose. "I've never been one to care about following the law."

She sighed as he grabbed the plate from where he'd set it on the coffee table and picked up a piece of carrot to feed her.

Should definitely be illegal.

46

No!

No, no, no!

She stared down at the piece of paper in her hand. She was back in her apartment. It was a week after Steele had taken care of her during her period. This past weekend, she'd spent Saturday night with them again. But this time had mostly been about them looking after her and having Little time.

She loved Little time with Daddy. The only thing that would make it better was if Grady would join them.

But she wouldn't push him into anything he didn't want.

Now . . . all thoughts of Little time were pushed from her head as she stared down at the letter in horror. A letter that stated someone was going for custody of Brooks. The first name of the person was unknown to her, but the last name wasn't.

This person shared Brooks' mom's last name. So it had to be a relative of hers. Effie studied the lawyer's name. There were contact details for him. The name was familiar, though.

Her mind went back to that phone call from a few months

ago where that lawyer had wanted her to allow Tanya to call Brooks.

Did this have something to do with that? Should she have let her call him? Could this have been prevented?

Her breath came in sharp pants. She had to get it together. Brooks had already left for school and Grady would be here in ten minutes to pick her up.

Grady and Steele now picked her up for work when they could. Mostly Grady, though.

And she loved those moments together. She needed to carve out more time for them without abandoning Brooks. But they'd both been telling her that he could come and stay as well.

Now, that all seemed like nothing. Pointless to worry about when she had something so much worse to concern herself with.

With a shaking hand, she dialed the phone number on the letter. After getting through his assistant, she heard that same lawyer's voice.

"Hello, Ms. Stephenson. How can I help?"

He sounded professional but smug.

Asshole.

"What is this?" she asked.

"I'm guessing you got the custody letter."

"You cannot go for custody of Brooks. He's mine."

"Actually, he's not. He has no blood or legal ties to you."

"He's lived with me for years!"

"Rather unfortunate."

Rather unfortunate? Was he kidding her?

"Unfortunate?" she whispered.

"Yes, my client didn't realize that his nephew was in the hands of a woman with no real familial ties to him. And now he wants to remedy that."

Nephew?

Brooks had an uncle? Tanya's brother?

"This won't happen. Brooks is sixteen. The judge will give him a say."

"And do you think the judge will be happy when he learns that Brooks is being cared for by a woman who is dating two men? At the same time? It doesn't speak well to your character, Ms. Stephenson."

"How . . . how do you know that?"

"You have a neighbor willing to attest to that fact. He's not happy with you. Then there's the fact that you work in a strip club, live in a terrible part of town . . . it's not looking good for you, Ms. Stephenson."

She ended the call, breathing heavily.

Do not throw up. Do not.

She took a few calming breaths. What was she going to do?

Tell Steele and Grady.

Right. Only . . . did she have to break up with them? She didn't want to, but this was Brooks.

They can help you.

The knock on the door made her jump, but she made herself move. She grabbed her coat and handbag and opened the door.

"Good morning," she said brightly.

He eyed her. "What's wrong?"

"I'll tell you in the truck."

He didn't like that, but he nodded. She locked up before letting Grady lead her out to the truck.

She blushed as she saw the booster seat in the front seat. "Really?"

"Safety first. Did you know there's a good shop for Littles in Billings?" he asked as he lifted her into the booster and buckled her seatbelt.

"Did you buy out half the stuff in it?" she asked.

"Yes."

He wasn't even joking. Yikes.

Once they were both in the truck, Grady set off toward Pinkies.

"Right. What's wrong?" He glanced over at her, his hands tight around the steering wheel.

She never felt unsafe with these guys while they were driving. They were always in control.

"I got a letter today."

"Right."

"A letter from a lawyer. I think . . . I think Brooks' mom, well, her brother, he wants custody of Brooks."

There was silence in the truck. "What. The. Fuck. Why would he think he'd get custody? Brooks is sixteen. It's been years since Joe died."

"I don't know," she whispered. "But, uh, I called the lawyer, and it seems they have some things they think will help them get custody."

"Like what?"

"Like a neighbor who will attest that I'm seeing two men. At the same time."

"Neighbor? What fucking . . . Roddy."

"Roddy." He'd moved out over the weekend, so she couldn't even confront the bastard.

"Fucking weasel. Don't worry, I'll take care of him. I'll take care of it all."

"Grady—"

"Little girl, you have two men now. Two men who have their own resources. We are going to take care of this."

"You'll take care of it?"

"I promise." He glanced over at her just as she spotted someone speeding backward out of a driveway.

"Grady! Watch out!" she screamed.

A large hand landed on her chest seconds before the car slammed into them.

The sound of screeching metal filled the car. Effie jolted forward, although her face never hit the dashboard thanks to the hand holding her back.

She sat there as they came to a stop, just trying to breathe.

She turned her head, wincing as pain shot through her entire body. "Ouch."

Grady stared at her, his face filled with fear. What was wrong? Was he hurt? She'd never seen him look like that. His mouth kept moving, but she couldn't hear what he was saying.

Why couldn't she hear anything?

Then Grady cupped her chin with his hand. The warmth of his skin hit hers. Suddenly, it was like her ears popped.

"Are you all right? Sweetheart, are you okay?"

"I t-think so."

"You think so?" Alarm took over the worry. "Are you hurt?"

"I . . . I don't think so."

"Are you sure?"

Not really. But the look on his face told her that she better be.

"Fuck. Fuck. I have to call Steele."

Okay, she really, really didn't think that was a good idea.

"Not a good idea."

His gaze shot to hers. "Believe me, if he hears this from someone else, he won't be happy. Where's my phone? Fuck, he's going to lose it when he learns we were in a car accident."

Car accident.

They'd just been in a car accident.

Like with Joe. They'd been in an accident and Grady could have died.

"Grady? Grady!"

"What is it?" He turned to her. He had his phone in his hand, but he'd been staring out the front window. "What the fuck is that bitch's problem?"

Grady's words tore through her panic for a moment. Effie glanced out the window to see the driver of the car that had smashed into them was now standing and looking at the damage. Her mouth was moving. And she was gesturing at them rudely.

"Steele? It's me. Just letting you know we've been in a car accident. We're both fine. I'm dropping you a pin." Grady ended the call.

Car. Accident.

"Got his voicemail," he said.

"G-Grady."

"Give me two seconds, sweetheart," he murmured as he fiddled with his phone.

"Grady. My legs. I c-can't feel my legs." She started hitting them. Why couldn't she feel them? Panic flooded her. "Grady! I can't feel my legs."

Alarm filled her. Panic had her breath coming in sharp pants.

"Sweetheart, it's all right. It's okay. Look at me. No, stop that." He grabbed her hands, holding them in his. "Look at me."

A sob broke free from her. "Are you going to die?"

Shock had his eyes widening as he gaped at her. "Sweetheart, I'm fine."

"Don't die. Please . . . please . . ."

"Okay, Little one. Listen to me. I'm going to get out of the car, and come around to check on you. Just keep it together for me for a little longer, all right?"

Keep what together?

Her sanity? She was pretty sure she'd lost that a long time ago.

"Just breathe and do not hurt yourself, understand me?"

She shook her head and the world spun. She didn't understand. "You shouldn't move. You might be hurt. Don't leave. Don't leave me."

"Little girl," he growled. "Listen to me. I am not leaving you. I will never leave you."

"I . . . I . . ."

"Listen to Daddy. You need to do as Daddy says."

"D-daddy?" Steele was her Daddy.

"You don't think I can be your Daddy?"

"Daddy G," she whispered.

His eyes widened with surprise. "Makes me sound like a bad rapper, but I'll take it right now. Daddy G is in charge, so you need to listen to me."

"Okay." Her breathing slowed, the panic clearing from her mind.

He wouldn't leave her.

He would never leave her.

"Tell me you understand," he said firmly.

"Yes, I understand."

"I understand, Daddy G."

"I understand, Daddy G."

"That's my good girl."

Okay. She liked that. Being his good girl.

Then he climbed out of the car and her fear returned. Her legs. She couldn't feel her legs.

She slammed her hands into them.

Why . . . why couldn't she feel her legs?

Harsh breaths filled the car, but it barely registered that they were coming from her. She slammed her hands down again. But it wasn't working. She couldn't feel anything.

Don't hit yourself.

Daddy G won't like it.

Okay . . . okay. She had this.

She stared out the window as Grady talked to the other driver. Although it seemed the other woman was doing all the talking. Grady shook his head at her and strode away.

That's when the bitch reached out and grabbed him.

Oh, hell no.

That, more than anything else, broke through her panic. Effie reached for the door handle, opening the door as he shook off her hold.

"Do not touch me," he told her coldly.

Whoa. She'd heard him cold before. But not like this. He was breathing pure ice at this woman. And that bitch stumbled back in shock, her rage dissipating for a moment.

What did she have to be angry about?

She was the one who'd caused the accident.

People were milling around, watching the drama unfold, but Effie barely paid them any attention as Grady turned back to her, striding to the open door.

She pressed her nails into her thighs. She was wearing a pair of thick pants, but surely she should have felt something?

Her legs.

Grady.

"Little girl, what did I say about hurting yourself?" He grabbed her hands, moving them away from her legs.

"I'm not . . . I'm not hurting myself. But I can't feel anything, Daddy G," she cried.

"Stop," he said firmly, taking her face between his warm hands. "Stop. You will not think. You will not worry. And you will not panic."

She wouldn't? Because she felt like she was doing all three right now.

"Because whatever happens, you are going to be all right. Understand me? You will be fine."

A sob broke free. "Are you . . . are you . . ."

"I'm fine, sweetheart. Not a scratch on me. I don't even have whiplash."

"Promise. Promise. I can't lose you."

Understanding filled his face. "I promise, sweetheart. I am fine." Taking her hand, he held it to his chest.

"Hey! Who the fuck is going to pay for the damage to my car!"

That came from the other woman and it was screeched. Grady's face grew cold, but he didn't turn from her. He gave her his full attention. And it was incredible. She soaked it up. She needed it. His calm. His surety.

"I don't want to move you until the paramedics get here, all right? I just need you to stay strong a bit longer. Can you do that for me, sweetheart?" He wrapped a hand around the base of her throat. It didn't feel like a threat, though. It felt like he was trying to infuse some of his strength into her. And she finally felt like she could breathe.

"Yes."

"Good girl. You are doing so well. Good things come to good girls, you know."

That hadn't been her experience in the past. But with them . . . yeah, good things had come her way.

Along with the bad.

The sound of a siren made her breath hitch. "She's so mad."

"Don't worry about her. She was the one in the wrong and she knows it."

A police car pulled up and the woman immediately went over to him.

"She doesn't think it's her fault."

"Don't look at her, Little one. Eyes on me. That's it. Everything will be all right."

She wasn't sure she believed him. But she wanted to. So she kept her gaze on him.

"Excuse me, sir. I need a word." It was the policeman.

"Later."

"Now. This woman claims you hit her."

"She's lying. She backed into us."

"Then I need your account."

"I'm busy looking after my girl. She's hurt. We need the paramedics."

"Right. What's wrong?" the policeman asked.

She glanced over at him and saw that he looked young. Then out of the corner of her eye, she saw a car pull up.

Uh-oh.

She knew that car. And she also knew that it probably wasn't a good idea that it was here right now.

Because the last thing they needed was Steele losing it in front of a policeman. And once he realized that this woman was trying to claim Grady was in the wrong and that she'd backed into Grady and risked hurting him...

Yeah. Uh-oh.

"Grady. Steele."

Grady turned and glanced over. "Fuck." Then he turned to the policeman. "My statement is that we were driving along and this bitch backed into us going full speed. Now, my girl here is injured and we need the paramedics. So how about you go arrange that?"

"That's not how this works."

"Grady," she murmured as she saw Steele striding toward them. He looked like a bull with a target. She just wasn't sure who the target was at that moment. But at least the woman who had crashed into them stopped screeching as she saw the thunderous look on his face.

"Fuck. Who the hell is that?" the cop asked, his hand moving toward his gun.

"That is someone you don't want getting involved," Grady

told him. "So I suggest you start interviewing these bystanders, see who witnessed the crash so you know I wasn't in the wrong, and then fucking leave."

"You can't talk to me like that."

What the young cop didn't realize was that Steele was standing right behind him. How he hadn't realized that she had no idea. It was like having a huge grizzly bear stalking you.

"He can talk to you however the fuck he likes," Steele snapped. "Now, get out of my way and go do your job."

The cop jumped and turned, looking up at Steele. She couldn't see the police officer's face, but she was kind of betting that he was shitting himself right now.

"You . . . you can't talk to me like that, either."

The driver started screeching again, and before she could stop it, a whimper escaped her. Both Grady and Steele zeroed in on her and she closed her eyes against the intensity.

"You," Steele growled.

She opened her eyes to see he was staring at the woman. "Shut the fuck up. And you," he turned to the cop, "go do your job before I make it my job to ensure you don't have one anymore."

The cop fumbled at his belt. "I could arrest you for threatening an officer of the law."

"Steele," Grady warned.

Steele moved his eyes back to them and stepped forward, ignoring the cop and the other driver. "Are you both all right?" His gaze went to her, then Grady. "Are you hurt?"

"I'm fine. But Effie isn't. We need to find out where the fucking ambulance is."

"What's wrong? What hurts?" Steele's face filled with fear.

For her?

"Effie can't feel her legs. We need to get her to the hospital and checked over." An ambulance drove up and she let out a small sob. She didn't want to go to the hospital. She didn't want to know that her back was damaged again.

She already knew that. Her breathing came in fast pants as the paramedics rushed toward her.

She couldn't do this. It wasn't happening. She couldn't.

"Effie. Baby girl. Look at me." Steele was suddenly in front of her. His gaze had almost turned gray. She focused in on him. "That's it. Listen to me. Everything is going to be all right. You are going to be all right."

"How do you know?" she whispered.

"Because I won't allow you to be anything else."

47

Steele paced up and down the waiting room. "What the fuck is taking so long?"

Grady glanced up at him from where he'd been typing something on his phone. How he could concentrate on work when their girl was back there being examined, Steele had no idea.

She couldn't feel her legs.

Worry flooded him.

He could have lost her. Lost both of them.

Just like Jacqui.

No . . . they were alive. Which meant he had another chance to take care of them properly.

He just needed to protect them better.

He stopped in front of Grady, studying him closely.

"I'm fine," Grady told him calmly. "The doctor cleared me. I barely have a scratch on me. It wasn't a bad crash."

It wasn't a bad crash.

No one had died.

They were still both here. Both his.

"No more driving," he stated. "Raul drives you everywhere from now on."

Grady raised an eyebrow. "I'm not your sub. And I wasn't at fault. The accident would have happened even if Raul was driving."

Because of that bitch.

"I want that other driver dealt with."

"Already onto it," Grady told him, raising his phone.

He should have known he would be.

Steele slumped on the seat next to him. "Why can't she feel her legs?"

Grady frowned. "I don't know."

"How are you handling this so well?"

Grady ran a hand over his face. "I'm trying not to freak out because you're doing enough for the both of us."

"I'm not freaking out."

Grady shot him a look. Okay, he was totally freaking out.

"This morning, Effie was upset when I arrived. She'd gotten a letter from a lawyer. It appears that Brooks' uncle wants custody of him."

Steele reeled back. "What the fuck?"

"Yes. I know. So I'm going to take care of it so she doesn't have to worry."

"He's sixteen. The judge will listen to what he wants."

"The lawyer got to that asshole neighbor of hers. He filled him in on a few things, like how Effie is dating two men."

"Motherfucker. I'm going to kill that bastard."

"Oh, he's on the list," Grady drawled. "But first, we deal with the uncle. Brooks will be here soon." They'd sent Raul to collect him from school, figuring it was better if he knew now.

Steele didn't like this.

He didn't like any of this.

He tried to calm himself down, but it wasn't working. Nothing was fucking working.

Leaning over, he placed his elbows on his thighs and took a few deep breaths.

When he'd gotten that voicemail from Grady, he'd nearly lost his fucking mind.

What had he been thinking, letting Grady have his own fucking vehicle? All right, so he wasn't the other man's boss and Grady didn't appreciate Steele telling him what to do.

But Steele gave less than a fuck about that.

Coming across them in a wrecked truck . . . that had nearly been his undoing. He thought he might have lost part of his sanity right then.

This isn't the same as Jacqui. They're both still alive. It wasn't a carjacking.

Somehow, it still didn't matter to him. The rage was real. The worry. The fucking fear.

This is why he didn't let people close.

But there was no keeping Effie out. No keeping Grady at a distance.

Even though Grady wouldn't let Steele fuss over him, the other man knew that Steele trusted him to keep himself safe.

But Effie wasn't an alpha male. And she was someone he could unleash his full protective instincts on. Someone he could coddle, wrap up in wool, and keep safe from everything.

She needed to be living with them. It was the only way he might now be able to sleep at night. He didn't want her out of his eyesight.

They'd both been in trouble and he hadn't been there to protect them. He clenched his hand into a fist.

He hadn't fucking protected them.

"Damon, you need to calm down. Stop working yourself up."

"You could have been seriously hurt."

"I wasn't though. I'm fine. I might be a bit stiff tomorrow, but I'm all good."

"You might not have been fine, though. I could have fucking lost you!" And that thought terrified him. Losing either of them wasn't something he could live with.

"Damon," Grady said softly.

"The two of you are my world." Reaching over, he drew the other man against him, hugging him tight. "What if I'd lost you both?"

Grady was stiff for a moment before he relaxed against him. Then he drew back and gave Steele a worried look. "You know you can't live with 'what if's."

Yeah, he knew that deep down. But fucked if he could make his brain steer away from that direction.

What if that bitch had been going faster? What if the car had caught fire? What if it hadn't been a random accident? What if someone had tried to get at them while he wasn't . . . fucking . . . there . . .

"This isn't the same as what happened to Jacqui," Grady told him, placing a hand on his back. "No one attacked us."

"I should have protected you both."

"You're not fucking Superman, you can't stop the people you care about from getting hurt."

"She could be fucking paralyzed!"

"What?"

The question came from the doorway. He turned to see Effie's boy standing there, looking pale and shocked.

Shit.

How had he not noticed the door opening?

He'd probably object to being called a boy, but he was only sixteen. And Steele now had the dreaded job of telling him about his aunt.

"What's going on? Why did you send your driver to get me from school and bring me here?" Brooks asked.

"Brooks," Steele said in a low voice. "Come and sit down."

Brooks shook his head, looking from him to Grady. "What is going on? What do you mean, she might be paralyzed?"

"Brooks, your aunt and I were in a car accident this morning," Grady told him.

Brooks grew paler, swaying.

Fuck!

Steele shot Grady a look. "You could have handled that gentler."

The other man had grown pale as well. "Brooks, I'm sorry."

"Is she alive?"

"Yeah, bud, she's alive. She's all right." Steele tried to make his voice softer. He wondered if Brooks would let him touch him. In the end, he just pointed to a chair. "Sit down."

"I want to see her. Right now."

Fuck, he was shaking. Steele knew he had to get the kid to sit before he ended up passed out on the floor.

"We're waiting for the doctors to come back and update us," Grady told him.

Thankfully, Brooks moved to a chair and sat. "You said paralyzed."

Steele shot his gaze to Grady, unsure how to proceed.

Kids didn't fit well into his lifestyle. A child would need a lot of protection and care. Just like a woman.

He'd never planned on having either.

And now he had both, it seemed.

"We don't know," Grady told him quietly. "The accident wasn't a big one. Some woman backed into us. It was jarring, but not a huge impact. However, Effie said she couldn't feel her legs. She's back there now, getting some tests."

Something strange filled Brooks' face. But before Steele

could try to figure out what he was thinking, a doctor walked into the waiting room.

"Are you the family of Effie Stephenson?"

Brooks jumped to his feet. "I'm her nephew."

The doctor eyed him, then looked past him to him and Grady. Probably wanting to speak to someone older. Fuck, he had a feeling this wasn't going to be good. "Are the two of you family?"

"They are," Brooks said, likely seeing the same thing Steele had. That this doctor didn't want to tell Brooks what was going on.

"I'm her fiancée," Steele said smoothly. "Grady is her boss."

Brooks shot him a look, but his expression didn't change. The kid was good.

"All right," the doctor said, turning to Steele. "Maybe we could speak alone."

Brooks scowled.

"Just give it to us, doc," Steele said gruffly.

"Steele," Grady warned.

"Brooks can handle hearing this," Steele said to Grady.

"I can," Brooks added determinedly.

"All right. We have run several tests and taken Ms. Stephenson for an MRI, as well as X-rays, and an ultrasound, and we cannot find any physical reason for her paralysis."

Huh?

He looked to Grady, who appeared just as confused, then over to Brooks, who had sucked in a breath. The kid still looked like he was going to pass out, so Steele moved closer.

Maybe he should have spoken to the doctor on his own.

"Then you must have missed something," Grady said. "She was hitting her legs. She couldn't feel them."

"We're very certain that there is no physical injury."

"You're saying she's faking it?" Brooks asked.

The doctor frowned. "No, that's not what I'm saying at all. Ms. Stephenson told us she was in a car accident six years ago where she injured her back."

"Yeah, with my dad," Brooks said. "He died a few days later from a brain bleed. And Effie, she . . . she injured her back really badly."

Fuck. Steele put his hand on Brooks' shoulder. To his shock, he didn't shake him off. So maybe he did need some reassurance.

"Do you think that has something to do with what's going on?" Grady asked. "Could she have re-injured her back and it's causing some sort of temporary paralysis?"

"I went over her old notes," the doctor said. "Back then, she had some numbness in her legs. I think that the accident today has triggered something in her brain. It's brought up old memories and stressors. This is something her brain is doing to her. She's not faking it. She truly cannot feel her legs."

"Fuck," Steele muttered.

"What I believe is that she needs a bit of time. Has she been stressed lately? Working a lot?"

"Not as much lately," Brooks said. "But a few months ago when she lost her job, yeah. Things were tight. We didn't have a lot of money for . . . for anything, but she never let me go without. I wanted to quit school to help, but she wouldn't let me do that. She jokes that I'm her ticket to the good times because I'm smart and I have to take care of her in her old age. But I know her . . . even when she's old she'll be taking care of me because that's just who Effie is."

The doctor's gaze softened at this. Then, a slightly worried look entered his face. "Does she have health insurance?"

"Yes, she has health insurance," Grady said coldly.

"Because she's in a private room—"

"Say one thing about money and this conversation is going to go very differently," Steele interjected.

"Ahh, right." The doctor swallowed nervously. "I think what she needs is some rest. Keep her stress to a minimum. Make sure she's eating well. Do you know whether she spoke to anyone professionally after her last accident?"

"I don't think so," Brooks said quietly. "She was too busy taking care of me."

"Not your fault, kid," Steele told Brooks gruffly.

The doctor nodded, looking slightly uncomfortable. "I'll let you go see her now if you like, but I would warn you not to add to her stress."

"Wait, have you told her that her paralysis isn't a physical thing?" Grady asked.

"Yes, I sat down and explained things, but I'm not sure she completely understands."

Shit. That wasn't good.

"You shouldn't have told her without us there," Grady snarled at the doctor, surprising Steele. And Brooks, who jumped.

"She has a right to know what is going on with her own body," the doctor replied huffily.

"Yes, and if her mental state is delicate, she needs people by her side who care about her. If we get in there and she is in any way upset, you can expect to hear from our lawyers."

The doctor left with a grumble while Brooks stared over at Grady in awe. "That was fucking awesome. You totally handed him his ass."

"The guy *is* an ass," Grady said. "Come on, we need to get to Effie."

Yeah. They needed to go take care of their girl.

48

There's nothing physically wrong with you.

Those words went around and around in her head.

So if there was nothing wrong with her . . . then what the fuck was *wrong* with her? Because, no joke, she couldn't feel her legs.

This was . . . terrifying.

It was actually worse than having a diagnosed medical issue in a way because how did she fix her brain?

And where was Grady? Why wasn't he here? The nurse and doctor refused to give her any information on him, citing patient privacy policies. But she just wanted to know if he was all right. What if he was hurt worse than first thought?

Her breath came in fast pants. She was on the cusp of a panic attack.

"Aunt Effie?"

She glanced over to see Brooks standing in the doorway, looking more uncertain and scared than she'd seen him look in a long, long time.

Shit. Why hadn't she thought of Brooks? Some guardian she was.

"Hey, honey."

He stood there, just staring at her. She held open her arms. "Come here."

He didn't rush at her the way he would have when he was younger, but he moved steadily toward her. Then he gently reached down to hug her.

"Effie," he whispered.

"I'm all right. I promise." She hugged him tight as she pushed all of her fears and uncertainties down deep. She needed to be strong for Brooks.

Which is why she needed to fix the fucked-up mess that was her brain.

He held on tight for a bit longer, then he drew back. His eyes looked haunted and he blinked rapidly.

She hated that. Hated that look on his face.

"I'm all right. Everything will be fine. I promise. Turns out I'm a bit messed up in the head, but we already knew that, right?"

Brooks drew back to glare at her. "Do not say stuff like that, Effie. I don't like it. You're not messed up in the head."

She gave him a shocked look. Although she shouldn't have been surprised by his words. Brooks was definitely his father's son. And Joe had also been a dominant man.

"Okay, honey. I won't. But I don't want you worrying. We'll be okay, you and I."

"Course we will," he said with more confidence than she had. But that was the beauty of being sixteen with your life ahead of you. "Because I'm quitting school and taking care of you."

"Nope."

"Aunt Effie—"

"I told you, Brooks. I need you to get a good job so you can take care of me in my old age."

"And I need to take care of you now. Auntie, you're paralyzed."

"Nope. Doc said I wasn't. I just need to get my brain sorted out. I'm sure that will only take a day or so. Although I might need some help getting out of here. I don't need to be here racking up a hospital bill."

She tried to shift over, to get her legs to damn well work . . . but they didn't.

What the hell was wrong with her?

"You don't need to worry about the hospital bill because it's covered by your job."

Relief flooded her as Grady stepped into the room. She hadn't noticed him lingering in the doorway.

Thank you, God. Thank you, God.

She had to hold back her tears of relief.

Nothing could happen to Grady. Or Damon.

Pull yourself together, Effie. No one needs to see you fall apart.

"You're all right," she whispered.

His gaze softened. "Of course I am, sweetheart. I might be a bit sore tomorrow, but other than that, I'm fine."

"No pains? No headaches? Did they run some tests?"

"They were all fine. I promise."

Okay. Now she could finally breathe a bit easier.

Steele walked in, his gaze even more intense than Grady's had been. He leaned over her, kissing her lightly on the head. "Baby. Fuck. I've been so worried about you."

Oh no.

She hated the thought of worrying him.

"I'm all right."

"Baby girl, don't make light of what happened. You were in a car accident and now you need some care. That's what we're here for, but you need to be honest with us. Got me?"

"I've got you." She turned to Grady. "I'm confused, though. I thought I had to work there six months before it kicked in."

"No."

She eyed Grady suspiciously. The guy looked innocent, like butter wouldn't melt in his mouth. But she was onto him.

He was a sneaky sneaky-sneak.

"Effie, everything." Steele gave her a stern look.

Why fight them? She couldn't afford to pay this hospital bill. It would send her further down the rabbit hole when she was only now in the black.

"And you will not be leaving school," Grady told Brooks. He'd obviously heard what he'd said to her before. "You're smart and you're going places. To do that, you need schooling."

To her surprise, tears filled her eyes. She'd never had anyone backing her up, supporting her, cheering her on for a long time. Not since Joe died. It meant so much that these guys were here for her like that.

Steele brushed her hair off her face, giving her another kiss on the forehead. That was pretty chaste for him. But maybe it was because Brooks was here.

Or perhaps it's because you're so fucked in the head that you think you're paralysed.

And they don't want you anymore.

Fuck. Fuck. Shit.

She tried to focus on the conversation rather than going into her brain. Looking around, she noticed Grady watching her intently.

Crap.

"Effie needs my help," Brooks insisted.

"Yep, she does," Steele agreed. "She needs to know that

you're good. That you're going to school, keeping up your grades, and staying out of trouble. That's what she needs from you."

"But who is going to look after her while I'm at school? She can't walk."

"Simple," Steele replied. "We are."

49

"I still don't think this is necessary." Or a good idea.

They couldn't possibly want her to stay here with them.

Not when she was completely fucked up.

It was the day after the accident. She'd spent the night in the hospital having additional tests. Betsy and Ink had come to pick up Brooks so he could stay the night with them. Betsy was utterly beautiful. Graceful. Elegant. Kind.

While Ink looked like a tattooed surfer. Slightly scary, although he'd been nothing but kind to her and Brooks.

Today, Raul would pick him up after school and he'd come back here.

To Steele and Grady's house.

Steele was currently carrying her into the house and up the stairs. He walked into his bedroom with her.

Wait. She was staying in his room?

"You'd rather we all move into your apartment?" Steele asked gruffly as Grady walked in behind them. "Tight squeeze, baby. And doesn't really make much sense."

"No, I just . . . I don't think you guys need to take care of me. You have stuff to do. Work. Lives. You shouldn't have to play nursemaid to the crazy lady."

As Steele placed her on the bed, she sensed the mood in the room change.

Glancing up, she took in the thunderous look on his face.

Then, looking over, she saw the way that Grady's face had grown cold.

Uh-oh.

"Crazy lady?" Steele whispered. He turned to Grady. "Did you hear that shit?"

"Yep. And I didn't like it."

"Well, it's the truth!" she cried. She hadn't slept last night. And she knew Steele hadn't either, since he'd watched her like a hawk the entire night. And today, she was exhausted, sore, and so worried she could barely keep herself from throwing up.

Luckily, she didn't have much in her stomach to throw up if she did.

"It is not the fucking truth. And if you say that again, I'll turn you over my knee and redden your ass."

"Steele," Grady warned.

"Not right now," Steele added. "Once you're feeling better."

"But I'm not actually injured. It's all in my dumb head. So how do I get better?"

"If you need a therapist, we get you a therapist," Steele said. "Need a physio, we get that. Nurse, we're onto it."

"I don't want to be an invalid! I don't want you to have to take care of me. You didn't sign on for that." It wasn't fair to them.

She didn't want to be a burden.

"Everything, Effie," Grady told her.

She threw her hands up in the air. "Everything doesn't include me being bonkers! I can't . . . I don't know . . . there's no happy in me." She rubbed her chest.

"What?" Steele gave her a confused look.

"I can't find the happy. There's no positive about this. Everything seems dark ... gray ... black. Where's the happy gone?"

Steele sat on one side of her, Grady on the other.

"What do I do?" She tugged at her earring.

"What you do is hold on to us," Steele told her, gently moving her hand away from her ear.

"We know about the dark, Little one," Grady added. "We've lived there for a long time."

"After my sister died, my whole world went black," Steele told her. "All that kept me going was Grady. And then along came my ray of sunshine. So sweet that she brought color to my life."

Dear Lord.

"So. Hold. Onto. Us," Steele said fiercely.

"I'm scared." Tears dripped down her face.

"Then you hold on harder," Grady told her.

"You'll hold me back?" she asked.

"We will never let you go." Grady gave her such an intense look that it took her breath away.

"What if I don't get better?"

"Then we put in an elevator, retrofit for a wheelchair, and figure out everything else you need. Do you really think Grady won't research the shit out of that? Start making lists? But that won't happen because you're going to get better."

"I can already tell that we're going to need to keep track of all the spanks she's owed," Grady said. "Starting with five for calling herself crazy. And another five for calling herself bonkers."

Oh God. She got the feeling that she wouldn't sit well at the end of all of this.

∽

The crash sent the car spinning!

Slam!

Pain screamed through her. She could barely breathe. Turning her head, she searched for him.

"Joe! Joe!"

She knew something was wrong and she started sobbing. But when she caught sight of him, it wasn't Joe's face she could see.

It was Grady's.

The scream broke out of her and she woke up, panting heavily.

"You're all right, baby girl. You're okay." Steele pulled her up so he was sitting with her on his lap.

The door to the bedroom slammed open and Grady raced in, looking frantic.

"Nightmare," Steele told him.

She shuddered, sobbing for breath. She hadn't had a nightmare in the hospital last night, so this one took her by surprise.

She was shaken and scared.

Grady climbed onto the bed and she threw her arms around him, dragging him to her.

"Oomph! Wow, for a Little one you sure are strong," he teased.

"I dreamed it was you. I dreamed it was you."

"Me, what, sweetheart?"

"In the car with me. It wasn't Joe's face, it was yours."

"Oh, sweetheart," he said, his voice breaking. "I'm fine. I'm here. It wasn't me."

He drew back, and she frantically ran her hands over his face and down his body, searching for injuries. "Not you. Not you."

"No, sweetheart, not me. I'm right here. You're all hot and sweaty. Why don't we get you in the shower?"

She nodded, just wanting to stay close to them.

Grady picked her up and held her against his chest. He nuzzled her neck. "I'm right here, sweetheart. I'm not leaving you."

Steele got up and turned on the shower. They passed her back and forth as they stripped off so she was in the arms of one of them at all times. Then Grady held her, singing quietly as Steele washed her body.

"It's going to be all right, Little one," Grady told her. "Just hold on."

When they were all dry, Grady placed her on the bed and they climbed in on either side. But she couldn't sleep. The nightmare played over and over in her mind.

"Why don't we try to help you sleep?" Steele murmured.

"I'll go get the bottle," Grady said, climbing from the bed.

Effie wanted to reach after him and pull him back, but she knew she was acting like a crazy person.

Unfortunately, even a bottle of milk didn't manage to calm her or make her sleepy. She was aware of the two men sharing an alarmed look before Steele got out of bed. She stared up at him with fear, wondering if he was planning on leaving.

"We could try swaddling," Grady suggested.

"You okay with that, baby girl?" Steele asked.

"Yes," she said croakily.

Grady came back with a large muslin blanket that had pictures of sloths on it. Laying it on the bed, Steele placed her in it and Grady wrapped her up tight.

An instant feeling of calm came over her.

Steele slipped her pacifier into her mouth and then picked her up in his arms.

Then he started rocking her back and forth.

Her eyes started to drift closed.

"We've got you, baby girl. We have you."

They had her.

She just had to hold on.

~

SHE STILL COULDN'T FEEL her legs.

And she was done.

Brooks seemed to have settled in well. It was Sunday, four days after the accident. Last night he'd gone on a date with Stella, just the two of them. And today he was with the twins.

She hated to uproot him. But she couldn't do this anymore. She couldn't hold on.

Not when she was going to become a weight around their necks... dragging them down.

Effie, no one wants someone who is a burden.

"I know that, Nan." She clenched her hands into fists. "I know it."

A knock on the door had her looking up.

The guys wouldn't knock.

"Hello?" A woman with dark hair and a big smile peered around the door.

What the heck?

"Oh good, you're awake."

Wait. She'd seen this woman before. But where? Oh, in the photos downstairs.

Millie.

But why was she here?

"Hi, I'm Millie and you're Effie. And I'm... I'm..."

What was she doing? Was she trying to drag something in here?

"Come on, Mr. Fluffy. I am not carrying you. You weigh over

a hundred pounds and the vet said that you've got to get more exercise. You can manage some stairs and then a few steps more."

Effie sat up, her mouth falling open in shock as Millie practically dragged an enormous dog into her bedroom. It looked like it was big enough to eat her . . . except it appeared that would be too much energy to expend.

The dog stumbled in, then flopped on the floor, letting out an exhausted sigh.

Millie put her hands on her hips and blew a breath out. "Seriously? That's as far as you'll go? Come and say hi to Effie."

The dog let out one deep woof, and then promptly went to sleep.

She'd never seen anything so ridiculous. And funny.

She grinned.

"Sorry about Mr. Fluffy. He tires easily. I asked the vet if there was something wrong with him, but the vet just diagnosed him as lazy. And because he's lazy, he's getting f-a-t."

"Fat?"

A grumble came from Mr. Fluffy.

"Shh." Millie waved her hands around in the air. "He doesn't like that word. That's why I spelled it out."

"He knows the word fat?" she asked incredulously.

Another grumble from Mr. Fluffy.

All right. It seemed he did know that word.

"He's really a very sensitive doggie, aren't you, Mr. Fluffy? Who's Mama's baby?"

Okay, it seemed that Millie was as nutty as her dog. And Effie thought that was hilarious. For the first time in days, some light was coming back into her world.

"Now, I'm Millie. Oh, drat. I already said that."

"It's okay. I'm Effie."

Millie beamed at her. "I know. You're Damon and Grady's. Which is freaking awesome! Spike now owes me fifty bucks, which I'm going to spend at that new Little store in town. They have the best dinosaur stuff."

It surprised Effie that she was so open about being a Little. Then again, maybe it shouldn't. Millie seemed very secure in who she was.

And why wouldn't she be when she was absolutely rocking it?

She wore a blue dress with a tiny print of T-Rex's in tutus dancing on it. It was cinched in at her waist, then flared out. And she had on a white cardigan and shiny shoes.

She was curvy and gorgeous.

"I told him that Steele and Grady would find someone to share. He said it would never happen."

That's what they'd bet on?

Millie perched on the armchair next to the bed, placing her enormous patchwork handbag down.

"Gorgeous handbag, I've never seen anything like it."

Millie beamed. "That's because it's one of a kind. An original Kate Spain."

Kate Spain?

"One of my friends. I could get her to make you one if you like. Actually, that's an excellent idea, seeing as you're going to be my sister-in-law."

What?

Shock filled her. Even if Steele was anywhere close to proposing . . . she didn't think that was actually the way it worked.

"Um, Millie, that's sweet—"

"They'll all want to meet you, of course. My friends. That's where we're off to after we leave here. To Nowhere. But Daddy needed to come here first to talk to Damon about this guy called Wolfe, who turned up at Reaper's the other night. That's the name of the bar that Reyes owns, where members of the Iron Shadows hang out. I have something for you."

"Nowhere?" she asked, her mind spinning as Millie drew a piece of clothing out of her bag.

"Yep, Nowhere. That's where I'm from. That's where we're going. My friends usually come here, but they're getting pretty old. I don't tell them that, though. Reverend Pat gets upset."

She was so confused.

"I made you this." She held out a bright pink T-shirt with a picture of a sloth on the front. "Damon said you liked sloths and Grady said you like bright colors."

Millie gave her a curious look as she took her creation. Yeah, she understood that look since she was wearing one of Steele's black T-shirts today and Slowly was hidden under the covers.

"It's gorgeous. Thank you."

"You're welcome. Oh, and . . . ta-da!" She drew out a jar filled with blue and white jelly beans. "They also said you like jelly beans, and that your favorites are the blue and white ones. So, I made the ultimate sacrifice and ate the others. Daddy wasn't too pleased, but he'll get over it."

She'd eaten all those jelly beans?

"Don't worry, I had help," Millie said as though reading her mind. "There were a lot of jelly beans."

"Ooh, thank you. I needed some magic beans."

"Magic beans!" Millie cried. "I love it. And you don't eat S foods?"

"Um, no."

"Fair enough. I don't eat meat."

There was a knock on the open door and a huge, bald man stepped inside. He folded his arms and gave Millie a stern look.

"Hi, Daddy. This is Effie."

Spike nodded to her, but his gaze went quickly back to Millie.

"Oh, all right," Millie said in response to something Spike seemed to communicate without words. "I know, I'm sorry."

He grunted. "Didn't have permission."

"But I had to give Effie the gifts I made."

"Coulda given it to Steele."

"But then I couldn't meet Effie," Millie argued.

"Two." He left the room.

"That's your Daddy?" Effie whispered.

"Oh yeah, isn't he sweet?"

Good Lord.

"Anyway, do you need anything? Can I help with anything?" Millie asked.

"Um, don't you have to go?"

Millie waved a hand through the air. "He said two minutes, but he really means twenty."

Yeah, Effie was convinced that he didn't.

She had to pee, but she wasn't going to ask Millie to help her and risk Spike getting grumpy.

"I'm fine. Thank you for the T-shirt and jelly beans."

Millie's face softened. "You're welcome. Are you all right? Are you sure I can't get you anything else? We're going away for a few days, but one of my other friends can come see you."

"Oh no, thank you. I'm fine. I mean, besides being messed up in the head and a total burden."

Crap. She hadn't meant to blurt that out loud. But there was something about Millie that made her easy to talk to.

"Oh, sweetie. You are not a burden or messed in the head."

"Millie, I can't feel my legs. And it's all in my head. The guys and I . . . we're still new, and they have to do everything for me.

They're soon going to figure out that I'm not worth all this work."

Millie's gaze turned fierce. "Do you think they're dumb?"

"What? No, of course not."

"Do you think they would move just anyone into their house? Take care of her like this?"

"No."

"That's right. No. Because you matter. You mean something. Spike said they haven't had a woman since Steele's sister died. Don't you think that means that you are firmly in their life? That you are everything to them and they would do whatever was necessary to take care of you? These are alpha men. They are badasses. They don't do things by half measures. When there's a challenge, they don't back down, they conquer it. So have a bit of faith, sweetie."

"Millie!" Spike called from outside the room.

"I gotta go. See you soon. Come on, Mr. Fluffy."

The dog let out a woof, then lumbered to his feet, shooting Effie a long-suffering look before he left.

"Keep the faith, Effie," Millie said at the door. "They'll see you out the other side."

She lay back once Millie was gone, feeling exhausted. Although how she could be exhausted when she wasn't doing anything, she wasn't sure.

But something had to give. Something had to change. Because she couldn't keep doing this.

You're moping. No one likes someone who feels sorry for themselves, Effie.

Maybe she should just get up and try to walk. If this was all in her head, then she should be able to just fucking walk, right?

Plus, she had to pee. So she slid to the side of the bed and pulled her legs over the edge.

Still not co-operating. She took a handful of jelly beans for good luck, eating them quickly.

"Right, listen, you two. You're gonna do what I need you to do without any arguments."

Crap. Now she was talking to her legs like they were people.

She heaved herself up, holding onto the nightstand so she was standing. Hey, that was better than she'd thought. And then she tried to move. And fell flat on the floor with a cry.

"Effie? Fuck, Effie!"

Great. Now there was a witness to her humiliation.

She stared up at Grady through blurry vision. "I'm leaking."

"Little one, what did you think you were doing?"

"Being an idiot."

"Are you hurt?" he asked.

"Just my pride."

Grady picked her up and set her down on the side of the bed. Then he crouched in front of her. "Effie, you should have called me."

"I need to pee."

"You still should have called me. That's twenty."

"Twenty?" she gasped as he picked her up and carried her to the toilet.

"Yes, twenty."

"What's going on?" Steele appeared in the doorway to the bathroom.

Grady set her down on the toilet. She wasn't wearing any panties.

"Another twenty to the tally. She tried to walk by herself instead of calling one of us."

"What? Are you hurt, Effie?"

"Just my pride," she said with a groan as her bladder protested. She really, really had to go.

Steele gave her a stern look. "Think that might mean an immediate spanking."

"You guys need to leave."

They both stared at her.

Good Lord.

But she couldn't hold it back, so with a quiet sigh of annoyance and relief, she peed, then cleaned herself up before Grady picked her back up and carried her to the sink to wash her hands. Then he took her back to the bed, setting her down. They both stood, looming over her.

"You won't spank me while I can't walk, remember?" They were treating her like she was made of glass. "I'm too much of an invalid for a spanking."

There was silence and she looked up to see them staring at each other. Not a good sign.

"You know what . . . I'm suddenly feeling tired."

"You just woke up two hours ago," Steele told her.

Drat. She glanced at the clock. It was only ten in the morning.

"Effie, what's going on?" Steele asked. "Why did you try to walk on your own?"

"This isn't fair to the two of you," she whispered. "None of it is fair."

"Baby girl, when are you going to get that it has nothing to do with fair and everything to do with the way we feel about you?"

She shook her head.

"Something has to change," Steele said, picking her up and putting her on his hip.

"Yes," Grady agreed.

Wait. What was changing? Oh God, were they finally realizing she was too much work? Were they going to get rid of her?

Steele started walking out the door. Would they just throw

her out? But instead of heading to the stairs, he moved farther back down the hallway.

He paused at a closed door. Grady opened it and Steele carried her into her dream room.

She gasped in delight. It was a mix of gray, cream, and bright neon colors. Maybe it shouldn't have worked, but it did.

An oversized crib with four sides was set out from the wall. Down the end of the crib was a matching changing table. And on one side of it there was a big rocking chair.

Directly across from her, in neon lights, was her name on the wall.

There was a tea set in another corner, along with a pretend kitchen. And then storage took up most of the wall.

But it was the ceiling that really shocked her. It was painted bright green and had ropes across it with sloths hanging from them.

The last area held a small stage with a disco light above it.

For dancing.

Tears trickled down her cheeks. "This is . . . it's amazing."

"You like it?" Steele asked.

"Like it? I love it." A sob escaped. "But I don't deserve it."

"Stop it, Effie," Grady said firmly.

"I've been a terrible girlfriend these last few days. Moping around and feeling sorry for myself."

"You've had a big shock. Joe died in a car accident so of course it's going to bring up bad memories. You are allowed to react how you react," Grady told her.

"I close my eyes and all I see is the crash," she confessed. "And I thought . . . I thought something had happened to you. I got all my memories mixed up. I couldn't stand it if something happened to you. To either of you. And I . . . I didn't realize it. I didn't consciously think it, I promise. But I think I was going to push you both away, make you give up on me so then I wouldn't have to risk losing you both." She started to sob and Steele moved to the rocker.

He sat and drew her onto his lap, holding her tight and rocking her back and forth.

A hand went up and down her back soothingly, and when she eventually calmed down enough, she opened her eyes to see Grady kneeling in front of them.

He used a tissue to gently wipe her face. "Blow."

She blew her nose. She was too tired to continue to fight them on everything.

"I can't believe you guys did this all . . . for me."

"Do fucking anything for you, baby girl," Steele told her gruffly, using his finger under her chin to tilt her face back. "Except leave you. Got it?"

"If we fell over at the first hurdle, we wouldn't be the men for you," Grady added.

"But we are the men for you because we fucking love you. I love you, Effie," Damon told her.

"What?" she whispered.

"I didn't know if I'd recognize love, if I'd ever feel it," Grady told her, running a finger down her cheek as she turned to face him. "But what I feel for you can't be denied. I love you, Effie."

More leaking. Great.

"I love you, Thomas Grady." Leaning in, he took her mouth. Slow and long and sweet.

When he drew back, he smiled. "You taste like sugar."

"Jelly beans."

"Least you ate something," Steele muttered, referencing the fact she'd barely been eating. Then he took her mouth with his.

When he drew back, she was dazed and grinned up at him. "I love you, Damon Steele."

He grunted. "Damn right, you do. And you're going to stop this fucking nonsense about this being too much for us. About you being a burden and whatever other shit is going on in your brain. You need help to do that, that's why we're here," he said, tapping her forehead.

"If you've got to stay in Little headspace to achieve that, we're down for that."

"Maybe not all the time, but I definitely want to play now."

"Then that's what you'll get. Right after your spanking."

"What? You were serious?"

50

Oh yeah, he'd definitely been serious. Steele did not like Effie shutting them out. He didn't want her listening to the shit in her head and pulling away.

And he did not like that she'd tried to walk without their help.

"You could have hurt yourself. That's unacceptable."

"And I think we've made a mistake in being so careful," Grady added. "I think you saw that as our relationship changing, when it was just us making sure that you recovered from the accident. You've been stiff and sore."

Steele studied her. "You didn't hurt yourself when you fell before, did you?"

"I want to say yes, so I don't get spanked. But I know I'd just get a delay."

"And get extras for lying," Steele told her.

"My back is fine."

"Good. I'm giving you ten. Then Grady will give you the next ten."

Steele was careful as he turned her. Then he drew the T-shirt up over her ass.

Fuck, her ass was gorgeous.

"I hope you know how precious you are to us, Little one," Grady said. "All we want is you, because you hold our hearts captive."

Effie sucked in a breath. "I love you both so much."

"And we love you enough to spank you when nonsense comes out of your mouth," Steele told her.

Steele went slow. Mostly because he wanted to be sure that she really was all right with this. But Grady was watching her carefully too, and he'd alert him to any signs that she couldn't take this.

When his ten was up, he stood with her in his arms so Grady could take his seat. He kissed her lightly.

"Love you." Now that the seal was broken, he couldn't stop telling her that.

"Love you too."

Then she was over Grady's lap and his hand began massaging her round ass.

Fuck, Steele had to adjust himself. That was so fucking hot.

Grady started spanking her firmly.

"No, no! Daddy G, stop!"

"You've got a few more to go, Little one," Grady told her.

Steele's eyebrows rose. Daddy G?

Grady eyed him for a moment, then he grinned.

Oh, he had left something out, hadn't he?

Then something happened. Something that had Steele's breath catching. Her foot moved. He saw it and pointed to her foot by tilting his head at Grady.

The other man gave her two more spanks. Both legs moved.

Thank fuck.

Grady spun her over, hugging her tight.

"W-what? Is that the end? Was that twenty?"

"Sweetheart, your legs moved," Grady told her in a hushed voice

"W-what?" she asked.

"They moved, baby girl." Steele crouched in front of her.

"Really?" she asked with a sob.

"Really," Steele told her firmly.

"I still can't feel them."

Steele didn't know why. He knew it was psychological. He knew she likely needed some professional help.

"Little one, you need to talk to someone," Grady said.

"What?" she asked.

"Someone who can help you," Steele told her gently. "Someone with the tools to help you with this because we don't have them. I hate that. Wish I could do it for you. But I can't and neither can Grady. You're gonna talk to someone. Get help with what's going on now, but also with losing Joe and that shit with your nan talking in your head."

God, let her say yes.

Because if she didn't, he knew he would have to get forceful. And he'd rather that she want to do this for herself.

"Okay," she whispered.

"I'll arrange it," Grady said immediately.

"But not today," Steele added. "Today is for fun. You want to explore your room, baby?"

She nodded. "Yes, please!"

∼

GRADY THOUGHT he might have felt more awkward.

Well, he definitely felt awkward. But not because he wasn't sure how to act with Effie. But because he was wearing a neon orange tutu, bright pink fingerless gloves, and an orange scarf.

"Daddy G, you look so pretty."

"So pretty." Steele grinned at him.

He knew the other man had been surprised when Effie called him Daddy G, but he hadn't said anything. Which was a miracle for Steele.

"What about Daddy, Little one?" Grady asked. "Doesn't he need to dress up for the tea party?"

"Ooh, yes." Effie clapped her hands from where she sat on a fluffy bean bag.

Steele had dressed her in one of her new outfits. She was wearing neon orange tights, a black skirt, and the bright pink T-shirt that Millie had made for her with a sloth on it.

"I think I'm fine as I am," Steele said hastily.

She pouted. "Daddy, don't you want to look pretty for the tea party?"

"Yeah, Daddy," Grady teased.

Steele shot him a look, then turned to Effie. With a sigh, proving there was little he wouldn't do for their girl, he nodded. "All right, but I doubt anything in there will fit me."

Everything wasn't miraculously all right. She'd moved her legs, but said that they still felt numb. And Grady knew talking to a professional was definitely the right way to go. But it could get rocky.

However, if he had to tie her to them to get her to hold on, he would.

"Here you are, Daddy!" She held up a green, fluffy scarf and a pink tutu.

"Baby girl, pink is not Daddy's color." Steele shook his head.

"Really, Daddy," she huffed. "Daddy G didn't complain about his outfit." She wiggled a finger at him. "You need to stop moaning so much. Or Effie might have to spank you."

Steele snorted. "That won't be happening, Spitfire. Keep up

that attitude, though, and you'll find yourself sitting in Time-out."

Effie bit her lip. Then she turned to him. "Daddy G, Other-Daddy is being mean to me. Will you tell him off?"

Other-Daddy?

Oh, even if she wasn't in trouble for trying to set one against the other, calling Steele Other-Daddy was going to get her in a world of trouble.

"No, I won't," Grady told her firmly. "Damon and I work together. We are on the same page when it comes to you. And there's no pitting one against the other."

Chagrin filled her face. "Sorry, Daddies."

"Other-Daddy?" Steele asked incredulously.

"Umm." She bit her lower lip.

"Time-out for you." Steele stood, picked her up and carried her to the Time-out chair.

And, wow, she had trouble with the concept of Time-out. She fidgeted, she talked, and she had it extended three times before Steele gave up, lifting her out and carrying her back to the bean-bag.

Then they had a tea party where she made them snacks from Playdoh.

"These are delicious, Twinkletoes," Grady told her, staring down at the mess of dough.

"You didn't eat it, though, Daddy G," she pointed out.

"Of course I did. See?" He pretended to munch on the burger.

"Daddy G, that's not eating it. You actually have to take a bite."

Brat. Her eyes were twinkling. But he loved that she was having such a good time. So he took a bite.

"Daddy G! No! Daddy! Daddy G ate the Playdoh."

Steele shook his head, looking amused. "Daddy G, that was silly."

"You're gonna get a tummy ache," Effie advised him. "You know what always helps me when I have a tummy ache? Magic beans!"

"No magic beans," Steele told her. "You've had enough sugar."

She pouted. "Daddy. So mean."

Grady walked into the bathroom and spat the Playdough into some toilet paper.

Gross.

He rinsed out his mouth before returning to play.

"Nap time for Effie," Steele announced.

"No nap time for Effie," Effie said.

"Definitely nap time. I've just seen you yawn three times."

"So did Daddy G."

He had. He felt exhausted. All the worry over their girl had taken its toll.

"Daddy G can take care of himself. Effie needs to do what her Daddies say."

She pouted as Grady picked her up and placed her down on the change table.

"Get her into her onesie," Steele said to him, pulling the onesie out of a drawer. "Padded panties for her nap in Little headspace. I'll get her bottle ready."

He undressed her. Easy.

Then he picked up her padded panties. They had bumble-bees on them.

"I can dress myself, Daddy G," she said.

"I have this." He slid the panties up her legs.

"You sure?" she asked.

"I'm just not used to dressing a woman."

"I'm not a woman, Daddy G! I'm just a Little girl!"

"You are," Grady murmured. "You're my Little girl."

"But I can dress myself."

"Not sure you can have it both ways, Little one."

"Daddy G! You don'ts have to be logical when you're Little. In fact, I think that's a rule. You should note that down. No logical Littles. Uh-huh, definitely a rule."

He grinned and shook his head at her antics. This was more like their girl.

Grady got her in one of the onesie's he'd bought for her. It had sloths on it and the feet and hands enclosed.

"Daddy G, you bought me lots of stuff."

"I did. I actually enjoyed it. There's a new shop in Billings that specializes in things for Littles. I went in there and the owner helped me. She was a sweet girl with an interesting, um, assistant. Besides, I bought you all of this because you deserve it." He sat her up and kissed her nose.

"I can'ts buy you stuff."

"No, but you give me much more in return. You give me happiness."

Her face lit up at that.

"And you gives me happiness. Those light-up shoes you got me give me lots of happiness."

He tickled her until she giggled. "Brat."

"I is not a brat. I is adorable."

"That too."

She smiled. "But I gots to say, you didn't need that silly Time-out chair."

"No?"

"Nuh-uh. Or that paddle with *Effie's Been A Bad Girl* written on it."

"I thought that was rather genius."

"Not cool, Daddy G. Not cool. I have to school you on this Daddy stuff. Daddies don't buy paddles or Time-out chairs."

"And if Grady believes that nonsense, he isn't as smart as he claims to be," Steele said, walking in with her bottle.

"Daddy! I didn't see you there."

"Uh-huh."

"Just to clear things up, I didn't believe a word of that," Grady told them both.

"You want to give her the bottle?" Steele offered.

Fuck yes.

He nodded.

"Are you going to swaddle me again, Daddy G?" she asked.

His eyes widened. "You want that?"

She chewed her lip. "I'm a bit nervous to be on my own, though."

"We have a baby monitor," Steele told her. "If you yell out, one of us will hear."

"I'll stay with you this time too," Grady told her.

"You will?"

"Yep. You say your safeword, I'll get you out immediately."

"Okay then, Daddy G. Do your worstest."

∞

EFFIE WAS IN SHOCK.

She wasn't sure she'd like being swaddled, but as Grady wrapped her up, she felt this sense of calm come over her.

"All right, baby girl?" Steele asked as Grady lifted her into his lap on the rocking chair.

She nodded.

"Our precious girl." Steele ran his fingers through her hair. "Look at our baby. So brave."

"Such a good girl for her Daddies," Grady added as Steele handed him the bottle. "Open up for Daddy G."

She parted her lips and he pushed the nipple into her

mouth. And even though she wanted to stay awake and watch them both, be with them, her eyes drifted shut.

It didn't matter that things weren't perfect because the two of them were perfect for her.

In every way.

51

"Effie, we need to have a talk." Grady walked over to where she was sitting on the sectional. Steele was behind him.

She had her laptop with her, trying to get some work done. She hadn't gone back to Pinkies since the accident a week ago.

But things were going better. She was doing better.

She had an appointment with a therapist at the start of next week.

And she'd managed to move her legs a few times, she'd always felt pins and needles. For some reason, her brain wasn't ready to let go completely, but she was no longer terrified of staying like this.

"I didn't eat all the magic beans! Someone else must have snuck in and stolen them! I swear!"

Grady paused and looked down at her. Then he glanced over at Steele, who staring at her sternly.

"No sugar for the rest of the week," Steele told her. He lifted the laptop away.

She pouted. "That's so mean!" Although all the jelly beans that Millie had given her were gone now anyway.

"I can add another week to the sugar ban," Steele threatened as he lifted her, then sat with her on his lap.

She'd noticed he liked to have her close, within touching distance.

"Rats," she muttered.

"That's what I thought."

Grady sat facing her. "I'm sorry, Little one, but I need you to be my Big girl for a while."

Since that day when she'd fallen over after trying to walk, she'd spent a lot of time in Little headspace. Maybe it was a form of hiding, but she'd needed it. She went back to Big when Brooks was home, of course. Although Brooks wasn't an idiot. She was pretty sure he knew what was going on.

"What is it? What's happened? Is Brooks all right?" He was due home any moment. Raul now took him to school and picked him up. Steele had made noises about teaching him to drive. Which made her nervous as hell. Her boy out in a car, driving? Yeah, she knew she would be a bundle of nerves.

But he was growing up. And all his friends were going to be driving.

Of course, that meant finding money for a car for him, but she was getting paid pretty well now.

"Brooks is fine. But he is part of the reason we have to talk," Grady told her.

"What? Why? Do you not like having him here?"

Steele squeezed her and she glanced up to see him scowling. "Gonna pretend you didn't ask us that because it fucks me off. Of course we like having him here. We love having both of you here."

"Indeed," Grady said. "And our plan is that you never leave."

"I say we say it right now. They ain't leaving," Steele stated.

"We're not leaving?" she asked breathlessly.

"No. You're not," Grady replied. "I'll get movers to deal with your belongings and talk to the landlord about your lease."

Move in? Could she do that?

Why wouldn't you do it? You love them. You want to be around them, and they wouldn't ask if they didn't want you living here.

"I, um, are you sure? I can be a lot to handle."

"No, Effie, you aren't a lot to handle," Steele told her gently.

"That's just your nan fucking with your head." Grady gave her a firm look. "You are our girl and you belong here with us. And so does Brooks. Although there will have to be some changes."

"Changes?"

"He's your kid, baby girl," Steele said. "But we aren't men to stay in the background. We want to help with him. Not saying he needs much, that boy is sixteen going on forty. But sometimes we want to do our bit with him, yeah?"

"I guess that would be okay." More than okay since she often worried that Brooks didn't have a father figure in his life. No one could ever replace Joe, but Damon and Grady were good men.

"And you're not going to argue about moving in here?" Grady eyed her with some surprise.

"No. I'm not going to argue. I love being here with you guys. But I do have six months left on my lease."

"Don't worry about that, Twinkletoes," Grady told her. "I will sort it. However, before Brooks gets here, we need to talk about the letter you got the morning of the accident."

A letter that she got on the morning of the accident?

Oh. Fuck.

"I forgot," she said in a panic.

Steele tightened his arms around her as she tried to move.

"I forgot about the letter! Oh my God! How could I forget?"

"Effie," Grady said firmly. "Effie, look at me. It's all right."

"It's not all right! I forgot!"

"Little one, you shouldn't beat yourself up after everything you've gone through. Besides, you might have forgotten but I didn't." Grady grabbed her chin in his hand. "I didn't forget."

Of course he didn't.

Grady didn't let things slide. Grady was on top of everything.

"Say after me: Grady is sorting this."

"Grady is sorting this," she repeated.

"Grady will make this all disappear."

"Grady will make this all disappear." She finally started to breathe easier. "You will?"

"Fuck, yes," Steele growled in her ear. "Nothing touches our baby or her boy."

"How?" she asked.

"This lawyer is slick, but he's no match for me," Grady told her. "Roddy, your neighbor, fed information about you. But taking care of that idiot was easy. He won't be bothering you again or talking to that lawyer."

"Lucy was another informant," Steele told her.

"What?" she asked. Lucy?

"This lawyer put an investigator on you," Grady said. "The investigator spoke to Lucy soon after we got rid of her and she told him a bunch of lies. And some truths."

Oh my God.

"Like that I work at a strip club? Oh my God, are they going to take Brooks?"

She couldn't do this!

"Sweetheart, we have this." Grady wrapped his hand around the back of her neck. "We've taken care of Roddy and Lucy. Both are retracting their statements and won't even answer the lawyer's calls. Also, all of the investigator's information has mysteriously disappeared."

Whoa, he was a miracle worker. She didn't know how he'd done all of that and she didn't care.

"And?"

"And we've totally taken the legs out of their custody claim," Steele told her. "There's nothing left. No judge would side with the uncle over what Brooks wants."

"I spoke to the lawyer today. He wasn't happy, but he knows he's beaten," Grady told her.

"Oh my God! Why didn't you lead with that!" She put her hand on her chest, trying to calm her racing heart.

"While the lawyer is effectively silenced, that doesn't mean that the person who employed him is," Grady explained.

"Brooks' uncle." Shit. "He could try again."

"Which is why I'm suggesting we tell Brooks," Grady said gently.

"What? Really?"

"He's a good kid," Steele said. "He deserves to know what's going on. This uncle might run away. Or he might try again."

"Or he might be someone Brooks would like to get to know and I haven't even given him that option."

"Baby, I doubt that." Steele shook his head.

The front door opened.

"Aunt Effie, I'm home."

Steele lifted her off his lap. Standing, he moved over to lean against the wall near the fireplace.

"Brooks, honey, could you come here for a minute?" she asked.

"Sure." He lifted his chin at Grady and Steele as he walked into the living room. He swung his bag down before striding to the sofa to sit facing her. Grady backed off as well. They were letting her do this but staying to support her.

God, she loved them both.

"Brooks, I need to tell you something." She went through all of it. The phone call from the lawyer. The letter. As well as the second phone call. Then, everything that Grady and Steele had done.

"My uncle wants custody of me?" Brooks asked.

"Yes, and I'm so sorry I didn't tell you earlier. I just . . . I wanted to protect you from your mom. Then the accident happened straight after the letter, and I honestly forgot. But this man is your uncle, and you have the right to make your own decision about whether or not you see him."

Brooks stood and started pacing. "No!"

"What?"

"Fuck that!" He scowled.

"Brooks." Lord, her heart was breaking for him.

"They think after all these years, I'd want anything to do with them? Mom or him? Fuck no, Aunt Effie. And this was a bullshit way to play things if they did. They come to me. They don't go getting a lawyer, investigating you, stressing you out. Just, fuck no." He grabbed his bag and she realized he was going to leave.

"Brooks, wait!"

He didn't stop, all she knew was that her boy was hurting and she needed to make it stop.

So, moving on pure instinct, she got to her feet and she ran after him. "Brooks!"

As he turned, her legs gave way on her. "Auntie!" He leaped toward her, catching her. "You . . . you were walking. Running."

She let out a surprised bark of laughter. "I was."

She wrapped her arms around him and he let her. "You're going to be okay, Aunt Effie. I know it."

"So are you, honey. Don't let them upset you. We don't need them. Not when we have each other. And now we have Steele and Grady as well."

He leaned back and nodded down at her, his eyes suspiciously bright. Then he straightened his shoulders. "You shouldn't be running like that, Aunt Effie. You could hurt yourself."

Alpha male in the making.

"Baby, you okay?" Steele leaned down to pick her up. She was surprised it took him as long as it did. But she guessed he was giving them a moment.

Grady ran his hands over her as she stood with Steele supporting her. She was smiling as she stared down at her feet. Thank God.

"You get my uncle's details and you give them to me."

She glanced up as Brooks said that to Grady.

"I'll call him and make things crystal clear. The woman who birthed me doesn't get to try and kill Aunt Effie, then think she can start calling me. And he doesn't get to be absent my entire life and then try to take me from Effie. No!"

"Wait. What?" Steele roared.

Oh shit.

Yeah, she'd forgotten about that part.

52

"I cannot believe that bitch tried to smack your head in with a steel pipe and you didn't think to tell us," Steele grumbled three nights later.

She couldn't believe he was still talking about this.

For the first two days after she'd managed to run, Effie had still felt a bit weak and grew tired quickly if she was walking.

But she could walk. And she was feeling far more like her usual self.

Which was why she was going to talk to her guys about things getting back to normal.

That meant she was going back to work on Monday.

It also meant them fucking her into oblivion. Right now.

She just needed to convince them she was up to it.

Which could be a problem.

They were still treating her like she was made of glass. As though she was fragile. She had to show them she wasn't and she had an idea how to do that.

They wouldn't even let her walk up and down the stairs. Nope. Tonight, Steele had carried her on his back.

Because she'd asked him to play horsie and he'd been in the mood to oblige.

Totally perfect for her.

Now the three of them were in bed.

And she didn't feel like talking about Tanya anymore. She felt like getting it on with her men.

"Let's not talk about it any longer. She was jealous of my relationship with Joe and she went after me. Joe stopped her. She went to prison for a long time. Now, who is going to fuck me?"

"Excuse me?" Grady asked coolly. "Is that any way to ask?"

"Wasn't asking, Big boy," she replied. "That was a demand."

"Are you hearing this?" Grady asked over her head.

Steele shook his head. "Seems we've neglected to discipline our girl. She's getting far too sassy. How much is she owed?"

"I'll go get the book."

"No, please! I'm sorry. Please, fuck me. Someone make me come. Pretty please with Effie on top."

"Not sure you're ready to be on top, Effie," Grady told her.

"I am. I'm good. I promise. I feel so much better."

They shot a look at each other.

"Please. I need you guys. And for more than just a finger fuck or your tongues. I need you to fuck me. I want you both to take me at the same time."

"You sure about that?" Steele asked. "You want one of us in your pussy, one in your ass?"

"Please."

"Fuck me," Grady murmured. "Perfect for us."

They had it wrong, but she wasn't going to correct them. Especially not when they set about stripping her and themselves. And then she was between them on the bed, their hands and mouths all over her.

Grady didn't usually sleep the night with them. But he

always waited until she fell asleep to sneak out. This time, she was hoping to tire him out enough that he stayed.

Steele rolled her onto her back, then his mouth moved to her pussy.

"Oh. Ohhhh."

"Don't come yet," Grady warned as he started to lube up his dick. She guessed he was going in her ass.

"Please. Please."

"Good girl for asking nicely," Grady told her. "But you can do better than that." His fingers tweaked her nipples. One, then the other.

She was so close to the edge.

Steele slid a finger into her pussy, then dropped it down to her back hole, rubbing it lightly.

Oh God! She couldn't hold back.

"Please let me come! Please, I need to so badly!"

"Not yet," Grady told her. "Don't you dare come yet, Effie, or I'll smack your naughty pussy."

Shoot.

"I want to feel you come around my dick." He tapped Damon's shoulder and the other man slid away from between her legs. His mouth was wet from her arousal.

And. It. Was. Hot.

Then Damon lay on his back and drew her over him, pulling her down onto his dick. She tried to move, to drive up and down. But he kept her still, holding her tight as Grady parted her ass cheeks, putting more lube on her hole.

"Relax and breathe out," Steele commanded as Grady pressed his dick into her ass.

Oh God.

So full.

It was incredible. It was too much, and yet, not enough. She wanted more.

"Move," she cried out when Grady was fully inside her.

"No, not yet," Damon told her.

"Move!"

Slap!

A hand smacked her thigh.

"Behave yourself," Steele growled at her.

And then... finally... they moved.

In tandem, one slid in while the other pulled out. It was magic. Heaven. It stole her away.

"I need to come," she cried.

"You know what to do if you want to come," Steele told her.

"Please, Daddy. Please let Effie come. I need it. Oh, please."

"Good girl," Grady told her. "So good for us. You can come. Come around our dicks."

The pleasure washed through her, taking her breath with it. It went on and on until she collapsed between them.

Best orgasm ever.

They continued to drive themselves into her. She heard Grady come first, then Steele roared his release.

But she was done. So tired, she could barely keep her eyes open as they cleaned her up and tucked her into bed with them.

"Such a good girl," Grady whispered.

"Perfect for us," Steele added.

53

She knew Grady wasn't in the bed as soon as she woke up.

For a few minutes, she silently debated what to do before she decided to carefully crawl out of bed.

She was surprised that Steele didn't wake up, but he'd been getting very little sleep lately.

Moving onto her feet, she stayed still, just making sure she had her balance.

Then, grabbing a shirt off the floor, she slipped it on and caught his scent.

It was Grady's shirt.

Stepping into the hallway, she decided to try his room first. She'd seen it before but hadn't spent any real time in it. It was smaller than Steele's and the bed wasn't as large.

When she stepped into the room, she saw that there was no one in the bed, but the curtains were open and she caught sight of him on the balcony.

Walking over, she slid the door open. He turned from the railing immediately, taking her in.

For a moment, she thought he was going to tell her to get lost and she froze. Then he held out an arm.

"It's freezing out here, sweetheart. Come here."

She went to him and he drew her close, holding her tight.

"Are you cold, sweetheart?"

"A little bit." She didn't want him to use it as an excuse to make her go back inside.

But instead, he moved them to a chair and pulled her into his lap. Then he grabbed a blanket from the other chair.

"Do you come out here often?" she asked.

"The air helps me think," he replied as he tucked the blanket around her.

"You always make me all snuggly," she told him.

"Do I? Good."

"It's not just about me, is it?"

He stiffened. "What?"

"I thought it was me that you couldn't sleep with because of the intimacy. But I've decided it's not really that. Or not entirely."

"Little one, I told you that you needed to give me time . . . I struggle with cuddling."

"But you don't have to cuddle me. I have a big snuggly ogre in my bed who will give me all the cuddles I need."

"I should still be able to do it."

"Rome wasn't built in a day, honey," she murmured. "But I don't think it's me, is it? It's him."

He stiffened. "Effie . . ."

"He loves you, you know."

"I know."

"But I don't think you see it in its entirety. I think the two of you have become so worried about losing the other person that you won't actually make a move. You don't want to do it because you think he'll reject you. So you hide your true feelings and fall into bed with women, but only when he's there. Because then it feels like being with him."

"Effie, that's not what it's like with you," he told her urgently.

"Oh, I know. I'm your world. I'm his world. Nothing will change that. I know if I don't say anything, things will continue on like this. Me, the Queen. You two, the peasants."

"Peasants?" he growled, squeezing her tight.

She giggled. "Sorry, servants."

"Someone's sassy mouth is gonna get them in trouble."

"I hope so." A sense of sadness filled her. "But it's no way to live, Grady. Feeling like you're on the outside looking in."

"I don't feel that way."

"Not with me. With him." She turned to look at him. "I never told Joe."

"Effie."

"I never told him that I loved him and I've regretted that for years. He died without knowing how I felt."

He squeezed her again. "Sweetheart."

"I mean, I think he knew. I tell myself he knew. I tell myself I was right to hold back in case he rejected me. But there's always that 'maybe'. You know? I loved him. I lost him. But now I have the two of you and it's hard not to feel guilty. Sometimes I'm so freaking happy, that I almost want to sabotage it. To test it. To make sure that it's real and won't crumble. Because sometimes I don't believe I deserve to be this happy when he's dead."

"Fuck, sweetheart. Don't do that. We're here, we're real, and we love you. And, of course you deserve this."

"So do you," she told him quietly. "I get you're scared, but I'm here now."

∽

So do you. *I get you're scared, but I'm here now.*

Those words played in his head as he sat out in the cold. He'd sent Effie back to Steele. She'd given him a kiss, but he'd sensed her disappointment.

Grady didn't want to let her down.

Didn't want to lose what they had.

But regrets were something that could eat you alive. So he got up and moved to their bedroom, climbing into the bed on the other side of Effie.

"Fucking finally," Steele muttered. "Do I have to tie you two to the bed to keep you here?"

"I love you, Damon," he blurted out.

Fuck. He hadn't meant to do this now.

"I know, man. Love you too."

"No, I mean as more than a friend. We've been together a long time, and, well, I've had these feelings for years. I was always too scared to tell you. But I . . . it's more than friendship."

Fuck. Fuck. Fuck.

Effie tensed slightly and he knew she was awake.

Steele sat up and turned on a lamp. He gave Grady a once over. "You mean you're attracted to me?"

Grady swallowed. "Uh, yeah. The thing is . . . I haven't slept with any women on my own for the last few years because I didn't want any of them. I wanted you. Until a certain Twinkle-toes came into the club, that is. She's my world. Will always come first. But I wanted you to know how I felt about you. I hope it won't change things." He climbed from the bed. He couldn't stay here any longer.

"Thomas."

He froze at the door.

"Come. Here."

He spun and scowled at Steele. "I'm not your sub. You can't order me around." Steele was leaning back against the pillows, while Effie had sat up to watch them both. She had a tight hold on Steele's hand.

But he seemed to be holding her hand back just as tight.

Steele grinned. It was slightly wild. Somewhat feral. "That's why I didn't think we would work. Not until we found our baby." He wrapped an arm around her.

"What?" Grady asked.

"I knew you were attracted to me. I mean, it took me a while to notice it. But we're both Doms, both like control. And I knew we'd tear each other apart if it was just us and that we'd end up miserable and alone."

"Grady was worried you'd reject him," Effie told Steele.

Steele gazed down at her, then up at Grady. "I'd never reject you. Fucking idiot."

"Damon," he growled, not liking the way he was talking to him.

Steele's eyes suddenly twinkled with amusement. "Guess I knew it was inevitable. No way anyone could resist a bod like this for long." He pointed to himself.

"Fuck me," he muttered.

"Yeah? You want that right now?" Steele asked.

His heart raced. Hard.

"Because I thought we might start with a blow job and work our way up to that."

"You're gonna give me a blow job?" Grady challenged.

"I thought you'd give me one."

"I'll give you both blow jobs," Effie offered.

They both turned to see her tugging at her earring.

"Baby girl, don't do that. Everything is fine," Steele soothed.

"I know. I know. It's just very testosterone-ish in here. I thought I was doing the right thing, giving Grady advice. But maybe the two of you won't work."

"We work just fine with you," Grady said. "So maybe we start there."

Her eyes lit up. "Yeah?"

"Good idea," Steele said. "Grady, get the ropes. I think our girl needs to be tied to the bed to make sure she stays there. She seems to have issues with staying where she's put."

∼

STEELE STARED down at their girl. He could scarcely believe she was theirs. They'd tied her wrists together and then secured them to the headboard.

And for the last fifteen minutes, they'd tortured her with their mouths and words.

His mind was still reeling from Grady's revelation. Not that it was a huge shock as he'd had his suspicions. His feelings for Grady had developed over the years, but he hadn't really let himself acknowledge them. But then, after their accident . . . well, those feelings had gone into overdrive. Still, letting them out wasn't easy.

Perhaps what they needed was their baby. Someone to help them make this work. He didn't know if they'd ever get to the stage of being able to be together without her. Maybe they wouldn't. They might always need her.

And that was fine with him. Because all he wanted was the two of them.

"You know, I've been a good girl," she said, panting heavily.

"Have you?" Steele asked, glancing down at Grady who was currently eating her out.

Grady looked up her body, raising a dark eyebrow. "That's why you're getting your pussy eaten, sweetheart."

"But I want something else. Please." She pouted.

Fuck. That pout. It was hard to deny her anything when she aimed that pout his way.

"What do you want?" Steele asked.

"Well, there's two things." She glanced down at Grady nervously. "I want you to play with me while I'm sleeping."

Shock, then hunger filled Grady's face.

"And I want the two of you to kiss."

Steele found himself holding his breath. Lord, she was a brat.

"You need a spanking," Grady growled.

"My sentiments exactly," Steele said, rolling her over so she was on her stomach, her arms out in front of her.

"Up on your knees," Grady said.

After she moved into position, they kneeled beside her, spanking her ass together, each taking a cheek. When her skin was pink and she was breathing heavily, Steele turned her back over and kissed her gently. Then he drew back so Grady could kiss her.

It was time. He could do this.

He was going to do this.

Moving to the other man, he grabbed him almost roughly by the shoulders and brought him in for an near-brutal kiss.

It was savage. Their tongues dueled as both fought to be in charge. But Steele figured he won by the smallest of margins.

Yeah, they might not be able to figure out who would bottom and who would Top. But maybe they didn't have to.

A hand wrapped around his dick, jacking him off, and he moaned. He knew it wasn't Effie's since she was tied up. He was shocked and thought about pushing Grady's hand away, but decided not to since it felt so fucking good.

Plus, this was what he wanted.

So he kissed his best friend. The only man he'd ever loved.

Ever wanted. And he let him jack him off to completion while their girl lay beneath them.

Fuck. So good.

⁓

That was the hottest thing she'd ever seen.

Watching Damon and Grady kiss. Seeing Grady give Damon a hand job until he spilled all over the other man's hand. Effie licked her lips. She wanted to clean him off.

Effie hated being tied down so she couldn't touch them. And yet at the same time, it was a good thing. Because it meant they had this moment together.

There might not be many, but that didn't matter.

They had this.

Steele broke off, slumping down against the headboard beside her, breathing heavily. "Fuck."

She turned to grin at him. "Did you like that?"

"You are such a brat," he mumbled back. But he did it grinning.

Grady left to get cleaned up and when he came back, his gaze was intent on her.

Uh-oh.

"Now it's your turn."

"My turn?" she asked.

"Yes." Grady climbed into bed and untied her wrists, before turning her to face Steele and slotting in behind her. She could feel how hard he was. Her body tingled, reminding her that she still hadn't gotten to come. Grady brushed her hair to one side. "You're going to sleep with my hard dick in your pussy."

"I am?"

"Yep. And at some stage, when you're sleeping, I'm just going to start playing with you."

A whole body shiver ran through her.

"I think she likes that idea," Steele said, his eyes heavy-lidded. "Thank fuck because I'm out. I need some shut-eye."

"Poor old man. Can't keep up," she said.

Slap!

That came from Grady. "Respect your elders, brat. Or I won't let you come later."

"Later? What about now?" she asked.

"No coming for you."

She had to fall asleep while turned on? So not fair. She started to pout. Then she felt him prodding at her entrance before his dick slid inside her.

"Do I have your permission?" he asked.

"Yes," she replied breathlessly. God, yes.

"Sleep, sweetheart."

Impossible. Not going to happen.

No. Way.

～

Grady woke with his dick hard. He'd slid out of their girl at some stage. Probably because the big ogre next to her had drawn her in for a cuddle.

She was lying on Steele's chest, one leg up on his thigh.

That worked for Grady. He moved in, getting to work with his fingers between her legs.

Fuck, she was wet still.

He knew she'd woken up when his finger slid over her clit. Sleepily, she turned to him as he licked her nipples, then sucked one into his mouth.

He moved over her, sliding his dick inside her. With a gasp, she wrapped her arms and legs around him.

"All right, sweetheart?" he asked.

"Please. More."

"Anything you want. Anything."

He fucked her long and slow. Making sure she came twice before he found completion. Then he slumped to the side of the bed and drew her against him. She stiffened for a moment, then relaxed.

"That was fucking hot," Steele murmured.

"Perv," he told the other man.

"Takes one to know one."

Steele stole Effie back and Grady fell asleep in their bed, cuddled against their girl who was cuddled against their man.

And he did it with a smile on his face.

·

54

Grady glanced up from his laptop as he sat at the kitchen island. Steele walked in, carrying a baby monitor. "You finally got her down?"

"Little brat was determined that she didn't have to nap this afternoon. Thinks she's fully rested and fine. Doesn't mean she doesn't need rest."

Grady nodded, feeling nervous. This was the first time they'd been on their own since he'd told Steele he loved him last night.

He could still feel the other man's mouth against his. The kiss he'd never thought that he would get.

It had been incredible.

But now he couldn't help but worry that Damon would regret it.

Steele walked to him and closed the lid of his laptop.

"Hey! What do you think you're doing?" Grady snapped. "I was working."

"It's Sunday," Steele replied.

"So?"

"We don't work on Sundays."

"We've always worked every day," Grady replied.

"Not anymore. Not now that we have Effie to spend time with. She needs time with us and we need time with her."

He made a good point.

"But she's napping."

"And we need to spend time with each other." Steele swallowed heavily. "Even though we've been best friends for years, I figure this part of our relationship is new. So we should make sure that we don't just ignore it or brush it aside. Fuck." He took in a deep breath. "What I'm trying to say is that you're important to me and I don't want to fuck this all up."

Grady stared at him in shock. This was unexpected. He'd kind of been expecting Steele to push everything aside. But he was the one laying things out there.

Grady turned to fully face him. "I . . . you're still good with everything that happened last night? I wasn't sure you would be today."

"It's weird. Wasn't unexpected, and yet at the same time it took me by surprise. Loved you for years, Thomas. You're my best fucking friend. But I guess I ignored any feelings for you because . . . well, a number of fucking reasons. I didn't want to ruin what we had if it went pear-shaped. Didn't know what to do with these feelings. Plus, we're both dominant guys. Didn't know how that would work. And I can't say I've ever been attracted to another guy before. Finding Effie . . . realizing I could let someone in like I did with her . . . I think it helped heal something in me. And then after the accident . . . when I realized I could have lost you both, I realized I've been an idiot."

This was so much more than he'd been expecting. "It's all right if you don't want to take things beyond what we did last night."

Steele narrowed his gaze and moved his hand to the side of Grady's neck, squeezing. "Didn't say that, did I?"

No, he hadn't.

"I want to explore this attraction. These feelings. I know it might take some sorting out. We both like to be in charge. Maybe we work better when it's three."

Grady placed his hand on Steele's chest. "Yes, I think we do. She's our glue. She brought us together. Having her softens your edges, while she helps me let go. I think we can both agree that she comes first. It's not about her being more important than me. It's about her being more important than everything. And that's the way it should be. For so long no one ever put her first. We do that for her."

"Agreed," Steele said immediately, the way Grady knew he would. "We work together to make sure her needs and wants are met. But we have to be strong to do that. And that means working on us too."

"When did you become a relationship expert?"

"I'm a fast learner. Don't worry, you'll catch up to me one day. Maybe."

"I made the first move," Grady said.

"I was planning on making it soon."

Liar.

Steele's hand tightened around his neck and then his face moved closer. The kiss was strong, almost violent. Grady felt the urge to fight for control but held back this time.

"Fuck, you taste good," Damon muttered, pulling back to stare down at him.

"There's other parts of me you can taste," Grady challenged.

Interest and arrogance filled Damon's face. "Yeah? Same goes for you. Are you gonna get on your knees and suck my cock?"

"Are you going to let me fuck your ass?" Grady asked back. He could guess it was a no.

But to his shock, Steele looked thoughtful. "Not today. But never say never."

Fuck. Arousal flooded Grady. Steele ran his hand down Grady's chest toward his dick. He was dressed casually in jeans and a button-up shirt. While Steele was wearing a T-shirt and gray sweatpants. Which Grady fucking loved.

He reached out and shoved the sweatpants down, revealing his thick, long dick.

"No boxers," Grady muttered.

Steele just grinned. It was a wicked, devious grin. Grady couldn't stop himself from grabbing his cock and running his hand along it in long, slow strokes.

"Fuck. Fuck me."

One day. Grady pumped him harder with firm strokes. Steele's breath came in sharp pants.

"Please tell me Brooks is still out."

"Yep," Grady muttered.

"Good." Steele reached for his jeans, and Grady lifted his ass so Damon could pull his jeans and boxers down to his thighs.

Then he sat again. And to his shock, Steele bent over and took his cock deep into his mouth.

Fuck. Grady felt his eyes roll back in his head. That felt so damned good. His breathing grew erratic as Steele drew him in, then slid back up his dick. Back and forth until the need to come was riding him hard.

Then Steele drew back and took his mouth with his. Steele wrapped his hand around Grady's dick and he returned the favor, pumping the other man's cock.

"Fuck," Damon muttered. "I'm so fucking close. You better come with me."

Grady nodded, groaning.

"Words," Damon ordered.

"Not your sub," Grady reminded him.

"Shit. Sorry."

Now, that was unexpected too. Damon Steele apologizing!

Then all thought fled Grady's mind as he came in a huge rush. He heard Damon grunt as he found his own release. Then Grady pulled back, letting go of the other man's cock as he fought for his breath.

Steele grinned at him. "Fuck. You're breathing heavily. Seems I'm just naturally talented at giving hand jobs."

Grady rolled his eyes. "You're so damn arrogant." Reaching back, he grabbed a hand towel to clean himself up.

"Well, it seems like I missed all the fun."

Grady glanced over with a frown as he saw Effie standing there. She was dressed in a sloth onesie and held Slowly against her chest. For a moment, worry filled him. Would she be all right with what they'd just done? Would she be upset at them being together without her?

Steele had stiffened, and he wondered if he was thinking the same thing.

"I can't believe you guys did that without me."

Shit. Fuck.

"Next time, can I watch?" she asked, moving toward them.

Relief flooded him and the tension seeped out of Steele's body.

"Yeah, baby girl," Steele said. "Next time, you can watch. Now, what do you think you're doing getting out of bed on your own? Didn't I tell you to stay put? And you shouldn't be walking down the stairs on your own. That's ten and some lines."

Effie groaned. "First, I miss the hand jobs, then I get a spanking and lines. This just sucks."

"Poor Twinkletoes." Grady finished cleaning up and handed the towel to Steele before righting his clothes and pulling her close. "There will be lots of other times."

"Promise?" she asked.

He stared at Steele over her head. His best friend. His lover. "I promise."

. . .

"Goody!" Effie clapped her hands together. She couldn't believe she'd missed all the fun.

Naps were so dumb.

Which is why, when she'd woken up, she'd decided it was time to get up. She didn't have time to just lie around.

Steele gave her a stern look. "You're still in trouble."

She pouted and took a step back as he moved toward her. "Um, Daddy, shouldn't you be in a good mood?"

"What makes you say that?"

"Because you just got to come! Effie didn't get to come. Effie might want someone to make her come."

"Too bad that Effie is going to get a spanking and lines instead, isn't it?" he said as she bumped into the wall behind her.

"Bummer," she muttered as he took her hand and led her back to the dining table. Pulling out a chair, he drew her over his lap.

"What about Brooks?" she asked urgently as Steele opened the drop seat of her onesie and drew down her panties.

"He's not due back for another two hours," Grady told her. "There's no getting out of punishment for you."

Drat.

"I'll go get a pad and pen for her lines," Grady commented.

Rats.

The spanking started hard and fast. Steele didn't give her much time to catch her breath or think as he reddened her ass, making it throb.

She kicked her feet, sobbing.

So mean.

She sniffled as he finished.

"Good girl. All done now," he murmured, rubbing her lower back.

"That was so so so mean, Daddy!" she cried.

"My poor girl. Effie deserved that, though, didn't she? She's got to learn to stay where Daddy puts her. And I don't want you walking up and down the stairs on your own when you're in Little headspace. And definitely not when your legs have just started working properly again."

Her legs were fine.

But she decided not to point that out.

As he moved her clothes back into place, Grady returned. "Here's the pen and paper."

"Good." Steele righted her, setting her in the chair next to him. Ouchie. That hurt her poor butt-butt. "Twenty-five lines saying that you will stay where your Daddies put you."

With a sigh, she wiped her eyes so she could see. But then Daddy G appeared with a tissue. He grabbed her chin, wiping her face and holding it to her nose.

"Blow," he commanded.

She knew better than to complain. Although sometimes that didn't stop her. But this time, she blew and got on with writing her lines. Steele's phone rang as she neared the end of her lines.

"I've got to take this, you got her?" he asked Grady.

"Of course. I'll get her bottle and put her back down for a nap."

"No nap!" she cried.

Daddy G sent her a stern look. "You will do as you're told, Twinkletoes."

Darn it.

Damon kissed the top of her head and moved out of the room, already on his phone.

She finished her lines with a triumphant shout. "Finished!"

Grady took the piece of paper, reading over it. "Very good."

"Thanks, Daddy G. I tried my hardest."

He sent her a soft look. "Let me get your bot-bot and then it's time for your nap."

"But I'm really not tired and I slept a little bit. Couldn't I just watch TV or something?"

"No. You need your rest. Remember what the doctor said? Lots of rest and no stress."

"TV isn't stressful."

"Yesterday, you cried watching a nature show."

"The lions were being so mean! That doesn't count."

The look he shot her was filled with doubt. He refilled one of her bot-bots with water and then handed it to her before picking her up and cradling her against his chest.

"Daddy G, I don't think I can sleep."

"What if I lay down with you?"

"Really? A special nap?"

"Special nap," he confirmed.

"Will you wrap me?"

"If you like."

"Uh-huh. And I gets to suck on your diddle?"

"If you swear to never call it a diddle again, you can," he said sternly.

She couldn't hold back a giggle. "Deal."

He set her down on the floor of the playroom next to the changing table. Then he laid a thin muslin blanket on the table. Lifting her, he placed her on top of the blanket and wrapped her up tight.

"Good, Twinkletoes?" he asked.

"Yes, Daddy G. Perfect." She already felt much more relaxed. Even more so when he picked her up and set her on his lap in the rocking chair.

He placed the nipple of her bot-bot to her lips and she started sucking back some water. Her eyes closed as he started singing her favorite nursery rhyme.

When she'd had enough water, she turned her head away. "No mores, Daddy G. Effie will have to pee."

"Do you have to pee right now?" he asked.

"No. Not yet. Effie sleep now. With Daddy G," she said demandingly.

"All right, we'll have to go sleep in my bed, though. There's not enough room for Daddy in your crib."

"Okay, Daddy G."

He carried her out of her playroom and into his room. Setting her down, he drew the covers back and placed some pillows along one side of the bed so she wouldn't roll out.

Her Daddies always took the best care of her.

As he laid her on the bed, he placed her so she was halfway down the bed before he stripped off naked and lay down next to her, pulling the covers up over her head. They were both on their sides, facing each other. Her face was level with his cock, and leaning in, she latched on.

He let out a sigh, running his fingers through her hair. "Sleep, Daddy's sweetheart."

And after a few minutes of sucking on his cock, that's exactly what she did. Safe with her Daddy.

~

"WHAT DO you think you're doing?"

Effie braced herself as she walked into the kitchen in her work clothes. She was carrying her laptop in the green case with a sloth on the front that Grady had bought for her.

Thankfully, Brooks had already left for school. She'd timed that on purpose. He didn't need to be here for the growling.

"I'm going to work today."

"No, you're not," Steele told her. "Go get changed into comfy clothes. You're on the couch today. Grady is staying home with you."

She put the laptop down as Grady turned from the stove to look at her. Then he looked at Steele and turned back to the food. Right. No help with her ogre from him.

"I'm going into work. I've had enough time off and I don't need any more."

Steele leaned his hands on the counter, staring at her sternly. "You're. Staying. Here."

"No. I'm going to work. Grady is needed at work. So am I. There's no reason to stay home."

"You're staying home."

"I'm not."

"Do you want a spanking?"

"You can't spank me for disagreeing with you!" She threw her hands into the air.

"Can't I?"

"Grady, you want to weigh in?" she asked.

"All right. Effie, you're staying home."

Damn it.

Steele grinned and crossed his arms over his chest. "That backfired, huh?"

Time to find a new tactic.

"I need to go to work. I need things to go back to normal. Things haven't been normal for a while and I need that."

Both men looked at her.

"I could just fucking fire you," Steele muttered.

She could get mad at that, but she knew he was just grumbling. He was an ogre, after all. Moving around the counter, she slid up next to him. He turned to face her and she put her hands on his chest. "Please?"

"Aww, fuck it." He glared down at her. "That damn pout."

Yeah, she had him.

She tried not to look smug about it, though.

"You won't work to the point of exhaustion. You're to take a nap in the afternoon. If I can't come get you, then Grady will. You'll stop working at five, but you can spend time with us upstairs. Then you and Grady are going home at nine. Understood?"

It was more than she thought she'd get, so she was happy.

"Understood, Daddy. Thank you!" She leaned up to kiss him.

He grunted but kissed her back.

Moving to Grady, she wrapped her arms around him, pressing her face to his back. "Good morning."

"Good morning, sweetheart."

"I loved what we did this morning." He'd woken her up with his tongue in her pussy. "Can we do that again sometime?"

He turned and hugged her tight. "Anytime, my sweet girl."

She smiled, then drew back. "What's for breakfast?"

"Omelet," Grady said.

"Yummy. I'll just have a cheese one."

"You'll eat what you're given," Steele ordered.

"Cheese, Daddy G," she said, ignoring the ogre.

"You need to eat more variety, Twinkletoes," Grady told her, then turned back to plate up the food.

"I don't think the two of you should be allowed to gang up on me. That's being mean to Littles."

"Only one Little here," Steele said, handing her a coffee.

Yummy.

"Yeah, so you're being mean to me. You're being mean to Effies. Effie doesn't like that."

Okay, so she was in Little headspace this morning. Not the best plan when she was headed off to work.

"Effie needs to learn to listen to her Daddies," Steele said, before disappearing into the utility room. He walked out carrying a supersized chair. It was high, with a tray in the front.

"What's that?" she asked.

"Your new high chair."

Good Lord.

She'd spent the whole day yesterday in Little space. Which is probably why she was having problems moving to being Big today.

Also, she'd put sloth panties on this morning.

"I don't needs a high chair, Daddy," she told him.

"Yes, you do. Little ones need to be secure. I don't want you slipping off your seat." He undid the tray and then picked her up, carrying her to the high chair and securing her in.

She was really glad Brooks wasn't here.

Grady set an omelet down on the table. She eyed it suspiciously. "Is there spinach in this?"

"Just a little bit," Grady told her.

"Do you not know how to spell spinach, Daddy G?"

"I do. And I also know that you can't continue not eating all S words." Grady sent her a stern look.

That was so rude.

Steele moved to sit down with his own plate in front of him. But first, he grabbed hers, cutting the omelet up and then spearing a piece with his fork.

"Here comes the choo-choo train."

She wanted to be annoyed by their behavior. But it was also so cute. And she kind of loved this high chair. Her feet could swing freely and everything was out of her control.

Leaving her with nothing to worry about.

Except the spinach.

She turned her face away as he got closer. "No."

"Baby girl," Steele warned.

"Nope. No."

"Do you want a spanking? It will make sitting at your desk interesting," Grady said as he sat and started to eat.

"Effie would like to lodge a formal complaint."

"Effie's complaint is denied," Steele told her. "You can eat your omelet, or I'll make you a smoothie and bottle-feed it to you."

That sounded better.

"With spinach in it," Grady added.

"What? Have you two taken shares out in spinach? This is not cool."

"Baby girl, just give it a try," Steele cajoled. "If you really don't like it, then Grady will make you another omelet."

It sounded like a hassle.

Sighing, she took a bite and made a face. All right, so she couldn't really taste it. But it was the principle of it all. And the principle said that she didn't like spinach and shouldn't have to eat it.

Grady stood. "I'll make another omelet."

But he hadn't finished eating his and she couldn't truly taste the spinach.

"I'll eat the spinach omelet, Daddy G, under protest and as long as you swear that you will never, ever feed me spinach again."

"How about I promise not to try to feed it to you for another week?" Grady countered.

It was better than she thought she'd get.

"Deal."

55

"Effie?"

She glanced up to see one of the new dancers standing in the doorway.

"Hey, Chantelle," she said with a smile.

"There's a young boy out in the parking lot wanting to see you. He says he knows you."

Hmm. That was weird.

"Okay, thanks."

Chantelle had a strange look on her face. "No worries."

Was it Brooks? But he was in class. Maybe a friend? Getting up, she grabbed her phone and headed out to the front of Pinkies.

She'd been back at work for a few days now. Things were going so well between her, Grady and Steele. They were going to move all of her stuff this weekend into their house.

Although maybe she needed to dump most of it.

Steele was in a meeting off-site and Grady had gone to check on something at one of Steele's other businesses.

She texted Brooks to make sure he was all right, but got nothing back.

Standing in the parking lot, she couldn't see anyone.

Suddenly, a car sped toward her from the street. She stepped back, getting a funny feeling. The window dropped open, and was that . . . was that a gun?

She froze, hearing the crack of a gun firing just as someone raced toward her.

"Effie! Down!" She ducked just as she swore she felt a bullet coming past her face. She knew that was ridiculous. But her imagination was in overdrive.

The person who had been running toward her, grabbed her and dragged her behind a car as another bullet came at her.

Breathing heavily, she stared up at the man who'd helped her as he peered over the car.

"All right, they're gone. Let's go."

There was a commotion behind them, people coming out of Pinkies and yelling.

"Get back inside!" the man yelled as he wrapped his arm around her and half-carried her into the building.

"Effie? Effie!" Her girls were suddenly there, surrounding her. She clung to them, her body trembling. She felt better inside Pinkies, but she knew she wouldn't feel safe until she had her men with her.

Where were they? She needed them.

"I . . . I n-need . . . I . . ."

Why was it so hard to breathe?

The room around her was spinning. Where were Grady and Steele?

"She's having a panic attack! Effie, look at me. Breathe in slow. Then out."

She peered up into the man's face. She knew him.

"You . . . banged into . . . pharmacy."

"Yeah. I've been, uh, watching you," he confessed. "I wanted to use you to get to Steele. Then I saw that asshole speeding up as you came out of Pinkies and I knew it wasn't good. Knew it really wasn't good when you were just standing there, frozen." He placed his hands on her shoulders.

"Any idea why someone would want to kill you?"

∽

STEELE TAPPED his fingers on his thigh as Raul raced them to Pinkies, trying to keep the panic from engulfing him.

He'd just gotten off the phone with Lex.

Someone tried to kill Effie.

Why would anyone try to kill Effie?

He should have been there. He'd nearly lost her again!

And he hadn't fucking been there!

Before the car came to a stop, he was out and running toward Pinkies. Lex was standing at the front door, but he couldn't stop to talk to him.

He had to find her.

"Steele, everyone is inside. That guy Wolfe is in there too."

He paused. "What? Wolfe? Was he the one who shot at her?"

Lex gave him a strange look. "No, he was the one who saved her."

Steele stormed into Pinkies. He needed her. Needed to see that she was all right. Everyone was in the main room, gathered around Effie.

Chardonnay and Tessie had her between them, but everyone was hovering close by. Because they all loved Effie.

Then he noticed the man standing off to the side. He was leaning against the stage, his gaze on Effie. But when Steele entered, that gaze went to him.

Wolfe.

"Damon!" she cried as she saw him. Jumping up, she raced toward him, nearly tripping over her own feet. Several hands reached out to grab her.

Steele swept her up into his arms, holding her against his chest.

She was all right. She was all right.

He could finally breathe since the moment he took that call.

Fuck. Fuck!

This couldn't happen again. He was wrapping her up in cotton wool. He wasn't letting her out of his sight, and if he had to, he was putting a bodyguard on her.

Nothing was going to happen to her.

"Are you all right? Are you injured?" He drew her back to frantically run his hands over her. "Effie?"

"I'm not hurt. I'm fine. I promise. I promise."

Fuck. He couldn't get a handle on himself. All he could think about was how he could have lost her.

"Effie!"

Turning, he saw Grady walking into the room. His gaze was intense. Hard. He moved to them, coming behind them to run his hands over her back.

"Is she all right?" Grady asked.

Steele nodded. Physically. But emotionally? That was another story.

Steele handed her off to Grady, who held her tight, talking to her quietly. His face was pale, and he looked as scared as Steele felt.

"What do you want us to do?" Nate asked, walking over to him.

"We're not opening. Tell Lex. No one leaves until I find out what is going on. Trev at one door. Lex at the other. Nate, you take care of everyone here. Wolfe."

The other man looked over at him. His face was hard. Angry.

"You're with us."

Steele led them upstairs. Wolfe, then Grady carrying Effie.

He couldn't hear what Grady was saying to her, but he could hear her soft sobs and it made him furious.

His fault.

He should have protected her better.

Steele pointed at the sofa. "Sit."

"You don't tell me what to do," Wolfe snapped. "For months, you've fucked with me, ignored and threatened me. I'm done."

Steele shoved him up against a wall, putting an arm over his throat. "Fucking talk to me!"

The roar filled the whole room, probably traveling downstairs. But he didn't care.

All he was concerned with was his girl.

"Daddy, stop!"

Steele glanced over to see that Effie was staring at him in concern. Grady had her on the sofa in his lap, holding her tight.

"He saved me. Please."

Steele reined his temper in. But only because he wanted to know what happened.

He stepped back, then started pacing. "Talk."

Wolfe coughed. "Fucker."

"Someone s-shot at me," Effie said. "Why would t-they do that?" Her face was splotchy, her hair a mess. Grady grabbed a tissue and cleaned her face.

"Fuck, fuck, fuck!" Steele yelled before turning to punch a wall.

"This isn't helping," Wolfe pointed out.

He wanted to kill the fucker. But he couldn't. Not yet.

"Have you got any enemies who might try to get to her?" Wolfe asked him.

"Maybe it was you. So you could play the hero," Steele accused.

"Fucker, that bullet could have hit me! I saved her."

"Why were you here?" Grady asked.

Wolfe looked shifty. Then his gaze went to Effie and he softened. Steele didn't like his gaze on her, so he moved between them, covering her with his body.

"I'm not going to hurt Effie," Wolfe snapped. "I don't give a fuck about the two of you, but I've been watching her for a while. I know what she is. She's a sweetheart. I wouldn't hurt her."

"Watching her?" Grady asked.

Wolfe sighed. "I was hoping to use her to get to you."

"You fucking asshole!" Steele yelled. "You did this!"

"I swear I didn't!"

"It wasn't Wolfe, Damon. P-please stop yelling," Effie begged.

He tried to rein his temper in. She'd been through enough. She didn't need to be upset any more.

"Why were you even outside?" Grady asked Effie.

"Chantelle," Effie said.

Steele turned to her. "What?"

"She said that a boy was outside, wanting to speak to me. I went out but no one was there. Then, a car sped up, and someone started firing. Wolfe yelled at me before grabbing me and pulling me to safety. He saved me."

Steele still wasn't convinced that Wolfe hadn't done this.

Effie's phone rang, and Steele recognized the ringtone as the one she had set for Brooks.

She answered it. "Honey? You okay?" Suddenly, she grew pale. "What happened?"

56

Grady stared down at the body of the man who was bound and in the trunk of the car.

He was breathing but unconscious.

They were standing in an abandoned warehouse on the outskirts of town. He glanced over at Ink, who was in the midst of an intense conversation with Baron and Royal.

Then he glanced back at Effie who was still pale. In shock. Brooks had his arms around her, holding her tight. He was pale too.

"You okay, Brooks?" Steele asked.

"Um, yeah. But I'm worried about Aunt Effie. She could have been killed."

After Brooks had called them, Effie had another panic attack. While Grady calmed her down, Steele had secured Chantelle in his office downstairs and Wolfe upstairs, each with men he trusted on them. Then he'd told everyone else to go home.

They'd sped here. To where Royal and Baron had parked their car in an abandoned warehouse they knew of.

When they got to the warehouse, Ink was already here, looking grim. He'd been the one to pop the trunk.

And reveal the bound man.

The man who'd tried to kidnap Brooks.

But he'd been overwhelmed by three teenage boys. Two of whom Grady was certain would either one day rule the world or make it rue the day they'd been born.

"I'm fine," Effie said. "You were the one who was nearly kidnapped. If it wasn't for Royal and Baron . . ." she let out a small sob and Brooks let her go so Grady could gather her close.

"This can't be a coincidence," Grady said. "It was a two-prong attack. Kill Effie and take Brooks."

"But why?" Steele asked.

"Maybe it was to do with the custody challenge," Brooks said. "Maybe this is my uncle."

Fuck.

Grady stared down at the unconscious man the boys had bound, popped in the trunk of the twins car, and driven here.

Was this Brooks' uncle?

Ink walked over with Baron and Royal.

"Hey, Brooks' mom, you doing okay?" Baron asked.

To Grady's shock, Effie let go of him and flew at the boys. Baron grabbed her, recovering quickly, nodding as she whispered something to him. Then she hugged Royal. He gave her a regal nod.

Turning, she came back to him. But she grabbed Brooks' hand, squeezing it.

"I'm better now," she said huskily.

Ink eyed her but nodded. "All right, this sounds like a professional hit to me."

"That's what I was thinking," Steele said. "But I don't recognize this guy. I can put out the word, but it might take a while for information. I think our best lead is Brooks' uncle.

Although how he'd have the money or means for this, I don't know.

"I looked into him," Grady said. "He seems ordinary. There were a couple of old arrests for theft, but nothing stuck. He lives a quiet life. But there's got to be more."

"My dad," Brooks said, then he cleared his throat. "He said something about the woman who birthed me having an uncle. But not a blood uncle like an honorary one. Dad said he wasn't a good man. Also, he said that Tanya had a weird relationship with him, like she worshipped him or something. But that one day they had a fight and he cut ties with her. Maybe it's him. Or something to do with him."

"Fuck, maybe we need to send someone to talk to her. Although whether she'll talk is debatable," Steele said.

"She probably won't," Effie whispered. "Tanya is stubborn."

"We need to question Chantelle and check the cameras," Grady said. "As well as speak to Wolfe again. I can do that."

"That leaves me with this guy," Steele said grimly.

"And me," Ink said.

"I figured you might take the boys with you," Steele said to Ink. "I'll need to take him somewhere more secure."

Ink shook his head. "You need back-up. I'll call Spike; he got home yesterday. I'll get him to come get the boys and Effie and take them to my place. It's secure."

"I want to stay with you guys," Effie said.

Grady squeezed her tight. He didn't want her or Brooks away from him.

"Effie stays with me," Steele said firmly.

Grady gave him a worried glance. He was holding himself together. But just barely. He looked like a powder keg about to ignite, and Grady knew why.

She could have been shot.

"I don't think Effie needs to see what's going to happen with this guy," Ink said carefully. "You trust Spike, right? We'll tell him to stay with her. And I'll make sure they're secure with plenty of guards. No one will get to them."

Steele looked torn.

"I'll go with Spike," Effie said. "I'll be all right, Damon."

"You'll do exactly as he says. He goes everywhere with you," Steele ordered.

She nodded.

"And we'll be there too," Baron said. "We'll keep Effie safe."

Steele looked about as worried as Grady felt about that. But there was no denying that the twins were resourceful.

"Fine. Fuck. Fuck!" Steele yelled, turning to kick a crate.

Effie jumped but didn't make a noise. Brooks tensed next to him. Then Effie tugged free of his hold and walked over to Steele, wrapping herself around him and whispering quietly.

He nodded, then straightened and turned, pulling her into his arms. He glanced around at everyone. "Sorry."

"No problem," Royal said. "If Effie was my woman, I'd want her under lock and key for the rest of her life."

Baron grinned. "He's not joking."

"Lord help me," Ink muttered. "Actually, though, I've got an idea." Using his phone, he took a photo of the unconscious guy and sent a text. "I'll send this to the Fox. If anyone might know who this guy is, it's him."

"Good idea," Royal said. "The Fox knows everything."

"Is it wise to bring him in?" Steele asked.

"Wise? No," Ink replied. "Will he help? Perhaps. It's hard to know. But I've also sent this to Brody. He'll get him to help."

"Who is the Fox?" Effie asked.

Grady shook his head. "Probably best you don't know."

"He was a paid assassin," Baron said. "But mostly, he took jobs where he killed bad guys."

"And he saved Ma," Royal added. "She was in a hole."

"A hole?" Effie whispered.

"In the forest," Baron added. "He saved Sunny too."

"He's saved lots of our women," Royal said.

Ink shook his head at Royal's words, his lips twitching before he sighed. "He's a pain in the fucking ass. Has a warped moral code and is arrogant. But yeah, he's also helped us a lot. And I think he'll have our back. Mostly." His phone went off. "Spike is coming in. Let's get ready to move."

∽

"I THINK he's given you everything."

Fatigue filled Steele. He looked at his watch. Ten hours had passed since Effie had been shot at. After they'd sent the boys and Effie away, it had taken a while to drive this guy out to his warehouse and wake him so he could work him over.

Steele looked over at Ink with a nod. He didn't bother looking at the man hanging from the ceiling. He knew he wouldn't lose any sleep over what he'd had to do.

Not if it kept Effie and Brooks safe.

"What do you want done with him?" Ink asked.

"I'll handle it. I've got connections."

Spike had taken the kids and Effie to Ink's security company. Betsy and Millie were going to meet them there.

He didn't like being away from her, but he knew Spike would guard her with his life.

Taking off his clothes, he left them in a pile. Then he washed off in the sink before pulling some fresh clothes out of the bag he'd brought in with him. He always kept spare clothes in his car.

"Where do you want to go now?" Ink asked.

"To Effie and Brooks. I'll call Grady on the way." He sent a coded message to his cleaner, knowing they'd come in and take care of the body and all other evidence.

They walked up out of the basement room.

"Took the two of you long enough to break him. I really thought you'd be quicker than that, Damon Steele."

Steele froze and turned, his hand going to his gun.

"I wouldn't do that," the voice warned coldly.

"It's our friend," Ink said quietly.

"Friend? Hmm, are we friends? I don't know. How is Betsy? Have you given her that ring yet?"

"Fuck, Fox, how did you know about that?" Ink griped.

"I know everything."

"What are you doing sneaking up on us?" Steele grumbled, searching the shadows for the assassin. But he couldn't see him. "I could have shot you."

"Doubtful," the Fox commented. "You know, I thought you'd be in a better mood now that you've got a girl of your own. Or are you still waiting for Grady to suck your sausage?"

"Motherfucker!" How did he know that?

"Calm down, this is what he does," Ink said.

"I've watched the two of you, any idiot could see he was into you. Except you. Which makes you even more of an idiot."

Fucking hell.

"Fox, why are you riling him up?" Ink asked.

"Just wanted to see if he and Grady have moved things along. Maybe I should give you some relationship tips, Steele."

Great. That was just what he needed.

Relationship tips from an assassin.

"Fox," Ink said. "We need to go. I want to get to the twins and Betsy."

"Those twins . . . they're going to rule the world one day. I can't wait. It was a professional hit, but not a professional doing it."

"What?" Steele said. He was tired, angry, and wanted to make sure that his baby was all right. He wasn't in the mood for a riddle.

"As soon as you texted me, I made a few inquiries about who might have taken a job in Billings. My town. Turns out, the professional hitman who was hired to kill your girl farmed the job out. And to an idiot. Which makes him a fucking idiot."

"A professional hitman gave the job to someone else?" Ink asked.

"Yes, he double-booked himself. Apparently, he had a wedding that his girlfriend was demanding he attend. I made it clear that I didn't appreciate him taking a job in my territory. He said he thought I was retired."

"Aren't you?" Ink asked.

"That doesn't mean I will allow anyone else to take jobs in my town."

"Did he tell you who he gave the job to?" Steele asked.

"Of course he did. I told him it wasn't good business practice to farm a job out. And that he shouldn't let his girlfriend dictate to him. He didn't appreciate that. Although now he owes me a favor since he fucked up. He's not happy that the shooter did such a poor job. I told him we were taking care of the kidnapper, who he knew nothing about, and he assured me he'd deal with the shooter."

"He's upset that the shooter did such a poor job?" Steele repeated incredulously.

"Am I talking in a foreign language? I know several. Australian is my favorite."

"Australians speak English," Steele told him.

"Do they?"

"Don't fall down the rabbit hole," Ink told him.

"Hey!" the Fox snapped. "It's a fox hole."

"I want the shooter and the professional hitman," Steele said.

"I can't do that. Professional courtesy."

"Fox, he shot at Effie," Ink said.

"And that means I should give up this man's name? Hmm . . . not sure of your reasoning."

"He'll try again! That's our reasoning!" Steele snapped.

"Oh. Now I see the worry. No, the professional won't try again. And the shooter certainly won't."

"Why not?" Ink asked.

"Because he'll be dead soon. I kind of thought that was implied."

"No, I mean, why won't the professional try to kill Effie again?"

"Because he gave me his word. Plus, he knows I'm not happy with him moving into my territory."

"And that's enough for you?" Steele asked.

"My word is law," the Fox said. "This man is not a friend. He's not someone I would ever go to bat for. I do that for you people again and again. So when I say he won't come for her again. He won't come for her again. He's embarrassed. And he's angry."

"Angry?" Ink asked.

"He was hired to make the kill. Not to kidnap a kid."

"The wannabe-kidnapper gave us the name of the person who paid him," Steele told him. "Steven Ford. Brooks' uncle."

The Fox grunted. "Makes sense. The guy's an idiot and a dead man since the professional hitman has already got his hands on him. He had a friend who was close and he sent him to collect him. Ford didn't tell him he was hiring someone to take the kid. Kids are the moral line this hitman doesn't cross."

Great. Good to know. Sub-contracting to kill Effie? Fine. Kidnapping Brooks? Not fine.

"So this man will take care of the shooter and Steven Ford,

Brooks' uncle," The Fox reiterated. "But you need to know there's more."

"What?" Steele asked.

"My this friend of the hitman has been interrogating the uncle. He just sent me an update. The uncle is a dumbass. Small-time criminal. The mother was the one pulling the strings. She's up for parole soon."

"Why does she want Brooks?" Steele asked, convinced it wasn't due to motherly love. Why would she go to the extreme of killing Effie and kidnapping Brooks?

"Apparently, this guy called Leopold Burns, fucking weird name, was a close friend of Tanya and Steven's father. So close that they both called him uncle. According to Steven, Tanya was infatuated with this guy. She fabricated this story in her head about how they were in love. Turns out, he didn't agree. When he told her that, Steven reckons she lost it and tried to go after him with a carving knife. He didn't press charges, but he cut her from his life. However, he must've been keeping tabs on her . . . that part is a bit murky . . . because he somehow found out about Brooks. When he died, Tanya still thought he'd leave her all his money. But in a weird twist, it seems Burns didn't have any children so he left his money to Brooks. My guess is he left it to Brooks because he's Tanya's son, and therefore, a descendant of his best friend. But he wouldn't leave it to Tanya and Steven because they're fucked-up assholes."

"What the fuck?" Steele whispered.

"Yeah. Tanya and Steven hired a lawyer and paid him off so he didn't contact your girl about the money he left Brooks. Instead, Tanya wanted Steven to get custody of Brooks so they could get access to the money."

Fucking bitch.

He closed his eyes. It was going to hurt telling Brooks this.

"What about Wolfe?"

"What about Wolfe?" the Fox repeated.

"Did he have anything to do with this?"

"What am I? A magic genie? I can't answer all your questions for you. I've got to go. Left a naughty Little one at home in need of a spanking."

"Fox? Fox?" Steele called out. Then he bit back his pride. "Thanks!"

"He's gone," Ink said. "Let's get you to your girl."

Fuck. Finally.

He needed to see with his own eyes that she was all right.

The drive to Ink's security company was done in silence. Steele got a text from Grady saying he'd meet them there.

Ink led him into a meeting room, where he saw Effie huddled between Betsy and Millie. As soon as she saw him, she got up and raced toward him. "What's going on? Are we safe? Are you okay?"

He drew her in tight against him, holding her as she shook with fear.

Fuck.

He hated that she'd been so scared. Kissing the top of her head, he rocked her back and forth.

"It's all right, baby. Don't shake. We're safe. We're fine."

"Where's Grady?" she asked.

"He's coming. Shh, baby girl. Shh." Picking her up, he carried her to the sofa where she'd been sitting.

The other girls jumped up and went to their men. Royal and Baron were sitting at the table with Brooks. But Brooks was watching Effie worriedly.

Steele sat with her on his lap.

"I need Grady too. I was so worried, Daddy."

Shit. She wasn't going to like that she'd called him that in front of Brooks when she realized it later. But the kid just gave him a small nod.

Right.

"She needs Slowly," Brooks said as she shook in his arms.

"Grady is bringing him." Standing again, he cradled her into his chest and rocked her back and forth while patting her back.

That seemed to calm her down slightly.

Then Grady slammed into the room, looking stressed, his hair on end, his clothes mused.

He'd never seen the other man look like that.

Effie turned in his arms. "Grady!" She tried to throw herself at him, but Steele tightened his hold.

"Effie! Careful!" he warned.

Grady rushed to her, gathered her into his chest, and after giving her Slowly, began whispering to her. Steele reluctantly let her go before moving in behind her.

"Is it over? Are we safe?" Brooks asked.

Steele held out an arm to him, uncertain if he'd take the offer. But the kid rushed toward him, joining them.

"It's over. We have to be careful for a bit until loose ends are tied up. But we're going to be okay."

"Was it my uncle?" Brooks asked, pulling away.

"Let's all sit down," Ink suggested.

They all sat at the table with Effie on Grady's lap. Spike studied him for a moment, then turned to Steele and gave him a grin. Spike knew Grady being this way with Effie was big.

Steele sat with Brooks next to him. "It was your uncle. And your mom." He went through everything they'd discovered but didn't say it had come from the Fox. That was to protect Brooks, although it was obvious the twins knew about the Fox.

"I have an inheritance from a man I don't know?" Brooks asked.

"Yep. But we'll have to research him, as this doesn't make me happy." Steele looked at Grady, who nodded grimly. No doubt he was angry with himself for not finding this connection. But there was no way for him to have known when this 'uncle' wasn't a blood relation.

"I can't believe that bitch did this," Brooks said, his face growing red.

"Brooks," Effie said. She climbed off Grady's lap and moved slowly to Brooks.

"Don't tell me it's okay, Aunt Effie. It's not. She's behind bars for trying to kill you, and yet she's still trying to hurt you. We need to pin this on her, make sure she doesn't do this again."

"I've got Brody working on it," Ink told him. "We'll make sure she doesn't get out of jail. We can get her visits and communication privileges revoked. Don't worry. Her life will be a misery."

"Good. Do it." Brooks gave Ink a grim look.

"Brooks," Effie said, clearly hurting for him. "Are you sure? She's your mom."

"No, she isn't, Mom. I have a mom and she's right next to me."

Effie gasped, her eyes filling with tears. Then she threw her arms around him. "I love you."

"Love you too, Aunt Effie." He stood and hugged her back.

"What about Wolfe?" Ink asked.

"I questioned him and he wasn't involved," Grady said. "Seems he really was there by coincidence. Well, not exactly, since he's been watching Effie."

"Fucking bastard," Steele muttered.

"Oh, and Chantelle was paid to lure Effie out," Grady said grimly. "She's being escorted out of town as we speak. Also, I made it clear to Wolfe that if he stays away from Effie and us, we'll steer clear of him."

Steele nodded. He agreed with that. He didn't like the man, but he did owe him. So he'd give him this.

"So I guess all that's left is to live a long, happy life," Millie said with a smile.

Yeah. A long and happy life with Brooks and the two people he loved. That he needed. That were his everything.

He'd basically given up on life, thinking he'd live forever in the black after Jacqui died.

But now he had so much color in his life . . . and it was so beautiful he couldn't even believe it.

EPILOGUE

Effie scowled at Steele, who stood in the bathroom with her. "You need to leave."

"No."

"I want to use the toilet."

"So go." He leaned back against the wall and gestured to the toilet.

"Damon!" She stomped her foot. There were times a girl needed some alone time and she needed that right now. A week had passed since she'd been shot at and Steele had put them all into lockdown, including Brooks, who'd been taking lessons online.

The old principal had resigned, and after Steele made a hefty donation, the new principal had been happy to let Brooks learn from home.

Effie was trying to be very patient with Damon, knowing that his overprotectiveness was due to what had happened.

But there was a line.

"That's cute. Not changing my mind." He crossed his arms over his chest.

"You are a very stubborn, frustrating man."

He just raised an eyebrow.

With a sigh, she knew she was going to have to bring out the big guns. She drew her phone from her pocket.

"What are you doing?" he asked.

"Calling Grady."

"You don't need to call Grady," he growled.

"I want to use the toilet on my own."

"You don't care when you're in Little headspace," he pointed out.

"I'm not in Little headspace right now."

"Should always keep you in Little headspace," he muttered. "Should just put you in diapers. Then you'd never need privacy."

"I would still need privacy! Now, are you leaving or am I calling in the big guns?"

"I'm standing on the other side of the door. And you won't lock it."

"Promise you won't come in."

He just glared at her.

"Damon. Promise."

"Fine. I promise. But you need to come here first."

She moved over to him and he swept her against him, kissing her hard before pulling away. "I know I'm being a pain in the ass. You still love me?"

"Always. I'll always love you. You and Grady are my everything."

∽

GRADY WATCHED Effie dance around the kitchen, singing to herself. It smelled divine in here–like vanilla and chocolate. She'd been baking again.

Brooks was sitting at the kitchen island doing something, and she danced behind him, then stopped to hug him.

Grady couldn't remember his mother ever hugging him. And if she had, it was when he was very young.

But Effie would never treat their children like that. She'd be an amazing mother.

Surprisingly, Steele wasn't looming over her, watching her every move. Three weeks had passed since she'd been shot at and Steele was having trouble letting her out of his sight.

Effie had been surprisingly patient with the big guy.

Grady was also feeling overprotective, but trying to tame it down to help Steele keep himself under control. For the first week, Steele hadn't let Effie do anything. He'd kept trying to follow her into the bathroom.

Grady often had to intervene just to let her have a tiny bit of privacy. But Steele had pretty much taken over her life. Feeding her, bathing her, dressing her.

Thankfully, he'd started to ease up.

Soon, they needed to get back to normal. He knew that. So did Steele. The shooter and the kidnapper had been taken care of. As had Brooks' uncle.

There were no more threats. They all needed to get back to their lives.

Effie's gaze lifted and her smile grew bigger as she spotted him. She ran toward him.

"Grady!" He kissed the top of her head. She was acting like she hadn't seen him in weeks rather than a couple of hours.

But he liked that.

"Hello, sweetheart." He kissed her. "Yum, you taste like sugar."

"I made cupcakes!"

Brooks looked up and smiled at him before gathering his

stuff up. He walked past them and Grady reached out his hand and lightly grabbed his arm. "You don't have to leave, Brooks."

"Don't worry, I'm finished. I'm going up to my room to call the twins. I get why Steele freaked and put us into lockdown, but I really want to get back to school."

"Soon," Grady told him.

When Brooks was gone, Grady picked Effie up, cradling her against his chest. "Come, show me these cupcakes you made."

"They're peanut butter and chocolate!" she said. "They taste sooo good, Daddy G."

"Do they?" he murmured, setting her on the island. Reaching over, he picked up a cupcake and held it out to her. "Want a bite?"

She took a huge bite, chewing happily. He took a smaller bite, watching her.

God, she was beautiful. What had he done to deserve such beauty?

"See? Good, right?"

"Delicious." Leaning forward, he licked some icing off the corner of her lips. "Just like you."

He might not think he deserved such beauty. But he would do whatever was necessary to keep it.

⁓

EFFIE KNEELED in front of the grave, tracing the name with her fingers.

"Seven years today, honey," she whispered. "A lot has happened since I last talked to you. I know Brooks has probably told you some things. I let him go first so he could catch up with his friends. I've met two men. I know, two! They're amazing. Smart, protective, sexy. I think you'd like them. They take care of me and Brooks. I know he'd rather have you. But they help fill a gap, I think. He needs strong men in his life. He's made some good friends and is doing well in school."

She took in a deep breath. "I've started seeing a therapist. I know you'd be proud of me for that. We did our first few sessions online because I've been on lockdown. I'll get to that. I needed to talk through losing you. And my childhood with Nan. The good news is, I'm finding it much easier to block out her voice. Not entirely, but I'm getting there."

She dug her hand into her pocket and drew out the packet of jelly beans she'd brought with her. Opening them, she spilled them into her lap. "Red and orange for you, right? Hmm. Who is going to eat the black and green? I can do black. But green is just gross. Where was I? Oh yeah, therapy is going well. Even though I feel exhausted after it, I think I'm getting somewhere. Lockdown . . . that's harder to talk about. Because it involves Tanya. Such a bitch."

She took him through everything that had happened. "But in the end, she lost and Brooks and I won. Because she's not getting out on parole and lost any privileges she had. I don't know how my guys did that. They also found out that that she'd called me a few times and then hung up, hoping to speak to Brooks. My men weren't too pleased that I hadn't told them about those calls. But I pointed out that we weren't together then. Oh, and the Fox assures us that the professional hitman isn't going to take any more jobs in Billings. I honestly don't know whether to be alarmed or relieved. I haven't heard from Wolfe again. My guys still aren't happy that he was following me, but they've stuck to their word."

She ate some of her jelly beans. "I know you might think it's crazy, but they give me everything I need. We're moving in with them tomorrow. I mean, we've been living with them for a while, but with being on lockdown, we haven't had a chance to move our stuff. Apparently, I'm not allowed to lift anything. Some of their friends are going to help them. I don't think they realized they had friends. But these are good people. They belong to an MC. I think I might join. No reason women can't join, right? I reckon I'd look great on a bike.

"They're overprotective. Sometimes, really overprotective." Steele had gone into overdrive this last month and she'd mostly let him. But he was going to need to ease up, and soon. She looked up and saw Steele standing just out of earshot, his eyes traveling around the area. Grady was standing on the opposite side, doing the same.

"But they're good men. The best." She sighed. "I'm sorry I never told you I love you, Joe. I hope you know that I did. And that your son is the most amazing kid in the world. I think you'd be proud of us both." She finished up the jelly beans, leaving the rest for him. "Bye, honey."

∼

"Effie! What do you think you are doing?" Steele yelled.

Eek!

She dropped the box she'd been carrying into the house and ran into the study to hide under his desk.

He'll never find me here.

Impossible.

"Effie?"

She glanced over as he appeared by the desk, crouching down.

"Oh, hi, Daddy!"

"Effie, what are you doing?"

"I just thought it might be dirty under here so I figured I would come and check."

"Out. Now."

With a sigh, she climbed out and he took hold of her hand, leading her from the room and up the stairs.

"Everything okay?" Grady asked from the bottom of the stairs where he stood, holding a box.

"Can you carry on for a bit?" Steele asked. "I have a naughty girl who needs tending to."

"Yeah, everything is nearly inside. Not like there's much. We'll unpack, then I'll come find you."

"Daddy G, save me!" she cried.

"What did you do?" Grady asked, following them up the stairs.

"She was carrying a box," Steele replied.

"Your ass is toast, Twinkletoes," Grady told her cheerfully.

Urgh. Yeah, that's what she figured too.

∽

"Daddy, can I come out of the corner now?"

"Nope. And sit still," Steele ordered from where he sat across the room.

She was sitting on her Time-out chair in her playroom. This room and the kitchen were her favorites in the house. Although she loved the porch too. Especially now that the weather was so much warmer.

"It was just one itty bitty box, Daddy."

"What were you told, baby girl?"

She sighed. "That all I was to do was direct things. I wasn't supposed to pick anything up. But it was so light."

It was late afternoon. Yesterday, she and Brooks had gone through their small apartment, chosen what they were going to keep and boxed it up.

Then, today, they'd been moving it all with the help of some friends. Although thankfully, they'd already left before Steele had caught her carrying a box.

"Daddy, this is boring and I have stuff to do."

"Well, unfortunately for you, you're about to get a spanking and put down for a nap."

"Daddy, nooo!" She turned to pout at him.

He sighed from where he sat in the wooden chair that he'd put in the middle of the room. "You really don't understand how Time-out works, do you?"

Well, she did . . . she just didn't like it much.

She smiled at him. "Come on, Daddy. You don't wanna spank Effie. Effie is cute."

"She is. She's also trouble. Come." He crooked his finger at her. When she got to him, he stripped off her shorts and panties, then tipped her over his lap.

"Now, do you know why you're being spanked?"

"Because Daddy enjoys spanking my butt?" she asked.

"No. Well, yes. But Daddy is doing this because you were naughty and disobeyed me."

Slap! Slap! Slap!

"You could have hurt yourself."

Smack! Smack! Smack!

"You will not do that again."

She lost track of the spanks. By the end, she was kicking her feet and sobbing. And her poor bottom was a hot, throbbing mess.

Steele cuddled her close before laying her down on the changing table to pull on a pair of padded panties. Then he swaddled her up and put her down for her nap.

And while she thought she wouldn't sleep at all, soon she was out like a light.

∼

EFFIE WOKE up with Grady's tongue in her pussy.

Her orgasm built up. She grew closer and closer to the edge. Steele rolled into her, his hand cupping her breast as he played with her nipple while Grady lapped at her pussy until she cried out her release. Her mind spun and she was barely aware of them moving her. But then she found herself on her hands and knees, her head at the end of the bed.

Grady stood in front of her, his hard dick right in front of her. Opening her mouth, she took him deep just as Steele entered her from behind.

They drove themselves into her, driving her into another blistering orgasm before they found their own release.

The three of them ended up in a cuddle with her between them.

"Happy birthday, baby girl."

She turned to kiss Steele.

"Happy birthday, my good girl," Grady added, taking her mouth with his.

"What a way to start the day." She sighed happily.

They ran their hands over her and she could feel her body stirring again. They were throwing a party for her tomorrow; all of their friends were coming. Some people from Pinkies, others from the Iron Shadows. She couldn't wait.

But today was all for them.

"I have a birthday wish."

"What's that, sweetheart?" Grady asked.

"Anything you desire, baby girl."

She was glad he said that.

~

"THAT'S IT, Daddy G. And now take a bow." Effie clapped her hands. "You look so pretty! And you did an excellent spin. You only stumbled once."

"I cannot believe you agreed to this." Steele shook his head, his lips twitching as he took in Grady.

The other man had on a tutu, a pair of boxers and nothing else.

He looked utterly ridiculous.

But Steele's gaze still ate him up. And he had to work hard to keep his dick under control.

"It's your turn now, Daddy." Effie turned to him.

His eyes grew wide. "Uh, no, it isn't."

She dug her hand into the jar of jelly beans and he reached over to grab the container, pulling it away.

"Hey, my bean-beans!" She made gimme signs with her hands. "Mine! Mine!"

"You've had enough."

"But it's my birthday! I want to eat my beans! You said that beans were a good form of iron."

"Actual beans, baby. Not jelly beans. These will just rot your teeth."

"But it's my birthday! I can eat whatever I want on my birthday."

"I'm afraid not. You can have some cake after dinner, but that's it."

"Daddy is being mean, Daddy G," she complained. "A poopy head."

"I believe there is such a thing as a birthday spanking," Grady said as he approached her. She jumped to her feet and looked around, as though searching for somewhere to hide.

But Grady grabbed her and, putting a foot up on the chair she'd been sitting in, he turned her over his thigh to give her several smacks.

Fuck.

Yeah. It was hard work keeping his dick under control.

Grady set her back on her feet with a grin. Effie turned to Steele and her pout turned into a smile. An evil smile.

"Your turn, Daddy!"

Great. Just great.

∼

"Hey guys."

Steele glanced up as Brooks walked up to them, dressed in his swimming trunks.

"Everything okay?" Steele asked.

He and Grady were sitting outside by the pool later that day. It was dark out, but the pool area was well lit. They'd all had a great day celebrating the birthday girl. Now they were giving Effie time to talk to her friend, April, before they went inside and took her to bed.

"Yeah, everything's good," Brooks said, taking a seat across the outdoor dining table from them. "I wanted to talk to you for a moment."

Grady took a sip of beer as he nodded.

"I just wanted to say this. Growing up, I can't remember a day going by where Effie wasn't laughing, dancing, singing. She was always so happy. My dad used to tell me it was because she felt safe. That she knew she was protected with us. Not just physically, but that we gave her a safe space where she could be herself."

Steele nodded. He knew Brooks didn't really need a reply. He just had to get this out.

"I never understood what he meant. Not until he died and Effie's sense of safety died with him."

Okay, that part Steele didn't like, but he kept his mouth shut.

"It took her a while to recover and I had to go into foster care. They were good people, they treated me well. But I had just lost my dad and the only mom I'd ever known. Aunt Effie came for me, though, as soon as she was well enough. She's always been there for me when I needed her. But she didn't sing or dance or really smile for a long time. And even then... it wasn't the same. She'd dance when she thought no one was looking. Or sometimes she'd sing in the car. And she'd smile and be happy. But she wasn't fully safe without Dad there to take care of her. And I couldn't really give her that. She hasn't had that since he died. Not until the two of you."

"Brooks, you are the world to her." Steele never wanted the kid to think that they were pushing him out.

Grady nodded in agreement but stayed quiet.

Brooks grinned. "Relax. I know my place in her life. I come first." It was said without boasting but with total confidence. Damn, Effie had done a good job with this boy.

Effie and Joe.

He glanced over at Grady, who was watching them both steadily.

"What I'm trying to say is thank you. I know things were different between Aunt Effie and my dad than they are with the two of you. But you've given her back that safe space where she can be herself and she knows that not only is she not judged, but she's loved and protected."

"Fuck, kid. You're far too smart for me," Steele muttered.

"Smart and caring," Grady noted. "Something we never were at your age."

"You forgot good-looking," Brooks boasted. "Of course, you two still ain't that." He shot up with a laugh before either of them could grab him and ran to the pool, jumping in.

Grady looked over at Steele.

"Can you believe him?" Grady commented.

"He's a great kid. With the job Effie's done with him, think about how she'd be with our kids. Never thought I'd have kids, but Effie has a way of making you see things differently." Steele glanced over at Grady.

They'd been taking things slowly. Making sure that the transition from best friends to lovers went smoothly. Also, since Effie loved to watch them, they hadn't had much one-on-one time.

But right now, it was just him, Grady, the moonlight and some beers.

Oh, and Brooks. But he was busy swimming.

Reaching over, he grasped the other man around the back of his neck and drew him close, pressing his lips to Grady's.

It was different from kissing Effie. She was soft and thankfully didn't have any facial hair. Not that he was complaining about Grady's. But she yielded instantly to his dominance, eager to give him whatever he needed.

Yet, between Grady and him, there would probably always be a fight for who was in control. Grady liked rules and order. It helped after his chaotic childhood. But Steele needed control too.

Grady's dominance was down below the surface. Locked up tight and only let out when Grady chose.

While Steele wore his like a second skin.

But that didn't mean that Grady would just submit like Effie did. And he didn't expect him to.

He drew back from the other man, his breathing quick and deep. His dick was hard, pressed against his jeans. Tight and uncomfortable.

"You ready for this? To give our girl the rest of her birthday present?"

"Yeah. I'm ready. Wouldn't be wearing a damn anal plug if I weren't."

Steele grinned. They were going to give their girl a show.

That's what she'd asked for her birthday. Dancing and to watch them touch each other.

She'd tried to take the last bit back, saying they didn't have to.

But they wanted to do that for her. And for them. It was time.

"You ready?" Grady asked.

"Fuck yes."

There was a splash and he glanced over to find Brooks was out of the pool. "I'm gonna go shower, then call Stella."

Steele gave him a chin lift. When the kid was gone, he turned to Grady. "Let's go find our girl."

∽

Effie was sitting on the bed, laughing at a story April was telling her about how her German shepherd, Patches, had spread mud throughout her newly detailed car when her men walked into the bedroom.

The look in their eyes had her heart racing.

She knew what that look meant.

"Listen, April, I've got to go."

"You bitch."

"What?" she asked, startled.

"I know that tone of voice. You're gonna get some and Trent's working late tonight."

Effie smiled. "Yeah, I am."

"Total bitch. But also, I love that for you."

"Me too," she whispered. "And I love you, Hairy Tits."

"Love you too, Droopy Bum."

She ended the call as Grady shot her a look. "Hairy Tits?"

"Yeah. That's my nickname for her."

"What's hers for you?" he asked while Steele locked the door behind him.

She gulped. Yeah, she was definitely going to get herself some. And it was gonna be good.

"Droopy Bum."

"I don't think her bottom is droopy, do you, Grady?" Steele asked, coming to a stop at the foot of the bed.

"Not at all," Grady said.

She cleared her throat. "Well, neither does she. Just like I don't think her tits are hairy."

"Well, I wasn't sure. She does live in the mountains of Wyoming," Steele said with a grin.

"Damon!" she protested.

His gaze heated. "Fucking love when you call me Damon, baby girl."

She knew that. Why did he think she did it? That, and she liked the way his name sounded coming from her lips.

Fire. Life. Protection that engulfed her.

That's what his name meant to her.

Then she turned her gaze to the other man who owned her heart. They didn't own pieces. They both owned it fully.

"Thomas," she whispered. He was beginning to like her using his first name. Not always, though.

That cool, almost detached gaze became laser sharp, focused. Lord, when he gave her his attention, she felt like there was no one else in the world except for her and Steele.

Ice. Calm. A safe place to land.

She licked her lips, watching them both as Grady came to stand beside Steele.

Her men.

"I'm so freaking lucky," she whispered.

"Do not pinch yourself," they ordered together.

She had to grin. "Aww, are you two gonna finish each other's sentences? That is so freaking cute."

"She said the c-word," Steele muttered.

"She certainly did."

"What happens when you use the c-word around us, Effie?" Steele asked quietly.

Excitement raced through her. Because she knew exactly what happened.

Punishment.

But not the sort of punishment that she shied away from. Not the kind that was actually supposed to deter her.

This was the sort of punishment she craved.

"But it was just the truth, you're both so cute," she told them, licking her lips.

"She licked her lips," Grady said.

"Saw that. That's even more punishment."

Grady shook his head. "Silly girl. Now, you're going to have to beg us to let you come."

Like they didn't love hearing her beg.

"Get the ropes," Damon ordered.

Grady retrieved them from the drawer while Damon helped her off the bed, then stripped her.

"Sit back against the headboard, sweetheart," Grady directed. He put some pillows behind her, then secured her wrists to the top corners of the headboard, leaving her legs free.

"Spread," Damon ordered.

She parted her legs and both men stood at the end of the bed, staring down at her. She still had moments of feeling self-conscious about her rolls. About her less-than-perfect body.

But when they stared at her like this, it was hard to remember the ways she wasn't perfect.

"Now, for your punishment," Steele murmured. "And your birthday present. You're going to sit there and watch. And you can't join in until we release you."

Oh fuck.

What had she gotten herself into?

And then she knew she'd gotten herself into a whole lot of trouble as the two men kissed. It was almost violent. Rough. A fight to see who was more dominant.

And it was sexy as fuck.

They practically tore at each other's clothing, revealing smooth skin, and plenty of muscle. So much yumminess that she swore she almost came just from watching them.

Then Damon shocked the shit out of her by going down on his knees and sucking Grady's cock into his mouth.

Holy. Crap.

She whimpered, pressing her legs together. Her clit ached and she pulled at her ties.

Grady glanced at her, frowning. Then he touched the top of Steele's head. The other man paused.

"We'll stop if you don't behave," Grady warned her.

Shit. Shit.

"Sorry," she whispered hoarsely.

"No pulling at your bonds and no closing your legs."

"Yes, Grady."

"Be a good girl for us and you'll get to come soon," Grady told her. "Be naughty, and I'll get you all hot and bothered, then make you sleep on my dick all night without coming."

Right. She quickly parted her legs.

"That's our good girl," Grady praised her.

Then Steele took him deeper and Grady's head went back on a moan. Steele worked him up until Grady was panting, his skin coated in sweat.

"I'm going to come!" Grady groaned as he pushed in deep, obviously finding his release.

Lord. So hot. She thought she might die there and then.

But at least now they'd untie her and she'd get to come. However, they didn't immediately move to her. Instead, Grady walked over to the drawer and returned with some lube which he squirted into the palm of his hand.

Steele stood, his magnificent cock at attention. She licked her lips again.

Could you blame her? It was fucking magnificent.

Grady grabbed Steele's dick in a far rougher grip than she'd ever dare use and jacked it a few times. It was the big man's turn to groan as he pumped his hips.

"Fuck. Fuck."

"Like that?" Grady asked.

She could hear the satisfaction in his voice.

"Fuck, yes."

"Good. I'm just going to get ready. You get her primed."

Yes. She liked the sound of that. As Grady walked into the bathroom, she watched him move.

Was that . . . did he have a butt plug in his ass? Then her vision was filled with Steele as he straddled her lap. He didn't give her his weight, protecting her like always, as he cupped her face and kissed her.

Slow and sweet.

Then deeper. Nastier.

She was here for it. All of it.

Then he moved down her body, tonguing her nipples before he reached her mound. But he rolled off the bed before his tongue could touch her where she really needed him to touch her.

However, it didn't matter. Because Grady was there, kneeling between her legs. He cupped her ass to lift her up to his mouth.

And he feasted.

And it was magnificent.

But not as mind-blowing as Steele stepping in behind Grady and pushing his way inside him.

"I want to see. Oh, please, can't I see?"

"More than you want to be eaten?" Steele asked as Grady paused.

"Yes. Yes."

So they rearranged themselves so that Steele was kneeling beside her while Grady's ass was toward her.

Then she watched Steele's fat, heavy cock push its way into the other man's ass.

And she swore she almost came as she watched. She didn't care that she wasn't being touched. Nothing was hotter than watching her two men together.

When Steele finally came in Grady's ass, he let out a loud shout of pleasure that filled the room.

Panting, both of them rested a moment before Steele slid free.

"Be right back," Grady said before moving into the bathroom to clean up.

Steele undid her binds, rubbing her wrists and kissing her gently.

Then he disappeared to get clean and Grady slid back between her legs. Steele returned, lying next to her, his mouth on hers as his finger drifted down to play with her clit. Grady moved to her other side. And together, they each pressed a finger inside her, moving them in and out, fucking her together.

One of them brushed her clit with his thumb and that was it. She ignited, her cries filling the room as her head spun dizzily.

Her men petted her as she came down. She ended up in her favorite position, pressed up against Steele, her arm over his stomach, one leg over his. While Grady pressed in behind her.

His dick was hard again and he slid it into her pussy.

"Ohhh," she said.

"I think our girl has more," Grady said.

"Yeah? You think you can stay still while I finger your clit, baby?" Steele asked.

"Umm. Yes?"

"Grady is going to stay pressing inside you, but he's not going to move. I'm going to play with that pretty pussy, but if you move, I stop."

Shit.

It sounded impossible.

"And you're going to have to beg to be allowed to come," he added.

Oh Lord.

Damon moved onto his side, watching her face carefully, ensuring she didn't move as he played lightly with her clit. Grady stayed still behind her and she knew he wouldn't come. He liked sleeping inside her while hard.

She clenched down around his dick, thrusting her hips back.

"Uh-uh, bad baby," Steele admonished, stilling.

"Please, I'll be good."

"Um, I'm not sure you will," Grady said.

"I will. I will, Daddies. I promise. I'm your good girl."

"Right now, you're our Little captive," Damon told her. "We can do whatever we want. Stay still."

He started again and it took everything she had not to move, to stay still.

"Please, Damon. Please, Daddy. Let me come. Please. Please."

"Beg some more. I love it when you beg."

"Please, Daddies. Please! I need to come so bad."

Steele moved his finger faster, harder.

"Come, our good girl," Grady said. "Come for us."

She screamed, pulsing around Grady's dick as Steele kissed her lightly. It took her a long time to drift down and then she let out a happy sigh.

"Happy birthday, baby," Steele said with a light kiss.

"Happy birthday, our good girl," Grady added.

"I love you guys so much," she whispered. "Ever since Joe

died, I've mostly lived inside my head. Dreaming up a fantasy or fighting off Nan's voice. I never found my way out of my head. But with the two of you . . . I no longer have to live in here." She tapped her forehead. "I no longer have to hide because you've both given me a fairy tale come to life. Because my life is so beautiful, I no longer have to chase a daydream. I am living my dream. Every day. And it's more amazing than I could ever have expected.

"Thank you for giving me magic."

Printed in Great Britain
by Amazon